INVISIBLE CHAINS

Michelle Renee Lane

Haverhill House Publishing

For Ronnie

You came into my life when I needed you most and showed me that I could be so much more than what other people expected of me. Thank you for showing me the history so many people wanted to keep a secret.

INVISIBLE CHAINS
© 2019 Michelle Renee Lane

ISBN: 978-1-949140-03-3 Hardcover
ISBN: 978-1-949140-04-0 Trade Paperback

Cover illustration © 2019 Errick Nunnally

Haverhill House Publishing
643 E Broadway
Haverhill MA 01830-2420
www.haverhillhouse.com

ACKNOWLEDGMENTS

First, and foremost, thank you, John M. McIlveen, Editor-in-Chief at Haverhill House Publishing, for giving this novel a home and making me feel at ease enough to act like I knew what I was talking about when I pitched the book to you at StokerCon last year. It was an absolute pleasure to meet you.

I would also like to thank Lucy A. Snyder, my second mentor in Seton Hill University's MFA in Writing Popular Fiction Program. At first, I couldn't get a sense of whether Lucy liked the book or not, but at our second mentor meeting, we had the mother of all brainstorm sessions that opened up so many possibilities and helped me figure out what this novel is really about. Thank you for your guidance, encouragement, and the poem that provided multiple methods for me to kill the vampire. And, thank you to Scott A. Johnson, my first mentor, who reminded me not to take myself too seriously and enjoy the ride.

My heartfelt thanks go to Timons Esaias, my friend and unofficial SHU mentor, who graciously listened to my anxiety-ridden rants about how I would never finish writing this book. Thank you for your writing advice, your kind words, and for teaching me how to make gumbo.

Thank you, Valerie Burns and Patricia Lillie, for staying up late with me during residencies at SHU and for always being there for me no matter how many miles separate us. I love you both and will never be able to thank you enough.

Thanks are also due to my SHU cohort, The Tribe: Jessica Barlow, Penny Thomas, Alex Savage, Matt O'Dwyer, Crystal Kapataidakis, Gina Anderson, Jeff Evans, Lana Hechtman Ayers, Anna La Voie, Dagmar Amrhein, Jacki King, Tiffany Avery, and Kenya Wright. I wouldn't have made it through the program without your kindness and support. Hazard yet forward!

And last, but definitely not least, thank you to my StokerCon roommates and fellow SHU graduates, Stephanie M. Wytovich (my witchy sister), Ryan DeMoss (our bearded cult leader), and Joe Borelli (our uncanny voice of reason). Thank you for all the laughter and inappropriate jokes. Thank you for being such good friends and listeners. You mean the world to me.

INVISIBLE CHAINS

Chapter 1

A hurricane nearly destroyed the plantation the day I was born. Moman Esther was in labor for half the night. She took shelter in the slave quarters, but the wind and rain rocked the shack right off its foundation. Great torrents of water soaked her skin until she thought she might drown. She claims the storm came just as her waters broke. I don't know if that's true, but my emotions and the weather have always seemed connected.

"Your first word was 'magic'," she told me.

Moman taught me everything she knew about our ancestors and the religion they'd passed down to her. Most children learn to count to ten and how to recognize the letters of the alphabet, but my first lessons were about the gods and goddesses of *Vodun*. It's hard to raise a child with your own beliefs when you're a slave, but Moman managed to do just that. She was a strong woman. I wanted to be just like her – smart, beautiful, brave, and powerful. Plantation life will use up your body and stomp your dreams right out of your heart if you let it. The trick is not to let life beat you down – no matter what.

Life isn't a fairytale. My story isn't about a prince rescuing a princess, and there aren't any *happily ever afters*. No goblins, trolls or dragons here, but there are plenty of other monsters.

Charlotte was Master's daughter. So was I, but since Moman was a slave, my birth didn't matter much to him beyond my value at auction. Master called his favorite little girl *Lottie*. That man spoiled her every chance he got. He never gave me a second glance except to ask for more biscuits. Like all his other bastards, I was invisible to him. I wish Lottie had ignored me, too, because at some point she got it into her head we were rivals. I had less than nothing, so why she felt jealous of a slave was beyond me. I don't know what injustice she imagined I'd committed against her, but for as long as I could remember, she loved to hate me.

We grew up together in rural Louisiana pretending we weren't related. My eyes should have been enough proof. They were the same dark blue, almost violet, as Lottie's. Master's wife hated me even more than my half-sister did. I was a constant reminder of her husband's infidelities. He had children with at least three other slaves besides Moman, so Lottie had a bunch of half-brothers and sisters. None of them got to spend as much time alone with her as I did. They were lucky.

Lottie received a new book of fairy tales for Christmas one year —I couldn't have been more than four or five— and she wanted to pretend to be every princess and damsel in distress. She read to me so that we could play together. In her versions of the stories, she was the most beautiful princess that had ever lived.

"When do I get to be the princess?"

She laughed when I asked to wear the crown of daisies. "Who ever heard of a pickaninny princess?"

She was always cruel, but I refused to shed a single tear over her. I wanted to be the princess. I yearned for my happily ever after. I didn't care if I had to sleep for a hundred years; I longed for the love of a handsome prince. I would have settled for being *Le Petit Chaperon Rouge*, but I was always *Le Grand Méchant Loup*.

Lottie refused to hear my protests. She didn't care if it wasn't fair. She always got the lead role.

"How do you know there aren't any pickaninny princesses?"

"Because there aren't any in this book." Lottie poked her finger at the cover.

The *Vodun* gods and goddesses were better than any old storybook princess, but I wasn't allowed to talk about them. Moman would use pictures of Catholic saints to represent the gods and goddesses on a shelf in the pantry, behind the flour, where she hid her altar – St. Peter for Damballah, Lazarus for Papa Legba, St. Expedite for Baron Samedi, and her favorite, Our Lady of Lourdes, for Erzulie Dantor. It was no coincidence that this hardworking dark-skinned woman who sought vengeance against those who tried to steal her power was our household goddess.

"We're *pretending* to be princesses. Dragons and ogres aren't real, either. Why can't I be the princess sometimes?"

"Well, you just can't. I'm always the princess."

I wanted to wear the crown of daisies even though breathing fire would have proven more useful. Moman wouldn't have to work so hard to get the stove lit first thing in the morning if I was a dragon.

I sat with my back to Lottie, arms folded tightly against my chest as she kicked me and screamed at me to accept a lesser role in our game of make-believe. I ignored her as best I could until she finally gave in. Knowing I had won, no matter how small the victory, was worth every scrape and bruise her shoe buckles left on my shins.

"Fine. You can be the princess just this once, but don't go

getting all high and mighty."

I put on the daisy crown and pretended to be Cinderella. She was my favorite. Cinderella was treated almost as bad as a slave before her fairy godmother cast the magic spell she needed to win the prince and escape her life of servitude. Not to mention that Lottie was a natural at playing one of the evil stepsisters.

Life would've been so much easier if I looked like a fairytale princess. At least that's what I believed until we both got a little older. Lottie had more freedom than me — she could read, write, play, eat when she was hungry, sleep when she was tired — but she was the daughter of a rich white man who made sure to keep her in line. Our father decided what books she could read, what she learned (or didn't) in school, and who she could or couldn't marry. Marriage for most women wasn't much different than slavery, except the children of rich white women didn't get sold off like livestock. On the plantation, Lottie witnessed the same horrors as me, but while I would hide my face and cry, she would scramble to get a better look with a big smile on her face. If princesses behaved like her, I'd rather be a dragon any day.

Moman worked in the house, which gave me access to the family mansion, the gardens, and best of all, the kitchen. She and I shared a mattress in the pantry, stuffed with clean, earthy-smelling straw. Warm in the winter, and cool in the summer.

On spring mornings before the birds woke, warm breezes brought in the comforting smells of sweet magnolia trees, mingled with the musky scent of sweating slaves working in the fields.

Moman wasn't born a slave. Before her Créole daddy died of yellow fever, he taught her and his other children how to read.

When Grandfather died, Grandmother had no way to prove she and her children were free. White folks didn't even recognize their marriage, because Grandmother had been a slave when they met. He never petitioned for her manumission, so it was only his word that had given her freedom. Grandmother was sold at auction. So were her children. They never saw each other again.

After Master bought her, Moman kept her education a secret. Feigning ignorance kept slaves alive. Moman had other secrets, too. She practiced the old ways, and she was the only Mambo for miles around. So, when she taught me how to grow herbs, make biscuits, build a fire, and collect eggs, she also taught me conjuring. She would draw *vévé* in the ashes beside the hearth, and taught me how to call upon the *loa* at night after all the work was done.

Her skills went beyond basic root work and charms. She taught me to take my dreams seriously too, because sometimes hers would come true. If I had a nightmare, she'd make me tell her as much as I could remember, and then she'd write it down in her spell book. From the time I could walk, I'd had nightmares about a man with pale skin, haunting green eyes, and a shock of dark wavy hair. He was always dressed in black and surrounded by shadows, so I could never quite make out his other features. I didn't dream about him every night, just often enough to make Moman worry. Somehow, I knew he was from another time, and from a faraway place. Bad things happened when he was around, even though he never hurt me. No matter how many times I dreamt about that man, I would always wake up screaming.

Along with my education in magic, Moman taught me how to read, too. By the time I was ten I could read most of Lottie's schoolbooks, and I stole copies of *L'Abeille de la Nouvelle-Orléans* and *Harper's* from the burn pile. I'd hide them under our mattress with Moman's spell book and would sneak off to read them behind the woodshed near the swamp. Cottonmouths and black widows kept me company under the cypress trees as I read every scrap of paper I could find. Nobody wanted to linger by the woodshed longer than necessary, so it was a perfect hiding place. I read about slave auctions in New Orleans, dry goods for sale, birth announcements, engagements, obituaries, stories about yellow fever outbreaks, runaway slaves, and everything else deemed fit to print. But I liked fairytales best.

Moman was proud of me, but she warned me never to show off my abilities in front of Master and his family. They'd make an example out of me. I'd get a whipping for sure, or worse. Smart slaves kept their mouths shut about their hidden talents, or they became dead slaves.

While Lottie learned how to play piano, sing, dance, and run a household full of slaves, all I wanted to do was read, write, and work spells. My chores — wood to chop, water to fetch, laundry to hang, rugs to beat, windows to clean, eggs to gather, and lots of other work — kept me busy from sun up to sun down. It was hard to find an excuse to hide behind the woodshed, but it was easy to sneak off on the days when Lottie's tutor was around. Michié Henri was almost handsome with his dark golden wavy hair, and funny little wire-rimmed glasses that kept you from guessing what color his eyes were behind the thick lenses. He came on Tuesday mornings after breakfast and would spend an hour teaching Lottie grammar. In the afternoons, she practiced music. Lottie took a fancy to Michié Henri, and gave him her undivided attention during those lessons. Lottie's mother made it known she did not approve of this infatuation and stayed close by to make sure it never went any further than "juvenile flirtations". It didn't matter how nice or smart Michié Henri was, he didn't make enough money to marry into her family. In her book, a lowly teacher was not much better than a servant.

One day, during Lottie's lessons, a fire broke out in the kitchen.

"Mamzèl, come quick!" Moman was coughing and gasping for breath when she ran into the house.

"Come here, girl," Lottie's mother said, and snapped her fingers at me.

I put down my rag and the silver fork I was polishing in the dining room and hurried to her side. Her mouth was set in a stern straight line as she stared down at me.

"I need you to be my eyes and ears, understand? I want you to tell me everything that happens in this room while I'm gone."

"Yes, Mamzèl." I bowed my head and took her place next to the settee.

She hurried off to help with the fire and left me to stand guard over her daughter's chastity. Shortly after her mother left the room, Lottie made her move. She professed her love for Michié Henri in a poem. When she was done reciting the flowery and somewhat inappropriate words, he faked a cough and tried his best not to laugh. A knot formed in my stomach and I held my breath as I watched a dark shadow pass over Lottie's face. Moman used to say that girl had the Devil in her. I could almost believe it when she got angry and her face changed so suddenly. All the color drained from her skin and her flesh shifted into an expressionless mask, blank as a clean sheet of parchment. Michié Henri was not as rich as Master, but he was raised in polite society and acted like a gentleman. He respected the feelings of others.

"Mademoiselle Charlotte," he said, "I am truly flattered, but I am engaged to a young woman in the next parish over. I'm sure another lucky young man will soon find himself bewitched by your beauty."

Lottie's face turned deep red. She was never denied anything she wanted, and she wanted Michié Henri. He stopped smiling, though, once he saw how angry she was. She glared at him, clutched her dress at the collar, and ripped it downwards. A pale pink nipple peeked out from under the torn cloth.

"What...what are you doing? Have you gone mad?" Michié Henri tried to stop her from doing any further damage to her clothes. She just kept staring at him with that look of hatred in her eyes and grinned, baring her teeth like a rabid dog. And then she screamed.

"Help! Someone, please!" She made tears fall from her eyes then turned to me and said one word: "Run."

I did as I was told and went to find Mamzèl. By the time we got back to the study, Lottie's older brother, Jimmy, had the tutor on the floor. Poor Michié Henri tried to protect his head as Jimmy kicked away at his ribs and ground his heel into his groin. He begged Jimmy to stop. As his pleas got louder, Jimmy stomped and kicked harder.

"What is going on in here?" Mamzèl demanded.

"Oh, Maman," Lottie cried. She wrapped her arms around her mother's waist and winked at me. "Monsieur Henri tried to...I can't even say the words. All I did was read him a poem I wrote, and he went wild." Lies and cruelty came easy to Lottie. "Ask Jacqueline, she saw the whole thing."

"Is this true, child?" Mamzèl glared down at me, arms tightly folded across her chest. Jimmy stopped his assault. I felt like the last piece of brambleberry pie at a late summer picnic. All eyes were on me.

"Speak up, girl." Lottie made sure I was looking at her when she spoke. She knew I was afraid of her, but if I said what she wanted me to say, I'd be lying to her mother. Lottie was scary, but her mother was a force of nature. If I lied to Mamzèl and she found out, I'd get a whipping. If I told the truth, her daughter would find far worse ways to punish me.

I thought back to the morning I'd caught her killing newborn chicks in the hen house when I went there to collect the eggs. She'd met my look of shock with a devious grin.

"They're just dumb animals. Who cares what happens to them?"

"They're helpless little babies, Mamzèl Lottie. How can you hurt something that's done you no harm?"

"Don't tell my mother or I'll tell her it was you." She ran off laughing and left me to clean up their limp, soft, yellow bodies. One little chick was still clinging to life. I put it out of its misery by breaking its neck. Later, I told Moman and she made me swear never to tell anyone about it.

"If Lottie finds out it was you who told, what you think she gonna do to you? *Les Blancs* think we're no better than beasts in the field. She sees no difference between you and those chicks."

Moman was right. Something was wrong with Lottie, and if I made her mad, no one would come to put *me* out of my misery. I wished I could speak up, tell the truth, and save Michié Henri, but I wasn't a princess, and I was no dragon. I was just a little black girl with no voice and no power. The threat of violence kept my mouth shut.

"Yes, Mamzèl. It's just like she said. I saw the whole thing. Michié Henri grabbed her and tore her dress. I ran as fast as I could to find you."

Michié Henri lay on the floor and stared up at me, his eyes so wide I could see more white than blue, like the look hogs get on their faces just before slaughter. I felt sick to my stomach. His mouth fell open, but no words were coming out. He rarely paid much attention to me, but he was never unkind. I'd lied to save my own skin. I wanted to feel guilty, but he could leave the plantation whenever he wanted. I couldn't. He might be badly beaten or crippled when he left, but he could still leave.

"That's all for now, girl. Go help Esther in the kitchen." Mamzèl's lips curled up at the corners in what I could only guess was her attempt at a smile. I went to help Moman clean up the mess from the fire. Before I left the study, I took one last look at Michié Henri lying on the floor pleading for his life. I was glad it was him and not me about to get the beating of a lifetime. I went about my business and wondered if he'd leave the plantation in a casket.

Chapter 2

Time passed, and Lottie switched the focus of her cruelty and hatefulness from small helpless animals to slaves. Master didn't hire another teacher after Michié Henri, and none of the adults seemed to have time for Lottie, so Jimmy became her minder. He was a few years older than her. Most of his education took place next to the overseer and Master, who taught him everything he needed to know about running the plantation and making sure the slaves did as they were told. He didn't care much for book learning. Some people are good at singing or playing a fiddle, and others can dance or paint pretty pictures. Jimmy's one true talent was being hateful to black folks. Lottie wasn't supposed to spend time around the field hands, but Jimmy wanted an audience for his violent games.

There was a boy I liked very much. Gabriel was a few years older than me. He worked in the fields, so his arms and back were strong from cutting and hauling cotton twelve hours a day. Since I worked in the house, we didn't see each other often, but sometimes I'd sneak him some cornbread and beans with pork fat. Field hands never seemed to get enough to eat, and he was always kind to me. Respectful. Moman liked him, too.

I guess Lottie noticed our interest in each other, because one day she singled him out and said she'd seen him stealing food from the kitchen. I'd wrapped some leftover biscuits in a clean cloth and given them to him on his way to the cotton fields before sun up. Sometimes gifts can be a curse to the recipient. Jimmy made him turn out his pockets. Gabriel had eaten the biscuits that morning, but crumbs fell to the grass when he pulled the cloth from inside his breeches.

"I told you he stole food from the kitchen," Lottie squealed with delight.

Gabriel didn't bother to defend himself. If he did, he'd have to tell them where the food had come from. I ran across the yard when I saw what was happening.

"Jacqueline, stop. There's nothing you can do for that boy that won't get you into trouble, too," Moman called to me.

I ignored her and kept running.

"Looks like we got us a thief here," Jimmy said to the overseer. "We punish thieves, but this is your first offense —and since you're such a valuable nigger, I'll let you off easy this time."

"What are you going to do?" Lottie bounced up and down.

"Normally, a thief would lose a hand for stealing, but Gabriel here is one of our best field hands. We can't afford to maim him, but we can make sure he thinks twice about stealing again." Jimmy took the whip from the overseer.

It wasn't fair that Gabriel should suffer for something that was my fault. I thought of Michié Henri and how I hadn't been able to help him. I didn't want any more violence on my conscience, not if I could help it. I ran toward Jimmy and begged him not to hurt Gabriel.

"What's gotten into you, girl? You lost your mind?"

"Gabriel didn't do anything wrong, Michié Jimmy."

Gabriel glared at me and shook his head.

"We caught him red-handed, crumbs don't lie."

"He didn't steal anything from the kitchen. I gave him those biscuits. They were left over from my breakfast."

"Well, Gabriel, looks like you're in luck today. This girl wants to take your place."

Tears brimmed in my eyes. I couldn't catch my breath. Fear nearly paralyzed me. Then I remembered a spell Moman had taught me to make others do as you command.

Lottie looked disappointed that Gabriel wouldn't be punished. I knew she wanted me to witness him being hurt. That was the whole point.

Recklessly, I grasped Lottie's wrist and nudged at her with the faintest touch of magic, and said, "Please don't let Michié Jimmy hurt me."

Lottie stared at me trying to understand the words I was speaking. She opened her mouth like she wanted to argue, but I forced a little more power into my touch. I thought, *tell him no, tell him no, tell him no.* She tried to fight against my influence, but couldn't. And then she turned away from me to whisper something in her brother's ear.

"Looks like luck is on your side today, Jacqueline," he said.

Luck wasn't on my side. Magic was.

Gabriel waited until Jimmy's back was turned and smiled at me before he headed back to the fields. I may not have gotten whipped that day, but the threat made me think twice about showing kindness to others. I didn't expect to be rewarded or thanked, but I certainly didn't think I'd be punished for a good deed.

Later, back in the kitchen, Moman scolded me. "I know you care about that boy, but that was just plain stupid. If *les Blancs* knew about your magic...my magic, what you think they'd do to us?"

I knew what they'd do. It was stupid.

"Promise me you won't use your magic like that again, Jacqueline."

I stared at the floor and mumbled, "I promise."

Moman grasped my chin and made me look into her eyes. "Swear it."

As much as I wanted to argue with her and tell her we should be using our powers to get free of that place, those thoughts were childish and dangerous. I knew better and never should have taken the risk of using magic to influence Lottie. Magic was useful and made life a bit easier on the plantation, but it wouldn't be enough to end slavery and set us free.

"I swear."

Chapter 3

On Sunday mornings, I usually had time to read down by the woodshed while Master's family attended church. After a quick breakfast of biscuits and gravy, Old Black Nate hitched up the horses to the carriage, and Master and his white kin rode the five miles up the road from the plantation. They spent several hours listening to the Catholic Mass, catching up with their closest neighbors, and making the trip back in time for late afternoon supper.

Not this Sunday.

Lottie's shrill laughter greeted me as I approached the woodshed. I stopped dead in my tracks and listened to see if she was alone. My half brother and sister must have lied to get out of going to church. They both needed an extra helping of religion.

"Come here, Lottie. Let me get a look at those little rose buds of yours." Jimmy's voice sent ice water into my veins. My own breasts had started to grow a few months back and everyone on the plantation looked at me differently now. I was hoping he hadn't noticed. I still hadn't got my blood, but my shape was changing. So was Lottie's. People weren't allowed to look at her the same way they looked at me, but that didn't mean no one noticed.

Lottie giggled. "Oh, Jimmy. Quit your teasing, now."

"I'm not teasing, I want to see them."

"No, what if someone catches us?"

"No one around except slaves. They won't say a word even if they do catch us."

"Why not?"

"Because I'll cut the tongue out of any nigger who says a word against me."

Lottie giggled at her brother's boast.

"Now show them to me."

I crept closer to the woodshed. My curiosity would surely be the death of me one day. I peered through a splintered knothole in the wood split by heat and heavy rains. A spider web caught my attention out the corner of my eye and I stepped back to make sure it wasn't occupied. After brushing away the sticky webbing, I quietly knelt in the damp grass to look through the hole again. You can learn a lot from watching people, especially if they don't know you're there.

They stood about a foot apart and Lottie carefully unfastened her bodice. When she opened her dress and exposed her small, pale, buds of flesh, Jimmy licked his lips like he was about to help himself to a plate of pork chops. He knelt before his sister and placed one of her breasts between his thin, cruel lips. A gasp of surprise escaped her, and she stood startled, looking down at the top of her brother's head. He stopped for a moment and smiled up at the confusion on her face.

"Let me see the rest of you," he said.

"No, Jimmy, that's for my *mari*."

He caressed her face and sweetened his tone. "I just want to see you. I won't do anything to ruin your wedding night."

Lottie was mean as a snake, but she wasn't stupid. She hesitated, as if questioning his sincerity, and then reluctantly agreed to his request. He helped her remove her dress and underthings and left her standing naked but for her stockings and shoes. He spread her dress out on the dirt floor, told her to lie down, and got undressed. She looked scared, but I also recognized in her the same curiosity I felt inside myself. I knew what they were doing was wrong, but I couldn't stop watching.

Jimmy sat next to Lottie and touched the soft hair between her legs. She giggled and tried to turn away, but he held her in place. At seventeen, his hands already looked like a grown man's, but when he touched his sister's fourteen-year-old body they looked like those of a giant.

"Stop, Jimmy, that hurts," she cried.

"Here, touch me here. It'll feel better soon."

Frustrated with her first few feeble attempts, he guided her hand. She caught on quickly and soon she relaxed and enjoyed the way he was touching her. She squirmed and sighed and pulled until her brother grunted and a creamy liquid ran down her hand like she was milking cows in the barn. He pulled away from Lottie and told her to get dressed.

"Touch me some more," she begged.

"Only whores ask for more, Charlotte." He wrinkled his nose up at her suggestion like he'd just got a big whiff of pig shit.

He dressed and left her alone in the shed. I was hiding behind a pile of wood that kept him from seeing me as he pulled up his suspenders and stomped back across the yard to the plantation house. Lottie lay on her back and touched herself until she achieved her goal.

I hurried back across the yard making sure Jimmy didn't spot me and when I reached the kitchen, my face was flushed.

"What's gotten into you, girl?" Moman was getting supper ready.

"Nothing," I said.

"Looks like you saw something you weren't supposed to."

I don't know why I bothered lying to her. She always knew when I'd done or seen something she'd warned me about. I almost told her what I'd seen in the woodshed, but I knew I'd get in trouble for staying to watch them for so long. It was only a matter of time before Jimmy took an interest in me, too. I was two years younger than Lottie, but my body was blooming a lot faster. I dreaded that day, because I knew he wouldn't spare me for my wedding night like he did Lottie. If I lived long enough to have a wedding day, it wouldn't matter to Master, Jimmy, or even the slave they gave me to if I was untouched or well-seasoned.

A few days later, while I was gathering herbs behind the kitchen, Lottie came looking for me. She still skipped across the yard like a younger girl, but I knew she had womanly intentions on her mind.

"There you are," she said, like I'd been missing. "I know Esther mixes herbs, and I've heard the niggers call her a conjure woman."

I didn't confirm or deny her statement.

"I need something from her, but I can't ask her myself. She'll tell my mother and we'll both be in trouble. Me *and* Esther."

"What you need from her?"

"She got anything to keep girls from having babies?"

She did, but that was supposed to be a secret from *les Blancs*. Girls and women came to Moman all the time. Making babies was easy. Birthing them was another story. I'd seen too many slaves die in childbirth. As much as I hated my half-sister, the idea of her giving birth to some monster child she'd made with her brother made me sick to my core. Jimmy would soon tire of the touching they did to each other. Soon he'd want more. If it weren't with

Lottie, it would be with me or one of the other slaves. I agreed to help her.

"Come back this time tomorrow. I'll have what you need."

"You better not say anything to Esther, or I'll send Jimmy after you."

That was all the threat I needed.

I asked Moman to show me how to mix the herbs Lottie needed. She didn't ask why. I was growing up fast and took after her in looks and smarts.

"Men'll be chasing after you soon enough," she said.

She took me out to the garden behind the kitchen after the evening meal. It was just before dusk. We had enough light to cut pennyroyal, rue, Queen Anne's lace, and a little wild fennel to improve the taste. Inside, we poured hot water over all the ingredients with a little lemon to make a tisane that needed to cool and steep overnight. Her recipe was thorough.

Moman knew a lot about babies. She was one of the plantation midwives and when any slave needed help birthing a baby, had pain during pregnancy, or didn't want to carry a child in the first place, they came to see her. Even slaves who didn't fully trust her enough to drink her potions took her advice and chewed cotton bark in the fields all day to keep from having too many babies. You could say she knew just about everything there was to know about bringing life into the world, but she also knew a lot about death. She ushered as many lives out of this world as she brought in.

"Life and death are separated by a very thin thread," she would say.

For slaves, that was even truer. Our lives depended on the whims of *les Blancs*. Overcook the bacon, you might get whipped. Serve the master spoiled food and make him sick, you might end up in the stocks or lose a finger, or maybe even an ear. Get caught putting poison in his food, and you'd end up hanging from the end of a rope. Moman checked the pantry for confused flour beetles weekly, made sure the dried meat wasn't rancid, and fetched fresh milk and eggs each day to prepare food for Master and his family. They ate like kings and rarely complained of stomach ailments. That was her way of protecting us from the whip. She'd taught me how to avoid punishment as soon as I was able to walk and follow her commands.

The night after Moman showed me how to make the unwanted baby tisane, I strained the herbs and poured the concoction into a small brown apothecary bottle. Light weakened some of the potions, so Moman always saved the brown, green, and cobalt bottles discarded from the big house. Master's wife had headaches almost every day, and each afternoon she added a few drops of her *medicine* to a glass of wine. The medicine varied, but laudanum and absinthe were her favorites, and they always had the same effect. She'd take a nap mid-afternoon on the sun porch stretched out on a daybed. There'd never be a shortage of empty wine or apothecary bottles. It was during one of those afternoon naps that I decided to sneak off to the woodshed. Lottie and Jimmy had the same idea.

I had Lottie's bottle in my apron pocket and was hoping to find her on my way to the swamp. After the midday meal, I didn't see her in any of her usual haunts, so I made my way across the yard in the hope of reading the next chapter in the book of fairy stories. Old Black Nate stopped me along the way and warned me he'd seen the Master's children heading in the same direction. I thanked him, and proceeded with caution.

I knew what I would find when I looked through the knothole this time. So, I wasn't shocked by what I saw. Lottie was going to need my tisane sooner than I thought. As she hiked up her dress, a water moccasin slithered across my bare feet and I screamed. Jimmy stopped what he was doing and turned his head towards the side of the shed where I was hiding.

Lottie lowered her dress. All the color drained from her face. She was just as afraid to get caught as I was. Jimmy pulled his breeches up but didn't bother to fasten them. He came outside and looked around the shed. I didn't have time to run and hide. I was caught, simple as that.

"What you doing out here, nigger?"

"I...I have something for Mamzèl Charlotte."

"Why did you come looking for her here?"

"Old Black Nate said he saw the both of you coming this way."

"What did you see in the shed?"

"Nothing. Can I give this to Mamzèl Charlotte?"

I held up the bottle.

"Come on in, Jacqueline," Lottie said.

I bowed to my half-brother and went inside the shed. Lottie's face was still pale, but she didn't look as worried as she'd been a few seconds earlier. I handed her the bottle.

Lottie held the bottle up to the sunlight streaming in from a gap in the wooden slats. "How much of this do I need to take?"

"Three drops each day should do the trick. Moman swears by it."

"Did you tell Esther who you were making this for?"

"No, she thinks it's for me."

"What are you two talking about?" Jimmy said.

"Esther gives this concoction to slaves so they don't have nigger babies every time they lay down with a man."

"How do you know it isn't poison?" Jimmy was standing a little too close to me.

"Esther never poisoned anybody. If she wanted to poison us,

she'd slip it into our food." Lottie was a lot smarter than her brother and usually sounded exasperated when she spoke to him. He was too dumb to notice she was talking down to him.

"I think we should make her drink it first," he said.

Lottie shrugged her shoulders and handed the bottle back to me. I took a drink and handed it back to her.

"Well, she drank it. Now what?"

"I think we should test it out," he said.

"How are we going to do that?"

He slid his hand inside his breeches with a sickening leer on his face. "I'm going to give her some of this. Come here and lift your skirt."

I tried to run. Jimmy caught me and threw me down on the floor. I scrambled to get up, but he held me tight.

"Come help me hold her, Charlotte."

Lottie stood for a second, staring at her brother. She pouted and stomped her feet.

"It was my turn," she said.

"I got plenty for both of you," he said, and leered down at me.

"Don't squirm so much, Jacqueline, you might like it," Lottie said.

She pinned my arms behind my head and Jimmy tried to pry my legs apart. He punched me in the face when I refused to spread my thighs for him. The pain was enough to make me comply. I screamed as I felt him ripping into my flesh. There'd be blood when he was done.

"She's tighter than you were, Charlotte," he grunted.

I focused on Lottie's face as her brother violated me for what seemed like days. She was smiling, but something lurked behind that smile. What was it?

"Make it hurt, Jimmy. Don't be gentle the way you are with

me."

Jealousy. It was jealousy.

"Holy shit, that was the best nigger pussy I ever had," he panted, and flopped down next to me on the floor.

"I'm good too, right Jimmy?" Lottie looked to her brother for approval.

"Not as good as that." He tried to catch his breath and wiped sweat off his brow. "I'm going to have to get some more of that later."

Lottie stormed out of the woodshed with tears in her eyes. Her brother laughed beside me and stroked my wound. Even after he kissed it, it still didn't feel better.

He loomed over me and pulled his breeches up. "You come back and see me here tomorrow, understand? Pussy that good, I'm keeping for myself. I don't want to see you messing with any of them nigger boys, you hear me?"

What could I say? He owned me. I didn't have any choice in the matter. All I could do was agree to meet him in the woodshed the next day.

He left me lying in a puddle tinged with my blood on the dirt floor. I wiped the tears from my face with the back of my hand, pulled my dress down over my legs, and got to my feet. I wasn't sure my legs would hold me, I was shaking so badly. Now that I was alone, the tears didn't just trickle down my face, sobs choked their way right out of my chest. I cried good and hard until I didn't think I'd ever be able to catch my breath.

Jimmy had ruined me. I was no longer untouched like the princesses in my favorite stories. I felt more like an outhouse than a princess. A handsome prince would never rescue me. Even Cinderella got to go to the ball. Moman was right. Those stories did more harm than good. None of the princesses in fairytales looked like me in any case, so what business did I have pretending to be one of them?

My thighs were sticky and sore as I walked back across the yard to the kitchen. I kept seeing Jimmy's horrible face leering down at me. Kept hearing his grunts in my head. My wrists were bruised where Lottie had held them behind me. I don't know why *she* was upset. She wasn't the one Jimmy was smacking his lips over. If she wanted him to do to her what he had done to me, she was crazier than I thought. Maybe he hadn't hurt her as much. It still didn't make sense why she'd want that disgusting pig grunting on top of her.

Moman was waiting for me in the kitchen. I didn't have to say a word. She took one look at me and knew what had happened. We held each other and cried. Once our tears had dried, she gave me a double dose of another potion she kept at the back of the pantry. This one tasted of black cohosh and licorice. She kept this on hand in case of rape and what *les Blancs* called 'accidents'. How can you call it an accident when you lie with someone, have full knowledge of where babies come from, and do nothing to protect yourself? Moman taught me that *les Blancs* liked to swallow a good healthy dose of bullshit. It absolved them of their sins and comforted them at night so they could sleep.

"Go wash up. I can smell him on you."

I could still feel his hands on me and it hurt to walk. With soap, hot water, and cotton wool, I tried to wash every last bit of him off me. When I was done, Moman gave me a salve to ease the pain between my legs. Then we got busy making the evening meal.

"He told me to meet him tomorrow," I said, peeling the life out of a potato.

"It gets easier." She put a pot of water on the stove.

"Is it going to hurt every time?"

She salted the water. "No. Some men understand how to be gentle with a woman."

"Is Master gentle with you?"

She gathered her thoughts before answering. "He can be gentle in his way, but that doesn't make what he does right. I've never had a choice. He takes what he wants when he wants it. But, no, he's never hurt me."

"Why is Jimmy so hateful? I've never done anything to deserve the way he treated me."

"A person can drive themselves insane trying to figure why *les Blancs* do what they do, Jacqueline. That boy's never been right in the head. There isn't always a 'why' to be had. Sometimes, you just have to accept they way people are and do what you can to protect yourself."

"He made me feel like filth."

"I didn't say you had to like it."

"How can I keep him away from me?"

She shrugged. "You're a strong girl. Your magic will see you through."

What else could she say? Maybe Master was easier to tolerate than Jimmy, but like me, he still owned her body and soul.

Chapter 4

As long as we did our work, followed the rules, and didn't try to escape, life could be bearable for a slave. I knew nothing about the rest of the world except for what I read in newspapers and magazines. True, my life was not my own, and every day, someone else would decide whether I lived or died. Life on the plantation was dangerous, but the unknown people, places, and things waiting for me out in the world were far scarier. Not all slaves felt the way I did; others felt freedom was worth dying for, and many died trying to reach it.

Light-skinned Harriet was always trying to run away. She came from the Carolinas and wanted to get back to her children so she could get them to safety up North. As many times as she ran, the slave catchers found her and dragged her back to the plantation. The last time Harriet ran she was gone for six days, and I thought for sure she was gone for good. Moman didn't think so.

"Why do you think she didn't get away?" I asked.

"Milk curdled yesterday." She stacked firewood near the kitchen door.

"It's been hot; milk always curdles when it gets hot."

"You ever see it turn blood red?"

Later that afternoon, Lottie came running into the yard where I was hanging sheets to dry on the line. I'd never seen her so excited. She was all smiles and giggles, clapping her hands and bouncing around like the circus was in town or something. I watched her out of the corner of my eye.

"We're going to have some fun today, Jacqueline," she laughed. "Did you hear? They caught Harriet in Baton Rouge getting on a steamboat headed up North."

I kept my head down and focused on the laundry.

"Didn't you hear what I said? The slave catchers are bringing her back right now. Jimmy's helping the overseer set up the cotton screw to punish that dumb nigger."

Even in my wildest imagination I couldn't figure out how they would use the cotton screw as a punishment. I didn't have long to wait before I found out.

"Here they come!" Lottie clapped her hands and squealed like a toddler on Christmas Day. The glee on her face made me sick to my stomach.

Four huge men dragged Harriet into the yard. Her hands and feet were shackled, and a collar with pointed barbs circled her neck. The shackles were so tight, her hands and feet were turning black. Harriet's clothes were torn and hanging in shreds all over her badly bruised skin.

The torture device was a large wooden structure with a screw at its center, attached to a large block of wood used for pressing and packing cotton into a box at the base of the machine. At the top of the screw was an arch-shaped piece of wood that hung out over the structure with hooks on either end. It stood in the center of the yard and Jimmy helped the overseer secure it to the ground with ropes and wooden pegs. Usually, two horses were harnessed to the hooks and driven in a circle around the machine to turn the screw and press the cotton. Jimmy only brought one horse. The other hook was for Harriet this time. Two of the slave catchers lifted her up off the ground and hung her on the hook by the chain connecting her wrist shackles. The others watched. She almost fainted from the pain, and blood started to trickle down her arms as flesh began to peel away from her wrists.

I recognized two of the men. Joseph and Allan Ogden, two of the meanest and loathsome bastards I'd ever seen. They prided themselves on how quickly they could track down and capture runaways, and made a healthy living off the bounties they collected. To them, catching slaves was about more than the money; they enjoyed the hunt. Catching and beating slaves half to death before turning them over to their owners was payment enough. Any slaves they caught would inevitably beg to be taken back to the plantation. No matter which punishment was in store for them at home, it was better than being alone with the Ogden brothers. Slaves told stories about them like they were bogeymen, and scared their children to warn them not to run away. The leers on their filthy, sweat-soaked faces made my flesh crawl.

"She's going to get it now," Lottie whispered. Her cheeks were flushed with her building excitement.

I tried not to watch, but I couldn't seem to take my eyes off Harriet. Jimmy smacked the horse's backside and set it at a trot around the machine. Harriet's body swung out away from the screw as the horse made its first turn and when she returned to the starting point, the overseer was there waiting with his whip. At some point, maybe after the second or third turn, her arms popped out of their sockets and she screamed. Tears, snot, and sweat dripped from her face and all she could do was moan each time the whip cracked and split open another wound in her flesh. The sweat mixed with blood and ran down her thighs like water in a dried-up river bed, in a slow and steady trickle. There may have been urine mixed in there, too, because after ten turns of the screw, Harriet was dead.

When they finally took Harriet's broken body down from the cotton screw, Lottie rushed over to get a better look. She was delighted by the taunts Jimmy and the other men continued to yell at the dead woman. They all laughed and congratulated each other on a job well done. Harriet would never run again. She wouldn't laugh, she wouldn't sing. And she would never hold her children.

I went back to the laundry and hid among the sheets, using the clean linens to hide my face and cover the sound of my sobs. The last thing I wanted was to draw attention to myself. I saw the look in Lottie's eyes. Never satisfied, she wanted more entertainment. I didn't want to take my turn on her stage.

Unlike Harriet, I was content to live on the plantation. It was my home. I knew nothing of the world outside and didn't want to know if it meant punishment at the hands of the Ogden brothers. I never wanted to experience the same fate. Lottie had frightened me ever since the day I saw her kill the chicks in the hen house, but after she'd turned on Michié Henri, she truly terrified me. But it was more than that; I was afraid of how I was changing due to her influence. It was just as much my fault that Michié Henri had left the plantation with two broken legs because I'd lied to save my own skin. I'd done whatever I needed to do to escape Lottie's attentions. But sometimes, no matter how hard I tried to be good, trouble found me anyway.

I feared Lottie, but I didn't hate her. I didn't hate anyone, even though *les Blancs* were often cruel and selfish. Not much I could do about that. Moman always said not to worry about things I couldn't change. The only thing I could really change was my own mind. Sure, Lottie was hateful and vicious, but hating her back didn't make my life any better. It just made me feel angry all the time.

Anger is exhausting. It's like a poison that eats away at your soul and leaves you feeling worse than any other person could ever make you feel.

At least, that's what Moman told me.

A few weeks after we planted Harriet's body in the ground, I found myself in another situation that completely changed the way I viewed my half-sister.

It was a hot day in June. There had been no rain in five days. Everyone was miserable, and tempers flared at the slightest mistake.

"Jacqueline, go run your pretty little ass down to the well and fetch some water," Jimmy called from the porch.

"Yes, Michié, right away."

Lottie giggled behind him, and a chill passed through me. I remembered the woodshed.

I grabbed the tin pail and placed it on the ground beneath the pump. I hated fetching water. The pump handle was too big and heavy, and it was hot from sitting in the sun all morning, so the metal scalded my hands as I strained to lift the handle. Once I'd primed the pump I could fill the pail in no time, but getting it started was no easy task. I was twelve that summer, but small for my age.

The handle wouldn't budge. I got my shoulder under it and tried to push up with my legs. Still, it wouldn't move. Sweat broke out on my forehead and upper lip. Jimmy didn't like to wait. My heart raced as I pictured his sweaty red face glaring down at me. I could almost hear Lottie encouraging him to do his worst to me as they planned my punishment. I pulled and pushed and tugged, but I couldn't prime the pump. Tears threatened to fall from my eyes as I cursed that iron monstrosity.

"Need help?" Gabriel lifted the pump handle and got the water flowing in no time. Cold water splashed into the pail. I turned to thank Gabriel, but he was already making his way back to work, across the yard. We hadn't spoken since I'd warned him about what would happen if Jimmy caught us alone together. Gabriel never laid a hand on me, but men like Jimmy think all men behave as badly as they do.

I splashed water on my face and neck. It felt good, but I couldn't linger. My heartbeat raced as I ran back to Jimmy, careful not to spill a drop of his water.

Jimmy snatched the pail from my hand, spilling more than half of the water on the ground. The soil sucked it up greedily. "What took so long? I thought I'd die of thirst."

Lottie mocked me as I knelt down to pick up the pail and tried to save as much water as I could.

"What's the matter, Jacqueline? You got the dropsies, girl?"

This was all just a game to her. I was nothing more than a toy or a pet, and I'd seen what had happened to her pets.

"I'll go back to the well and get more, Michié Jimmy."

He scowled at me and spat in the dirt. "Clumsy nigger! I'll teach you what it means to be thirsty."

He grabbed my wrist and dragged me to the barn where the livestock was kept. I screamed and kicked, but his grip tightened on my wrist as we drew closer to the gaping mouth of the barn door. The temperature inside the barn was a little cooler from the shadows cast by the big wooden beams overhead, which gave me a moment of relief from the heat. I looked around the large open space hoping to find another exit, but Jimmy and Lottie were standing between me and freedom. He threw me in the corn crib and slammed the lid shut, then hefted something heavy on top of the lid. Lottie giggled as she peered at me through a knothole in the wood.

"You can stay in there until you know what it means to be thirsty." There were threats of violence in Jimmy's voice. Lottie's laughter faded as they left me alone.

The corn crib was dark and hot. It should have been quiet in the barn since all the animals were out in the field, but something was rustling around in the corn. A small body covered in coarse fur brushed against my bare thigh. My leg jerked, and I pulled my knees into my chest.

A pointed wet nose poked into my ear. Whiskers scratched my cheek. Sharp little nails clicked against the bare wood as something sniffed me, pawed me, and then bit me. I screamed and cried and kicked them off, but they just kept coming. I kept screaming until my throat was too dry to swallow and my sides hurt like I'd been running from an alligator down by the swamp. I couldn't make another sound. The rats kept biting me. My tears mingled with blood as the salt from my sweat stung the cuts and scratches on my face. It was so hot my tears eventually dried up, but sobs shook my sides until my shoulders and back ached.

I couldn't tell if it was night or day. Hunger and thirst were the only reminders of time passing. I blacked out several times, but the rats never slept. I thought about eating the dried corn kernels, but, like me, they were covered in rat shit and piss. I prayed someone would find me before I died of thirst.

Voices in the barn woke me. I called out, but my own voice was gone. My dry, swollen tongue caught on the cracked skin of my lips. I gave up and kicked against the inside of my coffin instead. Whatever had been holding the lid shut scraped along the wood and fell to the ground with a thud. Covered in scratches, rat bites, blood and dried urine, I shielded my eyes from the bright morning sunshine streaming through the barn door. Gabriel's strong arms pulled me from my dark, hot, rat-infested prison. Exhausted and dying of thirst, I went limp in his arms.

"I found her," he called to the faceless voices.

"Water..." It was the only word I managed to utter before I fainted.

When I finally woke up a day later, I was back in my own bed. Clean, dressed in fresh clothes, my wounds treated and healing, I knew three things. First, I wasn't dead. Moman told me whatever didn't kill me made me stronger. Second, freedom may not be worth dying for, but I was willing to kill for it.

And third, I needed to stay alive long enough to see Lottie and her brother pay for the terrible things they'd done to me.

Chapter 5

About a month after Gabriel pulled me from the corncrib, a young man came to court Lottie. His name was James Lynch. His daddy was a slave trader who'd made his fortune in the West Indies. Michié Lynch had grown up on the Island of Saint Vincent, where there had been recent slave uprisings. After the brutal —but justified— killings of several white plantation owners and their families, Lynch and his mother were sent to live in New Orleans, where he planned to make his fortune as an architect.

He was handsome, I suppose, and Lottie was head over heels. He spent a few weeks at the plantation enjoying Master's hospitality. All day, he'd be at Lottie's side, taking walks in the gardens, reading under the magnolia trees, and eating picnic lunches in the tall grasses near the cotton fields. He was all flowers, smiles and romance; a perfect gentleman who met with Mamzèl's approval as a proper suitor for her daughter, and unlike Michié Henri, James Lynch didn't need to shield his privates from a good kicking if he paid too much attention to Lottie.

By day he was a model fiancé, but at night he kept company with Jimmy and the overseer. Every evening after dark, they'd stroll down to the slave shacks and help themselves to one or two. I felt bad for those women, but I was thankful Moman and I didn't share our sleeping quarters with the other slaves. They enjoyed themselves so much with one young girl that she ended up dead.

After they took turns with Lucille in front of her younger sisters, they took her out behind the shack and beat her until she stopped drawing breath. No one knew why they killed her. Sometimes, *les Blancs* didn't even have to bother making up reasons to kill slaves.

Lucille's grandfather, Old Black Nate, said they did it because they could. He'd found her half-eaten body in with the hogs when he went to feed them the following morning. All he could do was cry —once he was done throwing up his breakfast.

"They didn't have to kill her like that," he told Moman. "She did what they wanted, and in front of all those babies. They call us animals, but they're worse than beasts."

Moman comforted him and gave him a tincture to calm his nerves. That old man had seen so many horrors during his long life; it was a wonder he didn't pluck out his own eyes. I'd never seen him so upset. There was his grand-daughter: dead, broken, her face eaten away, and the rest of her covered in pig shit. Someone else had to bury her because he couldn't stop crying long enough to dig the hole. We all took turns doing his chores for a few days until he could rest up and get himself back together.

I wanted to show Lottie where Lucille was buried and tell her what I knew about her sweet, handsome young suitor. I didn't dare. What difference would it make anyway? She'd made up her mind that she was going to be Madame James Lynch and that was the end of that. I could have told her I'd seen him snatching babies out of cribs in the slave shacks to smash their heads against trees and all she would have said was 'Oh, Jacqueline, they're just dumb animals.' She didn't want to hear the truth about her fiancé. Lottie shrouded herself in lies. She thought she was a fairy princess, but she was more like a wicked witch.

Chapter 6

A week after I turned fourteen, Master gave me to my half-sister as a wedding present. I remember the day clearly. It was late October and the promise of cooler days floated on the air. The sky was a steely gray without a hint of sunshine, and the leaves turned up their faces to the breeze. All day it threatened to rain, but Lottie insisted on a garden wedding. Autumn flowers were in full bloom along the stone path leading to the garden where fat orange pumpkins grew on vines along the ground. Slave boys ran back and forth across the grass setting up chairs for the guests. I helped Moman prepare the fine foods and bake the wedding cake. We gathered little yellow and orange flowers to decorate the cake, which was covered in rich white icing.

Lottie's mother wanted the wedding to be perfect and yelled at everyone even if they were doing what they'd been told. The groom and his family were late. Lottie's aunts and cousins placed bets on whether he'd show at all, or if she'd be left at the altar like a spinster. Moman kept me busy and out of Mamzèl's way all morning. She was afraid I'd get into trouble. I spread crisp white linens on the tables in the dining room, set out the china and silverware, filled pitchers with cold water from the pump, and cut fresh flowers for the centerpieces. By the time the priest arrived at noon, everything was ready except for the groom's arrival and Lottie's final preparations.

Moman was Master's favorite slave, and he complimented her on how fine she looked that morning — a rare show of affection for her that unfortunately didn't escape Mamzèl's notice. Powerless to punish her husband, she made him punish Moman instead. While I helped Lottie dress for the most important day of her life, Master stumbled into the room. He'd gotten home late from the bachelor party and still smelled like whiskey and stale cigar smoke.

"Lottie, I have something to tell you...oh good morning, Jacqueline." I couldn't remember ever having heard him speak my name before.

"What is it, Papa, has James arrived?" Lottie fussed with her hair.

"No, but I have something important to tell you." He paused trying to find the right words. Since he never spoke to me, I couldn't help but pay attention to what he had to say next.

"Is something the matter, Papa?" Lottie looked worried.

Master covered his mouth and chin with his hand and stared out the window.

"Jacqueline, I don't know what Esther's told you, but I'm your father." This wasn't news to me, but he paused to allow his words to sink in.

"Oh, Papa, you're still drunk from last night." Lottie tried to laugh off what he said.

"Lottie, your mother wants Jacqueline gone, so I'm giving her to you as a wedding gift. Tomorrow, she'll be going to New Orleans with you and James."

Lottie had always been cold toward me even on the best of days, violent on the worst, but when she learned we were sisters, her whole attitude changed. The look in her eyes told me I had even more to fear from her. It made no difference that we'd grown up together and I knew more about her than anyone else in her life. She hated me, and that was that.

Guests arrived, but still no groom. Fortunately, Lottie was too concerned about her appearance and the fact that we were siblings to worry about the most important part of the day, the wedding itself. After Master's confession, she refused to let me help, and squawked at the bridesmaids like a deranged crow, demanding they fix her hair, button her dress, put her shoes on her feet, and apply her makeup. She was a monster, and I was thankful not to be in the wedding party.

The groom arrived with his kin, still drunk from the previous night's celebrations. I stayed in the kitchen with Moman where it was safe and warm, but we could hear all the commotion around the house. During the wedding, Moman set out the food, and the other slaves helped us serve the meal since there were so many guests. Twenty minutes after the groom showed up, it was time for Lottie to walk down the aisle. None of us were allowed to attend the ceremony, but I hid behind a large weeping willow and listened to the happy couple exchange vows. Lottie's dress, with its long white train and frilly lace, made her look like the cake Moman had made: pretty, sweet, and good enough to eat. If my half-sister were a cake, her center would be rotten.

Moman scolded me for watching the ceremony, but she went easy on me. Something had been weighing on her mind for days, but she wouldn't say what. Had she had a premonition about my leaving the plantation?

The night before I left my childhood home, Moman presented me with a small wooden box filled with dried herbs, charms, unguents, black cat bones, a few beeswax candles, straight pins, and a small bottle of her potion to keep me from becoming an expectant mother. Lottie had her dowry to take to New Orleans, and I had a box of magic for conjuring.

"Hide this in your sack. These odds and ends should hold you over until you can make your own. There's a clean dress, some biscuits, honeycomb, and salt inside the sack, too. Don't forget to lay a line of salt and brick dust across your threshold. It won't keep out *les Blancs*, but it will keep other evils away."

We spent our last night together on the mattress in the pantry. Neither of us got a wink of sleep. My feelings were all mixed up. I was scared, angry, and sad about leaving home and Moman. Who would take care of me in New Orleans? Who would keep an eye out for her here? I listened to the crickets singing to each other all night and my eyes were still open at first light.

Moman made me a special breakfast and salted it with her tears. We didn't speak the words that were hanging in the air around us. After breakfast, she combed and braided my hair and kissed me on the forehead. She hadn't done that since I was little.

Gabriel came to the kitchen that morning before heading to the fields. His hands were behind his back and he shifted from one foot to the other outside in the early morning sun.

Moman invited him to come in. "You got something you need to say, boy?"

He stepped inside but stayed near the door.

"I'm leaving today, before midday," I said.

He nodded his head and held his fist out to me.

"This is for you."

I held my hands out. Gently, he placed a small wooden doll in my palms. It had yellow yarn for hair, just like Lottie.

"I made it myself. You can get your hands on some of her hair, can't you?"

Moman laughed and covered her mouth.

"Thank you, Gabriel. I'll keep it somewhere safe."

He gathered me up in a big embrace before turning to leave.

"Be careful, that city's full of people waiting to eat you up," he said.

"I'll do my best to stay out of trouble."

Moman gave him some biscuits to eat on the way to the cotton fields. I waved goodbye to him.

"That boy will make a fine husband one day," Moman said.

"If he lives long enough to find love," I replied.

"He's already found it."

Chapter 7

In the fall of 1842, I moved to New Orleans. Soon after, Lottie's husband became the most sought-after architect in the *Vieux Carré*. Unlike his slave-trading father, he brought dignity as well as wealth to his family through his business dealings with some of New Orleans' more prominent families. Lynch was the first architect to add indoor plumbing to homes, and he designed the City Hall building. As his wealth and reputation grew, so did my half-sister's pride and vanity. He already owned three slaves, and, as part of Lottie's dowry, I became his fourth.

Big John, a large dark-skinned man, answered the door, tended the horses, and followed Lynch around the city while he met clients and oversaw his many building projects. I liked Big John. He always had a kind word and a smile for me, especially if he noticed I was having a hard time. Sometimes he'd pick flowers from the garden and bring them into the kitchen to brighten my mood.

Cook laughed at me when I giggled and blushed at Big John's attention. Her shiny round face would glisten with sweat all day long as she stirred the stews in the open hearth in the kitchen and baked bread in the large brick oven behind the house. "Silly child, actin' like Big John's your lover man. What you think? He gonna ride off with you and take you to freedom?" Big John was kind, but I didn't think of him as a lover.

Besides, he only had eyes for Mathilde. A few years older than me, she was quiet and walked with a limp. Her face was perfect even with the long-jagged scar that ran across her cheek. She had been severely whipped and hobbled as a child after trying to escape her first owner, who'd raped her repeatedly since she was eight years old. When she got her first blood, her master didn't want her anymore, and he sold her to Lynch. She shared the room next to mine with Cook. Sometimes her nightmares tore screams from her that would wake the dead. On those nights, Cook would calm her and help her fall back to sleep.

I slept in a small room at the back of the house, overlooking the cistern that supplied water for the Lynches' kitchen and bathroom. At night I mended and ironed clothing by candlelight and prayed to the *loa* to look after Moman, even though I knew she could protect herself. Having my own room was a small comfort. It gave me privacy to practice the spells Moman had taught me. Each day I spent tending to Lottie, I looked forward to the few moments I had alone at night before falling asleep.

As Lottie's body slave, I dressed her, bathed her, combed and styled her hair, kept her room in order, followed her to market, and attended to her every whim. I also ran her errands, which allowed me some freedom to move about the city on my own. There were free blacks, *les gens de couleur libres*, living in New Orleans, and even *les Blancs* who helped slaves petition for their manumission, or simply helped them escape up North. The wealthy Creole families hated the Abolitionists almost as much as they hated the Americans encroaching on their territory. The thought of running away did cross my mind at times, but my memory of poor light-skinned Harriet always made me return to the house on Royal Street.

Every Sunday morning, Big John would take the Lynches to church in the carriage. I made the beds, dusted Lottie's porcelain doll collection, and cleaned the indoor bathroom. Mathilde was usually out back beating the rugs clean. And Cook prepared the meal — roasted meats, cowpeas, stuffed mirlitons, and cornbread. We all looked forward to her Sunday suppers.

Sunday mornings were always quiet, and since the Lynches were out, we could go about our business, gossip, sing, and laugh to our hearts' content. But one of those mornings, Lynch claimed he wasn't feeling well and stayed home from church. He was a busy man, working six days out of seven, so he'd stayed in bed late to catch up on his sleep. Around eleven that morning I brought him his breakfast. I was surprised to find him awake and sitting up in bed with a book. I set the tray of biscuits, butter, jam, and coffee on the nightstand.

"You look pretty this morning, Jacqueline." His tone was playful, but his words made me uneasy. He was paying more attention to me of late, and his interest made Lottie jealous. Her life mirrored her mother's.

"Cook needs me in the kitchen," I lied. "Can I get you anything else?"

"I don't need anything but your company. Sit down." He patted the space next to him on the bed.

I stood near the door, muscles frozen and unable to move. Again, he called my name, with a deceptive gentleness in his tone. He even smiled. But what I saw was a mask that barely covered the lip-smacking grin underneath. I may not have gone to school like Lottie, but I wasn't a fool. Jimmy had educated me in the woodshed. Lessons in brutality and shame I'd never forget. I stood staring across a space of only ten feet between the doorway and the bed—a short distance that seemed to stretch on forever.

"I said *sit down*, Jacqueline."

It wasn't as if I couldn't hear him or didn't understand the words, but my legs refused to carry me across the floor. He sighed. I knew what he was capable of and I didn't want to make him angry. I thought of the poor dead girl with the missing face. Bile burned the back of my throat.

"Don't make me come to you, girl."

His smile was gone. He didn't like to wait. He was the master of the house and got what he wanted when he wanted it. I willed my feet to move, and stood before him.

"Get undressed."

I did as I was told. My hands trembled and I had a hard time unfastening the drawstring that held up my skirt. My fingers fumbled with the hook and eye clasps of my plain linen shirt. Although the room was warm, stifling almost, goose bumps covered my skin. I stood naked and shivering before him.

"Let me get a good look at you."

"Yes, Michié." I kept my eyes on the floor and did as he asked. I sat on the edge of the bed with my back to him, afraid to meet his eyes.

"Here, Jacqueline." He took my hand and slid it under the covers. "That's it. Just like that."

I wanted to run from the room and hide. But I had to do what I was told. Moman's voice shouted in my head, *Trouble, Jacqueline, les Blancs are nothin' but trouble*. She was right, but I was powerless to do anything about it. I dreaded what would happen next.

My body remained rigid. I closed my eyes tight, clenched my teeth, and tried not to scream. Once he'd finished, he collapsed on top of me.

"I knew you'd be sweet, Jacqueline."

I had no words. My insides felt black and diseased. I wanted to die. I quietly dressed and left the room to clean up before Lottie came home from church. Before I walked out the door he called to me.

"Same time next Sunday." It wasn't a question.

I knew Lottie suspected something, but apparently, she didn't care. The shame and fear I felt each time he touched me couldn't compete with the hatred I felt toward her for doing nothing about it. I shouldn't have been surprised. She'd watched her brother do unspeakable things to me. Why should things be any different with her husband? I hoped Hell existed and that the Devil would greet her with open arms the day she died.

I despised Lynch, but fortunately I wasn't being bred like an animal for profit. I once overheard the overseer telling Jimmy nothing was more valuable than a breeding nigger. I didn't want my value to double. Moman's herbal concoction worked just fine, but sometimes I got busy and forgot to drink it. So far, I'd been lucky, but I needed to figure out a better way to protect myself. One of the worst things I could imagine was carrying Lynch's child. Lottie was already jealous. She didn't need another reason to hate me.

One Sunday morning after I left Lynch's bedroom, Cook gave me a double take when I entered the kitchen. She stood and stared at me with her hands on her hips and clucked her tongue against the roof of her mouth. "Girl, you ain't careful, you gonna get yourself in trouble."

I didn't answer.

"How many weeks you been going up to that bedroom?"

"Five or six."

"Umm hmm. Didn't your moman teach you nothin' about protecting yourself from having babies?"

"She did teach me, but that man won't stop. I keep the potion hidden in the pantry, but I need something stronger to keep him away from me." I spoke in a harsh whisper.

The next week, Cook took me to see a conjurer. He lived a few blocks away in a poorer section of the Quarter, near the brothels. The tiny house made of white washed wooden slats was sandwiched between two identical houses that made it seem very ordinary from the outside. The narrow front door, painted pink to match the shutters, bore a simple sign that read: Squire Jean — Conjuring and Root Work: Appointments Only. Nothing else about the house made it obviously unique, but that was good. Unwanted attention could easily be avoided by blending in with one's surroundings. Hiding in plain sight usually kept folks with supernatural gifts safe from normal people. It also made it easier for the gifted to take advantage of regular folks. Talk around the Quarter told that old Jean was an abolitionist, too. He helped slaves connect with the Underground Railroad and organized escapes up and down the coast. The punishment for helping slaves escape was death, especially for black-skinned abolitionists.

Cook knocked gently on the front door and waited for an answer. A mulatto boy about my age greeted us.

"*Bonswa, Mamzèl*, do you have an appointment?"

"No, but I...I'm...in trouble and I need the Squire's help."

"*Bon*, I'll ask if he can see you this afternoon. Please wait here in the sitting room." He opened the door wider to admit us to Squire Jean's home.

An ornate six-foot-wide crystal chandelier hung above the main entranceway. It must have been beautiful when lit, but little light shone in the house at all. Dark red velvet wallpaper and matching garnet rugs adorned the foyer. Candles burned in wrought iron sconces along the walls that led down a long hallway to the back of the house. The rooms beyond were cast in shadows.

The sitting room was decorated in shades of blue and green,

with sheer ceiling-to-floor curtains that caught a gentle breeze and danced about the dimly lit room in a ghostly fashion. Cook took hold of my hand and patted it to calm my nerves. I don't know why I was so nervous. I wasn't afraid of the Conjure Man. I'd been around *Vodun* my whole life. What I hadn't learned from Moman, I'd picked up from Cook. She and Mathilde attended ceremonies in Congo Square on the rare occasions they were allowed to leave the Lynches' house, and were loyal followers of Squire Jean.

Squire Jean was a very attractive, petite man with skin almost as dark as Cook's. His black eyes scanned us suspiciously before he entered the sitting room.

"Why have you come here, child?"

"She worried about being in a family way," Cook said.

The conjurer stared at me with his hands on his hips. "Can't she speak for herself?"

"I don't want a baby. Slavery is no life for a child."

"Who tryin' to breed with you?"

"Michié Lynch."

"He own you?"

"He's married to my half-sister. She owns me."

"Stand up." He stepped closer.

I obeyed the conjurer.

He examined my eyes, made me stick out my tongue, and pushed and prodded every inch of me. "Your body is strong, but your spirit is weak. You need to be stronger. Up here," he tapped my forehead with his middle finger. "Understand?"

I nodded.

"I mean it. I will help you, but you need to summon your own strength. Dig deep and conjure your own magic or what I'm going to give you won't work."

Angry tears fell from my eyes. "He makes me lie with him. I

don't want his baby."

"Don't worry, child. I'll help you."

He turned toward the door of the sitting room and motioned for Cook and me to follow. We walked down the hallway to a shadowy room at the back of the house. Black fabric draped the walls and windows, snuffing all light but for the pulsing glow from two white candles on opposite sides of a crude wooden table at the center of the room. Behind the table, an open cabinet displayed glass jars in all sizes, colors and shapes. Inside the jars were dried herbs and flowers, stones and seashells, chicken feet and feathers, bones and teeth, and a lot of other stuff I didn't recognize. A man with a burlap sack over his head sat motionless in a chair next to the cabinet.

"Who that?" Cook asked.

"Him? Nobody."

Squire Jean went to the cabinet to gather everything he needed, and got to work. He crushed herbs in a stone mortar with a wooden pestle. The *véve* he drew with brick dust on the floor were unlike any I had ever seen Moman use. He murmured his spell quickly in a tongue I didn't understand and beckoned me towards the table. He grabbed my wrist, palm up, and sliced across the calloused flesh of my hand. Blood welled up along the shallow wound and dripped into the mortar to be mixed with the herbs. The *Hougan* chanted and combined the herbs with my blood.

The man in the corner stood up and moved herky-jerky towards the table. Cook gasped and grabbed my hand. The salt from her sweaty palm burned my fresh wound and I snatched my hand back from her grasp. Squire Jean forced the man face down on the table and cut off his head with one slash of a machete. I covered my mouth so I wouldn't scream. He must have goofered that man with graveyard dust. I don't know what he'd done to deserve it, but people rarely let you cut their heads off without a fight. The blade stuck fast in the wooden tabletop and the man's body fell to the floor. Only his head remained on the altar.

I should have been more concerned about the powerful dark magic in that house and what herbs went into the mixture, but I was too desperate to care. The longer I waited to do something, the greater the chance of me being with child. It didn't matter that Lottie's husband was raping me, somehow it would still be my fault. The conjurer smeared the dead man's blood all over his hands and came towards me, still chanting.

"Lift your shirt, girl!"

I obeyed and bared my stomach to Squire Jean. He pressed his bloodied hands to my bare flesh, leaving dark red handprints on my body. The chanting stopped.

"Do not wash the blood off for three days." He gathered the mixture in the mortar into a small glass mason jar. "You give this to him once a day in his food until it's gone." The conjurer wrapped the jar in cloth and handed me the bundle. "When the potion is gone, your problem will be gone with it."

I didn't ask what he meant.

"I can't pay you."

"Money ain't a concern of mine, child. Someday you will do me a favor as I have done for you today. There's more going on inside you than you know."

Cook and I stayed in Congo Square to dance and gossip with other slaves and *les gens de couleur libres*. It was one of the few places we could be open with our speech and not worry if *les Blancs* were listening. For a few hours, I forgot about my worries.

Chapter 8

Early the next morning, while I fixed breakfast, I heard Lynch say goodbye to Lottie. I quickly poured fresh milk into a mug, added Squire Jean's potion, a spoonful of sugar, and a dash of cinnamon.

"Michié Lynch, drink this," I said handing him the mug. "You'll starve without breakfast."

"Thank you, Jacqueline," he said, a queer expression on his face. He drank it all down in one gulp and wiped his mouth with the back of his hand. I took the empty mug from him and hurried back to the kitchen.

It was still dark when Big John drove him to the docks in the carriage. A new business client was coming to stay as a guest in the house. Normally, Big John would fetch the client alone, but this man was too important. Lynch wanted to greet him in person.

"We simply must make a good first impression. James will make a fortune off this man if he builds him a house," Lottie said. Pride, vanity, and greed — if there was a Hell, Lottie was surely headed there.

I spent most of the day helping Mathilde prepare for the guest's arrival. He'd requested special curtains be made and hung in his room. *Les Blancs*, especially the rich ones, could be as strange as they wanted. No one gave it a second thought. And, since the curtains were made at his expense, Lottie told me to accept the delivery and hang them the day before her husband's new client arrived.

All morning I fussed with those drapes. They were heavy and awkward. My arms ached from straining to lift the fabric and raising my arms over my head to pin them to the curtain rods high up at the top of the window casings. I was a hard worker with a strong body, but I couldn't get the job done alone. Eventually, I had to ask Mathilde to help me steady the ladder and hold the fabric as I pulled straight pins from the corner of my mouth to get them hung. It was noon when we got the sixth panel of dark green velvet tucked into place. Small flecks of the fabric dotted our otherwise clean white aprons. Thank goodness our heads were covered by our *tignons*, or we would have been combing dark green threads out of our hair for weeks.

We worked twice as hard to finish the rest of our chores for the day. It was Thursday and I looked forward to dusting the books in the library, but the leather-bound treasures were not at the top of Lottie's list of things to do. I swept floors, polished the large silver mirror, and made the bed in the guest room. After all the time Mathilde and I had wasted hanging the thick velvet drapes, I wasn't able to put fresh sheets on the bed. I could do that later in the afternoon, which would keep them crisp longer as the afternoon heat seeped out of the air. But first, I needed to accompany my sister to the market down by the river on Decatur.

Lottie snapped open an eggshell-white lace fan as Mathilde and I came out of the guest bedroom.

"Finally," she said.

A tiny gust of air pushed her curls back off her neck as she slowly flipped the fan back and forth in front of her face. It was already almost too hot to live, so there was no time to dwell on the heat.

"There's a lot more to do. Hurry up and get ready to go to

market, Jacqueline. I wanted to leave an hour ago."

"Yes, Mamzèl."

I quickened my step down the back staircase and hurried to find the market baskets. In the pantry, I slipped into my worn, brown leather shoes, one of the few luxuries Lottie allowed me. I could wear them when I ran errands, but I was not to wear them around the house and garden. She had given them to me when we moved to New Orleans. I'd never owned shoes on the plantation, so it took me some time to get used to wearing them. At first, they pinched my toes and made my feet sweat. When Lynch questioned the purchase, it was no shock that Lottie had bought them for her own satisfaction.

"No slave of mine is going to be seen walking barefoot at my side in the Quarter. It's uncivilized. She'll wear these shoes in the streets to show that we spare no expense, not even when it comes to outfitting our slaves."

Mathilde and Cook didn't have shoes. They left the house less often than I did, and were usually alone or with other slaves. Lottie almost never let me out of her sight. Trust wasn't the issue. Even though she hated the fact we were sisters, she still knew me better than anyone else in the city. She was crazy in love with her husband, but she didn't like his slaves. She barely tolerated Cook and Mathilde, and she'd never be comfortable with Big John in the house.

"It's not natural," she told me. "Boys like John should be outside, not in the house. I see the way he looks at me. A woman could die of nervousness worrying about a big strong buck like that staring at her all day."

Big John had no interest in Lottie. He only cared about Mathilde. Besides, he never raised his gaze above the knee when speaking to white ladies. She acted like she didn't want his attention, but that was all she talked about. How she ever got the idea he was dangerous was beyond me. He wasn't planning to take her out back to tear off her clothes and have his way with her. Sometimes, I think she hoped it would happen. Wanted it more than anything. I prayed she wouldn't do to Big John what she'd done to Michié Henri. Lies are dangerous things.

Newspapers showed pictures of dead black men swinging by their necks all the time, supposedly for raping white women. The idea that male slaves ran around the South like satyrs was ridiculous. There were more white men in New Orleans like Lottie's husband than decent white folks wanted to believe. *Les Blancs* liked lies. Lies made them feel better about themselves and allowed them to forgive all the evil things they were doing to each other and their slaves. I saw how the Creoles treated the Americans, and although the French could be cruel and hateful, they still treated their slaves better than the new crop of white folks who lived on the other side of Canal Street. To hear the Creoles talk, I expected to see the Americans down on all fours rutting like pigs in the street. They walked upright like everyone else, but seemed to hold their noses a little higher in the air.

I rushed to gather my things for market, but took a moment to rub a few drops of *eau floride* on my arms and neck before saying a prayer to *Ayizan*, the *loa* who protects markets and open spaces. The Quarter was alive with bad energy, and I didn't want to bring any of it home with me when I was done shopping with Lottie. She could generate enough negative feelings as it was, and I needed all the strength I could muster just to make it through the day.

I met Lottie in the foyer beneath the large crystal chandelier and followed her into the afternoon sunshine. I carried the square, reed baskets stacked against my hip. They would be full by the time we left the market, so Lottie had given Big John instructions on where to meet us with the carriage. We went shopping at least twice a week for fresh fish, scallops, vegetables, and fruits. Big John knew where and when to come fetch us.

We made our way along Royal Street towards the Cabildo for the third time that week to the *Marché aux Legumes*, my favorite section of the French Market. Lottie bought fresh fruit and vegetables, many of which were out of season and overpriced with just a few days until Mardi Gras. She spared no expense for such an important client. A client I'd hung drapes for to shut out daylight.

I was told not to disturb him until after sundown. On the plantation, even white folks rose early to see that all the work got done. In the city, I was allowed to sleep in a little later since we only had a few chickens to tend in the back and I didn't need to fetch water. It was still dark when I got up to gather eggs, make coffee, and roll biscuits. Lottie always loved Moman's biscuits and I knew her recipe by heart. Cook made the eggs, grits, and sausage gravy for breakfast each morning, but only I was allowed to make the biscuits. Like my flesh, Moman's biscuit recipe was part of my sister's dowry. Her husband treated himself to both as often as he could.

I carried the produce and other items Lottie had purchased in the large hand-woven baskets that rested comfortably on my hip. As I waited for her to finish haggling over a large redfish, I caught a glimpse of myself in a polished copper cauldron. I hated being pretty. Pretty or not, girls like me attracted unwanted attention. The way Lynch treated me, and the way men leered at me in the market, made me feel ugly. I worried about my safety in the house and on the streets.

Lottie's voice snapped me out of my thoughts. "Jacqueline, come here, you lazy thing. Didn't you hear me calling you?" She stood with one hand on her silk-adorned hip and a look of disapproval in her eyes. Her tiny bow of a mouth twisted, giving her usual bored look an edge of meanness.

I curtsied and cast my gaze at the ground. "No, Mamzèl."

"Well, hurry up, we still have a lot to do today. You must help me with my bath, iron my dress, and fix my hair."

I hadn't slept much the night before. I'd dreamt about the dark-haired stranger. He was showing up in my nightmares more often, so I was tired and had a hard time concentrating. Lottie continued to talk, and the words started to make less and less sense. All I heard was the shrill noise of her voice as she rattled off the chores I had to do before Lynch and Señor Velasquez arrived.

While I helped Lottie dress for the evening, I kept stealing glances at my reflection in her vanity mirror. The starched white apron was an attractive contrast to the dark blue of the dress. I had brushed and wound my hair up in a red linen *tignon* to hide my dark brown tresses.

"You look very nice, Jacqueline," Lottie said in a rare moment of civility.

"Thank you, Mamzèl." I styled her hair in a loose bun at the back of her head and added her favorite tortoiseshell combs. Lottie admired herself in the mirror and checked her hair from all sides. She was pleased.

"Here, Jacqueline, let's put a little color on you." Lottie dabbed her vermillion lip rouge on my mouth. "James wants you to be extra nice to Señor Velasquez. He's a very important client."

I couldn't hide the disgust on my face. The potion Squire Jean had given me had done its job with the help of my own magic to give it fuel. Lottie's husband hadn't touched me in weeks, but that didn't stop him from offering me up to other men.

"Don't worry, there's no guarantee Señor Velasquez will be interested in you," she chided.

My vision blurred, and I stumbled. I felt dizzy off and on throughout the day. It was probably from lack of sleep. A good night's rest would fix me right up. But I couldn't help thinking about the dark-haired stranger.

"Are you all right? You look a bit flushed."

I managed not to faint and crack my head on Lottie's vanity. "Yes, Mamzèl."

Lottie sat me down and asked Mathilde to bring me some water. Not sure what was wrong with me, she kept talking about our houseguest.

"If he does take a fancy to you, Jacqueline, it won't be like being ravaged by some old drunken overseer or dirty field nigger. Señor Velasquez is a nobleman, well-bred and dignified."

Her words did nothing to reassure me. She saw me as little more than an object to trade for what she wanted. She'd give me to this stranger without a second thought. She had stood by and watched her disgusting brother rape me. She'd turned a blind eye to her husband's behavior —why should I expect anything more from her now? I finished my water, held onto the vanity to steady myself, and stood up.

"Now," Lottie said, "let's go see how dinner is coming along. I need your magic hands to help with the herbs and spices." She wiggled her fingers at me like she was sprinkling pixie dust. "You know how Cook is always making things that taste so bland."

The subject changed quickly. The idea of giving me to a complete stranger to fill her husband's pockets didn't concern her. She didn't care what happened to me.

Lynch and his guest arrived much later than expected. Big John was putting the horses and carriage away, so I greeted them at the door. I was immediately struck by Señor Velasquez's appearance. He was a tall man, over six feet, with long, black hair that fell in soft waves about his face and rested on his shoulders. His charcoal grey suit conformed to his slim, muscular frame. As handsome as he was, something about him made his appearance unsettling. I couldn't decide if it was his unnaturally pale skin or his green eyes that glowed like a cat's. Maybe it was the glimpse of sharp canines that were just about visible when he smiled. It wasn't one thing or another that caused me to stare. He was hauntingly beautiful, yet repulsive at the same time. Even though we'd never met, I recognized him.

Lynch stepped inside the house as I held the door open for him, but his guest hesitated like he was expecting a formal invitation.

"Carlos, please enter. You are most welcome in my home."

Señor Velasquez stepped across the threshold. The air shimmered and rippled even though the day's heat had passed with the setting sun. A chill ran down my back as he entered the house. He arched an eyebrow and grinned at me when I took his overcoat.

When the stranger entered the parlor, Lottie rose out of her seat in a flurry of black silk and lace, like some strange lovesick turkey buzzard, and eyeballed him like he was a dead animal carcass ripening in the heat of the sun. She even licked her lips. I knew that look. She'd given that same look to her music teacher before he'd ended up beaten and broken on the floor. Every man who crossed her path was in danger of being eaten alive. Heaven help the man who didn't desire her as much as she desired him.

"Welcome, Señor Velasquez. We are so happy to have you in our home."

"Thank you, Madame Lynch." His accent was heavy, but he spoke French well. I had heard other Spaniards in the French Market, but never speaking my native tongue.

"Please, call me Charlotte. There's no need to stand on ceremony here." She was visibly shaken by his beauty. Her cheeks were flushed and she fanned herself like it was the hottest day of summer.

"That being the case, who is this lovely creature who greeted me at the door? James never mentioned her when he invited me to New Orleans."

He turned to me and smiled. I wasn't sure what he was up to, but he made me uneasy. I took a step back and almost tripped over my own feet. My nerves were jangled. Could he really be the man from my dreams?

"Jacqueline's one of our slaves. She'll show you to your room and see that all of your needs are met."

"While I have few needs, I doubt this young woman can satisfy *all* of them." He did little to hide his sarcasm.

I just stood there staring at him, not sure if I should run and hide.

"Jacqueline, didn't you hear me? Take our guest's bags up to his room." Lottie spoke the words through clenched teeth.

She was agitated by the stranger's interest in me and she fanned herself so quickly I thought she might snap the fan in half.

"Yes, Mamzèl."

I scurried to grab the two black leather valises by the front door and carried them up to the second floor. As I climbed the staircase, fear stabbed at me between my shoulder blades, like something was creeping up on me. I glanced over my shoulder. Señor Velasquez was walking a few steps behind me, his eyes boring a hole into my back. Another chill passed through me like someone had walked over my grave, and my arms broke out in goosebumps. Whoever this man was, I didn't trust him.

"If my bags are too heavy, I can carry them." He sounded sincere.

"No, Michié. Mamzèl Lynch told me to carry them."

"Do you do everything she tells you?" He joked with me in an exaggerated whisper.

"Have to. I'm a slave."

"I'm sure you break a few rules every now and then," he teased, and gently poked me in the ribs.

"No, Michié. I do what I'm told."

Was he trying to get me into trouble? If he was a friend of James Lynch, he must have an evil streak. No one that man dealt with was ever a true pillar of the community.

"Sounds boring to me. A little danger can be fun."

"Don't want any trouble, Michié."

The door to the guest room swung open as I nudged it with my foot. I carried the bags inside and placed them on the floor next to his bed. I stood up straight to release the knots in my back and reclaim a little dignity. Moman always told me to stand up tall, no matter how low I felt. A straight backbone on a slave was like spitting in the master's eye.

"Will I see you again this evening?" His tone was playful, but he blocked the exit.

"I'll be serving dinner." I spoke to a spot on the wall behind his head. I couldn't make eye contact, but I didn't want to seem rude.

"Am I to dress for dinner?"

He studied his coat sleeves and brushed road dust from them.

"Yes, Michié. You may use the bathroom for washing up. There's a cistern that feeds water into the pipes." I gestured behind me and down the hallway to the back of the house.

"How modern."

"Dinner is at 8 o'clock."

"Thank you, Jacqueline."

He made a bridge with his arm in the doorframe and forced me to pass under it to leave the room. I brushed past him and tried to avoid contact with his body, but he filled up most of the doorway. He smelled the air around me as I walked into the hall.

"Oh, and don't worry, I won't tell anyone your secret."

"W-what secret?"

"The air around you is practically crackling with energy. I can almost smell the magic." He folded his arms across his chest and leaned back against the doorframe, satisfied with his discovery.

"Are you a conjure man?"

"A what?"

"A *Bokor*."

"I don't know what that is, but I assume you mean a practitioner of magic. No."

"Then how do you know about me?"

"We all have secrets." He whispered the words with his mouth pressed to my ear, then took a step back and winked at me. "See you at dinner."

He closed the door and left me standing in the hallway. I stared at the door for a few moments and tried to get my thoughts together. Was he the stranger from my dreams? If he was, how did he know what was going on *inside* my head? I'd worked so hard to keep my secret. Maybe Señor Velasquez was lying about not being a *Bokor*. That had to be it. How else could he know so much about me? Unless he really *did* visit my dreams. I stared at the door until Lottie yelled for me from the kitchen.

"Coming, Mamzèl."

I hurried down the back staircase to the pantry. Lottie stood in the middle of the kitchen with her hands on her hips.

"What's gotten into you, Jacqueline? I called you three times."

I only heard her once.

"Something scare you, girl? You look like you've seen a ghost."

I wiped sweat from my palms onto my apron before I got to work and helped Mathilde chop vegetables for the salad. Cook was by the hearth stirring a big pot of gumbo over an open flame. Something *had* scared me. That man. If he told Lynch I was a Mambo, my life was over. Lottie knew about Moman, but she'd never said a word to her husband. Señor Velasquez's secret couldn't be worse than mine. It didn't matter. He was a white man. His word on any subject made mine worthless.

Lynch poked his head into the kitchen from the dining room. "Will dinner be ready on time?"

"Yes, Michié," Cook said.

"Smells delicious. Good work, Charlotte."

All she did was choose the menu. We did all the work. She never cooked a thing in her life. Loved to eat, though. That was one of the few things I liked about Lottie. No matter what you put on her plate, she never turned her nose up to a meal. She was like her daddy that way. Master's wife always complained about the food Moman set on the table. Meat was either over or undercooked. Vegetables were never fresh enough even if we'd picked them from the garden that day. Master always laughed at her and told Moman the food was good. I hoped he was still being kind to her.

"Is Señor Velasquez all settled?" Lynch asked.

"Jacqueline showed him to his room," Lottie said.

He looked at me. "Was he happy with the arrangements?"

"Señor Velasquez wanted to get washed up and change for dinner. He seemed impressed with the indoor plumbing," I said. I continued to chop the vegetables so I didn't have to look at Lynch.

"I think he took a shine to Jacqueline," Lottie said.

"She does look lovely in that new dress. Señor Velasquez might enjoy her company later this evening. A fine-looking girl like that shouldn't go to waste."

Lottie glared at me over her shoulder before following him out of the kitchen. Like it or not, I was in competition with my sister. At least in *her* mind I was.

"I don't like that stranger," I confided in Cook and Mathilde. "There's something not quite right about him. His eyes are like a cat's, and he has sharp teeth like a rat." I didn't say I'd seen him in my dreams.

"Stop actin' so high and mighty. You just don't want to be alone with him. They can't take your mind, but they own your body." Cook wagged a fat, greasy finger at me.

I shuddered again at the thought of the stranger touching me — ashamed it wasn't only a shiver of revulsion. The idea of having his hands on my body excited me as much as it frightened me. How could I be attracted to a man who made me so desperate to run away?

Mathilde rang the bell just before supper to let the Lynches and their guest know the first course was about to be served. I said a little prayer before bringing the oyster and artichoke soup to the table. I served Lottie, then Señor Velasquez, and finally Lynch, as I had been instructed to do. I poured the wine and stepped back against the dining room wall, imitating a shadow. I stood a few feet behind Señor Velasquez's chair, and although I tried to focus on what I had learned, I couldn't help staring at the back of his neck.

I admired the regal tilt of his head and the glossy sheen of his raven-wing hair.

Do you like what you see? The voice belonged to Señor Velasquez, but he hadn't spoken. The idea of him reading my mind frightened me, but even more than that, I was embarrassed that he could feel my gaze upon him.

I know you can hear me, Jacqueline. I asked if you like what you see. Do you find me attractive, or horrifying?

I ignored his voice inside my head and tried to pay attention to when I should bring out the next course. I noticed Lottie's not-so-subtle signal that she had finished her soup. I collected the empty bowls and hurried into the kitchen, relieved that I could escape the dining room for a few moments.

"Girl, you look like you got a haint chasing you." Cook set plates of salad down on the silver tray I brought to the kitchen.

I wiped away the sweat just above my upper lip.

"Are you feeling feverish at all?"

"No, that man just makes me so nervous."

"Well, you never can trust them white devils. I swear they ain't human like you and me. Too bad you used up all of Squire Jean's potion."

Sweat trickled down my temple, and my heartbeat thundered in my chest. As much as I hated the idea of the stranger putting his hands on me, I was more concerned about how easy it was for him to get inside my mind. I took a deep breath and returned to the dining room with the second course.

I didn't mean to scare you, Jacqueline. I was hoping we could become friends. His voice penetrated my skull and pushed its way deep into the secret spaces. *If you open your mind to me, I won't have to force my way inside.* His voice became more soothing as I gave in and allowed him access to my thoughts.

How can you speak with your mind? Can you read my thoughts? Are you the Devil? I was slightly surprised by my boldness.

I heard laughter inside my head. *I hope you aren't superstitious like so many of the slaves I have encountered in this country. You seem too smart for that kind of nonsense.*

My moman didn't raise a fool. She taught me not to trust les Blancs. You seem even less trustworthy than most.

Your madre sounds like a smart woman. I'm no devil, but I do have some unusual abilities. I promise I will not harm you. His voice reassured me. I became distracted by his words and missed one of Lottie's signals.

"More wine, Jacqueline." The impatience returned to her voice. "I swear, sometimes I think you're miles away. What good are daydreams to a slave?" She laughed conspiratorially to Señor Velasquez.

"Bring in the next course, Jacqueline." Lynch puckered his lips like he was expecting a kiss and winked. Lottie was oblivious, but Señor Velasquez saw the inappropriate exchange. He turned to me with a grin, which made me even more nervous.

When I returned to the dining room with the main course, Lottie's mouth was set in a firm line and her eyes had narrowed themselves into slits.

"Don't be upset, Charlotte," Lynch chided. "Carlos simply stated that he's taken a liking to Jacqueline. Maybe he's right. We shouldn't be so hard on her."

Lottie crossed her arms over her breast, rolled her eyes, and clucked her tongue in disgust. "Are you an abolitionist, Señor Velasquez?"

"Abolitionist? No," he said. "I am simply acting as Devil's Advocate here. What proof is there that *Blancos* are truly superior to *Negros*?"

"It says so in the Bible," Lottie almost shouted.

Señor Velasquez laughed and flicked his hand in response to Lottie's statement like he was shooing flies away. "I've read the scientific journals and listened to the speeches of politicians. What if everything we've been told is just a lie to justify the inhumane treatment of one group of people so that another might prosper?"

I almost dropped the silver tray I was holding. Señor Velasquez steadied it in my hands just as I let go. His eyes met mine. He smiled his seductive, sharp-toothed grin at me again. Somehow, I snapped back to my senses and finished serving the main course. I eagerly took my place against the wall when I was done.

Was this man, or whatever he was, out of his mind? Of course, I had heard abolitionists speaking of the evils of slavery and how we must fight to end it. They'd set up soapboxes in the square outside Saint Louis Cathedral, *les Blancs* and *les gens de couleur libres*, condemning slave owners to the Fiery Pit with their words. It was a nice dream, but I never believed anything would ever come of their speeches.

"Are you suggesting blacks and whites are equal, and the only difference between us is that we enslaved them first?" Lottie was furious.

"Your words, not mine." Señor Velasquez calmly took a sip of his wine.

"That's preposterous!"

"I don't think we can look to the Bible as the final word on anything." The dark haired stranger baited Lottie with his words.

"I've never heard anything so ridiculous in all my life. I grew up on my *papa's* plantation, and I know niggers are no different from cattle. It's our right as their superiors to use them as we see fit."

She sounded more like Jimmy than her *papa*.

"It's interesting you should feel that way, Charlotte, because I have a similar belief about all humans." Señor Velasquez wiped his mouth and stood up from the table.

"What's that supposed to mean?"

Maybe the stranger's secret was darker than mine.

"Charlotte, this argument has gone on long enough. Apologize to Carlos."

Lottie kept her arms folded over her chest and refused to speak another word. Sometimes I found her childish behavior funny. Most of the time it just made me sick to my stomach.

"No need for apologies." Señor Velasquez straightened his jacket and finished his wine in one gulp. "We're all entitled to our...opinions. Madame Lynch and I simply disagree."

"Carlos, this is a terrible way to begin your stay in our home."

"Not to worry, James. I'm tired after my travels, and unfortunately I seem to have upset your wife."

Lynch glanced at Lottie. She pouted like a child, her face as red as a sugar beet. "Jacqueline, show Carlos to his room. Mathilde can clear away the supper dishes." He wiped his mouth with a crisp white linen napkin and tossed it on the table. He stared at Lottie and stood until I took Señor Velasquez to his room.

"Thank you, Jacqueline. You are most kind," he said, after I'd drawn the drapes and turned down his bed for the night.

"There are clean linens on the dresser. Will you need fresh water for washing?" I still couldn't meet his eyes. He stepped a little closer to me. I backed myself against the doorframe hoping to escape.

"Jacqueline, I told you before I wouldn't hurt you." His voice was calm and almost reassuring. I wanted to believe him, but remembered Moman's words. *Nothin' but trouble.*

I retreated to the safety of the hallway. "Goodnight, Michié."

"What if I need something in the middle of the night?" His words held me in place —no matter how badly I wanted to run.

"There's a bell. You pull that cord." I pointed at the velvet-wrapped rope. "Big John sleeps in the kitchen. He'll hear the bell and come get one of us up."

"Oh? And where do you sleep, Jacqueline?" His words were laced with sugar and arsenic: tempting and deathly sweet.

"I...I sleep in the slave quarters at the back of the house." It seemed pointless to give him any more information. If he wanted it, he could simply pluck it from my thoughts. I'd given up the idea of being able to protect my body, but my mind had always been safe. Not anymore.

"I see. Well, hopefully I won't need to wake you during the night."

I curtsied and turned to go.

Goodnight, Jacqueline. Pleasant dreams. His voice invaded my mind again, causing my entire body to shiver. But it was the kind of shivering you do when you hear a good ghost story. You get excited at the promise of being scared.

Chapter 9

I was drifting off to sleep when a faint knock at my door startled me. Late night visits in the slave quarters rarely brought good news. I threw on a cotton shift and opened the door, hoping to see Big John.

Señor Velasquez was standing on the other side of the door.

"Y-yes, Michié?" I hated that he made me feel so afraid, so weak. "Can I help you?" Although the evening air was warm and humid, I felt a sudden chill and wrapped my arms tightly around myself.

"Sorry to bother you, Jacqueline, but James insisted I come spend some time alone with you tonight. What do you suppose he meant by that?" A devilish grin spread across his face as he stared down at me.

"I...I don't know."

"He seems to think you're quite the little tease and in need of a good...well, I won't bore you with his vulgarities. I think you get the idea."

My insides liquefied like murky swamp water, and I thought my cheeks were about to burst into flames. Lynch must have told him everything. Or, was this unsettling stranger simply baiting me, hoping I would crack and invite him into my room? He leaned against the doorframe but drew his arm back quickly. Blue sparks flew from his jacket. He stood up straight and stared at his arm in disbelief.

"Jacqueline, you naughty girl, you are superstitious." He shook a finger at me and grinned. "Don't tell me. Let me guess. Is it salt?" He taunted me, but genuine playfulness colored his tone.

I placed my hands on my hips, lifted my chin, and looked him right in the eye. "Salt and a little brick dust."

"Well, I'm impressed. There's more than just salt and brick dust, though." He tested the strength of the invisible barrier gingerly with his fingertips. Tiny blue flames sparked from his flesh and he pulled his charred fingers back quickly. "Is it a spell?"

I nodded and met his gaze.

"Does James know you're a witch? I bet he doesn't. Did he seduce you, or was it the other way around?"

My face grew hot with anger, and I felt the color rising in my cheeks. This stranger knew too much about me. More than most people did, and I had only known him for a few hours, unless you count his visits to my dreams. I knew next to nothing about him. For all I knew, he could've been the Devil himself.

"Well, Jacqueline. I'll keep your secret if you keep mine."

"What secret?" He knew my darkest secret, but I knew nothing about him.

"That I'm a monster, of course." His smile remained stitched in place.

"Oh." I knew there was something unnatural about him, but I still didn't know what he was.

"Aren't you going to invite me in, Jacqueline?"

"No."

"I must say I didn't expect *that* answer. Not after what James has been telling me."

I bit my tongue to hold back a string of curse words and a coppery taste seeped into my mouth. His taunts were becoming unbearable.

"What were the words he used to describe you? Eager to please, insatiable, willing to do anything, always begging for more...shall I go on?"

I felt as though I might choke on my anger and shame. I gritted my teeth and stood my ground at the doorway. "Go away." I heard the words coming out of my mouth, but I was sure someone else must have spoken them. I would never defy a white man.

"And here was I, thinking you a meek little creature. Always doing what she is told. Never misbehaving. A good little slave."

I was tired after my long day. All I wanted to do was climb back in bed. The sun would be up in a few hours, and my personal Hell would begin all over again. No rest for the weary. I was hurt, embarrassed, but mostly angry. My rapist had told this stranger about the most private and shameful moments of my life. More than that, he'd told him I'd enjoyed being raped. In that moment I hated James Lynch more than anyone else I had ever met. More than Lottie. More than the slave catchers. More than Jimmy. My hatred for Lynch ran deep.

"Go away, Devil." My voice came out in a harsh whisper.

"As you wish, Jacqueline. Perhaps another night." He bowed politely and walked back to the main house.

What was I thinking, telling the Devil he couldn't help himself to my body? Had I completely lost my mind? I watched him walk away and made sure he was gone before I closed the door and climbed back into bed.

I'm not sure how long I had been asleep when I heard Mathilde's muffled screams. I rolled over and covered my ears with my hands.

I was so tired, and I needed all the strength I could summon to get through another day in the Lynches' house. I also had conjuring to do to protect myself from the strange houseguest, for mere salt and brick dust would be no match for his persuasive tongue and handsome face. I was worried he would eventually wear me down and take advantage of me at the first sign of weakness. I decided to let Cook calm Mathilde down so everyone could get some rest.

But Mathilde kept screaming. The sun hadn't shown itself on the horizon yet. I wasn't sure what time it was, but I wasn't getting back to sleep. I never had been much of a morning person, but lack of sleep filled my head with a buzzing that slowed my thoughts to a standstill. It took me a few heartbeats to realize something was wrong before I scrambled out of bed and ran next door. Mathilde stood in the center of the room, but I could barely make out her shape until I lit a lantern. She stopped screaming, but her face was contorted into a mask of worry and dread.

"What is it?" My voice was strained, and my head was full of cobwebs.

"She...she won't wake up." Her voice was hoarse. She paced back and forth wringing her hands. A brownish red stain covered the front of her nightdress, and bloody footprints traced a pattern of her pacing on the bare floorboards.

I carried the lantern over to the bedside to get a better look. A jagged wound gaped in Cook's flesh where her throat used to be. I covered my mouth to hold in the screams that were trying to escape. The gash under her chin and the blood-soaked mattress sent chills up my back like tiny spiders racing across my skin. I backed away from the bed and grabbed Mathilde by the shoulders.

"Who did this?"

"She's cold, and there's so much blood." She was hysterical, and I tried to calm her to stop the shrieking, but she wouldn't stop. She'd woken Big John.

"Hush now! You gonna wake up the neighbors." He pushed past us and got a good look at what was left of Cook. Vomit spewed out of his mouth between his fingers. He stepped outside, ashen and shaking. He wiped his mouth with the back of his hand before turning back to us.

"H-how long she been like that?" He gaped wide-eyed at the ravaged corpse.

"I don't know." Mathilde paced and wrung her hands. "She was like that when I woke up."

Mathilde was shaking from head to toe. I grabbed the shawl off my back and wrapped it around her shoulders. She needed it more than me.

Big John was afraid to come back inside the room. I didn't blame him. The room stank like a slaughterhouse.

"Did you do this?" Big John asked.

Mathilde just stared at him.

"I asked you a question. Did you kill her?"

"No!"

"You were the only one in the room with her. What you think people gonna say?"

"She didn't...."

His head snapped around and he glared at me. "Nobody's talkin' to you. Go fix breakfast." I'd never heard a single unkind word out of that man's mouth before. His tone startled me, but my fear quickly turned to anger. I'd put up with *les Blancs* talking down to me day in and day out. No one else was going to speak to me like that.

"Last night, Señor Velasquez came to my door, but I turned him away. I saw him go back into the house. That doesn't mean he stayed there all night."

"You think he did this?" Big John's voice softened.

"There's something strange about him."

"What you mean?" Big John's tone made me feel like a child caught in a lie.

"Maybe he was angry because I didn't let him into my room."

"Now you're talkin' crazy. If he came in here and tried to hurt Cook, wouldn't Mathilde have called for help?"

"Not if she was too afraid."

"Afraid of what?"

"What if...what if he did something to Mathilde so she couldn't cry for help?"

"All the proof is here on Mathilde's nightdress." Sadness etched a shadow across Big John's face like morning stubble as he turned back to Mathilde.

Silence grew between us.

Someone was in that room last night. Blood soaked the mattress. Cook's skin had turned to chalky gray from shiny blue-black, and her dried, cracked lips peeled back from her yellowed teeth in a silent scream.

"Jacqueline. Get your high yella behind in the kitchen and fix breakfast. Michié Lynch'll take a switch to your backside if his breakfast ain't ready on time." Big John's voice wavered as he scolded me in a harsh whisper.

"Mathilde didn't kill anybody. You know that."

"I know she didn't, but who you think is gonna be blamed?" Tears formed in his eyes, but he wiped them away before they could fall.

"That's not fair. No one would ever believe she could do such a thing." I choked back my own tears.

"You ever known a single thing be fair in this life? Fair don't mean nothin' to slaves."

"You know she didn't do it!" The rage in my voice frightened me.

"Who you gonna blame for this so Mathilde don't get punished?" Big John rested his hands on his hips like Moman used to do when she scolded me. Her lessons had stuck with me. She taught me how to take care of myself and the people I cared about.

"Plenty of murderers and perverts in this city. Anyone could have slipped in here in the dark."

"You sayin' you want to tell Michié Lynch we had an intruder last night?" Big John's tone lightened a little.

"Why not? I'll even say I saw someone sneaking over the back wall. That a sound woke me."

"You gonna lie to Michié Lynch? That's dangerous, Jacqueline."

"It's worth the risk to protect Mathilde!"

"Stop!" Mathilde's shrieks rivaled a murder of crows. "Knowin' who killed her ain't gonna bring her back." She wiped snot and tears from her face with a bloodstained shirtsleeve.

"Michié Lynch gonna be up soon. Cook can't make his breakfast, Jacqueline. They gonna want to blame someone for somethin'. Go fix breakfast before you get in trouble, too."

Big John walked back into the death room. He gagged and covered his mouth and nose. He turned Cook's face to the side a little to get a better look at the wound, and her head nearly came off in his hand. He jumped back from the bed and hurried outside again. He looked like a catfish gasping for air on the riverbank.

The room closed in on me. I stood still and focused on keeping the contents of my stomach inside my body. Inhale. Exhale.

Señor Velasquez had been in that room. I felt it in my bones. He was the most likely suspect. Cook might still be alive if I'd invited him to my bed. But there was no sense in dwelling on what might've been. Nothing I could do about it now.

The service bell rang.

Big John had to tell Lynch. No way around it. I hurried back to my room and quickly got dressed. Lynch was waiting in the kitchen when I entered the house from the back garden.

"You're up early, Jacqueline."

"I...I heard the bell."

"Where's Cook? There's no coffee, and she's late making my breakfast."

"She's dead." I said it just like that. No preamble, no ceremony, no tears.

"What's that?" He looked at me like I'd gone crazy.

"She's dead."

"Where is she?" He still hadn't moved.

"Mathilde found her this morning. Big John's talking to her out back now."

Lynch grabbed a set of manacles off the wall by the back porch and ran out the door. He'd already decided Mathilde was guilty without asking any questions.

I stood by the gaping mouth of the hearth. It seemed to be laughing at me. They could blame Mathilde, but that wouldn't stop the murderer from killing again. It didn't matter that my veins felt like they were filled with icy water, or that my stomach twisted itself into knots just thinking about that room. I tried to shrug off the creeping dread. I fed the hearth more wood to stoke the fire that had died down overnight. I needed it good and hot to boil water. Lynch couldn't start the day without his coffee.

I rolled and cut out biscuits. Tightness in my shoulders and neck made the work harder, but working the dough relieved some of the tension. Experience had taught me that hysterical slaves were not tolerated. I needed to remain calm, act detached, and show no signs of knowing what might have happened. Play dumb, and numb myself to the outside world.

I didn't trust Señor Velasquez. If he was to blame, I didn't want to be next on his list.

Lynch rushed back into the kitchen with Big John at his heels. Mathilde must have run off. Dumb, but who could blame her? I'd probably run, too. Big John and Lynch hurried out the front door. If they couldn't find her, they'd set the slave catchers after her. I thought about the Ogden brothers dragging poor light-skinned Harriet to her death. No time to worry about Mathilde. I went about my business and got ready for the day. Lottie would be up soon, and someone had to get the undertaker. Someone had to clean up the mess when he was gone. With Cook dead and Mathilde on the run, that left me to do all the work.

Slaves didn't have the luxury of time to mourn the dead like *les Blancs*.

About twenty minutes had passed when Lynch and Big John came back into the kitchen. The Master of the House sat at the big wooden table in the middle of the room. I brought him his coffee. He stared at the cup like it was some mysterious object he'd never seen before. All the color had drained out of his face. His hands were shaking as he picked up the cup.

"Biscuits'll be ready soon," I called over my shoulder. I wanted to sit down, drink coffee, and talk about what had happened. But it wasn't my place.

"Jacqueline, go wake Charlotte and see if Señor Velasquez is up yet." Lynch's voice lacked its usual strength, and dark circles under his eyes made him look like he hadn't slept in a week. The herbal mixture I'd gotten from Squire Jean was giving him terrible nightmares and keeping him from sleeping right. He was too tired to chase after me, but he didn't suspect a thing. He sipped his coffee and winced at the temperature but eagerly drank it down. His hands were still shaking as he sat the cup back on the table.

"Should I fetch the undertaker, Michié?" Big John took over at the hearth. He pulled the biscuits from the oven to cool and warmed up some salt pork and red beans.

"After we talk to the slave catchers. The constable said they'd be here soon. We'll need some of Mathilde's clothes for the dogs to sniff her out."

I hurried up the back staircase. Lottie was awake and almost dressed since I was busy making breakfast. My half-sister turned away from her reflection to look at me. The corner of her mouth twitched in irritation.

"And just what is going on in the house this morning? All that racket woke me up and then I had to dress myself."

"Cook's dead. Mathilde found her this morning and she's run off. Big John's gone to get the slave catchers, but breakfast is ready."

"Where's James?"

"In the kitchen, drinkin' coffee."

"Are you sure she's dead? Who killed her?"

"Her throat's torn out, but we don't know who did it. Michié Lynch thinks it was Mathilde."

"That's ridiculous. Mathilde wouldn't...she couldn't...what proof does he have?"

"Her nightdress was soaked in Cook's blood."

"Did you see the body? How bad was it?" Lottie's morbid curiosity had gotten the better of her.

"Bad."

After I finished dressing her, we went down to the kitchen to see if there was any news on Mathilde. I fixed Lottie a plate and offered to set it at the big wooden table so she could sit with her husband.

"Monsieur Lynch can eat his breakfast in the kitchen if he likes, but I'll take mine in the dining room."

I followed Lottie with her plate.

"Ah, everyone is awake." Señor Velasquez entered the kitchen from the dining room. He was dressed in a long black velvet robe and wore dark tinted round spectacles that hid his eyes. Under his arm he carried a red leather-bound book and held an empty wine glass in his hand. "I hope I didn't wake the whole house. I was simply hoping to have a little more wine before I retire to bed."

He had rung the service bell earlier, not Lynch.

"Bed? At this hour?" Lottie's voice went up in pitch. "Haven't you been to sleep yet?"

"I was writing in my journal and lost track of time." He was overly polite. "I suppose if I'd had company last night, I would have gone to bed much earlier." All eyes were on me. Señor Velasquez had a smirk on his face.

"Well, you nearly missed all the excitement," Lynch said. "One of our slaves was murdered during the night, and another's run off." He finished his second cup of coffee, and I brought him more.

"Bad luck." Señor Velasquez shook his head in mock sympathy. Then I could hear his voice inside my skull.

No salt and brick dust on Cook's doorstep, Jacqueline?

I pretended not to hear him.

I know who killed her. Do you?

I pictured the blood-soaked mattress. Goosebumps covered my arms and my stomach wound itself into knots.

His voice was inside my head again. *Perhaps tonight, you'll invite me into your room.*

"Truly sorry to hear about your slaves, James. If I can help, please let me know." He stepped past us, craftily avoiding an early morning sunbeam, and climbed the back staircase to his room. We didn't see him again until nightfall.

Chapter 10

It was mid-afternoon before the undertaker came. If Cook had been a white woman, the police would've been called —and maybe even a doctor, to tell us how she'd died.

The undertaker was visibly rattled when he came out of her room. He covered his mouth and nose with a clean handkerchief and gave his apprentice and Big John orders on what to do with the corpse.

I knelt on the red bricks of the walkway surrounding the fountain in the center of the courtyard and gathered the herbs I'd need later for my spell work. I was invisible there in the garden listening to Lynch and the undertaker talking.

"Terrible mess." The undertaker attempted to make small talk with Lynch.

"What?" Lynch stared off into space and smoked his pipe.

"Terrible mess."

"Yes, terrible."

"That runaway slave of yours must have been as strong as an ox. Old woman's head was practically torn clean off."

"Mathilde's a tiny thing. She never showed any signs of that kind of behavior, but who knows? You never really can tell what's going on inside a nigger's mind."

"Are you sure? It looks like a madman tore her throat open."

"They say it's always the quiet ones."

"There were teeth marks on the old woman's neck and shoulder. Like an animal attacked her."

"Mathilde claimed she slept through the whole thing. The drunk who sold her to me said to keep an eye on her. Said she was wild and liked to run. I never saw any evidence of that until today."

Lynch shielded his eyes from the sun as he watched Big John and the undertaker's apprentice carry the corpse down the steps leading from the slave quarters to the courtyard.

"Maybe you're right." The undertaker cleaned his spectacles with his handkerchief. "I once saw a slave break his own fingers to escape his shackles. Who knows what motivates these savages?"

Lynch and the undertaker went inside to finish their business and settle payment for disposing of the body. When they were gone, I dragged the bloodied mattress into the alley behind the house to burn it. While the fire was growing, I brought down all Cook's belongings I couldn't use and threw them on the fire, too. There wouldn't be a funeral, but maybe in a few days Big John and I would say a few words about her, and then it would be over. Until Lynch bought another slave, or dragged Mathilde back to the house, I'd take on all the duties they'd left behind. I could cook, and as far as Lottie was concerned, I was better at it anyway. They wouldn't be missed.

I thought about my own life as I watched Cook's meager belongings going up in flames. Who would miss me if I died? Moman would miss me, but who would tell her I was dead? Would Lottie mourn my death? A dead slave was more of an inconvenience, a financial loss really. Lottie and I were sisters, and even if she hated to admit the truth, she had once viewed me as a playmate if not a friend. Any shred of kindness between us had died the same day our childhood did. I was no fool. I knew we'd never return to that simpler life we had on the plantation as children. All Lottie cared about now was money, power, and the status she had thanks to her husband's business deals. She'd decided long ago that slaves weren't people. Why should she feel bad if one died?

I didn't realize I was crying until Lynch crept up on me. Soot and blood from my hands stained my cheeks after I wiped away the tears.

"Why didn't you spend the night with Carlos last night?" He was angry.

"I...I don't know. He frightened me." It wasn't exactly a lie. He did frighten me, but not for the reasons Lynch probably thought.

"Did he come to your room?"

"Yes, but...I...I told him I was tired, and then he went away."

That was almost a lie, but I couldn't tell him the truth. He'd never believe me. If I revealed Señor Velasquez's secret, a secret I still wasn't exactly sure I understood, I'd have to reveal at least one of my own. It was better not to say too much.

"Was he angry?"

"No. He said he would come back another night."

That was the truth. Señor Velasquez wouldn't take no for an answer for very long. He would be at my door again that night, and the next night, and the next until I finally said yes and invited him in. I had no choice. I didn't want to end up like Cook.

"You *will* say yes tonight." Lynch squeezed my arm to make his point.

"Hopefully, he won't kill me, too." The words fell out of my mouth before I even knew I was speaking them. I stood stock-still with my hands clasped over my mouth, terrified of what would happen next. I braced myself for punishment.

"You think Carlos killed Cook? Think again. When the slave catchers drag Mathilde back to this house, I'll see her hanged by her neck."

"I...I'm sorry, I..."

"You better mind your tongue. Accusing a white man of a crime like that without any proof is dangerous business for a slave."

"Yes, Michié." I cast my gaze at the ground.

"Be nice to him, Jacqueline. I need his business."

"Yes, Michié." My heart ached and my head hurt. All I wanted to do was go to my room and cry myself to sleep. But there was more work to do. My tears would have to wait until the sun went down.

A circle of soft candlelight surrounded me in the dark library. It was silent in the house now that everyone had gone to bed, and I wanted to escape into the pages of a good book, although all books were good in my opinion. Each one held a world of knowledge just waiting to be discovered. Inside a book, I could pretend to be anyone or anything. There was freedom in knowledge. Words expanded my imagination and allowed me to run away with the characters living in the pages. Characters who felt like friends and occupied my mind while my body performed the toil of my daily life.

Sometimes I'd steal books from the library while I was cleaning and read them in my room. But after what had happened to Cook, I was in no hurry to sleep there.

I shrugged off the grim memory and chose a collection of ghost stories from the shelves. All the tales were written in Ireland, the birthplace of Michié Lynch's father. That little island seemed to have more haints than all the swamps and bone yards surrounding the Crescent City. There were still plenty of ghosts here, thanks to outbreaks of yellow fever, cholera, and the tendency for people to kill each other over such nonsense as gambling debts, adultery, and slander. If the dead decided to rise in New Orleans, the streets would be far too crowded to walk through. The gutters ran with blood and human waste, but I was sure tears were in equal measure with the rainwater.

The clock in the foyer had already chimed half past ten shortly before I had entered the library. I sat reading by my lantern for nearly an hour. I was lost in the pages reading about banshees, changelings, and kelpies. There was plenty of time before I had to turn in for the night. Taking care of Lottie meant rising before dawn. As long as I was in bed before the clock struck midnight, I wouldn't fall asleep in the library.

My legs were stiff from having them tucked under me on the armchair. I sat the book down, uncurled my legs and straightened them out in front of me. It felt good to stretch. I accidently knocked the book off the arm of the chair. I prayed no one had heard it hit the floor.

You've been a very naughty girl. Señor Velazquez was sitting in the chair opposite me. His dark clothing made him nearly invisible in the shadows outside my circle of light. How long had he been there?

I covered my mouth to silence a scream. Whatever he wanted, it would be better to stay quiet than let the Lynches find out where I was and what I was doing.

"Shall I tell your mistress what you've been up to in here?" His words mocked me, but at least he was no longer inside my mind.

"Please, Michié. Don't tell her."

"And why should I keep your secret?"

"Because I'm keeping yours."

He laughed. "Maybe you aren't as afraid of me as I thought."

"Nothing's scarier than my sister."

"Sister? Do you and Charlotte have the same father?"

"Yes."

He made a face like he'd tasted something foul and was unable to spit it out. "And she doesn't mind that her husband's been helping himself to your flesh?"

"She pretends it isn't happening."

He clicked his tongue in disgust. "He bragged about having you and said I was welcome to do the same. How often does it happen?"

"Whenever he wants. Lottie couldn't do anything about it even if she wanted to. But I've stopped him. At least for now."

He seemed very interested in what I had to say. "How did you stop him?"

I hesitated, not sure how much I wanted to share with him.

He placed a hand over his heart. "I swear I won't tell."

I still couldn't figure out how he'd gotten into the room without my noticing. I could swear I'd been alone. Where had he come from?

"A potion."

He nodded thoughtfully. "You used magic to keep him away from you. Why haven't you done the same to me?"

"Why are you so interested in me? Can't you find better company?"

He smirked at me and stood from his chair. He towered over me by nearly a foot. I had to look up to meet his gaze.

"Your sister is insane, and her husband is a sadist."

I crossed my arms in front of me and waited for him to tell me something I didn't already know.

"While my actions can be a bit unsavory at times, they both leave a bad taste in my mouth."

I trembled as he took a step closer. His hands were softer than I expected as he traced the shape of my face. He leaned down close to my ear and whispered. "Kiss me and I'll keep both your secrets."

That's all he wanted? A kiss? I expected to have my skirt lifted. To be humiliated yet again.

"Yes, Michié."

"Please, call me Carlos."

His soft, dry lips brushed against my earlobe like moth wings. When he said, "a kiss," I imagined the slobbering smears of spittle Michié Lynch left on my face as he grunted and rutted on top of me. That's not what I got.

Carlos held my face gently in his hands. He searched me with his eyes as if he sought some mystery there, and then he pulled me close in a gentle embrace. His lips parted mine with care. The kiss lingered, but not quite long enough. There was a gentle tug on my bottom lip when he pulled away. I swayed on my feet and he steadied me.

"Breathe," he whispered.

I sat back down and stared up at him, puzzled by what had just happened.

"You act as if you've never been kissed before," he laughed.

"Never like that." I couldn't look him in the eye.

"Well, maybe you should try it more often. It does wonders for your beautiful complexion."

He left me alone then. His footfalls were silent even on the hardwood floor. The clock chimed half past eleven. It was time for bed, but I was sure I wouldn't sleep.

Chapter 11

Just after dusk the next evening, Señor Velasquez sauntered down the back staircase into the kitchen. He was dressed in black and his dark wavy hair was tied back with a red silk ribbon.

"*Buena noche*," he said. "Something smells delicious." He came close to inspect my food preparation. With his eyes closed, he sniffed the air like he was savoring the most wonderful scent in the world.

"It's the herbs and spices I use. My moman taught me how to cook. She's got magic hands in the kitchen."

I bet you have magic hands in other rooms of this house. He took a step closer and his thoughts pushed their way into my mind. I tried to keep him out of my head, but his scent distracted me. He smelled like clean linen, autumn air, and just a hint of decaying flowers. It was an intoxicating blend of smells, but it needed a little something. Like a recipe, I imagined adding sweet or savory herbs and spices to complement his natural scent.

Señor Velasquez stood directly behind me with his nose pressed against my hair. "I can't possibly smell as good as you do."

"Thank you." I tried to sound polite even though I hated him for reading my thoughts.

"Will you join me in my room this evening, or should I come to yours?"

"I'll come to you." I still didn't want him in my room. Once I let him in, it would take more magic than I had to keep him out. It was safer to meet in his room. If he tried to harm me I could call for help. Big John slept in the kitchen and would come running if I screamed.

"If you're going to keep playing hard to get, I'll just have to work harder at tempting you with my charms." He wrapped his hands around my waist, pulling me close so I could feel his breath on my ear, and whispered, "It's only a matter of time before you let me have another taste, Jacqueline. You seemed willing enough last night."

"I'll come tonight." I gritted my teeth but managed to sound happy about being alone with him.

"Why so eager now?" It was his turn to distrust me.

"I don't want anyone else in this house to die."

"Not even Charlotte?"

"No."

"Or her lecherous husband?"

"Their deaths won't bring Cook back or make my life any better."

"I disagree. Their deaths could make your life much better. You know, Jacqueline, you could simply protect yourself and let them all die. Then you could be free."

His words were tempting, but I couldn't let everyone die to save myself. "Even if the Lynches deserved to die, I don't want you or anyone else to kill the other slaves."

"Do you still think I killed Cook? What could I possibly gain from that?"

"If it wasn't you, who was it?"

"I don't know, but whatever killed her, it wasn't me."

"You say 'whatever killed her,' like you know it wasn't a man. Why couldn't it be a man like you or Michié Lynch?"

"We both know there are more creatures in this world beyond animals and mortal men."

He was right, but I didn't want him to know how much I knew about magic and haints. He'd already guessed I was a Mambo, and that was enough.

"It wouldn't matter if you or anyone else killed the Lynches. I'd still have to buy my freedom. I belong to Mamzèl Lynch. I'd be returned to her father on the plantation if she and Michié Lynch died."

"I could give you the money to buy your freedom." He sounded sincere, but I still didn't trust him.

"What would I owe you in return?" Nothing in this world is ever given without a price. Bargaining with this man filled me with fear like I'd never known. I'd never set foot on an auction block, but it felt like my soul was for sale.

"Your loyalty. And perhaps, in time, your affection."

"What if I want more than freedom?"

He raised an eyebrow and tilted his head. "What do you want?"

I didn't get to tell him. Lottie entered the kitchen. "It's nearly 7:30, Jacqueline. Dinner should be on the table."

"Yes, Mamzèl."

"Are you joining us for dinner, Señor Velasquez?" She sounded impatient. "We should get out of Jacqueline's hair and let her serve dinner."

Señor Velasquez was annoyed by the interruption, but followed her to the dining room. *See you this evening, Jacqueline. I can't wait to continue our...conversation.*

I ignored him and ladled chicken and dumplings into a tureen shaped like a rooster. The white ceramic bird had been a wedding gift from a distant cousin. Lottie hated it, so I made sure to use it as often as possible. Maybe it was childish to tease her like that, but it didn't do any harm. A little fun at Lottie's expense would never balance the scales between us, but I did enjoy tormenting her whenever I had the chance.

The conversation was much more civil in the dining room that evening. Señor Velasquez chose not to debate the evils of slavery with Lottie, and asked her questions about her family instead. She rambled on about life on the plantation and how she missed it sometimes. We had that in common. Then she talked about how James had stolen her heart and moved her to the Crescent City. That's where we differed. Lottie had married James Lynch and had claim to all he owned. If she was his wife, what was I? I wasn't his mistress like the quadroon ladies who attended balls at the Salle St. Philippe. I was born a slave and would probably be one for the rest of my life. I wasn't his lover. He'd raped me the first chance he got, and unless I got more of that potion from Squire Jean, he would keep on doing it. He owned me. I was his property.

The clinking of glasses interrupted my thoughts. Lynch was giving a toast.

"To Carlos Diego Velasquez, may we be business partners for a long, long time."

"And to you James Lynch, for opening your home to me, for providing stimulating conversation, and for introducing me to one of the most beautiful young women I've ever met."

"Señor Velasquez, you've made me blush," Lottie giggled.

"I'm sorry, Madame Lynch, I was referring to Jacqueline."

And that was the end of the polite conversation. I covered my mouth to suppress a laugh, and Lottie stormed into the kitchen. I followed obediently. She threw her napkin on the floor and stomped up the back staircase without a word to me. I heard her bedroom door slam and that was the last time I saw her that evening.

I returned to the dining room to see if Lynch and Señor Velasquez needed anything. They were drinking bourbon, smoking cigars, and laughing when I entered the room.

"Speak of the Devil and she shall appear," Señor Velasquez said. His smile was genuine.

"I suppose Charlotte's gone to bed for the night," Lynch directed his words towards me.

"Yes, Michié." I cleared the table.

"She was livid after Carlos said you were the prettiest girl he'd ever seen."

He had called me a beautiful young woman, but I didn't dare correct him.

"I'd like to take a walk after dinner, but I fear I do not know my way around the city," Señor Velasquez said.

"Big John can take you in the carriage."

"I prefer to walk, and I would rather have Jacqueline's company."

I froze. I was never allowed out at night, a fact that comforted me when I would hear stories of what happened in the streets when the sun went down. In a city where all your wildest desires could be met, people often went too far and found themselves staring into the Mouth of Hell. Stabbings, suicides, lynching, absinthe poisoning, or death by duel — there were a thousand ways to die in the Crescent City.

"You aren't planning to run off with my slave, are you?"

"Of course not. I simply wish to get some fresh air, see the city, and enjoy the company of this young lady."

"There are women in this city who get paid for those services, Carlos."

Señor Velasquez laughed. "I promise to bring her back in one piece, James."

I thought of Cook's head hanging onto her neck by a thin, red sinew. She was almost in two pieces when the undertaker took her away. My chest felt tight like I couldn't breathe.

"I'll allow it, but don't get any ideas about stealing her away from us. She's been with Charlotte since they were children. I'd never hear the end of it if Jacqueline went missing. Besides, I've already lost two slaves. I can't afford to lose another."

I finished clearing the table and swallowed the bile burning the back of my throat.

The Lynches had gone to bed hours before I went to Señor Velasquez's room. I feared I would find him naked as the day he was born. Instead, he was dressed in a dark overcoat, ready to go out for the evening.

"Finally," he sighed. "I thought you'd never get here."

"I had chores to do after supper; they have to be done before I can rest." I did nothing to hide the irritation in my voice. I was too tired.

"No matter, you are here now. Put these on."

He handed me a long, dark green dress and a hooded black cloak. The garments were nicer than anything I had ever worn, but I was especially happy with the knee-high black leather boots he offered me.

"What are these?"

"Your costume, you'll need to wear these when we go out. Now, hurry up and get dressed."

I'd figured I'd be taking my clothes off when I got to his room; I certainly hadn't expected to be putting more on.

I clutched the clothes tightly against my breast. I didn't want to undress in front of the odd stranger. He must have sensed my unease, stepping out into the hallway without a word. I dressed quickly and admired myself in the vanity mirror. I liked the way I looked in the beautiful new clothes and wondered if he'd let me keep them. I stood on tiptoe to see as much of the outfit as I could in the mirror and was still admiring myself when Señor Velasquez entered the room.

"Pretty as a princess," he mused.

He took me by the hand and spun me around to get a good look. As I turned in a circle, faster and faster, the fluttering in my stomach, like moths around a candle flame, made me laugh. Then I caught sight of myself in the mirror. My dance partner cast no reflection. I stopped laughing.

He noticed the change in my mood, stopped dancing, and looked at the mirror. "Do not be frightened."

"What are you?"

"Before you start screaming or throwing salt and drawing symbols with ashes on the floor, please hear me out."

I wanted to run, but listened instead. He knew more about conjuring than I thought, and that made me uneasy. I already feared for my life.

"Explain yourself, demon." I folded my arms across my chest and looked him in the eye. More than anything, I wanted to hide under my bed, and pretend I didn't know anything about the things that lurked in the dark. But the lies we tell ourselves are often the most dangerous.

He laughed, showing me his sharp teeth. "I assure you, I am no demon. I have been unfortunate enough to meet demons, and I cannot claim to have such power and influence as they."

"Then what are you?"

"Many people have different names for what I am — incubus, ghoul, *strigoi* — I think the most common name for me in this century is *vampire*."

He sounded more like a scholar than a monster, but that didn't make me distrust him any less. Slowly, I took a step back, trying to hide the fact I wanted to run. Predators wanted you to run. They enjoyed the chase almost as much as killing you. *Les Blancs* like Lynch and Jimmy thrived on scaring slaves into doing what they wanted. The fact that they took pleasure in my fear made them monstrous men. Moman had taught me to do what I was told, but never show them I was afraid. If you showed them your fear, they'd treat you worse the next time. Now that I knew Carlos Velasquez was a *real* monster, I'd do everything in my power to hide my fear.

"That's why you sleep during the day. What do you do at night when everyone's asleep?"

He paused and studied my face before answering. "Sometimes I read, or write in my journal. And sometimes I sneak out to feed."

"What do you eat?" My voice trembled slightly.

"I think you already know the answer to that question."

"Did you kill Cook?"

"No."

"Was it another vampire?"

"I'm not aware of any other vampires living nearby, but the murderer was not one of my kind."

"But Cook's throat was torn open and there was blood everywhere."

"Exactly. I would not have left that much blood behind."

That made sense, but his answer didn't comfort me. I pictured Señor Velasquez ripping Cook's throat out and gorging himself on her blood. As much violence as I'd seen, it wasn't hard to imagine.

If he didn't kill her, who or *what*— did?

"Are we really going out?"

"If you like. But you need not come with me if you are afraid."

"Afraid of what? Drunkards? Cutthroats? Slave catchers?"

"I admire your spirit. Are you ready to go?"

I nodded once and put up the hood on my cloak. He put on a mask to fit in with the other Mardi Gras revelers.

I wasn't used to being out at night. Big John was the only one allowed out after dusk, and he was usually with Lynch. Darkness held too many possibilities for escape or worse, being raped or murdered by the drunks and thieves that roamed the Quarter at night. Vampires are terrifying creatures, driven by an insatiable cannibalistic hunger and murderous urges. I was glad to have one at my side when I left the safety of the Lynches' house.

Chapter 12

We walked through the dark, dirty streets of the Quarter in silence for several blocks. He scolded me for walking behind him and insisted that I take his arm like a free woman might while walking with a gentleman.

The streets were busier than usual, and music floated on the humid air all around us, drifting out of people's homes and late-night drinking establishments. Some of the masks scared me, but the excitement in the air quickly made me forget those fears.

"Tell me what you heard after Cook's body was examined."

How did he know I had listened?

"The undertaker said she had teeth marks on her —like an animal's. *You* have sharp teeth." For some reason, I felt safe speaking my mind to him.

He laughed. "True, but not sharp enough to tear Cook's head off."

"You think that happened in one bite?"

I sure didn't want to meet anything large enough to take off a head in one bite.

"What kind of creature could do that?"

Before he could answer, we heard a woman's screams echoing around us. His muscles tensed under my hand. He placed his index finger against his mouth and nose and pushed me into a dark corner. He mouthed the words, "stay here," and walked toward the screams.

I pulled my cloak tight around my shoulders. My body shook with chills even though the night air was warm and moist. I pressed myself against the brickwork of the building, trying to blend in with the shadows. The stink of garbage and sewage rising up from the gutters made it hard to keep my supper down. I had no business being out after dark. It was too dangerous, even with a vampire escort.

I don't know how much time had passed, but I was relieved to see Señor Velasquez appear out of the darkness.

"They captured Mathilde. There was nothing I could do." He sounded sincere.

"We need to get back to the house," I said.

"What difference will that make?"

"She'll be scared. Big John's there, but he can't protect her or show her the kindness she needs right now."

"It is too dangerous for you to interfere," he said, and took a step closer.

"I can't stop them from hurting her, but maybe if I'm there she won't feel so alone."

He gawked at me like he was seeing me for the first time, some oddity he'd never witnessed before. Childlike wonder lit up his expression.

"Unless you have other business, I'd like to go back to the house," I said.

The house was quiet and dark when we took our evening stroll, but now it was lit up like the Lynches were expecting guests. Big John stood at the front door with tears in his eyes. He wouldn't look at me or answer my questions.

Señor Velasquez entered the house. "Don't come inside until I tell you to," he whispered.

Loud, angry voices that promised violence reverberated through the house, pitting themselves against Mathilde's screams.

"What is happening, James?" Carlos entered the kitchen. I couldn't see him, but I could hear him clearly.

"The slave catchers found Mathilde. We were just about to teach her a lesson for running off," Lynch said, with delight in his voice. "Where's Jacqueline? Did you take her with you?"

"She's outside. I told her to wait for me there. Do I still have your blessing to use her as I wish?"

What was he up to?

"Be my guest, but you'll miss all the fun here in the kitchen. My brother-in-law's in town, he helped capture my runaway. At least let me introduce him to you," Lynch insisted.

"Of course, where is he?"

"He's gone to fetch neck irons and a scold's bridle."

Brother-in-law? Knowing Jimmy was in the house reminded me there were fates worse than death.

"Jimmy, this is my house guest and business partner, Carlos Velasquez. This man is going to make me rich," Lynch said.

"Pleasure to meet you, Carlos. Care to join us?" Jimmy's unmistakable voice sent shivers through me. I gripped the doorframe to keep my balance.

"Already invited him, but he's got other pleasures in mind, right, Carlos?"

"Indeed. James has been kind enough to offer me one of his slaves to keep me company tonight."

"Well, if she's as pretty as this little bitch, you're in for a real treat."

"Jacqueline is certainly easy on the eyes," Lynch said.

"Not my Jacqueline," Jimmy said.

"Your Jacqueline? I thought she belonged to Madame Lynch."

Mathilde had done was run because she got scared. That was enough of a crime to be stripped, beaten, and chained to the stove.

It had taken less than a day for the slave catchers to find Mathilde. Lucky for her, there'd been another murder like Cook's in the Quarter. This time it was a white woman who'd died. A prostitute was found torn apart in an alley behind one of the brothels in Storyville. The undertaker was quoted in the *Times Picayune* saying he had seen similar wounds on a slave belonging to James Lynch.

This time they were certain an animal was to blame. Teeth and claw marks made the dead woman's face unrecognizable. They'd figured out who she was by asking the other whores who was missing. Mathilde was no longer a suspect, but she was still being punished.

Chapter 13

A few days after the second murder, I found Lottie in the pantry holding the potion I kept hidden behind the sacks of cornmeal. She uncorked the apothecary bottle and pressed her nose to the rim. She knew what was inside. Her small frame shook. Rage was building in her. A shadow passed over her face as she clenched her teeth and her eyes turned to slits. She hissed at me like a snake and smashed the bottle on the floor.

She growled before lunging at me to tear the *tignon* off my head to get at my hair. I thought she'd rip my braids out. I'd never seen her so angry. I covered my eyes to protect them from her nails, but she clawed at my face and tore the flesh.

I made the mistake of defending myself. I slapped her face as hard as I could to calm her down. A tiny drop of blood fell from her nose and stained her lip. Her mouth hung open in disbelief. Everything seemed to slow down in that moment. It got very quiet and very still in the pantry. She took great panting breaths with her hands pressed to her ribs. Her corset was making it hard for her to catch her breath. I didn't envy the level of vanity she fell victim to each day when she got dressed. She brushed a strand of hair back from her cheek and took a shallow breath. For a second, I thought it was all over. Then she screamed.

"James!"

Her face was as red as the Devil's ass.

"I'm sorry, Mamzèl Lynch. Please don't call Michié Lynch. I got scared. I lost my mind."

I didn't move for fear of agitating her even more.

"James!"

I tried to reason with her. "Please, Lottie. Don't tell Michié Lynch."

I thought flames would shoot out of her eyes.

"Don't speak to me in that familiar tone. I am your better and you will show me the respect I deserve."

"I didn't want your husband to touch me. He raped me like Jimmy did to both of us."

Lottie's blonde hair was a mess; it framed her face like the halo of a deranged saint. Strands had pulled free from her hairclips when I slapped her. Blood still trickled from her nose. I hadn't meant to hit her so hard.

"I see the way you walk around here. Showing off in front of all the men in this house."

She pointed a finger inches away from my nose.

"That's a lie. You know it is." The hatred in my voice shocked me.

Her feet traced a pattern back and forth on the stone tiles of the pantry floor.

"James! Where is that man?"

I tried to remain calm, but my instincts told me to run. I turned my back on her and ran into Lynch. Jimmy was right behind him.

"What's all the fuss, Charlotte? I was with a client."

He held me steady and looked into my eyes. Confusion replaced his grin.

"How long have you been sneaking around behind my back?"

"Honestly, Charlotte, I didn't make much effort to hide it; nor should I have to. She's my slave. I can do whatever I want with her.

You're my wife, and I don't have to listen to that tone of voice from you."

"How dare you! That nigger isn't bringing her half-breed babies into this house. I don't have any children of my own yet, James."

"I thought you niggers knew tricks to prevent that sort of thing."

He looked at me for confirmation and I nodded my head. I kept my mouth shut. My head hurt, and my heart was beating so fast I thought I might faint.

"She was taking that potion to keep you from putting a baby inside her," Charlotte said.

"The potion you spilled when you smashed the bottle?" He pointed to the dark puddle on the floor.

I thanked the *loa* Lottie hadn't found the concoction I'd been putting in her husband's food. She would have been happy to know why I was giving it to him, but he wouldn't.

One of his hands gripped my arm like a vice, and the other was balled into a fist at his side.

"I was angry," she pouted.

"How did you know what that potion was for, Charlotte?"

She became silent. He waited for her to answer, and quickly became impatient.

"Well, how did she know, Jacqueline?"

Telling the truth wouldn't save my skin. I only told him part of the truth. Whole truths were too dangerous. Lottie would kill me on the spot if I told him everything. Besides, Jimmy was standing right there.

"My moman used to make it on the plantation for the slaves. We watched her make it so many times, she knows the recipe."

"You two spend a lot of time together as children?" He kept his eyes focused on me.

"They were together almost every day." Jimmy answered the question for me.

"Why would the master's daughter play with a little nigger girl?" His question was for Lottie.

"She's my sister. Happy now, James? You've been fucking my sister!"

"Ladies don't use language like that, Charlotte. It's unbecoming. So what if she carries my bastard? She's your sister. Light as she is, that baby might even look like *you* when it's born."

"I want her punished," Lottie said.

"For what?" He laughed at the suggestion.

"For making me look like a fool in my own house. You've had your fun, but it's over. I can't punish you, James, but you can punish her."

His fingers dug into my arm. Lottie had pushed him too far.

"Charlotte, I'll allow you to speak to me like that once, because I know you're upset. Don't make it a habit."

Lottie glared at him. She didn't like being told what to do. But she knew her place.

"Yes, James," she said with a forced smile.

He dragged me out of the pantry and my heel slid through the puddle of spilled potion. A piece of broken glass grazed my foot and made a small cut along the side. It hurt, but I didn't dare make a sound. Once we were near the back door, he told Mathilde to go find Big John. She had just enough length of chain to reach the courtyard and front door. A few moments later, Big John entered the kitchen with Mathilde dragging her irons behind him.

"Jimmy, bring me the whip and meet me out back," Lynch said.

I screamed and fell to the floor at his feet. I grabbed at his pants leg and pressed my forehead against his boots. "Please don't do this. I'm sorry, Lottie. I didn't mean for this to happen."

She turned her back on me and wiped the blood from her face with a white lace handkerchief.

"Mathilde, I need you to fix my hair," Lottie said, unlocking Mathilde's shackles with a key on her chatelaine.

Mathilde ran upstairs to get what she needed from Lottie's vanity. I didn't blame her for smiling. She'd been wearing those chains since the night she was caught. The end of her own punishment outweighed whatever was going to happen to me next.

Lynch and Jimmy grabbed my arms and dragged me out to the courtyard behind the house. I fought them as hard as I could, but I couldn't get away. I was terrified. The whipping I imagined I had coming would make my time in the corn crib seem like a dream come true.

"Stop fighting, you'll only make it worse on yourself," Lynch said.

Lottie sauntered out the back door with her hair neat and tidy. The look of happy expectation on her face made my stomach hurt.

"Please, don't whip me. I'll do whatever you want me to, but please don't do this." Tears ran down my face and I choked the words out between sobs. I was down on my knees again begging him for mercy.

"Charlotte won't be happy until I do this. Just pray to God I won't have to sell you," Lynch said.

Jimmy lifted me up and carried me to the fountain in the middle of the courtyard. "I hate to see that tender flesh of yours torn up," he whispered.

I kicked and screamed and hit him all the way. The gentle babble of the water should have been soothing, but there was nothing peaceful about having my hands tied in front of me as I embraced the copper statue at the center of the concrete structure. I looked up into the nymph's face. Drops of water splashed my cheeks and mixed with the tears. I wished my body were solid like the statue the first time the whip struck my back and split it open. After the fifth lash I lost count. Each time he struck me a new gash opened on my back. The pain was so bad I couldn't catch my breath, which made it harder to scream. My dress was in shreds and so was the skin on my back. Blood and sweat mixed into a salty sticky mess that ran down my sides, stinging my open wounds, and dripped into the fountain. Salt, musk, blood, and leather combined into a perfume of odors which, on their own, would normally have pleased me. Now, they would only remind me of pain and fear.

My eyes were shut tight. I cried and begged, but no one heeded my pleas. Then, all of a sudden, the beating stopped. My back tensed as I waited for the next blow, but it didn't come.

"What are you waiting for? Strike her again, James," Lottie shouted.

"Hush, Charlotte. I heard something in the alley behind the house."

Near the rear wall of the courtyard there was a low growl. I opened my eyes and looked down into the fountain. The water had turned pink. I didn't recall throwing up, but vomit floated in the water, too. The growl came again, but I couldn't see what was making it.

"Jimmy, go see what that is, but come right back. We're not done here," Lynch said.

I held onto the nymph to keep my balance, but my grip was slipping. All the strength had left my body. Pain covered every inch of me. I couldn't fight now if I had to. More than anything I just wanted to lie down and die right there in the garden. They could bury me under the herbs for all I cared. I was about to fade from exhaustion when something jumped over the wall and attacked Lynch. Lottie screamed.

With the little strength I had left, I turned to see what could only be a wolf tearing its way through Lynch's throat and chest. It was the biggest animal I had ever seen. At least as tall as a man, taller, and covered in course black fur. It stood on its hind legs and treated itself to a meal of that bastard's flesh. It picked Lynch up and shook him from side-to-side in its jaws and then dropped him to the ground. Then it came at me. Out of the corner of my eye I saw Lottie crawling across the yard to kneel beside her husband's corpse.

I was so tired and scared I couldn't even scream when the animal fell forward onto its front paws and started walking towards me on all fours.

Big John came around the corner of the house with an axe in his hands. He raised it over his head and ran at the animal, but he wasn't fast enough. The wolf turned and snapped his teeth at Big John. He jumped back just in time and didn't get bitten, but the wolf bore down on him and chased him toward the house.

Lottie rose up on unsteady feet. Blood covered her hands and the front of her dress. She pressed her forearm to her mouth to hold in another scream and quietly backed away from Lynch's body. She followed Big John into the house.

No one was coming to save me.

The wolf turned back to me and approached the fountain, stopping short just a few feet away. Watching me. It didn't come any closer. I thought for sure it would kill me. Instead, the creature bowed its head then looked me in the eyes. I must have lost my mind, because I swear that animal was smiling at me. Then it turned and leapt back over the wall.

My body finally collapsed against the copper statue. I don't know how long I was out, but when I came to, Señor Velasquez was untying my hands. A wide-brimmed black hat and his little round dark spectacles kept the sun off his face, and leather gloves covered his hands. He lifted me into his arms and carried me to my room.

He placed me face down on the bed and examined my wounds. Gently, he removed my tattered dress. Pain and exhaustion kept me from caring about modesty. I had escaped death that day. What difference did it make if Señor Velasquez saw my naked body?

"Jacqueline, can you hear me?"

"Yes," I whispered. My throat hurt from screaming.

"You lost a lot of blood. Your back is...your skin is badly torn. Will you allow me to help you?" His words were clipped and tense.

"Yes, Señor Velasquez."

"My name is Carlos." Some of the anger left his tone.

"Carlos?"

"Yes?"

"Am I going to die?"

"Not if I can help it."

"Did you see the wolf?"

"I did. We can talk about it after you rest."

I turned my head to look at him kneeling next to the bed. I had never seen a white man so worried before. A frown twisted his beautiful mouth and his eyes were glassy like he'd been crying. Had he watched Lynch whipping me?

Carlos removed his hat, gloves, and spectacles, and set them on the small table next to my bed. His cold fingers soothed away some of the pain as he examined my back. My muscles tensed beneath his touch, expecting more pain. He peeled shredded scraps of my dress from inside the wounds. I gripped the blanket and bit my lip to keep from screaming. My back was raw, sore, and sticky.

"Your wounds are much worse than I thought," Carlos said. He held my hand and I saw there was fear in his eyes.

"I'm not dead yet."

My vision blurred. I had to close one eye to focus. He stroked my cheek and brushed away strands of hair that had become stuck to my face with sweat. The coolness of his hand comforted me. I wanted to drift off to sleep, or even death, but the pain wouldn't let me.

"Jacqueline, I am going to heal you. Without my help, you will die. You lost a lot of blood when James beat you. Unless you want to become like me, I must heal you before you lose more blood."

"How...?"

He stood and took off his long, black coat, rolled up his white shirtsleeve, and pulled a pocket knife from his vest. He pierced the flesh in the crook of his arm, lifted my head, and placed his arm against my mouth.

"Drink," he said.

The first taste was bitter. His blood was heavy on my tongue, almost too thick to swallow. But soon, it flowed down my throat with ease. Warm and wet, my dry lips and sore throat gulped down the bitter liquid greedily. With each swallow, I could feel my body growing stronger. The pain eased up faster than I could've imagined possible. I sat on the edge of my bed to face Carlos, still clinging to his arm and drinking deeply. His lips parted to reveal sharp eye teeth as he watched me fight for my life. I could almost smell the lust in him, but he made no move to touch me. He pulled his arm away. I grabbed it and tried to drink more of his blood. I didn't want to stop.

"That's enough, Jacqueline," he said, and pushed me away.

I reached for his face and drew him toward me for a kiss. He hesitated only for a second. Our mouths were impatient to taste each other, and I shared his blood on my lips between us. He moaned and pulled me closer to him. His black, wool trousers scratched my skin as I wrapped my bare thighs around his waist.

"No." His voice was stern when he pushed me away again.

I stared at him, startled not only at my own behavior, but also by the fact that he didn't want me. The first time I'd ever approached a man of my own free will, and he'd rejected me.

"Am I not pretty?"

He stood and turned his back to me, and ran an unsteady hand through his dark mass of curls. After a few moments he turned back to me and knelt beside the bed. He took my hands in his and kissed them.

"You are the most beautiful girl I have ever seen. There is nothing in this world I want more than to part your thighs and lose myself in your flesh, but I do not want it to happen like this. Not here, and not now. You are weak and vulnerable. Those are qualities I seek in my victims, not my lovers."

"But you saved my life. You healed me with your blood. I want to thank you." I guided his hands to my breasts and tangled my fingers in his hair. He kissed me again. My whole being was on fire for him. He wanted me, but resisted the temptation.

"My blood is making you feel this way. You only think you want me. Tomorrow, things will be back to normal. You will distrust me once again."

"How could I not trust you after you saved me?" I wanted to cry as he backed away from me.

"People rarely have trouble coming up with reasons to distrust a creature like me." He laughed without smiling.

He found a clean dress and helped me put it on after he'd

washed away the dead skin and dried blood from my back and arms with a damp sponge. He ignored his urges and cared for me like a mother cares for an infant.

"Try to sleep, Jacqueline. My blood will heal you, but your body needs time to rest."

"Why are you leaving?"

"I want to see what is happening in the house. Your sister has probably lost her mind by now. I will offer to help with whatever she decides to do about James' body."

"Be careful. Jimmy is meaner than a snake," I said.

He smiled. "Are you concerned about my safety?"

I quickly changed the subject. "You said you would tell me about the wolf."

"Later. Tonight. You drank a lot of my blood. I need to find more and sleep. I risked a lot coming out in the day."

"Will you die?"

"No, but the longer I stay awake, the weaker I become. I will come to you later. Sleep."

He donned his hat, spectacles, and gloves, and went back into the sunlight.

Soon after he left, I fell into a deep and troubled sleep. Nightmares haunted me. I dreamed about Carlos, but he was different somehow. We walked side-by-side on a long stretch of road until we came to a door. The door wasn't attached to anything; it just sort of stood there in the middle of the road. I reached for the doorknob and tried to open it, and then Carlos attacked me. He pinned me to the ground and drained my life away. I was powerless against him. Just when I thought I would surely die, the wolf appeared. I'd never forget its smile. The dream clung to me long after I awoke. I don't know why, but I felt at peace.

Chapter 14

At dusk, Carlos entered my room. I was awake, but it felt good to lie in bed. The last time I'd stayed in bed like that, I'd been sick with the fever. My body was completely healed now, and I had dead man's blood to thank for making me feel more alive than ever.

Carlos sat next to me on the bed. "Are you awake?"

I opened my eyes slowly and smiled at him. I took his hand in mine and he smiled back. With his free hand, he placed a mason jar of water on the table next to me. I eagerly drank the lukewarm rainwater he'd drawn from the cistern. It never did taste as cold and fresh as the water from the well on the plantation. I wiped my mouth with my dress sleeve and handed him the empty jar.

I gently touched his sleeve. "What's happened?"

He turned his head slightly and looked at me over his shoulder, still not making eye contact. He was hiding something.

"Charlotte was rambling on about wolves roaming the streets of New Orleans. The doctor gave her a heavy dose of laudanum to sleep through the night."

"Did the doctor believe her?"

"James' death marks the third animal attack, but she raved on like she was insane. The police are investigating. Even though one of the victims was a prostitute, two of the victims were *Blancos*."

"What was that thing? It was bigger than any animal I ever saw, and it walked on two legs. It picked Lynch up off the ground and shook him with its mouth."

"There are many kinds of shape-shifters, but what you saw today was an *hombre-lobo*. I think the French call it a *loup-garou*."

"That thing used to be a man?"

"And still is, most of the time. For some reason this particular *loup-garou* is interested in this house, and judging by what I saw today, it is especially interested in you."

"What did you see it do?"

"It killed James to stop him from killing you."

"It smiled at me."

Carlos clucked his tongue in disgust and stood up to pace across my floor.

"Did I say something wrong?"

It suddenly mattered what he thought about me. Feeling like I might die because I wanted Carlos so badly was the worst pain in the world. I hoped it was just his blood making me feel that way. Earlier, he'd said the effects would wear off by the next day. I prayed that was true. I wanted to undress and give myself to him. I was ashamed of my recklessness.

He stopped pacing and came back to my side.

"You did nothing wrong. I am worried about your safety."

"Why? The *loup-garou* didn't want to hurt me. It wanted to protect me."

"If it...he wants you, he will come back. Not as a wolf, but in his human guise. You will not know who he is until it is too late."

"Are you worried about my safety or jealous of him?"

He didn't answer right away, just stared at me with a frown tugging at the corners of his mouth. The lines on his face were carved by emotions, not age. It didn't matter how many years he'd walked the Earth, he didn't look a day over twenty-five.

"Both," he said.

"Most men wouldn't admit they were jealous."

"You already know I am not like most men."

I offered him my hand and pulled him close. We listened to each other's thoughts as we embraced. I made room for him on the bed and he lay down next to me on top of the blanket, our arms still wrapped tightly around each other. Moments like this were rare. I soaked up as much of the good feeling as I could.

He lifted my hand and held it against his cheek, and then he brought my palm to his lips and gently kissed it. His mouth moved up to my wrist and placed playful nips and kisses there. A shiver ran through me and I moved closer to him on the bed. He cupped my face in his strong hands and parted my lips with his tongue. We kissed, but then he pulled back and stopped me from coming closer again. His fangs were bared and his eyes were darker than usual, a deep green ringed in black.

"We must not," he whispered.

"But you're the only man I've ever wanted."

He swallowed and rested his forehead against mine.

"I am very flattered that you want to give yourself to me. It is very hard to say no to you, but what you feel will not last forever."

"Why are you fighting your nature? I can see in your thoughts what you want to do to me."

"And you are not frightened?"

"Only a little."

"I fear that if I touch you the way I want to, I will want more than you are willing to give. I have yet to feed tonight and unlike my victims, I truly desire you. I want to be in control when we make love. I do not wish to hurt you."

"How will you feel if I never again want you the way I do tonight?"

"Disappointed. Hungry. Cheated. But, hopeful."

I stroked his hair and kissed his forehead. I knew what it was like to desire something you wanted but couldn't have, like the freedom to govern your own actions. The feeling was worse when someone else knew and tormented you by reminding you that you could never have it. People never let me forget I was a slave.

"Thank you for not taking advantage of me."

"I hope it makes you want me even more," he sighed, and stroked my hair.

I wasn't sure how I could possibly ever desire him more, but we both needed to focus on more important things. James Lynch was dead. A *loup-garou* had killed him, and would most likely return to kill others. Carlos believed the creature wanted me. To distract us both from temptation, I changed the subject.

"Did you tell the police about the *loup-garou*?"

"I said I didn't see what happened."

"That's a lie."

"The constables seemed convinced, and Charlotte's brother corroborated my story."

I'd forgotten about Jimmy.

"I was in the courtyard, too. Didn't the police want to speak to me?"

"I told them you were recovering from your vicious beating. I said I'd found you in the courtyard after the attack."

"What did Jimmy say about the *loup-garou*?"

"He said he saw a wolf jump over the wall and kill his brother-in-law."

"Did they ask why you didn't watch Michié Lynch whip me?"

"I told them I opposed that sort of violence." His fangs were still exposed.

An image of Carlos ravaging me in the dream I'd had that

afternoon crept into my mind. My blood stained his face. His eyes were black with lust. I shuddered. "Only *that* sort of violence?"

"When it's done to someone I care about."

Despite the lingering images from my nightmare, I wanted to kiss him again. My heart pounded in my chest and I knew he could hear it. It hurt not to touch him, but my instincts told me not to.

"You're gonna tell me something I don't want to hear," I said.

He buried his nose in my hair and took a deep breath. Then he kissed my face softly. His hunger was quieter.

"Are you feeling well enough to perform a spell?"

"Best I've felt in a long time. Maybe ever."

"I need you to create a protection spell for the whole house. Mathilde said she would help you prepare."

I leaned back to get a good look at his face. "Does she know what you are?"

"I don't think so, but she saw the *loup-garou.* She doesn't want it to come back either. Not after what it did to Cook and James. She's scared. I told her you would protect the house, and she wants to help."

"I need a few things, but they're easy to gather. If Lottie doesn't wake up, I can go get what I need tonight."

He shook his head. "No, I don't want you out alone. Tell me what you need and where to get it."

"The *loup-garou* won't come looking for me tonight."

"The streets of New Orleans are dangerous enough without one of those things stalking you. Besides, the blood I gave you will make you feel stronger than you really are. I don't want you getting into trouble or falling prey to the lustful advances of some drunken sailor."

"I'll make a list. There's a man down on Burgundy with a shop. Squire Jean. He'll have everything I need."

He handed me a slip of paper and a piece of charcoal he pulled from his vest pocket. I placed the paper flat against my bare thigh and wrote out the list of ingredients I needed for the spell work. I felt much better and wanted to get to work right away.

Carlos stroked my thigh as he read the list.

"I will get your supplies and then I must leave for a few days."

My chest ached at the thought of being away from him. I couldn't catch my breath.

"Why are you leaving?"

"Because some of my habits make me suspicious. I told Charlotte I would be gone for a few days to take care of some business. I can't be here while the police investigate. My odd behaviors will be questioned."

"The spell will keep you from entering the house, too."

"I know. I want you to come to me."

"You want me to run away?"

"Now seems like a good time."

"How...?"

"I rented a small house on Esplanade. You will be my *placée*. At least that's what we'll tell everyone. I don't expect you to live as my wife. The goal is your freedom."

"Even if Lottie is out of her mind, Jimmy would never let me out of his sight."

"I'll take care of Jimmy. You just focus on protecting the house and keeping out the wolf."

He disappeared over the edge of the balcony and his long, black coat unfurled as he silently landed in the courtyard below. I peered over the banister and he blew me a kiss before fading into the shadows.

After he was gone, I went to find Mathilde. She was in the kitchen finishing up chores. Someone had chained her to the stove again. I hushed her as I entered the house. I didn't want to run into Jimmy. She signaled that it was safe to come in.

"Big John's standing guard at the front door. He'll be there all night. You want something to eat?" Mathilde poured me a cup of coffee and sat it in front of me. Steam rose up in perfect gray curls from the lip of the cup. I was amazed at the detail of everything around me. *The blood*, I thought.

"I'm not hungry, but thank you for the coffee," I said.

"I didn't expect to see you out of bed after the beating you took today," she said. "Did you use root work to heal yourself?"

"Carlos healed me."

"With what?"

I didn't answer right away.

"Jacqueline, I saw how bad you were beaten. You ain't got a scratch on you. How did he heal you?"

"His blood."

"I knew something was strange about that man," she said.

"He's trying to help." I sounded like I was trying to convince the both of us.

"That kind of magic is dangerous, and you know it. Where's he at now?"

"I sent him to get what we need to protect the house."

"Did you see it, Jacqueline? Big John said it almost bit him."

"I saw it. Thought it would kill me, but it didn't."

"You're lucky to be alive. Mamzèl Charlotte lost her mind after seeing Michié Lynch tore up like that. When the mortician came to collect the body, Michié Lynch's head came off."

"I didn't see anything after he dropped dead in the yard. I must have fainted."

I hated to lie to Mathilde, but I couldn't tell her about the creature's smile. She'd think I'd lost my mind, too. Besides, I didn't have time to wonder what that smile meant. Carlos seemed to think the man who became the beast was infatuated with me for some reason. How could that be? I rarely left the house on Royal Street. Sometimes I was out to run errands, but I never paid too much attention when men looked at me. In fact, I tried to ignore them as much as possible.

Mathilde took a sip of her coffee and rubbed the kinks out of her neck. Then she placed her hands over mine and made me look her in the eye. "Tell me what that man is," she said.

"What man?"

"Señor Velasquez. You know him better than anyone else does in this house."

"Why do you say that?"

"Because I see the way you two talk to each other. Mamzèl Charlotte wishes he talked to her like that. And now, you got him running errands for you. He's different from other men. Why does he sleep most of the day? Is he ill?"

"He's a vampire."

She laughed and covered her mouth. Slaves weren't encouraged to enjoy life.

"You wanted to know why he acts so strange, and I told you. He's a vampire."

"Why hasn't he killed everyone in the house, then?"

"Because I have morals," Carlos answered her question.

Mathilde stood and bowed her head, a habit we'd learned to practice when in the company of *les Blancs*.

"Stay seated, Mathilde. I didn't mean to startle you," he said.

He approached the table and set the basket of items I'd requested down in front of me. His frown told me he was unhappy I had divulged his secret.

"Can I get you something to eat or drink?" Mathilde couldn't relax in his presence.

"Some wine would be nice," he said, and sat next to me at the table. He took my hand and kissed it while Mathilde's back was turned.

Mathilde brought him a bottle of red wine and a crystal goblet. She fidgeted and wrung her hands. All her chores were done, but even if she wanted to leave, she didn't have enough length of chain to do so.

"Please, join us." Carlos poured himself some wine and gestured to the other seat at the table.

She hesitated before sitting down across from me. Her hands were shaking as she took a sip of her coffee.

"What do you know about vampires, Mathilde?" Carlos drank his wine and casually wrapped his arm around my waist. He smelled like sweat, night air, and just a hint of rosewater. I edged a little closer to him.

"I don't know much, Michié." Her voice shook.

"You know that I drink blood and sometimes kill people, right?"

"Yes, Michié."

"If we are going to be friends, I want you to call me Carlos."

"We're not supposed to talk to *les Blancs* like that. Too familiar. We get punished for speaking like we're the same as them," I said.

"How are you different from them?"

"Our skin is different, and they have all the power," Mathilde said. She sat up a little straighter in her seat.

"In my country, my people were treated like animals because our religion was different. We were punished for our beliefs. I come from Spain, but my parents were Jews. My father changed our surname to protect us from starvation. He was a merchant, and no one would buy goods from Jews after the Catholic Church made it illegal."

"Michié Lynch hated Jews as much as he hated Negroes," Mathilde said.

"Too bad I didn't have a chance to kill him myself." Carlos finished his glass of wine. "*Papistas.*" He spat on the floor.

"What do we do now?" Mathilde asked.

"The two of you need to work the spell to keep the *loup-garou* out of the house. I will pack my things and be ready to go before first light. In a few days, I will send for you, Jacqueline. Mathilde, you are welcome to join us."

Mathilde couldn't make eye contact with him. Her days of running were over.

"By the time you send for me, Lottie will back on her feet. She'll need our help to make plans for the funeral. And Jimmy will be watching us like a hawk. We'd never be able to leave then," I said.

"Charlotte and her brother are a problem. I would be more than happy to remove those obstacles."

"You mean kill them," I said.

He shrugged his shoulders. "Well, yes. What else would you suggest?"

"Hasn't there been enough killing?" Mathilde spoke up.

"I thought by now the two of you would realize death is part of life. You both experience violence on some level every day. Sometimes, in order to survive, someone in your way must die. I don't need to tell you this."

"This house stinks of death. I don't suppose one or two more will matter that much," I said.

Mathilde stood up and walked away from the table, avoiding eye contact with Carlos. "How can you say that? I'm glad Michié Lynch is dead, because I saw how he treated you. And Lottie can be mean as a snake, but she's your sister. How can you joke about killing your blood kin? That's not like you, Jacqueline."

"Perhaps I am a bad influence." Carlos laughed at his own remark.

"My whole life, she's treated me like filth. We grew up together, have the same father, and were abused by the same men, but she has never once shown me kindness. In fact, she hates that I even exist. If she had the chance, she'd kill me first."

Mathilde looked like I'd taken the wind out of her sails and sat back down at the table with a heavy sigh. "Wait," she said. "Won't the protection spell keep Carlos out of the house?"

"Yes," I said. "The spell keeps ghosts, vampires, *loup-garou*, and any other evil spirits from getting in."

"Maybe that's a good thing. Once we protect the house from the *loup-garou*, we should keep him out, too."

"And I thought we were getting along so well, Mathilde. That hurts my feelings." Carlos frowned and pretended to be sad.

"Don't you want to be free, Mathilde?" I asked.

"Yes, but I don't want to kill anyone."

Carlos patted her hand. His expression was like a Mardi Gras mask—exaggerated happiness that bordered on grotesque.

"I'll take care of that for you. I've killed a lot of people. Once you get over the initial shock of the first kill, it gets easier each time."

Chapter 15

Three days after the *loup-garou* killed James Lynch, Lottie sent me to the apothecary for smelling salts. Glad to be away from the house, even for a little while, I took my time. If it were up to me, I'd have spent the whole day wandering the streets of the Quarter. Blisters on my heels would have been a welcome pain compared to the headache I had from listening to Lottie yammer and moan all morning about making funeral arrangements. Her grim mood cast a dark shadow that seemed to seep into the walls and floorboards, from roof to foundations.

I welcomed the sunshine on my walk to see the pharmacist. The doctor had given Lottie strict orders to use laudanum throughout the day when her nerves were on edge. Taking the tincture at night wasn't a problem, but during the day, sleep wasn't always convenient for the mistress of the house. She would receive visitors and needed to remain conscious during social calls. The smelling salts would revive her if she fainted or drifted into slumber. On that particular day, she was interviewing men to guard the house at night, and needed to have her wits about her.

She was convinced the creature that had torn apart her husband and Cook would be back to do the same to her. Tragedies always happen in threes, don't they? She rambled on about locking eyes with the beast and seeing the true face of evil, which Mathilde and I found amusing since we figured she already saw that every time she looked in the mirror. Now that Carlos was gone, she wanted more men in the house to protect her from the slavering jaws of the *loup-garou*. Earlier in the day, she'd sent Big John down to the docks where men gathered looking for work loading and unloading steamboats along the river. He must have found some fools willing to stand around outside at night, because when I returned to Royal Street, there were twelve men at the back entrance of the house. What had he told them the job would entail?

I brushed past the rabble and entered the kitchen. Before I removed my shoes in the pantry, I made sure I hadn't trampled in anything: mud, tobacco juice, or animal dung would have done me no favors.

A black stain on the floor marked where Lottie had thrown the potion days before. I hoped I wasn't going to need it anymore, because Lottie would never let me out of her sight long enough to gather the ingredients. Now more than ever, she wanted me within earshot. Not because she believed I could protect her from the *loup-garou*, but because she was afraid of being alone. Since she was born, she'd always had an audience—family members, teachers, and slaves. She couldn't stand to spend any time alone with herself. That's all I ever daydreamed about. Time alone to read, enjoy a sunset, rest my body, or just simply sit quietly and listen to the sound of my own heartbeat. She had no idea what luxuries those things were.

Mathilde entered the kitchen as I straightened my *tignon* and put my apron back on. Lottie must have made Jimmy remove her neck irons. She stared out the window at the gathered men and shook her head slowly. I knew it was hurting too much for her to turn her head. She'd been wearing those irons for more than three days.

"Mamzèl Lynch was asking for you," she said.

"I just got back from the apothecary." I showed her the package of smelling salts. "Is this what she wants?"

"She said her vision was blurry and she needed a little something to help her wake up. I'm making tea. You want some?"

"In a bit. I'll go see what she wants." I sighed. "How many men has she seen this morning?"

"I don't know. Five? She's talking to one in the parlor right now." Mathilde placed the kettle over the fire and measured loose tea into a large porcelain pot.

I stuck a smile on my face and prepared myself for Lottie's company. The hallways were darker than usual with all the mirrors draped in preparation for Lynch's funeral. His family and Lottie's were all due to come to the house in a few days, and we had plenty to do before they arrived. Why she wanted to waste time talking to these men now was beyond me. She needed to rest and plan the funeral. Big John and Jimmy could look after the house between them. Besides, if Jimmy was kept busy, he wouldn't have time to come bother me.

"Finally," Lottie said, as I entered the parlor. It took everything in my power to keep that smile on my face.

"Here are your smelling salts, Mamzèl Lynch."

She snatched them out of my hand and broke open one of the small glass vials. She held it under her nose and inhaled deeply. Her eyes went wide and a little color came back to her cheeks, although the dark circles under her eyes made her look even more pale than usual. She had tried to cover the signs of fatigue with too much lip rouge, which made her look like one of the whores over in Storyville. Once she'd regained her composure, she handed the vial back to me.

"Jacqueline, I want you to meet Monsieur Gale. He'll be

helping Big John and Jimmy guard the house at night and he'll also be doing some odd jobs around the place during the day. Show him to Mathilde's room. She'll sleep in your room now. I've asked Big John to replace Cook's mattress, and you can help him get settled with whatever else he needs."

"The name's Aleister." He sounded like an Irish dockworker who'd read a few books.

Aleister Gale stood from his chair and turned to me. He was a handsome man but wore years of hard labor —or possible sorrow— on his face. Eyes can be deceptive sometimes, showing only a glimpse of the mind behind them. His were a beautiful blue like the cobalt glass bottles at the apothecary. They sparkled with just a hint of mischief, but wisdom lived there, too. Not the kind of wisdom men get from books, but the kind they learn from hard lessons. His thick mane of reddish-brown hair was slightly mussed from the cap he had tucked under his armpit. Dark golden hair covered his lean, muscular arms where his white shirtsleeves were rolled up to the elbow; in an instant, I knew why Lottie had hired him. She wanted his company as well as his brawn. Her snake of a husband wasn't even in the ground yet and here she was, looking for his replacement.

Gale offered me his hand. I didn't take it right away since it was unusual for *les Blancs* to shake hands with slaves. I accepted his labor-scarred hand eventually, and was comforted by its warmth and strength. His callouses, cuts, and chapped skin mirrored my own, and the back of his hand bore a tattoo in deep blue ink, a symbol I didn't recognize. A hum of energy passed between us. His grip tightened when he felt the charge. His eyes locked on mine like he was trying to see inside my head. He couldn't read my thoughts like Carlos could, but Gale was more than he seemed. He let my hand drop and took a step back from me. He was sizing me up, but I had questions of my own.

"Quit staring at our guest and get on with what I told you to do," Lottie snapped.

"Do you have any bags with you, Michié?"

"Just this," he said, lifting a small, worn brown leather satchel off the floor and holding it close to his chest. "I can carry it myself."

"After you show Monsieur Gale to his room, send the other men away," Lottie said.

"Mathilde is making tea; would you like me to bring you some?" I asked.

"Monsieur Gale, may I offer you some tea?"

Lottie would never have treated a common day laborer with such geniality. The thought of her preying on this man gave me plenty to smile about. Hopefully, Aleister Gale would be tough enough to survive Lottie's predatory flirtation.

"I could murder a cup." He grinned and looked between the two of us for what to do next.

"Such a colorful phrase," Lottie said, while fanning herself.

"Beg your pardon, Missus. I just meant I'd love some tea."

"Please, sit." Lottie gestured toward the chair closest to hers.

I left the two of them there and headed back to the kitchen to fetch the tea. Gale was so familiar, but I couldn't think why. Had I seen him in the market? Down by the docks, perhaps? I shrugged off the thought and grabbed the silver tea service from the pantry while Mathilde poured hot water into a teapot and let the leaves steep. She placed sugar, fresh cream, and sliced lemons on the tray along with teaspoons and linen napkins. Then she set some small teacakes on the tray.

"Is she seeing any more of those men?" Mathilde asked, carefully tilting her head back toward the door.

"She told me to send them away. She's chosen the one she

wants."

"That was quick."

I laughed. "Did you see that man? Handsome as the day is long."

"You want me to take the tea in while you tell the men they can go?"

"Trying to get another look?"

She laughed and waved her hands at me like she was trying to shoo me out of the kitchen.

"Hush your mouth. You know I ain't got eyes for nobody but Big John."

"Any more deaths in this house and the two of you can run off and finally be together."

"That's an awful thing to say."

"Don't tell me you haven't thought about what you'd do if Lottie died."

She wouldn't look at me, but a smile played at the corner of her mouth.

"Speaking of Big John, he was supposed to bring a new mattress for Cook's bed. I need to put fresh linens on it for Michié Gale. Looks like you and I will be rooming together."

Mathilde never said a word, but ever since Cook died, she'd hated sleeping alone. She was probably relieved to have an excuse to sleep in my room.

"Haven't seen Big John since early this morning." She peered out the back window into the courtyard and her face lit up with a grin. "Here he comes."

Big John kicked dirt off his boots on the mat outside the door before stepping into the kitchen. Some of the men wanted to know how much longer they'd have to wait. He shrugged and came inside.

"There's a new mattress on Cook's bed," he said, wiping sweat from his forehead. "Mathilde, your bed's in with Jacqueline's now."

"Mamzèl Lynch has chosen one of the men already, Big John. Can you tell the others we don't need them?" I asked.

"She only wants one?" He seemed puzzled.

"That's what she said. Michié Gale's in the parlor. Mamzèl Lynch wants him to start right away."

"She told me she wanted men watching the house round the clock." Big John shook his head before heading back outside to dismiss the gathered men.

"I guess that means you, her brother, and Michié Gale."

Mathilde headed to the parlor with the tea, and I went to make Gale's bed. The sky was the color of slate. I hurried to get the fresh linens inside before it started to pour. Not that it mattered to me if Aleister Gale slept on damp sheets, but Lottie would throw a fit if her new house guest were uncomfortable. She prided herself on the care and hospitality shown to her guests. After the beating I'd taken in the courtyard, I wanted to avoid Lottie's wrath.

I carried Mathilde's things from her room into mine. She didn't have much, but what she did have was important to her. I made space for her belongings in my dresser. I liked Mathilde, but hoped we didn't have to share a room for very long.

Mathilde's room still had a faint odor of blood in the air; the stench had worked its way into the grains of the timbers. The dimly lit room was clean, but cobwebs in the corners made it dreary. I grabbed a broom and swept the corners ceiling to floor. After refilling the oil lamp, I made the bed and took another look around the room to make sure I hadn't missed anything. I turned to leave and stumbled into Aleister Gale. I gasped, and the broom clattered against the wooden floor. I hadn't heard his footsteps when he'd climbed the stairs.

"I didn't mean to startle you," he said, apologetically.

I got a hold of myself and picked up the broom.

"Clean sheets are on the bed, and the oil lamp is full." I tried to brush past him to get on with my other chores.

"I hope I haven't caused you any extra work."

"No, Michié."

I had one foot out the door, but he blocked my way. Standing that close, I got a good whiff of him. He didn't smell like the other men who'd come to the house that day. Instead of stale liquor and tobacco, foul breath, and body odor, I caught the scent of autumn air. Most laborers stank of mud, fish, and the dark waters of the Mississippi. His smell was more animal than human. Not like livestock, but something wilder. Familiar, but queer and mysterious at the same time.

"Did you see the animal that attacked Mister Lynch?"

I glanced at his face but didn't make eye contact. No one else seemed to care if I'd seen it. It's like everyone forgot I'd been tied to the fountain and whipped before the *loup-garou* had arrived. It was ridiculous to think my punishment had any meaning to anyone but me. Carlos wouldn't forget it, but he was in the minority.

"I did see it."

He stepped into the room and circled it, taking in his new accommodations. His footfalls were still silent even though he wore thick-soled boots.

"Was it as terrifying as Missus Lynch described?"

I glanced at him over my shoulder.

"It ripped apart two people in this house."

He took a few steps closer and I could feel his breath on my neck.

"Two?"

"Yes, Michié."

He paused as if he was trying to figure something out. "You don't seem as afraid of the beast as Missus Lynch."

I turned to face him.

"I can protect myself."

"Aren't you even a little worried about it coming back?" He was trying to catch me in a lie.

"What good is it to worry? It'll either come back or it won't. I hope the creature stays away, but I have no control over what it decides to do."

He smiled and tossed his hat on the freshly made bed. Again, I was struck by how familiar his face was to me. Especially when he smiled. I knew I'd seen him before but couldn't think where.

"You seem like a smart girl. Much wiser than your years betray."

Compliments were rare in my world, and praise that didn't involve slurs about my body parts was even rarer.

"Thank you, Michié."

"Call me Aleister. We both work for Missus Lynch. I'm no better than you."

True, we both worked for Lottie, but he received pay for his labor, and when his work was done, he was allowed to go wherever he chose.

"You seem like a nice man, and I don't mean to be rude, but I'm trapped in this house until I die, Mamzèl Lynch dies, or someone decides to abolish slavery."

I left him standing in stunned silence and went back to my chores.

Chapter 16

Aleister Gale ate his dinner in the kitchen with the slaves. Lottie took hers on a tray in bed. The fatigue of the day had finally caught up to her late in the afternoon and she'd retired before sundown. She was barely awake when I entered the room.

"Is that you, Jacqueline?"

"Yes, Mamzèl. I brought your dinner. Mathilde made soup and there's pie."

"I'm not hungry," she said, shielding her eyes as I turned up the gas lamps.

"You should try to eat something."

"The laudanum makes me a little nauseous, but I'll try the pie."

Lottie loved my biscuits, but she'd eat Mathilde's pie off a pile of horseshit in the street and ask for seconds. Mathilde had made Lottie's favorite, black walnut chess pie. I helped her sit up and propped the pillows behind her before setting the tray of food across her lap. Once she had her fork in hand I turned to leave.

"Sit with me while I eat."

I sat on the settee next to her bed and folded my hands over my apron. My dinner would have to wait. Luckily, Mathilde would keep it warm for me. My hands were restless in my lap. They needed something to do. I straightened the *bibelots* on the mantel, stoked the fire, and fluffed the pillows on the settee. I hoped Lottie would get irritated and send me away. She hated when I fussed at things like that.

"Do you miss him?" She took another bite of the pie and stared at me waiting for my answer.

"Michié Lynch?"

"No, you idiot, Señor Velasquez. I see the way you two talk when you think no one is looking. He likes you."

I wasn't sure how to respond.

"What'd you do? Bewitch him? You can tell me. I know how hard it is to catch a good man, and now that James is dead I'll probably never meet someone as handsome and rich as he was."

The laudanum had loosened her tongue.

"He's only kind to me out of pity."

She laughed and almost choked on the piecrust she had in her mouth.

"You sure do like to play dumb, don't you?"

Playing dumb had kept me alive so far.

"I've been onto you for a long time now, Jacqueline. You think you're smarter than me. At some things, maybe, but don't ever think I'm not paying attention."

She sat up and pointed a finger at me.

"I knew James was messing with you, and I told him to stop it, but he laughed at me and said it wasn't my business. Not my business? When my husband lies with my sister, you better believe that's my business. It doesn't matter if you're a slave or not, he should have had more respect for me."

I remained silent.

"I know you hated every minute of it, but you took it, just like you put up with Jimmy. How could you stand it?"

I was sure she had lost her mind.

"I used to think you were jealous of me, but I know better now. I disgust you. You think you're better than me because you don't let them into your heart or mind. Men can only touch your flesh. You act like some kind of saint or martyr, walking around here with your head held high like you're first in line to get into Heaven."

I wanted to run from the room. The walls seemed to be closing in. My collar felt tight at my throat.

"I'm glad I made James whip you before he died. Beating you like the bitch you are makes up for every time he committed adultery with you."

That was nasty even by Lottie's standards.

"You think Señor Velasquez is going to save you? Take you to freedom? He's no different than the rest. He'll whisper sweet words in your ear until you give him what he wants, and then he'll move on to someone else."

Part of me agreed with her. I still didn't know what motivated Carlos to want to help me. He was no knight in shining armor. He was a monster, plain and simple. I was half right when I'd said he pitied me, but he also saw something in me that others either ignored or mistook as my being uppity. He believed the darkness inside me connected us, made us kindred. His attention made me feel like there might be more to my life one day, but I never wanted freedom if it meant preying on the lives of other people. Life lived at the expense of others wasn't a life worth living. I'm sure Carlos had found a way to justify the murders he committed over the centuries. I hoped I'd never have to comfort myself with lies like the ones he told himself.

"Drink this, Mamzèl," I said, and handed Lottie a glass of sweet tea mixed with a heavy dose of laudanum.

"Did you make the tea sweet enough this time? You know I can't stand the taste of that nasty medicine." She wrinkled her nose and then frowned at the glass.

"Yes, Mathilde made an extra sweet batch this evening," I said.

She swallowed the liquid in three gulps.

"You'll stay with me all night, won't you, Jacqueline?"

"Yes, Mamzèl."

"If that thing comes back, I don't want to be alone."

I didn't bother telling her that Mathilde and I had worked a spell to keep the *loup-garou* out of the house. I enjoyed seeing Lottie in her agitated state. I liked the fact she was afraid. All the terrible things she'd done to me, she *should* be scared for once in her life.

"There haven't been any more sightings of the beast in the Quarter," I said, and sat back down.

"Just because no one has seen it, doesn't mean it isn't still out there." Lottie wiped sweat from her upper lip. Crazy or not, what she was saying made sense. It was still out there. Waiting. For what, I wasn't sure.

I stood to open the window. Cool night air blew across my face. The room was stuffy, and I was sweating too.

"Have you lost your mind? Close that window, you simpleton," she shouted.

"I thought you were too warm, I only wanted to make you comfortable."

"Don't you dare talk back to me," she spat. "If James was alive, I'd make him whip you again."

"Well, he isn't," I said, and turned to walk out of the room.

"Wait! Don't leave me alone," she pleaded.

"Just let the laudanum do its work and go to sleep. No one is coming to kill you in your bed."

I stepped out into the hallway, shocked at my own behavior. Never in my life had I talked back to Lottie, or any *les Blancs* for that matter. I spoke my mind to Carlos, but even then, I was careful about choosing my words. He allowed me to speak my mind, so even if I did get overly emotional and use harsh words, I knew he wouldn't punish me for my honesty. He encouraged me to bare my soul.

Lottie's sobs pulled me out of my thoughts. I was about to return to her room to quiet her when someone knocked on the front door. Big John was stationed by the front gate. If someone wanted to enter the house, he would let them in. He wouldn't leave his post unless he had to.

I poked my head inside Lottie's bedroom. "Someone's at the door."

"Where are Big John and Monsieur Gale? I told them to watch the house all night." Her voice became shriller with each word.

"I'm going to see who it is."

I slowly descended the grand staircase to the foyer. The gaslights on the lower level of the house were turned down for the night. Shadows crept out from every corner, and the dull flicker of flames made them dance. The hiss of gas in the pipes sounded like whispers passing between the shadows as they slowly slithered across the floor. I knew it was my imagination playing tricks on me, but the whispers hushed when I stepped off the last step.

"Big John," I called, in hopes of rousing him from a nap. No answer. I crept stiff-legged toward the front door. Fear gripped every muscle in my body. My heartbeat quickened and a cold sweat prickled across my forehead and at the back of my neck. My hands were shaking and it took me three tries to turn the brass doorknob. What if it was the *loup-garou*? I knew he couldn't cross the threshold, but a man who becomes a beast must know a little something about magic.

Carlos claimed to know next to nothing when it came to spell casting and the ways of magic, but dark energy coursed through him. I could feel the vibrations when he was near. And he admitted it was my power that had initially caught his attention. What if all magical beings were somehow connected by that energy? Could the *loup-garou* somehow influence me to let him into the house? I couldn't ignore the knocking forever.

"Who's there?"

"It's me, Jacqueline, hurry —let me in," Carlos said.

I opened the door and invited him across the threshold. He had to step over something to come in. I stared at the black man's corpse lying on the front steps. Big John's throat had been torn out. The *loup-garou* had come to the house and killed again. Carlos gently nudged me out of the way and ushered me to the parlor. He turned up the gas on one of the light fixtures and sat me in a chair. I was in shock.

"Here, drink this." He handed me a glass of brandy.

I stared at the amber liquid until my sense came back. I drank the brandy and handed him the empty glass.

"Did you see it?"

"No, I was upstairs tending to Lottie. I sat with her after she took her medicine. Someone knocked. Big John didn't answer the door, so I came down to see who it was."

Carlos put his hands on my shoulders. "You're still shaking."

I pressed my head against his chest and sighed. "I'm so glad you came back. I couldn't get away to come to you."

"Is Charlotte sleeping?"

"Should be. I gave her a pretty heavy dose of laudanum. She screamed at me before I came downstairs, though."

"We could use this situation to our advantage."

"How?"

"Well, someone outside the house will notice Big John's body before morning and try to rouse someone in the house. When no one answers, they'll call for the police. And the police will find not one, but two bodies."

"I don't follow you."

He let go of my shoulders and paced back and forth in front of me.

"Go pack your things and tell Mathilde to get out of here."

"What are you going to do?"

He stopped pacing and met my gaze.

"I'm going to kill your sister."

I hesitated for only a second. I inhaled deeply and stood from my chair. Halfway up the staircase I turned to look at him. He was right behind me and I startled him slightly.

"What is it?"

I placed my hands on both sides of his face and kissed him. He melted into my arms and returned the kiss with equal passion.

"What was that for?"

"Thank you for coming back."

"I couldn't stay away. And, I promised that you would be free. It's time to make that happen. Go. I'll come find you when Charlotte's dead."

"What about Jimmy?" I'd dreamed of the day those two would meet an unsavory end.

"I'll take care of him, too."

Carlos made his way up the staircase to Lottie's bedroom, and I followed close behind.

"Oh, Lottie hired another man to help watch the house."

"What man?"

"An Irishman, but he's got better manners than Michié Lynch ever had."

Chapter 17

The smell hit me first. The sick, sweet stench of death—salty, metallic, and fetid—crawled up my nose and made me gag. The aroma of blood was overpowering, and it brought even Carlos to his knees. His eyes flashed an unearthly green and his fangs were out the moment I opened Lottie's bedroom door. He panted like an animal in heat, and sniffed the air with his mouth open, savoring the scent. His excitement disgusted me. It was all I could do not to faint, but I vomited on myself. I gripped the doorframe and sank down to the floorboards. My legs were too weak to hold me. Blood was everywhere. On the walls, across the ceiling, sprayed on the curtains and settee, and the bed was a mess of unidentifiable body parts and innards swimming in a sticky pool of red. Unlike Cook and Lynch, Lottie's head was still firmly attached. Jagged claw marks ran along both cheeks, making her face almost unrecognizable.

I wiped vomit from my mouth with the back of my trembling hand. As many times as I had wished for Lottie's death, I had never imagined the details. In my fantasies, she was simply dead and gone. In my wildest imaginings, I never would have pictured such a violent end for her.

Carlos regained some of his composure. He kept his distance like he was afraid to touch me. I was thankful for that, given the look on his face, which was somewhere between lust and starvation. Something told me that if he touched me at that moment and I asked him to stop, he might not be able to stop himself. I suddenly regretted kissing him.

"It came back," he said. "Did something go wrong with the spell?"

I stared at him like he was speaking gibberish. It had killed Big John outside the house, but how could it get inside? And where was Aleister? Had the beast killed him, too? I needed to warn Mathilde. I couldn't live with her death on my conscience. Besides, I wanted an excuse to get away from the carnage and away from the mindless fiend Carlos was becoming before my eyes. If he touched me, I was sure I would vomit again.

"I'm going to find Mathilde and Aleister."

"Aleister?"

I tried to stand, but my legs were still shaking. Carlos offered me his hand but I drew back from him. For a second, I thought he would grab me, but he took a step back and allowed me to stand on my own.

"I told you, Lottie hired him to help Big John and Jimmy guard the house."

I swallowed and cringed at the taste of bile on my tongue.

"Does Aleister have a surname?"

I coughed and tried to catch my breath without gagging again.

"Gale. Aleister Gale."

It was Carlos's turn to be confused. I was sure I had spoken clearly.

"Did you say Gale?"

I shook my head and wished I hadn't. The room tilted. I was in danger of fainting. I turned my back on the gruesome scene, unable to bear the silent scream frozen on Lottie's face a second longer. She was dead, and as she feared, the *loup-garou* had killed her. Sometimes it doesn't pay to be right.

"When did Gale arrive?"

"The day after you left. Why?"

"Gale is the *loup-garou*." He raked his fingers through his raven-wing curls and shouted the words mere inches from my face.

Aleister couldn't be the beast that killed Cook, Lynch, Big John, and now Lottie. *Could* he? His smile. I had seen it before. When the beast approached me in the garden. Aleister Gale was playing a game with us.

"How do you know Aleister is the beast?"

"We're old enemies. All this," he waved his arm toward the gore-smeared bedroom, "is for my benefit."

How many other people had Gale killed for Carlos's benefit? I had allowed another monster to get close to me. Trusted him. Slept in the room next to his and took no additional precautions to protect the other people in the house. I stupidly assumed the spell I'd used to guard the thresholds would keep that thing away, but I never thought we'd invite him in. Fools, we were all fools with no real chance of hope in a world where monsters walked among us.

"This is your fault?"

He didn't answer me.

"Gale killed at least four people for what reason? To impress you?"

Anger replaced the lust and hunger on his face. "I think he wants me blamed for these killings."

"You are to blame. He wants to see you punished."

"Semantics."

I didn't know what that word meant, but I'm sure it had something to do with his refusing to take responsibility for the deaths of four people I knew. Two I'd cared for a great deal, and the other two I had wished dead too many times to count. Cook and Big John didn't deserve to die the way they did.

"Am I in danger?"

"I won't let him harm you."

I didn't believe him. In the short amount of time it took for me to answer the door and climb the stairs back to Lottie's room, she was dead. She hadn't even had time to scream. The *loup-garou* was probably still in the house. Listening to our conversation. Laughing at us. How long had it been watching us? If Gale wanted to hurt Carlos, why didn't he kill me? He must have seen how close we'd become.

"How can you protect me from something that can do...?" My voice trailed off as I gestured toward Lottie's disemboweled corpse. "Besides, haven't you done worse? You did something to grab Gale's attention."

He was silent.

"I don't know him well, but he seems like a rational man."

My head snapped back as Carlos suddenly pressed his nose against mine. He glared down at me with green flames in his eyes, intense with heat, but somehow, I felt chilled to the bone.

"Rational? That *man* you speak of has hunted me across two continents and won't stop until he sees me ripped apart like your dear sister in there."

He silenced me.

"Velasquez, it has been such a pleasure getting to know your little pet here. So beautiful, strong, and clever, you've outdone yourself this time. You always did like girls with a bit of piss and vinegar."

I jumped at the sound of Aleister's voice and pressed my back against the wall to create some distance between me and the monsters. As usual, Aleister's footfalls had been silent. Even Carlos was startled. He spun around, fangs exposed, and faced his enemy.

"You've made your point, Gale, but nothing will bring your harlot back from the grave."

Aleister took a step toward me and grabbed my arm. His grip was tight, but he didn't hurt me. His gaze met mine and he gave me a reassuring smile.

"I'm not going to hurt you. You've suffered enough at the hands of your own enemies. I consider us allies."

"What game are you playing, Gale?" Carlos took a step closer to me.

Aleister ignored Carlos and kept his focus on me.

"I don't know what lies this viper has told you, but he's very good at making promises. One day, this vile excuse for a man will turn on you. When he does, I know you will have the strength to fight him. If I can assist in that fight, all you have to do is ask."

That sent Carlos into a rage. "Are you going to listen to this filthy beast who killed four people just to get my attention? You saw what he did to poor Cook and Big John. And even though James and Charlotte were despicable people and got what they deserved, he tore them apart."

Gale arched an eyebrow and tilted his head as he kept eye contact with me. "I've only killed three people in this household. I regret killing Big John," he said.

It suddenly dawned on me that Carlos had killed Cook. My initial instincts had been right, and I had ignored them.

"Why do you think you're any less of a monster than Gale? It's a very fine line between drinking people's blood and eating their flesh," I said.

Carlos had nothing to say.

Both men claimed they wanted to protect me. One way or another, I was going to get hurt.

Chapter 18

Word of Lottie's death spread fast, and with it came a hundred different versions of who had killed her and why. Most people assumed that because Mathilde and I were missing we had done the evil deed. People said we'd gone crazy, killed Big John, and then killed Lottie. Maybe we killed Cook and James Lynch, too. People wanted to believe we'd killed our masters, but judging by the state of the bodies, I don't see how they could. I did my best with protection spells, *gris gris* bags, and potions, but I only had so much magic to keep the people in the house on Royal Street safe. Too many people to look after, and I had to worry about my own hide. Don't matter how much power a mambo's got if she's too busy warding off evil from her own door. It was a relief when the Lynches died, but I only got to enjoy the peace for a moment.

When my father caught wind of Lottie's death, he sent The Ogden Brothers to help Jimmy track Mathilde and me down. I read about it in *L'Abeille de la Nouvelle-Orléans*. The reporter mentioned that Aleister Gale, "a man working in the Lynch household at the time of the tragedy," had offered his assistance, and the four men formed a band of slave catchers to inspire enough nightmares for a lifetime. Jimmy reported Big John and Lottie's deaths the next day. He wasn't in the house when Aleister killed them. He'd been in Storyville gambling and spending his winnings on prostitutes. That part of the story wasn't mentioned in the paper.

I had no idea where Mathilde ran off to, but Carlos and I hid in plain sight. We stayed in his rented house on Esplanade. Fortunately, he did not force me to provide all the services expected of a *placée*. For a monster, he was capable of acts of kindness.

I slept on a cot in one of the four small rooms and he slept in a well-shaded shed under a cypress tree in the courtyard behind the cottage. For two weeks, I stayed inside the humid little house and worked on protection spells to keep us hidden. Most days I ate fresh foods I didn't have to cook, or something easy that I could simmer over a fire, but when Carlos returned from his nightly hunts he brought me lime water with sugar cane, petite pastries, candied violets, and other delicacies. Lace gloves, a pearl necklace, a silk coin purse, and a cameo brooch were all unexpected gifts lifted from the bodies of his female victims. This strange romantic gesture was one step above grave robbing, but I didn't want to refuse the gifts for fear of seeming ungrateful. I kept the *memento mori*, objects that were surely cursed, in the wooden cigar box Moman had given me for root work. I wasn't sure how I would use them, but they might give a little extra power to my conjuring. I worried about the consequences of keeping the objects, and Carlos worried that he might have to sell them to get us out of New Orleans.

"I don't care about the trinkets," I told him. "All I care about is my life...and yours."

I meant every word. I did care about Carlos, and I wanted him to be safe. Maybe that made me a fool to care about a monster who looked like a man, but he'd shown me tenderness, and in his strange way, treated me with respect.

"I have lived a long time," he said. "I am no stranger to being hunted. No ignorant slave catcher is going to harm you —or me."

"The Ogden Brothers aren't ordinary slave catchers. Jimmy and Aleister Gale have enough personal motives to want to catch both of us. If they find us, I'll be sold or hanged." I did nothing to hide the anger in my voice.

"Or worse."

"What's worse than that?"

"I think you already know the answer to that question."

I did know what was worse than being lynched. A memory of Jimmy flashed into my head, punching me in the mouth while he raped me. It was a miracle I still had all my teeth.

"Aren't you worried Gale will expose you for what you are?" I asked. "He was trying to frame *you* for those deaths, not me. A lot of people in this town believe in magic, so it won't be a stretch for them to believe in vampires."

"If he exposes me, he risks exposing himself," he said.

A fist pounded against the front door. Terror squeezed my heart with all its might. I dropped to the floor and scrambled under my cot. I ignored the dust and centipedes and covered my head with shaking hands. Dying was easy. My fear came from not knowing what would happen to me before I was allowed to peacefully drift off into nothingness. Carlos was strong and fast and scary, but if a mob showed up to hang us, he may as well have been facing a dragon.

"Ah, Carlos, I was worried something terrible had happened to you, too," Jimmy said, from outside the front door.

"How did you know where to find me?" Carlos didn't invite him in.

Jimmy laughed. "People talk in the Quarter. Before she died, Charlotte mentioned you had some business to attend to, but I wasn't sure if you were still in the city."

"I did have other business dealings, but they've concluded. Now that James and Charlotte are both dead, there's really no reason for me to stay on in New Orleans."

"It's a shame. James was so excited about building your house. There are other architects in the city who might be able to complete the project if you decided to stay."

What was Jimmy up to? Why did he care if Carlos stayed in New Orleans?

"I have considered that, but other matters have caused me to reconsider settling here. Especially the threat of dying at the hands...or rather, *mouth* of a wild animal that still hasn't been caught," Carlos said.

"Speaking of wild animals, have you seen Jacqueline or Mathilde?"

"Pardon?"

"The two runaways from the Lynch house," Jimmy said.

"Why would I see them?"

"Well, it looked like you were getting nice and cozy with Jacqueline, and she might trust you to hide her if she was in trouble."

"Are you accusing me of harboring fugitive slaves?"

"I'm not accusing you of anything, but one of your neighbors said he saw you in the company of a young *fille de couleur*, possibly your *placée.*"

"People should be more in the habit of minding their own business," Carlos said, between clenched teeth.

Jimmy laughed. "Personally, that's why I prefer the plantation to the city. Too many people with too many opinions about how you should live your life."

"I'm sorry I can't be of more help to you," Carlos said.

"Well, at least we can rule out your house as a safe haven for runaways." Jimmy didn't sound convinced.

"Best of luck in your search," Carlos said. He was somber, but he wanted Jimmy to go away. I could feel his anxiety radiating off him like waves of heat.

"And best of luck to you in whatever your future plans may be," Jimmy said.

Carlos shut the door of the cottage. I stayed hidden under the cot.

"It's safe to come out, Jacqueline."

I wasn't sure I believed him. If I didn't know any better, I would have sworn that Jimmy knew I was in the house for certain. Did Aleister Gale tip him off? Maybe the *loup-garou* had smelled me while spying on the property.

"We can't stay here," I said. "They know."

"They know what?"

"You're smarter than that. You know as well as I do that Jimmy was only toying with you to see if you'd get nervous. He already knows I'm here. They've been watching this place, noticing when you come and go. They'll be back for me later tonight when you go out to hunt."

"They won't find anything if they do," he said.

"Why not?"

"Because we'll be gone," he said.

The only person I knew who could safely get us out of New Orleans was Squire Jean. Not only was he a powerful *houngan*, but an abolitionist to boot. Cook told me he helped slaves escape all up and down the Mississippi and he claimed to know Harriet Tubman, the freedom fighter who ushered freedom seekers along the Underground Railroad. Carlos insisted he knew how to get us to safety, but he'd never traveled with a runaway before. We needed as much help as we could get. I wasn't about to end up swinging from a rope just because my sister was in the wrong place at the wrong time.

We packed only what we could carry into Carlos's leather traveling satchel and left the small, bright yellow cottage on Esplanade. On the way to Squire Jean's, we stopped at a pawnbroker's to sell the trinkets Carlos had given me. I was happy to see them sold. The money would help us escape from New Orleans.

According to rumors floating around the Quarter, Squire Jean had studied root work in Haiti under a powerful *Bokor*. He had the sight and knew we were coming. He sat on his porch swaying back and forth in his rocking chair swatting flies from his face with a paper fan.

"'Bout time you got here, girl. I've been worried sick about you. Saw the wanted posters in the French Market yesterday."

"Can you get us out of New Orleans safely?" Carlos asked.

Squire Jean ignored him and addressed me directly. "You gonna travel with this here vampire?"

"Yes, Squire," I said.

"I don't advise it, but it might help you get further faster. Here in New Orleans you can keep up the lie of your *mariage de la main gauche*, everywhere else you'll have to pretend to be his slave."

"Why can't we say she's free?" Carlos was getting angry.

"No proof. Nobody freed her, so there's no Certificate of Manumission. You don't need to show any proof she's a slave, because that's what everyone wants to believe anyway."

"So what do we need to do?" Carlos insisted on being in charge of the situation.

"You need to get her some new clothes and hop on a riverboat heading up the Mississippi. I've got folks to connect you with along the way. They'll get you as far North as you want to go. Some folks might not take too kindly to your vampire, but they'll still help you."

"Aren't you afraid of offending me, old man?" Carlos gritted his teeth.

Squire Jean was the only one I knew who could get me to the North. I was scared that Carlos would do something stupid, like hurt him.

"Afraid of you? Now why would I be afraid of you? I'm helping you, ain't I? At least, I'm helping this girl you seem to care about. Why else would you be here? If you care about her, prove it. Get her out of New Orleans and help her get up North where she'll be free."

I didn't need to worry about Squire Jean. He'd run away from his master twice before he was free, once on a broken leg. I trusted him to send us in the right direction.

"What do you want in exchange for helping us?" I was prepared to give him money.

Squire John handed Carlos a small, cobalt blue apothecary bottle. "Here, vampire, fill this with your blood."

Carlos snatched the bottle from the conjurer's hand and laughed. "I knew there would be a price. My blood is quite valuable to practitioners of black magic."

I had never heard of vampire blood being used in conjuring, but after seeing how quickly it had healed me, I was sure it would be a powerful ingredient.

Chapter 19

We boarded the steamboat Caledonia that night. I had a new dress, a warm cloak, and Squire Jean had given me a few odds and ends to add to my cigar box. Herbs mostly, a few coffin nails, and a couple *gris gris* bags made specially for me. Carlos had the names of the people we'd be looking for along the Underground Railroad written in his journal and tucked safely in the pocket of his long, black wool coat. It didn't matter if I was his *placée* or not, I was not permitted in the whites only sections of the riverboat. I stayed below deck with the other Negro passengers. A coffle of slaves that were to be sold at the Forks of the Road Slave Market in Natchez, shuffled into the hold shortly before leaving port. Among them was my childhood friend, Gabriel. He didn't see me at first, but I recognized him right away. His head was lowered to avoid eye contact like the other slaves chained on either side of him. Fear of what would become of them after they were sold in Natchez kept them quiet.

"Gabriel? It's me, Jacqueline," I said, in a low tone.

He slowly raised his head like a sleeper escaping a perplexing dream.

"Jacqueline, what are you doing here?"

"I...I'm heading north with a new owner," I lied.

I had a note in my pocket, and a pass Carlos had written for me to show anyone who doubted my ownership. Slavers got greedy sometimes and even tried to sell free blacks into slavery if they couldn't prove they weren't runaways.

"Someone buy you from Mamzèl Charlotte?"

"Yes, one of Michié Lynch's business clients bought me."

"He treat you right?"

"Right enough. How'd you end up here?"

He shook his head and laughed. "I tried to run. Michié Jimmy wanted the Ogden Brothers to teach me a lesson, but Master wouldn't hear of it. Said I was too valuable. They argued about it, but finally decided to reap a profit rather than maim me or worry about me trying to run off again."

"Where were you running to?" His family was on the plantation, and as far as I knew, he didn't know anybody else.

"Thought I'd come look for you," he said, and took my hand.

I choked back tears and put on my best smile for him.

"I missed you, and wondered if you were doing all right in the city."

"I missed you, too. Running away from that plantation is like asking to be lynched. What were you thinking?" I scolded him, but my tone was gentle.

"Well, none of that matters now, because I got to see you," he said, and squeezed my hand.

The air down below was stale and smelled like fetid breath, unwashed bodies, and human waste from the overflowing barrels we were expected to use. Having Gabriel for company made me care a bit less about the inhuman conditions.

We spent the next few days catching up and recalling old times. He told me how Moman and some of the other slaves were doing, and I was glad to hear everyone was healthy and that not much had changed. Aside from Gabriel, no one had been sold off or punished too severely since my departure a year earlier. I stayed near him in hopes that I could keep his mind off the slave market. It was one of the first stops up the river from New Orleans.

Late one night, three, maybe four days into our journey, I awoke to the blast and terrible vibrations of an explosion, and screams coming from the decks above. All around me, people were scrambling to see in the darkness, trying to find the doors that led to the upper levels. Panic cut a pathway from passenger to passenger as someone tried to open the door and found that it had been locked. Men pounded on the door, and when no one came to open it, they worked together to break it down.

In the chaos around me, Carlos's voice soothed my mounting terror.

I'm coming for you Jacqueline. Focus on your surroundings, and guide me to you.

Even in my head, he sounded panicked.

We're in the first cargo hold. Men are trying to break down the door, but it won't budge.

The screams overhead made the men's efforts to open the door more frantic. Babies and children cried, and mothers tried to calm them while their own fears rose to the surface. The boat shifted suddenly at an odd angle. We were taking on water, but not on our side of the vessel.

I called to Carlos. *Is the boat sinking? What happened?*

I think one of the boilers exploded. No word from the captain yet, but there's a giant hole where the paddle engines used to be. Stay calm. I'm almost there.

What was keeping him? He should have been able to move through the boat quickly unless frightened passengers were blocking his way. Men were working on opening the door and women all around me were praying that the cargo hold wouldn't become our tomb.

A woman near me didn't have enough arms to hold her three scared children so I lent her mine. Side-by-side, we rocked the babies in hopes of easing their fear and ours.

"It's going to be all right. We'll get out of this. You'll see," I said.

She nodded, her eyes wide with fear. She didn't believe me. I wasn't sure I believed myself either.

Tell the men to stand back from the door. Carlos's voice gave me hope.

"Stand back from the door. Someone's coming to help," I shouted above the pounding and screaming.

"What you mean? How you know someone's coming to help?" A man with sweat pouring down his face directed his fear and anger toward me.

"I...I just know."

"You some kind of witch? A seer?" The man's tone accused me of something. He came toward me and two other men followed.

"I don't want any trouble," I said, and took a step back from the man. The baby rested in my arms.

"This girl is helping me quiet my children. She didn't do nothing to you." The mother holding the other two children stood up and faced the three men coming toward me.

Gabriel spoke up. "If Jacqueline says help is coming, then help is coming."

"Ain't nobody comin' down here to save a bunch of niggers," the man said with that same accusing tone. "All they gonna worry about is gettin' white folks off this sinking boat. We gonna die like animals down here."

The door splintering in half and falling inward with a loud crash interrupted his tirade. Carlos ran to my side and lifted me up in his arms.

"I came as fast as I could. Are you all right?" He set my feet back down on the swiftly tilting floor. I fell forward into his chest and he steadied me. Gabriel gazed in wonder at Carlos, but didn't say a word.

"I'm fine. We need to help these folks get out of here," I said.

"I saw a way out, but we'll have to swim. All the lifeboats were gone when I left the main deck. They didn't have enough for all the passengers anyway," he said, between gritted teeth. "How many children? Can everyone swim? I'm not sure how close we are to shore or how deep the river is, but it's our only hope of getting everyone out."

The man who'd felt threatened by me spoke up. "Infants and children who can't swim can float next to us. We'll take our time and get to shore. Those of you who can swim, help anyone who can't."

"Follow me," Carlos shouted, and led the way off the sinking steamboat.

Gabriel grabbed my arm before I could follow. "That man didn't buy you to be his slave, he's in love with you."

I laughed. "So he says."

"You don't believe him? Not many slave owners would risk their lives to save the life of a slave or agree to help other colored folk at her command."

"True, but even if he does love me, at what cost?"

"Our lives as slaves might only amount to a bill of sale, but you can't live your life weighing and measuring how people feel about you. At some point, you're going to have to feel something, too. Allow someone into your heart."

He was right, but now wasn't the time to dwell on it.

"Jacqueline, hurry." Carlos called to me and I raced to his side.

Men scrambled to put out the fires burning out of control in the boiler area, and a hole bigger than a barn door gaped open so that we could see the starry night sky and the black rushing waters of the Mississippi.

People are going to drown; we can't save everyone, Jacqueline.

He was right, but I didn't want him to be. If we could save some I'd be happy, but I wanted to save them all. I was most concerned about the coffle of slaves, bound together by heavy links of chain connected by shackles on their wrists and ankles. It was unlikely any of them would make it to shore.

Can we try to separate them? Break the chains? I pleaded with Carlos.

We don't have the tools or the time. I'm strong, but I can't break through iron.

I was thankful for my gift in that moment. The people standing around us couldn't hear us deciding their fates. Then I remembered something Moman taught me long ago. She said if I ever found myself in trouble and really needed help, I should call upon the *loa* and draw them down. I'd never allowed the gods to mount me before, but Moman had shown me how to become a *chèval*. There wasn't time to do a full ritual, but maybe I could channel enough energy from the people around me to draw the *loa* down.

"Everyone, gather in a circle and join hands," I shouted above the deafening noise of the hull cracking.

They did as I asked, including Carlos. The boat tilted again and we were thrown against the walls of the paddle engine room. I remained calm. When all hands were linked, a hum of energy passed through the circle. There was fear on some of their faces, but they were desperate for help. Like the slaves in the cotton fields, I spoke the words to call upon *Agwe* and *La Sirène*, and they repeated the chant back to me. Before I could invoke the power of the *loa*, another boiler exploded. The boat split in half and separated one side of the circle from the other. Carlos's hand gripped mine, but I watched as the coffle of slaves slipped over the jagged edge where the hull finally broke in two. Their screams echoed through my entire body as I ran to the edge. I caught a glimpse of Gabriel's head before it slipped beneath the whirlpool the sinking boat had created.

"Gabriel," I screamed. I leaned over the edge to see if he would resurface and almost fell into the water after him. Carlos grabbed me just in time.

He shook me by the shoulders. "Are you trying to die?"

I couldn't speak. My childhood friend, the boy who treated me like a human being, was gone. Swallowed up by the river. Pulled to his death by the rushing current with fourteen other men and women.

Fires broke out on the upper deck and the other men, women, and children fended for themselves and did their best to swim to shore. I have no idea how many of them survived. I was in a fugue and Carlos had to take charge. I wouldn't step away from the edge. I kept hoping Gabriel would come back to the surface. I kept calling to him. Finally, Carlos slapped me hard across the face and brought me back to reality.

"I don't know what that boy meant to you, and I'm sorry he's dead, but I'm not going to let you put your own life in danger just because you're upset. We need to get in the water now." Carlos was stern, but not angry. "Do you trust me to get you safely to shore?"

I nodded my head, but still couldn't find words.

"Climb on my back and hold tight. Don't let go."

I did as I was told. I wrapped my arms around his neck and my legs around his waist and held on with all my strength.

"Close your eyes," he said.

I did, and then he jumped over the edge of the boat and we landed with a loud splash. The water dug its icy fingers into my flesh and I gasped for air even though my head was well above the surface. Carlos swam like a sea creature with me on his back. Even though it would have been soaked and heavy with water, I wished I hadn't left my new cloak behind. I'd need it sooner or later and it was too late to go back for it.

I don't know how long we were in the water, but Carlos didn't come up for air once. Further proof that he was not like other men. I said a prayer for Gabriel, but I couldn't do anything else for him. Why would the gods bring him back to me just to take him away? Moman taught me that the gods had a plan for all of us, and we should never question their ways. I wanted to curse them but knew it wouldn't bring him back to me. I tightened my grip around Carlos's neck and waist, and fought to hold on as my limbs became numb in the icy water. I was glad to have a monster for my traveling companion as he got us farther and farther away from the wreckage of the Caledonia.

Chapter 20

When I climbed out of the river, my clothes clung to me, heavy with water. Exhausted, I collapsed on the muddy bank near a dark wooded area. Carlos fell down next to me with a thud. Turning my head slightly, I rested my cheek in the crook of my arm to get a better look at him. He was lying on his back, staring up at the night sky. His skin glowed an eerie white in the darkness, except for one dark spot. Something moved on his neck, black, slug-like, and it seemed to be feeding on him. It quivered slightly and changed color from black, to grey, to white, like cinders in a dying fire. As the color changed, so did its shape. At first glance, it was fat like my thumb, but soon it shriveled and fell to the ground. Was it dead?

"Something dropped off your neck. I think it's dead now."

"What?" He turned to me and I pointed at the thing.

He picked it up and examined it. A smile spread across his lips.

"What is it?" I propped myself up on my elbows to get a better look.

"A leech. It must not have liked my blood," he laughed.

I sat up quickly and peered down the front of my body. I was covered in black, shiny leeches. Modesty went out the window; fear and disgust gripped my thoughts, and I tore off my soaking wet dress. I stood naked, covered in vile, bloodsucking parasites. There were so many of them that I was becoming light-headed from blood loss. I stumbled, and Carlos steadied me.

"Let me help you." That seemed to be his new favorite pastime.

I nodded, on the verge of tears.

He got to work right away, removing the leeches by scraping his sharp nail under their slimy, black bodies until he pried their mouths loose from my skin. He tilted his head back and swallowed each and every blood-engorged leech with a moan of pleasure. Twenty bites in my flesh wept blood. Carlos took several steps back and covered his mouth. His fangs were exposed, and his eyes had darkened. His bloodlust was aroused. He had tasted my blood.

"Stand by the water and rinse off the blood carefully. The scent is driving me wild." His voice was heavy with desire.

I washed away as much blood as I could, and dressed quickly in my wet, tattered clothes. I was so cold I would have sold my soul to bask in the glow of hellfire. Gooseflesh and chills ran up and down my bitten and bruised limbs. I was shivering so much that my insides hurt.

"I need to get you somewhere warm. Are you strong enough to walk a little further? I smell smoke through the trees." He kept his distance.

Too tired to speak, I gestured for him to lead the way. His strides were longer than mine, so I had to work to keep up, but I managed to walk through the woods, tripping over my feet only once or twice. The woods opened onto a meadow that must have been beautiful in daylight. I pictured butterflies and wildflowers in every color imaginable, but now, the meadow was draped in shadows, and dim moonlight shone upon a small cabin with a wisp of smoke rising from its narrow chimney.

"Stay here," he said.

He approached the cabin with caution. Blending into the

darkness, his feet made no sound on the ground that was littered with broken twigs and dried weeds. He peered into one of the grease paper windows and motioned for me to come closer.

I was careful not to make any noise as I made my way to his side.

"I can still smell your blood," he whispered.

"I...I'm sorry I didn't wash better," I stammered.

He turned to face me. "I wasn't chastising you, I just meant...I want to taste you."

Tiny rivers of blood carried on trickling down my skin.

"Will you be able to stop the bleeding?" I looked up into his eyes.

"Yes."

"Promise not to hurt me," I said, quaking.

"I promise. I'll tend to your wounds once we're inside," he said with a smile.

"How many people are in there?"

"I saw only one man, but others may be sleeping where I can't see them. I can hear only one heartbeat, though."

He crept around the side of the house to the front door and motioned for me to stay hidden. I pressed my palm against the rough wooden boards to give myself a little extra support. My head was spinning again, and I was afraid I might faint. If I didn't sit down soon, I'd *fall* down. I hadn't had a proper night's sleep since we left New Orleans.

Carlos knocked on the door, three gentle raps.

"Who's there?" The heavy wooden door muffled an older man's voice.

"Travelers," Carlos said. "We need a warm fire and maybe a place to rest for a few hours. We'll be gone by daybreak."

"Travelers? How many?" The man wasn't in a hurry to open his door.

"Just me and my slave. We survived a steamboat accident a few miles upriver; we washed up along the stream bed." Carlos sounded charming and sincere. I knew he was starving for blood.

"Your slave can sleep in the shed with the horse. There's fresh straw." The man still hadn't opened the door.

"May we dry off by your fire before bedding down for the night?" Carlos motioned for me to come stand next to him. For a moment I wished he were human so we could share what little heat our bodies held between us. I couldn't stop shivering.

"I don't usually let niggers in my house, but I suppose you can sit by the fire," he said, and finally opened the door. He took a good look at both of us and motioned for us to come in with the barrel of his rifle.

"Thank you, Señor," Carlos said, and ushered me to the hearth where he made me kneel before I fell over.

"You're not from around here, where you from?" Suspicion crept into the man's voice.

"I'm from Seville, Spain, but I've been living here in the New Country for a few years. We came from New Orleans," Carlos said.

I swooned and lost my balance. I righted myself and moved closer to the fire. My clothes dried almost immediately and the chill left my bones.

"What's the matter with her? Is she sick?" The man placed his gun on a large wooden table in the center of the one-room cabin.

"No, just exhausted from our travels. And, leeches bit her while we were in the water. I need to tend to her wounds," Carlos explained.

"I don't have any clean cloth to make bandages, so I'm not sure how you're gonna patch her up," the old man said.

"I'll manage," Carlos said. He placed his hand on my shoulder to let me know he was beside me. I had drifted off to sleep.

"She's in bad shape, huh?" The old man stood next to a shelf by the stove that held dried goods, canned goods, and other food items. "When'd she eat last?"

"I don't know, a day or two?" Carlos shrugged.

The old man shook his head. "You gotta treat your slave better than that, Mister...."

"Velasquez, Carlos Velasquez."

The old man set out some Johnnycake and lit a flame under the kettle on the stove.

"I feed my horse every day and make sure she has clean water twice a day. You don't care for your slave right, she'll die."

Was the old man really that concerned about me, or just giving advice on the upkeep of livestock?

"I'm going to have to take your dress off to clean your wounds, Jacqueline. Is that permissible?"

I looked at the old man without making eye contact and nodded at Carlos. He helped me out of my damp, torn dress, and I covered my nakedness as best I could with my hands and arms.

"Young enough to still be modest," the old man said. "I may have something she can put on after you look after those leech bites." He disappeared behind a privacy screen where his bed and a few other pieces of furniture stood.

While the old man was busy, Carlos opened a gash in his wrist. I mouthed the word "no". I didn't want to drink his blood again.

"You don't have to drink it, I'm going to use my blood to heal your wounds. I'm just going to place it over the bites. That should work just fine," he reassured me.

Carefully, he spread his blood over the bites with his fingers and let the magical properties work on their own. When the wounds were treated, he offered his wrist to me. "Just take a little to boost your strength."

I couldn't make eye contact with him, but I accepted his wrist and drank from him. The healing effects were immediate. My fatigue subsided, the aches and pains in my back and legs were gone, and most of my bruises vanished. And, more than anything, I wanted to kiss him. His blood had awakened my craving for touch. What other effects would his blood have on me?

Carlos sensed my longing and pulled me close for a kiss. My eyes fluttered shut and I allowed myself to enjoy the pleasure of his embrace. The cabin, the woods, the world outside faded away around us. His kisses put me in a dreamlike state. My skin tingled at his touch. The kettle whistled, but we ignored it.

"Water's ready if you want to make tea." The old man stepped out from behind the room divider. He stopped in his tracks at the sight of Carlos worshipping my body before the fire. "I'll have none of that in my house, you hear?"

Carlos ignored the old man.

"I don't know how you do things in New Orleans, but round here, we don't mix with the niggers," our host said in a raised voice.

That was a lie. If *les Blancs* owned slaves in these parts, then they were helping themselves to the bodies of black women, and men for that matter.

Carlos stopped kissing me when he heard the old man cock his rifle. The barrel was pointed at the back of the vampire's head. My legs were wrapped around his waist, so it took him a few seconds to sit up. He offered me his coat to cover my body.

"That'll be quite enough of that," the old man said. "Here." He tossed a dress at me. "Put that on, get something in your belly, then the two of you need to be on your way."

"I'm sorry if we've offended you, Señor. I have a fondness for this girl that goes beyond the savagery I've witnessed in most slave owners." Carlos stood, and I quickly dressed.

"You can do whatever you like in the privacy of your own home, but treating niggers like they're the same as white women just ain't right."

The old man lowered the barrel of the gun, which gave Carlos the opportunity to grab the man by his neck and raise his feet off the ground so that he was eye-level with him. The swiftness with which Carlos shifted from passionate lover to enraged murderer startled me. He was going to kill this man. Not because he was a threat to either of us, but because he had insulted me and questioned Carlos's motives.

In his mind, it was nobody's business who he chose to love. He tightened his grip around the man's neck and planned to snap it.

I thought of Gabriel drowning in the river. How many others had died that night? I knew I'd never be able to talk Carlos out of killing him, but I'd seen quite enough death for one night. I also knew the man would alert the authorities about us if he had the chance.

"Make it quick," I whispered.

Before the body had a chance to cool, Carlos helped himself to a healthy dose of the man's blood.

Wearing a fresh dress, I took the whistling kettle off the flame and made tea. I ate Johnnycake until I was full and downed two steaming mugs of tea with honey. I felt almost human again. Carlos wiped blood from his nose, mouth and chin while he watched me eat.

"Now, where were we?" Carlos pushed the empty mug onto the floor and climbed across the table to kiss me again.

My fear made my heart beat faster and pound against my ribcage, and my desire made my pulse thump between my thighs.

I soon forgot about the dead man on the floor. I eased my conscience by telling myself that the man had been a threat to us. Carlos needed to kill him to protect me. Us.

"You had to kill him," I said into Carlos's ear.

"Yes, if he didn't try to kill us, he would report that he'd seen us."

"Right."

"You don't like that I killed him?"

"I don't like that you kill anyone."

He sat up and offered me his hand. The romantic mood was broken.

"You need your rest. Sleep. I'll keep watch tonight and you can take watch at sunrise. We'll begin our journey again at dusk tomorrow evening."

"Goodnight," I said, and kissed him once more.

"Goodnight, Jacqueline."

Carlos took the old man's body outside to bury it. I tried to stay awake to talk about where our next stop would be, but I couldn't keep my eyes open. I was asleep before he came back inside.

At dusk, we were on the move again. I wrapped the rest of the Johnnycake in a clean towel and tucked it in with my belongings in Carlos's leather satchel. My boots had dried, and I was glad of them as we cut our own path through the thick woods. We weren't sure where we washed up, but we were closer to Natchez than New Orleans. If we were lucky, Aleister Gale, Jimmy, and the Ogden Brothers hadn't gotten too far ahead of us to post wanted signs. I trusted Carlos to keep me safe, but I honestly didn't think he knew which way to go.

"Did the names Squire Jean gave you get washed away in the river?"

He pulled his leather journal from his inside coat pocket. The pages were damp at the edges, but the writing was still legible. We were looking for a woman by the name of Agatha Mae. Squire Jean said she'd get us as far north as I needed to go for a time. I wasn't sure what that meant, but Agatha Mae lived in Jackson, Mississippi. That was a long way to walk. Boots or no boots, my feet would only carry me so far.

"If I was on my own I could travel further faster," Carlos said.

"I'm sorry I'm holding you back," I said.

"Don't you know a spell to get us there quicker?"

"Magic doesn't work like that."

We trudged on through the woods. The moon had been full the night before and still provided plenty of light for me to see. Carlos could see in the dark like a cat, but I didn't possess the same supernatural abilities.

Full moon. I wondered if the *loup-garou* would reveal itself to the other slave catchers. Carlos never came right out and told people what he was until they either guessed at his nature, or it was too late. Neither did he try to hide what he was. Aleister Gale used deception to hide the fact that he was a monster. When he wasn't a wolf, he appeared to be just like other men. His life was a perpetual lie. He hunted Carlos for revenge, and maybe to stop him from killing, but that made him a hypocrite, because he killed people, too. Maybe he thought his motives were more honorable, but murder is murder.

We walked for three nights, and on the second, I tripped over tree roots, fell over an embankment, and rolled into a muddy ravine. It happened so fast I didn't have time to register the pain I was in. Carlos rushed down the embankment. He looked terrified when he found me at the bottom. I was stuck in the deep mud and he had to pull me out. That's when I lost my boots. My feet were already sore, and now I'd have to make the rest of my journey barefoot.

Carlos checked me for serious injuries, and then we were on our way. We had to keep moving. We only stopped to eat or sleep. Exposed to the elements, each night before dawn, Carlos dug a shallow grave for us, with his bare hands. In the dark, he could look after me and still be safe from the coming dawn.

Carlos wrapped his arms around me. "Are you cold?"

"I'll be fine." I clutched his collar and pressed my lips to his cheek.

"You're safe with me."

I desperately wanted to believe that, but a voice inside my head warned me to trust my instincts. My instincts told me that sooner or later, all men showed their true faces. This monster was more of a gentleman than most men I had met, but like all predators, it would be foolish to let my guard down around him. Maybe Gabriel was right. Someday I'd have to trust someone enough to let them into my heart, but that day wasn't today, and that person wasn't Carlos Velasquez.

When we finally saw the lights of Vicksburg, I thought Carlos might weep. The city was bustling with life, life that provided him nourishment. In the woods, he survived on animal blood, which he found disgusting. He hadn't fed off another human since he'd killed the old man. Almost a week. He was starving for human blood.

I could barely walk when we reached Vicksburg. Despite his

hunger, Carlos insisted on carrying me. My feet wouldn't have held me up even if I wanted them to. Without the boots, my feet took a beating in the woods from prickle bushes, twigs, rocks, and all manner of things that poked, scratched, and cut them up. We must have been a sight. A crazed white man carrying a slave in his arms, both of us dirty from sleeping in the ground. It's a wonder we weren't arrested.

Chapter 21

The train ride from Vicksburg to Jackson was more trouble than it was worth, but my feet finally had a chance to heal. The blisters on my heels and toes tore open and got infected from the dirt and mud caked all the way up to my ankles. Carlos insisted that I be allowed to ride in his compartment rather than in the back of the train with the other slaves and livestock.

By the time we'd boarded, I had a fever. Carlos pushed past all the people waiting on the platform and carried me onto the train. Our meager belongings were slung over his back, and he scowled at the conductor attempting to block our entrance. He refused to argue with the man. I would sleep in his car and that was final. He demanded hot water, fresh towels, and bourbon.

"Sir, slaves can't sleep among the white passengers," the conductor said, and tried to stand his ground.

"She is sick and needs medical attention. She is my responsibility. I can't look after her if she is kept with the cattle."

"But, Sir, the other passengers will be angry."

Carlos pushed his nose against the conductor's, snarled, and flashed his fangs at the startled man.

"If anyone complains, send them to me."

He stormed off to our cabin and left the conductor to argue with the back of his head. Fresh towels, hot water, and bourbon arrived a little while later. The black porter brought some food on a tray. I was almost asleep; exhausted from the fever, bone weary from walking fast enough to keep up with Carlos's stride, but the smell of the food pulled me awake. Beans, cornbread, and a little salt pork. I barely noticed the pain when Carlos wiped the caked mud from my feet. We rode in a first-class sleeping car. It was quiet, clean, and comfortable. Almost as cozy as the one-room cabin we'd left behind seven days earlier.

"There's dried witch hazel, belladonna, and a little all-heal in the sack. Crush them up and let them steep in the water," I said, through a mouthful of cornbread.

He pulled my cigar box out of his leather satchel.

"These?" He held up the dried herbs and looked up at me for guidance.

"Yes. Now crush the herbs between your hands to release the oils and put them in the water. Hand me the bourbon."

After he added the dried herbs to the basin, he grabbed the dark brown bottle and pulled the cork out with his teeth. He handed me the bottle and I took a hefty pull. The smoky, sweet liquid slid down my throat, burned my chest, and sent its warm tendrils down into my belly. I closed my eyes and leaned back against the padded bench.

"This is going to hurt. Take another drink," he said.

He waited for me to take two more pulls. Then the pain came. Using his sharp thumbnail, he sliced open the blisters that hadn't burst yet, and rubbed the herbs into my feet in the hot water. I winced at the burning sensation in my feet that clawed its way up my calves, but I refused to cry out. I didn't want to draw any more attention to us. I wanted to sleep next to Carlos on the train. I bit my lip and kept quiet.

"You're doing a good job," I said. Tears streaked my dirty face.

"I can take the pain away if you let me."

He invited me to drink his blood again. I couldn't. It was dark, powerful medicine. I would not allow myself to drink from him to heal every little cut and scrape. His blood tied me closer to him. I could read his thoughts more clearly, sense when he was near sooner, and when he called me, I was unable to ignore his commands. His blood healed me quicker than any root work I knew, but it scared me to not be in control of my own body. With his blood inside me, I didn't want to fight him. How long before I gave in and became a creature like him? As tempting as it was to give in, I would not allow that to happen.

"May I have some of that?"

I handed him the bourbon and he took a long swallow from the bottle before replacing the cork. He sat next to me on the bench and moved closer so that my head could rest on his chest. My feet soaked in the herbal bath. We rocked to the motion of the train and the pain slowly faded.

"Why are you so afraid to drink my blood? It saved your life, twice."

"I am grateful for your kindness, but I want a normal life as a mortal woman. I want children and grandchildren. If I become like you, that won't happen."

He folded his arms over his chest and turned his back to me. He was angry, but couldn't argue with facts.

"Try to get some sleep," he said.

"We'll arrive in Jackson tomorrow."

"I hope we reach Jackson close to nightfall. I'd rather not be exposed to sunlight without proper rest and sustenance."

"I'll go sit in the cattle car when I wake up."

"You'll do no such thing," he said.

I smiled and pressed my cheek against his back. He believed we were the same. Maybe not equals exactly, but he saw no reason for me to be treated like an animal, just because my skin was darker than his. As long as he was beside me and had the will and strength to fight, no harm would come to me. Everyone else around us was a potential victim, but he didn't see me the way he saw others. The thought delighted and terrified me at the same time. I'm sure the Devil is perfectly well mannered and charming until you anger him. Carlos protected me because he saw something in me he didn't see in other humans. I hoped I'd never find myself on the wrong side of his kindness.

"You need to rest, too. You can watch over me tonight while I sleep, and in the morning, I'll tell the porter to make sure no one disturbs you. I'll sit with the other slaves until we reach Jackson."

He pulled me closer and kissed the top of my head before kneeling again to dry my feet and wrap them in soft cotton fabric. Then he lifted me up onto the bunk.

"I need to find something to eat," he said.

"You mean someone."

He removed his filthy shirt and tossed it in the corner. He pulled his last clean one from the leather satchel and pulled it on over his head. After raking his fingers through his hair to remove the tangles, he tucked the shirt into his trousers and flashed me a grin that would have made the Devil proud. His dark curls were like a halo around his pale face, and his eyes shone like emeralds in the lamplight. He was beautiful. I almost envied the person he chose to slake his thirst with that evening.

"I'll be back before you miss me. Don't let anyone else in."

I grabbed his wrist as he turned to leave.

"Come back soon," I said. I was suddenly afraid to be alone.

"I won't be long. I promise."

He kissed my hand and grinned before he disappeared into the passageway. I stared at the door and tried to stay awake, but the bourbon, the fatigue, and the motion of the train made my eyelids heavy and I fell asleep moments after he was gone.

I awoke to the distinct sounds of passion. Not the genteel muffled sounds of upper-class white folks, but the guttural grunting and rutting of beasts in the field. Carlos decided to dine in our sleeping compartment. His bloodlust won over reason. His true face was showing.

I peered over the edge of the bunk where I was hidden from sight in the dimly lit train car. Carlos had a woman on all fours with her face buried in the fabric of her enormous hoop skirt. His trousers circled his ankles and the clean white shirt was hung on a hook. I squirmed under the covers, ashamed to be aroused by the scene before me. He sensed me staring at him and looked up to meet my gaze. His smile was lascivious, mocking, and yet somehow inviting.

If you're feeling better, come join us.

His thoughts penetrated my head. The invasion still reminded me of Jimmy and Lynch forcing their way inside my body. No matter how much I trusted Carlos, when he was inside my head I wanted to run and hide. My head was the only hiding place I had on this earth, and even that wasn't safe from his intrusions.

I'll kill her now and lie with you instead. Just ask.

I ignored his taunts, but couldn't look away.

You won't say no to me forever.

He closed his eyes and I knew he was close to satisfying his lustful cravings, which meant that he would soon satisfy his hunger. I hated that he made me watch. He must have known how I felt. Why I pulled away from his touch. All touch. When I agreed to be close to him it was out of necessity. Fear always won out over my desires.

The woman cried out when her needs were met. He helped her stand and cover herself with the yards of fabric that made up her pretty dress. My dress was torn and dirty. I needed a bath. My hair was a mass of tangles under my *tignon*, and I could smell myself. It had been at least three weeks since I'd washed with soap or combed my hair. I knew it made no difference if the white woman was prettier, richer, or cleaner than me. If a man wanted to use a woman's body to satisfy his lust, she didn't even need a head.

"I think you might be the best I ever had," the woman said.

"I don't know if I'm the best, but I may be your last," Carlos said.

His facial expression shifted from seductive to homicidal in a split second—teeth bared and eyes solid black. I had seen this look before. It meant that the gentleman Carlos chose to be was gone, and the ravening beast inside him was hungry for blood. I could see that look hundreds of times and never stop being afraid of him.

"You can do whatever you want to me, but please don't kill me." The woman's voice came out in a harsh whisper.

"No need to kill you, I just want a taste," he said, and sank his teeth into her throat.

Would this be my end too? Would he turn on me and give in to his hunger? How could I believe his kindness to be genuine when he killed people to feed his terrible hunger? How could I have feelings for this man? This monster?

He satisfied his thirst and let the woman go. She quickly gathered her clothes and whispered, "Thank you," before making her escape. His face was smeared with red as he collapsed onto the padded bench. A smile spread across his lips as he licked blood from his fingers.

"It's all over, Jacqueline. You can come down from your hiding place now."

I stayed in the bunk and turned my back to him. I covered my mouth and nose to keep the smell of blood and sex at bay.

"Wash up before you come to bed," I said. My stomach twisted in knots fighting the waves of nausea. Sex always sickened me. It wasn't as bad to watch as it was to have it done to me, but it was worse to watch Carlos. At least he'd spared the woman for my sake.

When he was done enjoying himself, he used what was left of the water in the basin to clean up the car and himself. I pretended to sleep when he climbed onto the bunk. As always, his body was too close to mine. He removed my *tignon* to smell my hair and pressed his cold nose against my scalp.

"You smell like a wild animal," he whispered.

"You smell like that woman."

He laughed and wrapped his arm around my waist as if we were lovers. I shrank from his touch.

"I'm still excited from drinking her blood."

"Don't touch me. Please."

"I...I would never...never without your permission."

"Why am I so different from that woman or your other victims?"

He took a moment before answering and created some space between us on the small bunk.

"There's something special about you, Jacqueline. Besides, I'd hardly call her a victim. She wanted me to ... she allowed me to seduce her."

"Only because she didn't know you are a vampire. If she knew what you were, she never would have been alone with you."

"She wasn't alone with me. You were here too."

I made him angry. He turned away from me and we lay back-to-back on the bunk. The motion of the train reminded me of the motion of his hips before he fed off the woman. I cursed myself for thinking about the curve of his back, the muscles in his thighs, and the steady motion of his hips. I could say no to him a thousand times, but eventually I would die in his arms.

He wormed his way inside my mind.

It could be so sweet, our bodies together rocking in time with the train. I still have enough energy before dawn to satisfy you three or four times. I promise not to hurt you.

"Get out of my head!"

"Why do you hate me so?"

"You just seduced and drank from another woman in front of me, and now you want to whisper sweet words to me? How can I bend to your will when I know that it is your nature to kill me whether you want to or not?"

He was silent for the rest of the night. No more words about how I was different from his victims. No more invitations to enjoy his flesh. No more intrusions into my mind. I knew he wasn't asleep. He wouldn't sleep until dawn. He wasn't angry, either. What I sensed from him was altogether new.

Somehow, I'd managed to offend him. His ego was hurt. Like a fool, I wanted to apologize. Make him forgive me. I had feelings for this murderous creature. And if he could exist in this world, surely there must be a Hell. The Devil would greet me with open arms when my time came. And my sin wouldn't be standing by while this monster killed one person after another. No. My sin would be knowing he did it and still finding a place in my heart for him. I cried myself to sleep and was grateful he didn't try to comfort me.

Chapter 22

I awoke at first light. Carlos was deep in his death-like sleep next to me. I climbed over his cold, solid form to get down from the bunk. I stopped a moment and rested on top of him to gaze at his face. So peaceful. So handsome. But I knew the truth. Loving him would only lead to more pain, more terror, and most likely my own death. It was stupid to think he even had feelings, but my words had hurt him. What I thought about him mattered. I couldn't completely trust him. His behavior frightened me. Disgusted me. That wasn't the whole truth. He knew my true feelings. It wasn't his fault he could never live up to my dream of being rescued by a prince like the princesses in fairy tales.

Monsters didn't rescue princesses.

Yet, he had rescued me from my evil half-sister. He was no prince. But, I was no princess, either. Not with my grime-streaked face, torn dress, and bird's nest hair. He didn't care that I wasn't a princess. Why should it matter to me that he wasn't a prince?

I hopped down from the bunk and tried to clean myself up a bit. I was going to sit in the train car where slaves were permitted to ride. It was best to make the move now before too many white folks woke up and saw me coming out of Carlos's sleeping car. We didn't need to draw any more attention to ourselves. The woman he fed on might not say anything for fear of being marked a whore, but the slave catchers were still after us. The water left in the basin was cold and cloudy from my foot soak and the woman's blood, but I was able to wash away some of the dirt on my face and hands. I retied my *tignon* over my matted braids and tried to make my dress look a little less wrinkled. I gave up and unwrapped the fabric Carlos had used to cover my feet. They were still tired and sore, but the herbs had taken away some of the pain and swelling. They'd heal in a few days. I was glad not to wear shoes, but I'd need boots soon if we got any further north. My feet would freeze walking through creeks and mud in the colder weather. Would we see snow? Slaves talked about snow once in Congo Square, but I'd never seen any living in Louisiana.

Before I left the quiet luxury of the sleeper car, I noticed a note with my name on it sitting on top of a small bundle wrapped in waxed paper. I picked up the bundle and found a thick piece of fresh cornbread. I took a small bite just as my belly rumbled from the sweet smell. The note was from Carlos. There were only two words written on the inside of the small piece of folded paper: *Forgive me.* I could barely swallow the crumbs in my mouth. Here was proof. My words had stung him. Knowledge of my new power filled me with pride, wonder, and fear. I could hurt monsters with my words. Control over others can be exciting for some folks, but as a slave, experiencing how it twisted people, I wasn't sure I wanted that kind of power over another person.

I pocketed my cornbread and the note and made my way to the back of the train. The conductor who'd tried to bar our entrance onto the train the night before was about to knock on our door. He glared at me as we passed in the narrow passageway. I ignored him and kept moving. In the next car, I met the porter who'd brought us the tray of food and the bottle of bourbon. He smiled and said good morning as I shuffled past.

"Hey, girl," he called to me.

I turned to listen.

"You hungry?"

"Starving."

"Go on back to the last car. I'll bring you something to put in your belly."

"Thank you."

I walked to the back of the train with my head down. No one paid any attention to me. Sometimes being invisible came in handy. When I finally reached the last car, fresh horse manure hit my nose and made me feel a little sick on my empty stomach. There were several slaves lying in different positions all over the bare floor of the train car. The animals were in pens along the walls of the car, and these pens took up most of the room. At least they had straw to keep them warm and comfortable. There weren't any benches or bunks like in the fancier passenger cars near the front of the train. I found a place to sit on the cold floor and rested my back against one of the horse pens. I hadn't slept much the night before and my head still hurt a little from all the crying. I fingered the note in my pocket and drifted off into a restless sleep.

The porter nudged me awake and handed me a steaming cup of coffee. I stared at the cup for a moment, a little confused and half asleep. The man's voice brought me back.

"Drink this to get warm. I brought some sausage biscuits, too. You look like you ain't eaten in days."

The coffee burned my tongue and the roof of my mouth, but it warmed the rest of me and took away the early morning chill. I blew on the surface of the inky liquid before I took another sip. The smell of chicory reminded me of mornings on the plantation, and I wondered if Moman missed me as much as I missed her. I ate both sandwiches and enjoyed every salty, greasy bite. My belly filled up fast, but I didn't leave a crumb of the sausage biscuits. I might not have another treat like that once Carlos and I got off the train.

"That man you're traveling' with, does he own you?" The porter poured a little more coffee into the tin mug between my hands.

"Yes," I lied.

"He sure does take good care of you. Not too many white folks would let their slaves ride with them on the train."

"He can be good sometimes."

"Is he your papa?"

"No."

I was glad he didn't ask any more questions about our relationship.

"Where you headed?"

"Not sure, but we'll be getting off the train in Jackson."

"We should be there by dusk. You get some sleep. I'll check on you in a few hours."

I looked the man in the eye when I thanked him for his kindness. He smiled and went back to his regular duties of serving the white folks on the train. Slaves usually had to fend for themselves. I was lucky he'd taken pity on me. The cornbread Carlos had left for me was tucked in my pocket. I saved it for another time when I would really need it. My eyes struggled to stay open and I fell into a deep dreamless sleep.

The rough shove of a man's boot against my backside woke me. The conductor's angry face reminded me I was still on the train.

"Get up, girl. Your master's looking for you."

Was it dusk already? The porter must have let me sleep all day.

I was thankful, but my head was full of cobwebs. I rubbed my eyes, stretched, and stood up slowly. It took me a few beats to get my balance with the motion of the train.

"Hurry up. Your stop is coming up soon. He wants you to meet him in his car. Don't know why he can't just meet you on the platform like everybody else." He checked his pocket watch for the third time and shook his head at me before heading back to the main cabins. I followed him, but didn't try to keep up with his pace. I shuffled a few steps behind him as he led me to Carlos. He didn't want me roaming about the train alone.

"I found her at the back of the train where she belongs," the conductor said.

"Ah, there you are," Carlos said. He greeted me with a smile and ushered me into the car. He ignored the conductor and shut the door before the man could say another word. Carlos cursed the man in Spanish and spat on the floor.

"Our stop is next," I said. My head was spinning from jumping to my feet after a long rest. I needed more sleep, but I was happy to sit on the padded bench. My rear end was cold and numb from the floor of the train car. We'd be on the run again soon and I had no idea when I would get that kind of rest again.

"We'll arrive in Jackson within the next thirty minutes. How are you feeling?"

"I'm fine. Rested."

He knelt before me and gently rubbed my feet as he inspected them to see how they were healing. He gripped my ankles in both hands and raised my toes up to meet his mouth and kissed them. I couldn't help but laugh.

"I'll get you a pair of new shoes in the next town. The weather will change soon."

"I wish I hadn't left those beautiful boots behind."

"Would you like another pair? You can have whatever you want."

I picked at a hole in my dress and frowned.

"You'll need warmer clothes. A dress, some frilly underthings, and boots."

"How will you pay for all that?"

"The same way I always do."

I thought of the trinkets Carlos had brought me when we lived in the little house on Esplanade. He had his own money in banks all over the world, but without a bank at hand to arrange transfers, he resorted to stealing from the dead. He was my provider. I wouldn't question his methods any further.

Moments before the train pulled into the station, the conductor knocked on the door to warn us our stop was next. Carlos put the leather satchel on his shoulder and offered me his hand. I took it and gazed boldly at the conductor, daring him to say something rude. He glared at us, but didn't say a word. He'd be happier once we were off the train.

"Squire Jean said we could find a conjure woman in this town. She'll give us a place to stay and show us how to reach the next station along the Underground Railroad. Free coloreds live near the railroad tracks. Once we find them, we should be able to find the Mambo."

"You guide, and I will follow. I can protect and provide for you, but I need you to lead us to safety."

Again, I was reminded of how much power he placed in my hands. My own energy seemed to be getting stronger and the spell work came easier. I felt surer of myself, even when Carlos wasn't at my side. Separate, we each held considerable strengths, but together we were a force of Nature.

We pulled into the station.

Chapter 23

The shotgun house sat about a mile from the train station on the opposite side of the tracks, nestled comfortably near the woods. Two big oak trees spread their branches and cast protective shadows across the whitewashed bare boards and tar paper roof. With no numbers to guide us, we asked the people willing to talk to us how to find the house. Some folks looked at us like we were crazy for wanting to find it. One woman warned us not to go near the place.

"That's the Devil's stomping grounds."

Carlos laughed in her face and she made the sign of the cross as she scurried away. Sadly, her faith probably wouldn't protect her from the monsters roaming this world in plain sight, side-by-side with the rest of us. I wasn't even sure my own magic was strong enough. Bad thing for a conjurer to doubt her own power.

We stared at the single-story house for several heartbeats. Three, maybe four.

"Are you going to knock on the door, or shall I?"

"She's expecting me."

Carlos snorted. "If she's half as good a seer as that conjurer claims, she's expecting both of us."

"I'll be welcome in her home."

He didn't say anything. He shoved his hands in his pockets and turned his back on the house.

A gust of wind rustled the remaining leaves on the skeletal limbs of the oak trees and I thought I heard my name whispered among the branches. It was time for me to go to the door.

"I'll wait here for you." He attempted a smile.

Carefully, I approached the front door. Any smart witch will lay hexes to ensnare her enemies. A Devil's Trap will keep an unwanted visitor rooted on the spot where it is drawn until the conjurer comes to set free whatever she's caught. I didn't have time for such carelessness. Carlos and I needed to reach Freedom. The *loup-garou* made sure we'd have plenty of angry men on our tails. Wanted signs near the docks and railway stations offered a $5,000 bounty for Carlos's capture, for the murder of the Lynches. They showed a rather flattering sketch of my traveling companion, but I was only mentioned briefly at the bottom of each posting. As a fugitive slave, I would bring $200 to my captor. Master had paid $200 for Lottie's piano, and at $7 an acre, Carlos's bounty could buy a small plantation and slaves to work it. Aleister Gale would have his revenge even if I got hurt in the process.

The wooden steps leading up to the little shack creaked under my weight. The wind had picked up and the trees made a high-pitched whine as they rocked back and forth in the night air. I pulled my cloak a little tighter around my shoulders. A chill crept under my skin and made its way for my bones. Before I could knock, the door opened, and a Negro woman dressed in a white cotton dress with skin the color of rice flour and kinky pale orange curls peered out at me through milky pink eyes. A large snake was draped lazily around her neck and shoulders. Its yellow scales and pale eyes made the witch and her familiar quite a matched pair. My mouth fell open and I stared at her like a child with no manners.

"What's the matter, girl? Cat got your tongue?"

"A-agatha Mae?"

A gap-toothed smile spread across her ghost-like face.

"Wasn't sure you were gonna make it."

My hands trembled, but not from the cold wind.

"Squire Jean said you could help me get to Freedom."

She raised her chin and stared without seeing past my shoulder at Carlos.

"I suppose you'll be bringing him, too," she said.

"Can you help us?"

She gestured for me to come closer and I obeyed. Before I could blink, she had my hand in hers and sliced open my palm with a tiny, razor-sharp blade hanging from a silver chain around her neck. She spat on the wound and mixed her spit with my blood. Moman never would have spit on anyone, but each witch does her own thing. She studied my hand with her fingers and those creamy rose-colored eyes.

"We can get you close to Freedom. Within a day's walk. Going all the way would take us too far off our planned route."

"Planned route?"

She ignored my question.

"Says here," she tapped my palm, "you can interpret people's dreams and make potions. You'll be able to earn your keep in no time."

"My keep?"

"I know what you can do, what can your vampire do?"

"I can do this," Carlos said as he landed silently beside me like a cat after jumping from his perch in a tree.

"You'll fit in with the rest of the freaks in the circus," she said.

Carlos bristled next to me and ground his teeth together to hold in the thought that slammed into my head. *She had better bite her tongue before I bite it for her.*

"Agatha Mae means medical curiosities."

A large man wearing a sleeveless, white, button-down shirt that showed the colorful tattoos covering both of his arms, appeared in the doorway behind the albino witch.

"No, I don't. I said freaks, and that's what I meant."

The man chuckled warmly. As he stepped into the moonlight I could see that his face was perfect except for a jagged, angry scar running along his jawline from temple to chin. Whoever gave him that scar wanted to see him dead. His bright blue eyes and generous grin made the deformity easy to ignore.

"You'll have to excuse Agatha Mae. She only joined the circus after meeting me. She's still not used to our strange ways."

Again, Carlos forced his way inside my head. *Is she really going to pass judgment on other people's deformities?*

"Well, you better come inside. Smells like rain."

Agatha Mae patted my hand and guided me towards the door.

"You can bring your vampire inside, too."

She turned to the man in the doorway and touched his arm affectionately. He kissed the tight marmalade curls on top of her head.

"I'm Emil." He extended a hand. Carlos and I shook hands with him and he stepped aside for us to enter their home.

"We don't get company too often," the seer said. "Emil, this is Jacqueline. She's a conjurer from New Orleans. And this is Carlos. He's a vampire from Spain. This is my husband."

Carlos stared at the strange woman openly with a distinct air of distaste. I almost laughed at his pompous attitude. The idea that he found Agatha Mae unsettling was funny.

He addressed Emil, "How long have you been a circus performer?"

"Most of my life. My family is Romany. Traveling with a circus felt natural to us."

Agatha Mae was busy putting water on to boil and fetching biscuits and tea from tins on a shelf next to a cast iron stove. She took down three cups and measured out the loose tea leaves. Then she lifted the snake from around her shoulders and placed it on a perch in the corner by the stove. It slithered around until it found a spot it liked and curled itself into a figure of eight, as if it might eat its own tail.

"There's biscuits, salt pork, and tea if you're hungry," Agatha Mae said. "Hope you ate before you got here, vampire."

"I had a bite on the train," Carlos said, sneering at the weird witch.

Next to the stove sat a small wooden table with four chairs. The chairs were red with tiny yellow flowers painted with care along the back rungs. The shelf near the stove was painted to match them. Pretty yellow curtains tied with red ribbons hung at all the greased paper windows, and a matching quilt covered the mattress of the double bed that sat in the corner opposite the stove and snake perch. Not much room for anything else in the small house, but several steamer trunks and valises in various colors and sizes were stacked neatly at the foot of the bed and in another corner by the door. In the fourth corner of the house, opposite the stacked trunks, was a makeshift bed made from wooden train pallets, blankets, and homemade pillows in vibrant blues, greens, and purples—a perfect place for travel-weary visitors to sleep.

"Agatha Mae, your home is so beautiful, did you do all the decorating?" I asked, turning in a circle to take it all in.

"I can't take credit for that, child. Emil here did all the painting and sewing. Artistry is in his Gypsy blood."

Agatha Mae invited me to sit at the table with her in one of the painted chairs. It felt good to sit down after the walk from the train station. I bit into the salt pork biscuits greedily and eagerly sipped the hot, black tea. The food recharged me, but I still needed a good night's sleep. At least a few hours of rest so I could think more clearly about the journey ahead.

"Eat until you're full, child. There's plenty to discuss, but we can talk in the morning after you've slept."

I hoped Agatha Mae didn't have access to all my thoughts, but more importantly, I hoped she'd be unable to get a clear reading from Carlos. Having access to his thoughts was sometimes like walking through the landscape of a nightmare. People say some words are better left unspoken, and I believe some thoughts are better kept secret.

Carlos lurked in the corner near the makeshift bed of pallets. "Where shall I sleep, witch?"

Emil stood from his seat at the table and crossed to the center of the room in three steps. He bent to lift a worn woolen rug that was most likely the inspiration for the house's color palette. A door hid beneath the rug of rich golden hues and rusty reds.

"This is the safest place we have to offer," Emil said. "I made this hiding space for...emergencies."

Carlos stared down into the dark crawlspace. "What kind of emergencies?"

Agatha Mae spoke up. "Most folks don't take too kindly to circus people when they settle down. It upsets the people who view themselves as good Christians."

"Has there been trouble?" Carlos stopped gazing into the darkness and glanced up at Emil. The dark stubble framing his lips and peppering his jaw line gave him an angry appearance. A shave and a comb run through his ebony mane of curls would tame his wild appearance.

Emil closed the wooden door and replaced the rug. "People hate white men who treat black women like wives even more than they hate circus folk."

"In Spain, my people treated Gypsies with suspicion and I'm sure that hasn't changed much over the centuries."

"People still scare their children when they wander off, with stories about Gypsies stealing them," Emil said.

"Has anyone threatened you?" Carlos strode across the room and took a seat at the table next to me. He took my hand in his.

I stared at our interlaced fingers and a chill ran through me. He was concerned for my well-being, but he was also hungry. I felt the pulse of his lust pass through his touch. My senses were getting stronger.

"There's a group of men in town who keep threatening to burn me at the stake," Agatha Mae said. "Protection spells and good, old-fashioned fear keeps most folks away."

"The townspeople blame us when anything goes wrong. We're even responsible for the weather and crops failing," Emil added.

My tea had gone cold, but I finished the last few swallows. I had learned to take comfort from the mundane activities of daily life while growing up on the plantation. Simple pleasures like taking a walk, sleeping on clean linens, planting seeds in the garden, or sipping tea could lessen the burden of fear and anger in situations that were beyond one person's control. As a slave, I rarely had a say in how I would live my life. Meeting Carlos had changed the way I thought about the future, and made me believe I might be able to have a hand in shaping the rest of my days. Freedom was a real possibility for me, and Carlos wanted to help me achieve it. I didn't always agree with his methods and habits, but he never hurt me. Not physically.

Somehow, he managed to keep himself in check when he was

near me, no matter how much he might want to help himself to my flesh. I didn't want him to kill people who didn't deserve to die, but I was powerless to stop him. Sure, I could ask him not to, and he might agree to try not to kill. For a little while, he might be content to feed without killing his victims. I knew he was able to practice restraint when his own safety was in question. But, eventually, he would succumb to his cravings.

I was too weary to think about what might be. More than anything, I wanted to curl up on the guest bed and fall asleep. Usually, Carlos would watch over me until dawn, but I knew he was going hunting instead. His questions about threats from the townspeople were more than just polite inquiries. He wanted a name.

Agatha Mae must have gotten a similar feeling from Carlos. She cleared the plates and brought a bottle of whiskey and four cups made of horn to the table. Emil poured generous amounts of the smoky amber liquid into the cups as his wife sat back down at the table.

"It's none of my business how you choose to live your life, vampire, but keep in mind that every time something goes wrong in this town, it's the circus folk who get blamed," Agatha Mae said.

Carlos took a hefty pull from his cup and savored the whiskey. His tongue darted out of his mouth and he licked his lips.

"I'll be discreet," he said. "Just tell me who's been threatening you."

Emil poured more whiskey into Carlos's cup.

"Williams. James Edwin Williams. He and his cronies set fire to one of the vardos parked in the woods behind the house. They tried to scare us off, but this land and house belong to me. To us." Emil placed a hand on Agatha Mae's shoulder and squeezed gently.

"Was anyone hurt in the fire?" I asked.

Emil shook his head. "No, but a lot of equipment was destroyed. It couldn't be replaced, so our aerialist quit. We don't have anyone to perform the high-wire and trapeze acts."

"I'm willing to work without a net," Carlos said, with a grin.

"Don't let Williams' death be traced back to the circus," Agatha Mae warned.

Carlos turned to me and took both of my hands in his. "Will you be comfortable here while I'm gone?"

"We'll look after her," Emil said.

Carlos waited for my answer.

"Go, but be careful. Promise to be back before dawn."

He kissed the tops of my hands and stared into my eyes. "I promise." And then he was gone.

Agatha Mae placed a small tobacco tin on the table, packed a pipe with sweet-smelling herbs, and offered it to me. I placed the pipe between my lips and lit it with a red-tipped match.

"It's my own blend; it will help you sleep," she said.

Emil added more wood to the stove to keep the cold creeping between the knotholes at bay. He stoked the fire and spoke over his shoulder. "Would he have obeyed if you'd asked him not to go?"

I exhaled a perfumed, gray cloud and felt pleasantly light-headed. "I don't get between him and his hunger. No matter how much he thinks he cares about me, his appetites always come first."

"You're wise for your age," the albino witch complimented me. She smoked from the pipe and handed it to Emil. He passed it straight to me.

"Someone needs to keep a clear head tonight just in case," he said. "I'll sit up until Carlos gets back, but the two of you should get some sleep. Big day tomorrow."

Agatha Mae took another drag from the pipe and handed it back to me. Her eyelids drooped lazily over her milky eyes.

"I think I've had enough." My vision was slightly blurred, and my body had that floating quality I would sometimes experience just before slipping into a deep slumber.

I was happy to sleep in my clothes. The wind raged outside, and I was glad to have the warm blankets my hosts provided. I drifted off soon after my head hit the jewel-toned pillow. Then, the nightmares came.

I was standing inside a house I didn't recognize. It was nighttime and everyone in the house was asleep. I could hear them breathing. Someone snored in a gentle rhythm, and the only other sounds were from the floors and walls settling, as if they knew it was now safe to relax after a long day of holding up the roof. It was quiet, but I knew someone or something else was lurking in the shadows upstairs. Something familiar.

I slowly crept up the staircase to the second floor. Five doors waited for me upstairs—one facing me at the very top of the staircase, and two on each side of the narrow hallway. Each door was closed, which made the hallway much darker than the downstairs. I didn't know the house or the people inside, but I knew they were in danger. I made my way to the first room on my left, closest to the front of the house. I pressed an ear to the door and heard the gentle breathing of two young children. I did not enter for fear of waking them.

I moved to the next room and listened at the door. More gentle breathing, but the sleeper was restless, as if troubled by dreams. And then I heard sobbing that reminded me of my own. Tears of shame after so many violations. I had so much sadness and anger inside me that I sometimes cried in my sleep. I couldn't tell if she was awake, or even if she was alone. I hesitated before turning the knob. Anyone could be in there—a suitor, a stranger, a brother. In my experience, any man could lay claim to a girl's body whether he had the right to touch her or not. I took a deep breath and opened the door slowly. The room was bathed in the gentle glow of moonlight shining through the open window. Someone had let himself in. As my eyes adjusted to the dim light, I could see the girl, not much older than me, stretched out on her bed with the covers disturbed. Her chemise was raised above her waist and her legs were parted at an obscene angle. A closer look revealed a small pool of blood between her thighs. Someone or something had fed on her, but she wasn't dead. Her breathing was weak, but she would live. Whatever had entered her room only wanted to taste her, not kill her.

I closed the window, covered the girl up, and shut the door behind me as I continued down the hall. The door at the top of the stairs was an office with a high-backed secretary and Windsor chairs. I moved to the next room, which held a sewing machine and a dressmaker's mannequin. I flattened an ear against the fifth and final door. Carnal grunting greeted me, and again I hesitated to turn the knob. What if I didn't want to see what was happening on the other side of the door? That thought lasted for only a moment as my curiosity outweighed my fears.

Carefully, I turned the knob and was shocked to see Carlos between the thighs of the lady of the house. She glanced at me with terror on her blood-smeared face. Carlos was too busy satisfying his hungers to notice me. He rode the woman and drank from her at the same time, while paying no heed to her husband's corpse on the bed beside them. I didn't recognize the dead man or his wife, but Carlos's dark curls, alabaster body, and cat-like movements were unmistakable. Was I dreaming? It all seemed so real. He grunted and panted as he lost himself in his cruel pleasures and he didn't notice when the life left his victim's eyes. He rode the woman until his hips snapped forward and he moaned loudly like a beast in the wild. Our eyes met. He was as startled as I was.

"Jacqueline?" Confusion, fear, and a slight hint of guilt registered on his gore-covered face. He righted himself and stood to face me, but kept his distance. Despite the guilt on his face, his body told another story—he was aroused. "How...?" He reached out to touch me, and as his fingers made contact with my arm, everything went black.

When I opened my eyes I was lying on the guest bed in Agatha Mae and Emil's house. My arm tingled from a phantom touch. By the dim candlelight I examined my arm where the sensation was strongest. Blood streaked my sleeve in the shape of a man's fingers.

My scream startled Emil awake. He had fallen asleep at his post. "What is it?" He fell to his knees at my side.

I showed him my arm. "I got these in a dream."

He gently grasped my arm to get a better look at the bloody fingerprints. "How?"

"I don't know. Carlos was in my dream. He made these marks."

Agatha Mae was awake too. She made her way to my side and Emil helped her sit next to me. She touched my arm and shivered. "You weren't just dreaming."

"I don't understand."

She turned her sightless eyes to the door. "He's coming."

"What happened to her, Agatha Mae?" Emil paced back and forth in front of us.

"She traveled to the house and watched the vampire killing Williams," Agatha Mae explained.

"Traveled? She's been in bed all this time."

I was getting scared. "I don't remember leaving the house."

"You didn't leave the house, girl. Your spirit did."

I knew that dreams were sometimes more than they seemed. Moman could sometimes see inside my dreams when we slept together. Not every night, but she could visit my dreams, and she also taught me how to control them when the nightmares got too scary. Vivid dreams were nothing new to me, but it felt like I had really been in that house. Carlos had seen me. Touched me. Mrs. Williams' blood was on my dress.

"Carlos and I have a connection. We can hear each other's thoughts, but I've never traveled to him in my sleep."

"It must be the herbs you smoked. They may have made the connection stronger." Agatha Mae tilted her head and regarded me as if she could see my face. "At least, the herbs could have transported you, but that doesn't explain how you were able to bring something back with you."

The front door flew open and Carlos stormed in with a flurry of black wool as the wind billowed his coat all around him. He hadn't bothered to button his shirt or clean the blood from his face. He was scared. Taking two long strides from the door, he came toward me and fell to his knees.

"Were you really there?"

I showed him my arm. He stared at it and his hand was shaking as he touched his own fingerprints.

"How much did you see?" His voice shook.

"Enough." I pulled my arm away from him. His touch sickened me.

His eyes glistened with the promise of tears. He could see the revulsion on my face. Felt me pulling back as he tried to get closer.

"Are they dead?" Emil's voice seemed louder than it needed to be.

Carlos kept his eyes focused on me. "Williams and his wife are dead. The children are alive."

"You tasted his daughter. Did you rape her the way you raped Mrs. Williams?" My voice caught in my throat as I fought back tears. Rage, fear and disappointment mingled inside my chest. Carlos was no better than Jimmy or Lynch. He would do the same to me someday. I was foolish to think I was any different from his victims. As soon as I got to Freedom, we would part ways. I wouldn't need him after that, and hopefully I would have the will to resist his charms.

Without a single word to defend his actions, he crawled away from me on his hands and knees. He pushed the rug aside and slunk down into the dark hole in the floor. He had nothing to say in his defense. No witty or sarcastic remarks to take the sting out of what I had witnessed behind that final door. The memory would be with me forever.

Chapter 24

Most nights I enjoyed the quiet that darkness brings. I missed the privacy of my room at the back of the house on Royal Street. That was the only thing I missed about Lottie's house. I could read, conjure, or just lie there and gorge myself fat on the silence. Midnight to sun up was my time. I took no joy from lying awake in the dark that night. I was too afraid to sleep—afraid of my new abilities, afraid of Carlos, and afraid of the feelings he stirred inside me.

Dawn slapped me awake from my restless sleep and the harsh light made my pulse throb at my temples. I was exhausted. I managed to get a little sleep, but each time I closed my eyes the nightmares returned. I lay facing the wall, absently picking at a knothole with my index finger, and running the dream that transported me to Carlos through my head. How was I able to travel without using my body? Why was Carlos able to touch me? Maybe it had something to do with drinking his blood. It had magical properties I couldn't hope to ever understand. He appeared to be able to live forever without ageing a day.

As a conjurer, I knew magic was real. I used it myself to shape the course of events and influence the world and people around me. Although I had a fairly firm grasp of how it worked, I still had no real concept of why I was able to make certain things happen by combining ingredients, drawing *vévé* on the floor in brick dust, and chanting certain words. I knew it was true and I accepted it at face value. Moman had taught me about the old gods, and there were times I would invoke their names to bring more power to my spell work, but I had never seen proof of their existence. Again, I simply accepted that they were real. I guessed the best thing for me to do was to also accept the fact that I could now travel to places in my mind and bring a physical form of myself along. Moman never mentioned having this ability to me. I hoped Agatha Mae would have more answers.

"You doing all right this morning, Jacqueline?" Emil was at the stove, boiling water for coffee. He slept even less than me, keeping watch all night in case Carlos hadn't covered his tracks properly. The bodies wouldn't be discovered until the children woke up. Carlos didn't kill the young ones, but they were still his victims.

"She'll be fine once she has a chance to get some real sleep," Agatha Mae said from beneath the blankets on her bed.

"No time for sleeping in today. I'm heading back into the woods after breakfast to meet with the other circus folk. Before you know it, it'll be time to head out on the road." Emil placed three tin coffee cups on the table.

"You should meet them today, Jacqueline. It might do you some good to be around other people, no matter how strange they appear." Agatha Mae sat up and swung her legs over the edge of the bed.

"I'm looking forward to meeting them. I've never been to a circus before."

Lottie and Jimmy went to the circus in the neighboring parish every year. Master loved it too, and made sure they went each spring when the traveling circuses arrived with the first fresh blooms. Lottie always came home with stories about the elephants and the ladies in pretty outfits who rode them. She liked the clowns, too.

I didn't have to go to the circus to see clowns. People dressed up like them for Mardi Gras each year. I didn't like clowns. They made me uneasy. I never understood why people thought they were funny. A clown never once made me laugh, but they certainly did make my skin crawl.

"There are only two clowns in this circus, and their make-up doesn't obscure their faces." Agatha Mae was reading my mind again. I didn't like it, but at least she didn't force her way into my thoughts the way Carlos did.

Carlos. I hoped his sleep was as troubled as mine, but I doubted it. The only reason he was upset about his actions from the night before was because I had witnessed them. If I hadn't caught him satisfying himself with that woman's corpse, he would never have thought to feel guilty. He may have stayed longer to play with the dead woman's daughter if I hadn't been there. I shuddered at the thought of him touching me and leaving evidence of his crime on my body. My forearm tingled where his crimson fingerprints stained my dress.

Agatha Mae pulled me out of my thoughts. "No sense in dwelling on that nonsense all morning, Jacqueline. Have some coffee and a bite to eat and then you can go help Emil down in the woods."

I slowly sat up and Emil pointed me to a washbasin sitting on the table. I splashed a little of the warm water on my face, drank some coffee, and straightened my hair using a mirror that hung on the wall beside Emil and Agatha Mae's bed. It took a little time, but I was able to comb through all the knots and braid my hair before retying my *tignon*. I pinched my cheeks to bring a little color back into them, and brushed some of the wrinkles out of my dress. I wanted to look halfway decent before meeting the circus performers.

"Don't worry about impressing the freaks. Besides, any man dumb enough to pay attention to you when that vampire of yours is around deserves whatever he gets." Agatha Mae chuckled to herself as she sipped the coffee Emil had brought to her in bed.

I wasn't interested in meeting any men. It was just polite to look your best when greeting people for the first time. But, there was some truth to her words. Any man who approached me was in danger of incurring Carlos's wrath as long as he believed he was in love with me. That was all well and good when someone made unwanted advances, but what would happen if I met someone I really cared about? Would I ever be allowed the simple pleasure of loving a normal man who felt the same way about me?

"Are you ready to meet the other performers?" Emil smiled through the steam rising from his coffee cup.

"I'm ready."

He downed the last swallow of coffee and placed the empty cup on the table. He grabbed my shawl off the back of the chair I had sat in the night before and wrapped it around my shoulders with care. Then he opened the front door and waited for me to pass through it before shutting it behind him. We walked down the creaking wooden steps and took a stroll into the woods behind the shotgun house. He had mentioned the vardos the night before and I had expected to see them as soon as we stepped into the woods, but the woods were empty. Only trees and undergrowth greeted us.

"Where...?"

Emil took a few steps ahead and waved his hands in a half-circle while speaking words in a language I didn't recognize. When he completed the phrase, the woods directly in front of him shimmered like heat rising off the ground on a hot day. A door appeared in the woods. There wasn't anything fancy or unusual about the door, aside from the fact that it appeared out of nowhere. Just a plain wooden door with chipped red paint and worn letters in black that read: CIRQUE DU OMBRES.

The heavy red door swung slowly open with a loud creak that sent shivers down my spine. A little lard on the hinges would solve that problem. I was more concerned about what lay on the other side.

Where Emil and I stood, the haze of early-morning sunlight brightened with each passing moment and dried the dew on the grass underfoot. But on the other side of the door, it was night. A sharp fingernail moon cut through the sky above the trees, and just beyond the trees was a haunting strain of music like nothing I'd ever heard before. I recognized some of the instruments—fiddles, accordion, and drums—but the pattern of notes was unfamiliar. It was a magical sound and I wanted to dance to the swirling rhythms that snaked between playful and ominous. The music enticed me and I stepped through the doorway to discover its source. My hips swayed to the melody. I was about to venture into the dark grove of trees, but Emil stopped me.

"It's easy to lose yourself on the other side. You're a smart girl. Don't be fooled by what you see. Understand?"

I nodded even though I didn't fully understand what he meant, still distracted by the music. Seconds after I stepped through the door, it creaked again and slammed shut. Emil stood next to me in the dark woods and pointed toward a line of burning torches ahead of us. Their flames shuddered with a gentle gust of warm air. Shadows danced about the fiery glow and illuminated a half circle of tiny houses on wheels.

"What are those?" I pointed toward the shadowy shapes ahead.

"Vardos. They're the homes of the performers, and in some cases, they double as attractions. Agatha Mae sets up shop reading tarot and tea leaves in our vardo. We would live in it year-round if it were up to me," Emil said.

"Why doesn't Agatha Mae want to live in it all the time? They look...cozy."

Soft, gray tendrils of smoke rose up from small chimneys on top of the rounded roofs.

"Not enough room for her taste. Plus, she doesn't want to live behind the door."

I wasn't sure I liked being behind the door either. It had been morning on the other side, but here it felt like midnight or later. Despite the warm air, I drew my cloak closer to my body. My skin still prickled with goosebumps.

Emil offered me his hand like an old friend. "Come, stand by the fire."

As we approached the campsite, I got a better look at the funny little houses. They reminded me of the witch's cottage from *Hansel and Gretel*. Each wagon was painted a different bold color—red, green, blue, yellow—and accented with pictures of flowers, birds, lions, horses, and mythical creatures as well. They were so beautiful. How wonderful it must be to live in one.

"You'll get to travel in one of those when we take the circus on the road," Emil said.

"Really? I'll have my own?" I couldn't contain the excitement in my voice.

"You'll probably have to share one with Carlos. I only have so many to go around."

"Oh."

Emil's reminder dashed my hopes of spending time alone in one of the lovely little houses. I wasn't happy about traveling with

Carlos in such a confined space. My skin prickled where he'd left bloody fingerprints. I closed my eyes against the memory of rat claws and whiskers scraping at my flesh. I shivered and moved closer to the fire.

"What did you see last night that upset you so much?" Emil squeezed my hand gently.

"He killed those people."

"That can't be the first time you've witnessed violence. Agatha Mae still has nightmares from when she was a slave."

"No. I've seen plenty of terrible things. Had things done to me, too." My voice trailed off at the end of the last sentence.

"Then why are you so shaken by what you saw in the dream? Is it because it really happened? Have you never had prophetic dreams before?"

"I've dreamed things that have come true before. What really scares me is how much he enjoyed hurting them. Killing them. It reminded me...the look on his face...he raped that woman before he killed her."

Emil placed a hand on my shoulder and I jerked away from him.

"I'm not going to hurt you." His voice was soft and calm. He took a step closer to me, but didn't box me in. "You knew what he was, but you thought he was different from the man who hurt you."

"Men," I said.

"I see. I'm sorry those terrible things happened to you."

Tears trickled down my cheeks. "I can't...I won't let him hurt me."

"It seems he already has," Emil said.

"I want my own vardo. I don't want to share it with anyone."

"What will you tell Carlos?"

"I don't know."

"He'll come after you."

Emil was right. Carlos would be furious if I left him behind. Or worse. He'd be broken-hearted. Love was far more dangerous than anger. I was going to have to convince him we needed to go our separate ways. Make him believe I would be safer without him.

"The slave catchers will have a harder time finding us if there are two trails to follow. Aleister Gale wants Carlos, not me. I'll be protected and hidden behind the door. Carlos can lead them away from me."

"Sounds like a noble thing for a man in love to do. Even if he doesn't truly love you, his ego won't be able to resist."

"I'll promise to meet him again when it's safe."

"Agatha Mae will help with your deception. She'll be pleased to know you want the vampire gone."

The heat of the bonfire burned away the chill seeping into my bones. Within the circle of vardos, a group of five or six people was gathered around the fire. As we got closer they each turned to us. Their true faces were hidden behind masks.

"Ah, good. Some of the performers are awake. I'll introduce you," he said.

Agatha Mae's voice rang out inside my head. *Freaks.* Some people spend their lives dreaming about running away to join the circus. The Cirque du Ombres could only promise nightmares. I grasped Emil's wrist and moved closer to him to peer at the gathered group from behind his broad shoulder.

"I won't let anything happen to you," he whispered.

A tall man in a black stovepipe hat stepped forward to greet us. He removed the hat and bowed to us with a flourish of long limbs and flapping coattails. Beneath the hat, his head was clean-shaven, and protruding on each side of his forehead, directly above his temples, were two horns about the length of my index finger. They were the color of bone, like a deer's antlers, and sharp at the ends. When he stood erect again to his full height, he put the hat back on and turned to Emil. Unlike the other performers, he did not wear a mask.

"Jacqueline, this is Old Nick. He's the ringmaster," Emil said.

Old Nick extended his hand to me. A jolt of magic pulsed between us when he placed a soft kiss across my knuckles.

He pretended not to notice the surge of power. "Such tiny hands. Still a child and brave enough to step into our world. What talents will you share with us?"

"Agatha Mae says she's a powerful witch," Emil said.

Old Nick sized me up and took a step closer. My grip on Emil's wrist tightened.

"She's pretty enough to be a dancer. I'm sure we'll find something for her to do around here with that shapely waist and beautiful face." His eyes sparkled in the firelight, and for a moment I caught a glimpse of myself screaming in their depths. I jerked my hand back. He winked at me and gestured toward the others gathered around the fire. "Allow me to introduce some of the performers to you," he said.

I stayed close to Emil. Why I trusted him more than the people who lived behind the door, I couldn't tell you. He was part of the circus, too. Something about him was different, though. He didn't appear to be a threat. But Carlos was proof that I was capable of misjudging people.

To Old Nick's immediate right was a set of twins standing almost back to back, but slightly angled so they could both look toward the fire. The young women appeared to be in their late teens or early twenties. Their masks were similar, but slightly different. One twin's mask was black with white scrollwork and symbols that reminded me of the *vévé* I'd drawn in the ashes of the hearth back home. Her sister's was white with black symbols. On closer inspection I realized the twins weren't just standing close together. Their dresses were fashioned from one large piece of cleverly tailored gingham. They were Siamese twins. Attached at the waist.

"I see you've taken an interest in Alice and Ida. Say 'hello' to Jacqueline, girls," Old Nick said.

"Hello," they said in unison, and waved.

I waved back and tried not to stare at them like a slack-jawed idiot.

A few feet away from the twins was a bearded man in a dress. I'd heard about men who liked to wear women's clothing, but hadn't ever seen one in person. His mask was red with a long, pointed nose that covered his cheeks, leaving only his mouth, chin, and beard visible.

"This lovely hirsute lady is Jezebel," Emil said.

"Pleased to meet you," Jezebel said. Her voice was unmistakably feminine, despite the long shock of auburn hair covering her breasts.

Again, I tried not to be rude. "Nice to meet you, too."

Agatha Mae was right. These people were freaks. And each one I met got stranger. To the right of Jezebel, on a stool that was about waist high, sat what appeared to be half a man. His upper body was complete – head, shoulders, arms, torso, and then he just stopped, like he'd been sawed in two. The lower part of his body was missing. All I could do was stare and wonder how he got around. How did he relieve himself? Was he born like that, or had he been in a terrible accident?

"That's Roy the Half Boy," Old Nick whispered in my ear.

"H-hello," I stammered.

"Pretty as a flower," Roy the Half Boy said. "I hope you'll be staying with us."

"Hm. Roy seems to like you," Old Nick said. "Maybe the two of you can get acquainted later."

An image of Roy edging toward me, using his strong arms and large hands to move along the ground, and grinning like a pervert flooded my mind. Had Old Nick put that vision in my head? Another shiver ran through me. If he could get inside my head like Carlos, I was doomed. I needed to ask Agatha Mae if there was a way to keep people out. Block my mind. I prayed none of these circus people would visit me in my dreams. After my experience with Carlos the night before, I might never sleep again.

Chapter 25

The Mask Maker's vardo was hidden deep within the trees, far from the firelight and other carnival folk. Unlike the cheerful wagons back in camp, this vardo was black and painted to look like the night sky with stars and comets in gold and a fat, silver full moon. I was grateful for the lantern clutched in my fist and the circle of light it cast around me. Why Emil had sent me to find the Mask Maker alone, I didn't know.

My pulse thumped in my throat as I approached the wagon that mimicked the velvety black heavens. After meeting some of the performers and seeing masks that ranged from queer to grotesque to nightmarish, I was nervous and a little excited to meet the person who made them.

I knocked on the door three times. A rustle of movement reached my ears and measured footsteps crossed the floor before the door swung open and a large man filled the frame. His warm smile and sparkling blue eyes slowed the nervous patter of my heart.

"Come in, come in. We've been expecting you," he said, and made room for me to enter his home and workshop.

"How...?"

"My ravens saw you coming. And I saw you in a dream a few nights ago."

Two large black birds sat on perches in a silver cage in the center of the vardo. They eyed me suspiciously and gave a ruffle of their feathers.

"Do you know why I've come here?" I hoped he had some answers. There were many more miles ahead and I had no idea where that path was leading me. I knew I had to outrun the men who wanted to drag me back to the hell of slavery. I couldn't. Wouldn't go back.

"I made you a mask," he said.

He put a kettle on the tiny stove in the corner and placed two mugs the color of moonlight on a small table. The wall behind him was covered in masks hanging on tiny metal hooks. Each finished piece was unique, but they all bore a striking family resemblance to the maker himself.

"You made all these?" I gestured to the wall covered in faces, both human and monstrous.

"Mask-making is a labor of the soul. There's a little bit of mine in each of my creations." He stared at the kettle as if willing the water to boil.

"They're scary, but beautiful," I said.

The kettle whistled, its urgent scream jangling my nerves. The birds squawked and beat their wings as they danced about on their perch. They bowed to each other, circled twice and settled down in their new spots.

The Mask Maker handed me a cup of steaming tea that smelled like licorice with a hint of chamomile, and watched as I took a sip. I hadn't gotten much sleep the night before. The herbs were sure to make me drowsy. Just as the thought entered my head, my vision blurred and the walls tilted at an odd angle. I felt like I was falling, but knew I was upright. At least for the moment. The Mask Maker's tea remained untouched. He took a step closer.

"They keep me awake at night," he said.

"The ravens?" The words struggled to get out of my mouth like an animal stuck in quicksand.

"The masks."

I awoke in the Mask Maker's bed. A thick layer of warm blankets and a black bear skin didn't stop me from shivering at the sight of the faces staring down at me. I raised myself up on one arm. My head ached and the room leaned to one side. My clothes were gone but there was no sign that I had been violated. In fact, my skin was clean, oiled, and smelled of spices. My hair fell in loose curls around my face and shoulders. It had been brushed and treated with scented oil, like my skin.

The Mask Maker entered the vardo. "You needed to rest." He answered my unspoken question and sat in a chair against the wall of masks. I swear I heard them murmuring.

I pulled the blankets up to my chin.

"Still so modest after so much violence and intrusion upon your flesh. Or maybe it's fear. I will not couple with you unless you wish to show me affection."

"W-where are my clothes?"

"Drying on the line outside."

"You washed them?"

"And you," he said with a wistful look on his face. "You've traveled a long way. Your dress was in need of mending and a good wash."

He had dirt caked under his fingernails and he smelled like the woods—dead leaves, moist earth, and spring rain.

"The tea...you poisoned me." The anger in my voice surprised me. Life as a slave taught me to bite my tongue and hide my emotions. I learned to keep my tone steady even when rage and pain boiled beneath the surface of my painted-on smile.

"Not poison, just a sleeping draught. You were suffering from exhaustion. Rest was the best thing for you."

"Why didn't you ask me if I wanted to rest?"

"Because I knew you would say no."

I didn't know if he was treating me so well out of the kindness of his heart or if he wanted something in return. Most people do.

"How long was I asleep?"

Candles still burned brightly inside the vardo, and since there were no windows I couldn't tell if it was day or night.

"Long enough," he said, with a smile.

He went to the stove and lit the burner. He covered the flame with a small frying pan and placed a beautiful earthenware bowl on the counter next to the stove.

"Are you hungry?" He reached into the large pockets of his leather apron and produced three brown eggs. He cracked them into the bowl and gently whisked them with a fork. He set the eggs aside. Using a knife plucked from his belt, he chopped a pile of fresh mushrooms and herbs. The pan heated up and he poured a greenish amber liquid into it then added the eggs. The mushrooms and chopped herbs went in next. The smell was delicious, and my stomach growled beneath the blankets. The last meal I'd had was with Emil and Agatha Mae. I was ravenous.

The Mask Maker slid the omelet onto a plate and placed a single fork next to it. He grabbed a chair and sat next to me. Balancing the plate in one hand, he cut through the spongy golden delicacy with the side of the fork.

"Shall I feed you?" He suspended the fork before my face.

"Only if you take a bite first," I said.

"Fair enough," he said, and took a bite of the omelet. "Now will you eat?"

I nodded eagerly, and he slid the warm eggs with earthy mushrooms and fresh dill into my mouth.

"That is delicious," I almost moaned. I licked my lips and opened my mouth for more.

He fed me until I had eaten the entire omelet. With my belly full and the lingering taste of mushrooms and dill on my tongue, I felt sleepy again.

"I have more work to do. You're welcome to stay in my bed and read." He pointed to a shelf of books. "Or you can sleep until your clothes are dry."

"What kind of books do you have?"

"Do you read French or English?"

"Both, but I do better with French since it's my first language."

He placed the empty plate and fork on the counter and turned his attention to the books.

"Let's see. Well, I only have a few texts in French, and honestly they may not be to your taste."

I tried to get a better look at his collection without climbing out of bed.

"I'll read almost anything," I said.

"In that case, this will probably be the most interesting one. It's a story about a girl who's a lot like you." He handed me a thin volume with a red leather cover. The title, *Justine, ou les malheurs de la vertu*, was printed on the inside with several illustrations.

I made myself comfortable and dove into the pages of the book. The Mask Maker went about his business and gave me the luxury of peace and quiet. I admit that as the tale unfolded, I was a little shocked by some of the passages. I'd seen all kinds of things most people only see in nightmares, but I'd never read about them in books. What surprised me most was the fact that no matter how bad the young woman's situation got, she never gave up on her ideals and hopes of living a virtuous life even though people took advantage of her and used her body to satisfy their vile lusts. No one needed to explain to me that it wasn't safe to be alone with some men.

Long before I was ever raped, I knew I could do nothing to prevent it. Fighting back wasn't an option for slaves. But now that I was free, that would never happen again. No man would take from me what I didn't give willingly. I'd rather die than let a man take advantage of me. That didn't mean I hated all men. Some men were kind and never raised a hand to harm another soul. They were few and far between in my world. As I read and rested, I listened to the Mask Maker working at his table sculpting and painting his leather faces. I prayed his kindness wouldn't turn to cruelty. Or worse, his generosity would act as currency to buy access to my body. No one aside from Carlos had ever asked me if I wanted to be touched. They just took what they wanted and left me to patch myself up afterward. It didn't matter if he treated me better than his victims. Now that I knew the truth about him, I'd never let him touch me again.

I hoped the Mask Maker was different. The masks murmured again, and the ravens became agitated in their cage. Could they hear my thoughts? I glanced at the wall of half faces with their sightless eye sockets and noticed a new one had appeared while I slept. It looked different from the others, but somehow familiar. The new face staring back at me was my own.

The masks twittered and shook on the wall. I climbed out of the Mask Maker's bed and moved closer to them to hear what they were trying to tell me. Garbled whispers and mocking snickers. The only mask that remained silent was the one with my face. It stared down at me, mirroring the confusion on my face.

How did it get there? When did he make it?

"You're up, did you enjoy your rest?" The Mask Maker stood next to me.

"H-how...? W-when...?" I couldn't stop staring at my mask. Did it belong to me just because it resembled me?

"Don't be alarmed. I didn't create it to hurt you or control you. I made it to protect you." His voice was soothing.

"Protect me from what?"

"I have seen the vampire in my dreams. He means you nothing but violence. His words of love are false. He has been guiding you down a path that is familiar to him that leads to a graveyard full of his victims." He took a step closer.

"How will it keep me safe?"

He took my face down with slow, careful movements. "Come, sit with me at my workbench."

He offered me his hand and guided me to sit on a chair catty-corner from his.

"As you've probably guessed, my masks are special. I mentioned that I craft them using my own face and each one bares a whisper of my soul. Old Nick uses my masks to control the other performers. They must wear them at all times. The sliver of my soul that exists in each allows me to walk in their dreams and see their desires. If anyone dreams about running away or stealing Old Nick's power, I can see what is in their thoughts and warn him."

"You spy on people's dreams?" Disgust and disappointment must have tainted my voice.

"Please, understand, I don't do this because I want to harm others. I too am kept here against my will. I, like you, am no stranger to bondage."

"But your powers, why can't you use them to escape and free others?"

"He holds me here under magical influence, a spell I am unable to break. But yes, my powers were once great, and I only used them to help others."

I placed my hand over his and he followed my gaze to the mask in his hand.

"Tell me how this mask will help me."

My smile lifted his spirits.

"It is different from the others, because I made it with your face and there is now a small part of you living inside it. Not only will it protect you while you travel with the circus, keeping me out of your thoughts and dreams, but that tiny flame, that sliver of your soul, will protect you from darkness. Darkness will tempt you. Not only from outside forces, but from inside as well."

I listened carefully to his words. I took them in. Memorized them. Words are the power behind spells. Knowledge of the future and how to prepare for it are some of the most valuable magic you can hope for. The mask and his words were gifts to keep me safe and make me strong at a time when I felt most weak.

"You're very kind."

"You deserve kindness and so much more. I only hope you will consider me a friend long after you have left the Cirque du Ombres."

I lifted his hand and placed it against my heart. "You will be here wherever my travels lead me."

A shy smile spread across his kind face.

"Thank you," he said.

"For what?"

"For reminding me that there are still things in this world worth fighting for."

Chapter 26

The next night, Emil came to find me.

"Would you like to see your vardo?"

The Mask Maker was asleep at his workbench, snoring on top of one of his creations. I wanted to thank him for his strange hospitality, but I didn't want to wake him. Besides, I was sure I'd see him again before I left *le cirque*. He offered to let me stay with him in his little home on wheels, but it didn't feel right. It would never really be mine, because it didn't belong to me. And I wasn't ready to call anywhere home until I got further away from slavery and found a safe place to settle.

As tempting as the Mask Maker's offer was, I had to keep moving. He was kind, and meant well, but he couldn't give me what I needed – a chance at a life I would define for myself without the weight of the invisible chains I carried. The ravens fluttered their wings, but remained silent as I closed the door behind me.

"How long have we been gone?" I followed Emil to a small clearing away from the other performers.

"Time moves faster on this side of the door. We've been here for three nights. Only a few hours have passed back on the other side."

I let that sink in. For me, it felt like more time had passed. I had been able to think about what Carlos had done to the Williams family and how I had been there to see it all. I wasn't happy about sharing my vardo with Carlos, but I would do whatever it took to get away from the slave catchers. Traveling with the *Cirque du Ombres* would be a lot riskier than I first imagined, but Emil and Agatha Mae were kind enough to provide passage for Carlos and me. I caught only a glimpse of the other performers, but I saw enough to know that new and unusual dangers awaited behind the red door.

We stopped in front of a deep green vardo with white trim. The glow of torches illuminated the bright yellow door with its brass fixtures and a shiny brass handle. In the center of the door, just under a tiny round window, was a hand-painted red heart framed by cream-colored wings—a heart in flight. I wasn't sure why, but it made me smile.

"This will be your new home as we make our way to your next destination," Emil said. "I painted it myself."

"Can I look inside?" My hands were clasped against my chest. I couldn't wait to see what was behind the door.

"Go ahead, it's all yours...unless you decide to bring Carlos with you."

I didn't think I had a choice in the matter. Carlos was coming with me whether I wanted him to or not. Agatha Mae was a powerful witch, and she seemed to think the same of me. Between the two of us we might have been able to prevent him from coming along, but I didn't want to risk her safety or Emil's. Once Carlos joined me on the other side of the red door, things might be a little more equal between us. Hadn't I made at least one friend with magical abilities? I knew he was watching out for me, maybe others would too.

Inside the vardo were little cabinets with doors painted bright white, which made a beautiful contrast to the deep blue walls. Against the opposite wall was a set of bunk beds covered in thick wool blankets. The sight of the two beds filled me with relief. I hoped the sleeping arrangements and Carlos's guilt would keep him from crawling into my bunk. And I hoped the guilt was eating him from the inside out.

"Well, what do you think?" Emil stayed outside while I inspected my new home. It wasn't as nice as the Mask Maker's, but it was mine. I'd allow Carlos to share it with me if he promised not to touch me. Otherwise, he'd be on his own. Something about having my own place gave me a new sense of confidence. That was a rare feeling for me. I liked that little taste of power; it was sweet.

"It's beautiful. When can I move in?" I sat down on the edge of the bottom bunk. A smile lingered on my face. My spine felt a little straighter too.

"As soon as you're packed and Agatha Mae decides she's ready to go. I have a few things to take care of here on this side before we head back. Will you be all right on your own?" Emil glanced at his pocket watch before turning his attention back to me.

"How long will you be gone?"

"Not long, I need to confirm some details with Old Nick and figure out our travel schedule before we pack up."

I giggled. "I'll make myself at home."

He laughed. "I'm glad you like it."

I waved to him and then he was gone. In the cabinets were dishes and cups for me to use while we traveled. A washbasin and water pitcher sat on a small wooden chest that hid more blankets, and a chamber pot was tucked under the bottom bunk. With Carlos around all the time, I'd most likely just do my business in the woods.

"You didn't say goodbye," the Mask Maker said, making me jump.

"I...I didn't want to wake you," I said. A slight tremor passed through me.

"The ravens didn't alert me when you left. Did you bewitch them?"

"Did I...? No. I didn't sneak away. Emil came to find me and told me my vardo was ready. *Le cirque* will be leaving soon, and I need to settle in." Why did I feel like I was being accused of something?

"Will you invite the vampire into your bed like I invited you to mine?"

And there it was. A claim of ownership. My fears confirmed. His generosity came with a price.

"I don't see how that's any of your business," I said.

"He only means to harm you. I told you, I've seen it in my dreams."

"And what do *you* do with me in your dreams?"

He was quiet, but still darkened my doorstep.

"I just want to spend a little more time with you. It's been so long since I had such a lovely companion." His voice trailed off.

I liked his company too. Maybe we could be friends in another time or place.

"I will come visit you, I promise." I said the words as truthfully as I could manage.

"Your vampire won't allow it," he said.

"He isn't *my* vampire!"

"To whom do I belong if not to you?" Carlos appeared in the clearing a few feet behind the Mask Maker. Dressed all in black, his head seemed to float in the darkness.

I took a step in front of the Mask Maker and faced Carlos. "How did you find me?"

"I followed your scent," he said, with a smirk.

"Agatha Mae told you."

"She took some convincing, but I finally got it out of her."

"Did you hurt her?"

"No, but she's appropriately frightened of me now. She won't use that rude tone with me again." The guilt from the night before had worn off. His cruelty and desire to dominate me had returned.

I turned to the Mask Maker and placed a hand on his forearm. "I think you should go."

"Aren't you going to introduce me to your new friend?" Carlos stepped into the glow of torchlight and blocked the Mask Maker's path.

"No," I said.

Carlos laughed so hard his shoulders shook. A split second later his hands were around my throat.

"I don't know how you came to be in that house last night, but I never meant for you to see that. I never wanted you to see me kill." He tightened his grip.

"I believe what she did is called astral projection," the Mask Maker spoke up. "When Jacqueline realizes her full power, you'll regret the way you've treated her. Will treat her."

Carlos's grip loosened from around my neck and his hands fell to his sides.

"Who is this man?"

"This is the Mask Maker. He's a friend. I stayed with him for a few nights."

"A few nights? It's only been a few hours since I saw you," Carlos said.

"Time works differently here behind the door," the Mask Maker said.

"It's always night here," I added.

"That will be convenient," Carlos mused.

The Mask Maker switched places with me to protect me from Carlos.

"So," Carlos said, inches from the Mask Maker's nose, "did you get a taste of her sweet flesh? Or did she play hard to get with you, too? She likes to pretend that she's innocent, but she's no stranger to the desires of men."

His words dug into my chest and my heart pulled back away from him. He was trying to make the Mask Maker angry. It didn't matter if my feelings got hurt in the process.

The Mask Maker remained calm. "I admit I have fantasized about lying next to this beautiful and exciting girl, but her body isn't mine for the taking. As old as you are, I'd think you would know better than to take someone like her for granted. Keep threatening her with violence, and she'll fight back. Keep treating her with disrespect, and one day she'll be gone."

"Your friend seems to have gotten to know you well in just...what was it? Three nights? I've known you much longer and still can't claim to understand what goes on in that pretty little head of yours." Carlos pretended to pout.

"He has visions and prophetic dreams. He's seen my future. Our future."

"So he's a voyeur with access to your dreams. Sounds trustworthy," Carlos said.

"I do not wish to harm her like you do," the Mask Maker said. "In fact, I hope she finds the freedom she seeks to govern her own life."

The Mask Maker might prove to be a valuable ally someday. In the meantime, he would make an excellent neighbor.

"Why don't you see if our new home meets your standards, Carlos?" I attempted to change the subject.

"Ah yes, our cozy little love nest. Where will I sleep?" He brushed past the Mask Maker and me to step inside the vardo. He had no trouble crossing the threshold.

"I'm sorry," I said to the Mask Maker.

He took both my hands in his. "Don't be. You've done nothing wrong. You're a strong girl. Don't be afraid to use your power. And, if you need me, for any reason, you know where to find me."

Then he was gone.

Emil was surprised to see Carlos stretched out on the bottom bunk when he returned.

"When did he get here?"

I stepped outside to speak with him.

"Shortly after you left."

"Are you all right?" Emil was genuinely concerned.

"I'm fine, but you should check on Agatha Mae. Carlos...threatened her to find me."

Emil growled deep in his chest and ran up the steps of the vardo. He grabbed Carlos by the shirt collar and lifted him up to face him before the vampire had time to react.

"Did you hurt my wife?"

Emil's quick movements and strength stunned Carlos.

"N-no...of course not. I wouldn't jeopardize Jacqueline's chance at freedom. I frightened her, but I didn't touch her."

I never heard Carlos stammer. Was he afraid of Emil? Why?

"I'm going back to the other side to get Agatha Mae. We're leaving at moonrise," he said to me. Next, he addressed Carlos. "If there's even one hair out of place on Agatha Mae's head, I'm coming back here to hammer a stake into your dead heart, *strigoi*. We don't need your help to get Jacqueline to safety."

Would a wooden stake kill Carlos? I knew he could be hurt, but didn't know if he could be killed. Could you kill someone who was already dead? Knowing his weaknesses took away some of his power. Maybe I'd eventually have the power to run away from him.

"Jacqueline, you're welcome to come with me if you don't feel safe here," Emil said.

"I'll be fine."

"Old Nick may seem a little frightening at first, but if you ever need help, you can go to him." Emil turned to leave.

I placed a hand on his shoulder. "Hurry back."

"Your new-found confidence is rather attractive." I didn't hear Carlos approach me.

"Moman always said to trust my strengths. I'm discovering new ones each day."

"I'd love to meet your *madre*," he said almost wistfully.

"I don't have any plans to go back to the plantation."

"Right," he said.

A small band of performers stepped out of the woods into the clearing. The Siamese twins, Alice and Ida, three clowns of varying sizes, the shortest of whom barely reached my waist, and a man who surely had an alligator for a daddy. He was bald, and every inch of his exposed skin was covered in scales like the 'gators I used to run from in the swamp. He grinned at me, and inside his mouth were two rows of sharp teeth that looked like straight pins. I tried to keep my disgust from showing.

"Good evening, Jacqueline," Alice, or was it Ida, said. "We haven't seen you since you arrived, and wondered how you were settling in."

Was the Mask Maker's vardo off limits to them?

"I'm doing well," I said. "It's kind of you to check on me." I made sure I could see the twins' traveling companions at all times. I wouldn't turn my back on a single one of them.

"We see you have a visitor," the other twin said.

"Carlos Velasquez, pleased to make your acquaintance." He bowed and kissed each twin's hand in turn.

Alice and Ida giggled and their cheeks took on a rosy blush in the flickering torchlight.

"Would you ladies be so kind to give me a tour of the grounds?" He was really going out of his way to prove himself a gentleman. He was up to no good.

"Do you mind if we borrow your handsome gentleman caller, Jacqueline?" The twins spoke at the same time.

"Be my guest," I said, and hoped the clowns and alligator man would follow. Being alone in the dark would have been better than their company.

"Won't you join us, Jacqueline?" Carlos took pleasure in teasing me.

"It's been a long...night. You go on without me."

"Suit yourself," he said, and walked off with his arm around the twins' shoulders.

My wish came true. Soon I was stretched out on the bottom bunk, alone in the vardo. Or so I thought.

"I've got my eye on you, little witch." Old Nick stood in the open doorway and blocked the cool night breeze.

I sat up and prepared to defend myself.

"That vampire of yours is an interesting character, and quite popular with the ladies. Well, until he gets hungry, right?" He winked at me.

I didn't respond. Life as a slave had taught me how to tell when someone wanted to talk *at* you, or have a conversation. Most times, *les Blancs* didn't expect you to answer. Old Nick had that same tone. He wanted me to know he knew things about me, but he didn't care about my thoughts on the subject.

"Am I going to be able to trust you to keep a tight leash on him? *You* are my guest. It is your responsibility to keep an eye on your monster. Understood?"

I did understand. If Carlos hurt anyone while we were traveling with *le Cirque*, it would be my fault, and I would be punished with him.

"It is a pleasure to have you with us even if it is for a short time. Too bad you won't be joining us forever."

Once again, I saw myself screaming in the fires that burned in his bottomless dark eyes.

"Pleasant dreams, Jacqueline." He disappeared into the woods.

Chapter 27

I wasn't sure how the carnival traveled from place to place, but Emil assured me we were getting closer to my final stop on the Underground Railroad. Many nights passed behind the door and I lost track of time. The performers were excited to have audiences again, and the closer we got to our first stop on the tour, the air buzzed with more magical energy than usual. Even Carlos was in good spirits.

"Where are we headed?" I asked.

Carlos stopped writing in his journal to thumb through to Squire Jean's list. He threw his head back and laughed.

"What's so funny?"

"Freedom."

I didn't get the joke.

"What?"

"The name of the town we're going to is Freedom."

Funny name for a town, but freedom wasn't a place. Freedom was a way of living.

He saw I was deep in thought and stopped laughing. "I didn't mean to make light of your situation, Jacqueline. I know freedom means more to you than anything. We're almost there."

"Well, we may be headed to a town called Freedom, but I won't be free until Gale, Jimmy, and the Ogden Brothers are off my tail."

"I'll figure out a way to stop them. We'll figure out a way together." He was desperate to mend the rift between us, but I couldn't forgive him for what he'd done to the Williams family. His attempts to seduce me stopped soon after he arrived at *le cirque* and saw how much my feelings for him had changed. I put up with him to avoid more tragedy. Each day I denied him access to my body, my heart, my soul, he grew more impatient. Soon, he'd do something to provoke me.

"Who are we supposed to look for when we get there?"

Carlos checked the list again. "It doesn't say. He only wrote the name of the town."

Strange. How would we know who to contact?

The first stop on the tour was a small town on the outskirts of Memphis, Tennessee. Emil suggested I ease into my career as a circus performer by selling tickets to the public. He posted me outside the door in a small wooden ticket booth with a roll of tickets, a cash box, and a stool to sit on. I hadn't been on the other side of the door since Emil had brought me to *le cirque*. Walking through the red door made me dizzy, confused. Once I got settled on my stool and started selling tickets, I was fine. Carlos wanted to join me, but Emil had other plans for his talents.

The sun set, and a line formed in front of me. People of all walks of life wanted to see what was behind the door.

"Is this where we buy tickets for the carnival?" A young man dressed in his Sunday best approached me with a shiny nickel in his hand.

"Step right up, folks and get your tickets for the Cirque du Ombres!"

"You're a natural barker, Jacqueline," Old Nick appeared out of nowhere and whispered in my ear.

"T-thank you," I said. "Lots of customers tonight, better get back to work." I kept my eyes straight ahead and focused on the gathering crowd.

"We call them rubes, not customers." He spoke the words against my earlobe. "Although, I suppose we do sell fantasies. You must tell me all of your darkest desires someday, Jacqueline."

He disappeared as silently as he arrived.

I don't know how many tickets I sold that night, but the cash box was full. Selling tickets wasn't the hardest job I'd ever done, but I was tired. I couldn't wait to climb into my bunk.

The Cirque du Ombres was still in full swing, and the haunting music that played my first night behind the door filled the air and made my hips sway. I gave in to the rhythms and danced my way home.

I passed the Mask Maker's vardo. He was cooking a lamb on a spit over a fire under the stars. My mouth watered at the smell of the roasting meat and I remembered I hadn't eaten dinner.

"Hungry?" He held out a plate with sliced meat, bread, and fresh greens from the woods.

"Starving," I said, and eagerly accepted the meal.

"How are you? You look well," he said.

"I can't complain. You?" I asked, between bites.

"I miss your company. You should visit more." He ate from his own plate.

I was content to share a meal with the Mask Maker under the stars by his fire. I was tempted to sleep in his cozy vardo that night, but it wasn't meant to be. It was late. I was tired, and if Carlos didn't find me in my bunk he'd search every vardo, tent, and dark corner until he found me.

"Next time, I'll make dinner for you." I thanked the Mask Maker and bid him goodnight.

"Jacqueline," he called to me. "There's something I need to tell you. Something important."

I stopped to listen to my neighbor. He looked around in the dark before he spoke. The Mask Maker was afraid. He beckoned for me to come closer and lowered his voice.

"Your life and the vampire's are in danger."

"What do you mean?"

"Old Nick likes you. He wants to keep you."

"Keep me? But Emil said we're getting closer to my next stop."

"None of us are really free here," he said.

"Does Emil know?"

"Emil means you no harm, but he must do as he is instructed."

"What do you know?"

"The vampire will be tempted, and he will succumb to his nature," he said.

"When?"

"Soon. I wish I could tell you more, but others are listening."

"I thought you were Old Nick's spy."

"I'm not the only one," he said.

Agatha Mae stepped into the clearing. "Good evening, Jacqueline. Beautiful night, isn't it?"

"Perfect weather for sleeping," I said, and hurried home.

Inside the vardo, I wished I could lock the door, but I needed to speak to Carlos, and there was only one key. Mine. I made a pot of strong tea and sat up to wait for him. The tea helped, but I struggled to keep my eyes open.

Carlos shook me gently to wake me. Blood stained his face.

"It's too late," I said. "You've already done the deed."

"It was the twins," he confessed.

"We have to get out of here. We've been set up. Old Nick means to keep me."

"Keep you? How do you…?"

"The Mask Maker told me."

"You still trust him?"

I didn't answer right away.

"It won't be easy to leave if there is a plot to keep you here. There's only two of us, and too many of them," he said.

He had a point.

"I promised I'd get you to the North so you'd have a chance at being free. I'm going to keep that promise," he said.

Fists pounded the door, a sound that was becoming too familiar. Voices raised in anger circled the vardo. Torchlight blazed through the tiny windows. The Mask Maker's warning had come too late.

"Can you fight back?"

"Yes," I said, and concentrated on focusing my powers.

"If I don't open the door, they'll kick it in, and I know how much you like it," he said, with a laugh.

"I'll open it." I stepped in front of him and turned the shiny brass handle.

Outside was a mob of freaks with torches raised and violence in mind.

"Give us the vampire!" A chant rose among the gathered mob.

If Carlos died, I'd be on my own. I was getting stronger, but I didn't think my power could compete with Old Nick's.

"What has he done?" I challenged the crowd.

Old Nick stepped forward. Torchlight glinted off his sharp horns. Still dressed in his blood red coat, the Ringmaster raised a hand and commanded silence from the throng.

"No one blames him for giving in to his nature, Jacqueline. We all do bad things sometimes. However, he killed one...well, two of our own. That's punishable by death," Old Nick said.

"They seduced me, and asked me to drink from them," Carlos spoke up behind me.

"Yes, yes, the Devil made me do it. I'm familiar with that excuse," the Ringmaster said.

"We'll go," I said, "and never return."

"Don't be silly, Jacqueline, you've done nothing wrong, but I did warn you if you didn't keep a leash on your vampire, you'd both be punished."

"If we leave, he can't do any more harm here," I said.

"He can't do any more harm if he's dead either," Agatha Mae said from the back of the crowd.

Her betrayal hurt, but she'd taught me a few tricks I could use against the mob to escape.

"His punishment will be death," Old Nick said. "Your punishment is to stay here with me." Fire flashed in the depths of his eyes.

"Like the rest of us are being punished?" The Mask Maker spoke up.

I knew I could trust him.

"Don't be a fool, Mask Maker, I own you, remember?"

"No one is going to own me," I shouted, and released a wave of energy to snuff out all the torches.

Everything went black.

Carlos grabbed my hand and we ran into the woods.

"*Feuer!*" Old Nick lit the torches with a word and chased away the darkness.

We didn't get far. The mob and Old Nick caught up and performers grabbed both of us at their master's command. They tied Carlos to a tree and took turns beating him with axe handles.

Agatha Mae made sure my hands were bound and put a gag in my mouth so I couldn't use magic. I screamed and cried against the fabric, but no one helped us. Carlos weakened with each blow. The men laughed and taunted him. Lottie had laughed like that at poor, dead, light-skinned Harriet. Rage burned inside me. I pushed my thoughts inside the Mask Maker's head.

Prove your friendship, and help me.

How? They'll kill me.

The masks. Control them.

I don't...

Touch me. Use my energy.

Everyone was focused on watching Carlos take a beating. The Mask Maker knelt beside me, untied my wrists, removed my gag, and placed both hands on my bare skin. Blue sparks flew between us. His spell began. The magic was different than mine, but I helped him channel it. Together, we got inside the heads of each performer.

The ruffians got bored hitting Carlos, so they set him on fire. I screamed. Power surged between the Mask Maker and me. Old Nick turned toward the sound, but it was too late. The performers dropped to the ground, lulled to sleep by the Mask Maker.

"Sweet dreams," he said, and collapsed next to me.

I ran to Carlos's side and smothered the flames with a heavy cloak I pulled off one of the sleeping performers. His skin was blackened and cracked, but he wasn't dead.

"Thank you," he whispered.

Old Nick took a step toward us. I had enough power left to push him back a few feet with a wave of magic.

I untied Carlos and set him free on the motionless bodies around us. He drank his fill, but it would take time for him to heal. The Ringmaster did nothing to stop him.

"You're much stronger than I thought," Old Nick said.

"You don't have the right to keep me here."

He laughed. "Big talk for a fugitive slave."

"I promised to take you to your next destination," Emil said. "That's what I intend to do."

"Where were you?" Anger colored Old Nick's voice.

"Counting tonight's take. Looks like I missed a lot," Emil said.

It was time to leave the *Cirque du Ombres*. We'd worn out our welcome. Emil and Old Nick escorted us to the red door.

"This won't be our last meeting, Jacqueline," the Ringmaster whispered in my ear. "I'll be watching you."

I refused to meet his gaze. I'd seen myself swimming in flames enough times to understand the message.

Carlos was like a statue next to me. The beating had humbled him. Silenced him. It would take longer for his pride to heal than his charred skin.

"You owe this girl your life, vampire. Don't squander that kindness if you can help it," Emil said.

The red door swung open with a loud creak. On the other side was a field of fresh green alfalfa with new purple buds. Spring was on its way. And so were we.

Chapter 28

Across a bare cornfield, toward a small town in the distance, Carlos limped beside me. A hand-carved sign made from old wooden planks told us where we were headed. Carefully nailed together and painted with whitewash to accent the letters, the sign read: FREEDOM. We stared at each other for a moment and almost laughed, but I was too tired, and his mouth was hurting too much for laughter. He hid the raw, angry burns on his face with a black wool scarf. For my sake, or maybe his own pride, he pretended not to be in pain as he limped along the crude dirt road.

When we left *le cirque* three days before, he was thankful to be able to go to ground at daybreak. I had to help him dig his shallow grave. The fire had taken its toll on his body. I tried to stay awake and keep watch over him, but the amount of magical energy I'd spent to get us away from the angry performers had drained me too. We were camped in the woods again, and the sound of a roaring stream lulled me into a deep sleep. I guess he was frightened when I didn't wake up right away. He was shaking me hard when my eyes finally opened.

"Carlos?"

"We need to keep moving."

It was just past dusk when we set out again. Without the magical protection of *le cirque*, Gale would be able to find us if he picked up our scent again. Hatred and greed kept Jimmy and the

Ogden brothers on our trail. At some point, they might give up the search, but Aleister Gale was driven by his desire for vengeance. Unless he had a sudden change of heart, we would be running for a long time.

Now, we stood at the crossroads outside Freedom. It was close to midnight.

"Can you make it the rest of the way?" I placed a hand on Carlos's back like Moman used to do to comfort me.

He stood against a wooden fence post to get his balance. "I can make it."

"Do the burns still hurt?"

The blackened skin that covered his face had peeled away to reveal a layer of red, blistered flesh. I couldn't imagine what it felt like to be set on fire.

"They will heal faster when I have fresh blood."

"Human blood, you mean." Deer and a few smaller animals had gotten him this far.

"It is a little late for me to pretend to be something else, Jacqueline."

I didn't have time to argue with him about right and wrong, we needed to keep moving.

Soft lamplight spilled out into the darkness from only one window as we entered the town. It came from a small log cabin with a sturdy door. Smoke snaked from its stone chimney. We stayed hidden in the shadows of the churchyard among the headstones, and waited to see if anyone moved about the streets of the tiny farming community. No one stirred that night, not even a barking dog greeted us. We approached the house with caution and silently shared our thoughts.

Stay behind me. Whoever answers the door may take pity on me, but your injuries will be hard to explain.

Carlos followed my lead. He hung back in the shadows and kept watch as I approached the wooden door with a pineapple painted on it. I knocked three times and waited for someone to answer. A few seconds passed before an elderly woman answered the door. She had a neat mound of white braids held on top of her head by a bright orange scarf. She squinted out at me from a weathered, kind face, then scanned the street behind me.

"What you want this time of night, girl?"

"Please, Ma'am. I'm looking for a place to rest and maybe a meal. I don't have money, but I work hard."

"Runaway."

It wasn't a question.

"Yes, Mamzèl. I won't be any trouble."

"What about your friend over there? Will he be trouble?"

"No, Mamzèl."

"Good evening." Carlos stepped out of the safety of the darkness and made himself vulnerable.

"Keep your distance, devil."

Was his nature so apparent that an old woman could immediately sense the danger? It usually took people longer to recognize what he was, and by that time it was too late. This woman was different. She knew what he was at first glance.

"I swear, I mean you no harm. I only seek safety and comfort for my companion," Carlos said.

"That may be, but I don't trust you."

The old woman welcomed me inside her home. Her golden eyes narrowed and she searched his face with suspicion. She refused to let Carlos step across her threshold.

"You can sleep in the barn come sun up, demon."

"As you wish, *anciana*." A polite tilt of his head and then the shadows swallowed him up.

I expected more of an argument from him. The urge to fight must have been beaten and burned out of him. He still wanted to be my protector, but since we were allowed to leave *le cirque*, our roles had reversed.

Cinnamon, cloves, and other sweet smells invited me into the house. Embers glowed in the sturdy stone hearth and my skin sighed at the warmth. Dried sage, catnip, and thyme hung above the fire. The mantle held lighted candles, and tiny glass jars full of natural treasures like feathers, polished stones, seashells, and dried wildflowers all in a neat row.

Is this woman a conjurer? I thought.

"Girl, are you out of your mind? Ain't you got any sense? That man is a monster."

"He's never hurt me." That wasn't entirely true, but when most people ask if you've been hurt, they don't mean your feelings.

"I bet he's the reason you had to run in the first place."

I didn't answer.

"Maybe you'd be better off dead than keeping company with a creature like that. He feed off you? Offer to make you like him?"

"No."

"How you keep him from feeding from you?"

"He never asked."

"Creatures like that, they don't ask, they take what they want."

"Not from me."

"What makes you so special?"

I didn't have an answer.

She looked at my torn, dirty dress, my matted hair, and shook her head. "Girl, you look a mess. You hungry?"

"Yes, Mamzèl. Haven't had a decent meal in three days. Survived on roots, mushrooms, and berries."

"How you know what's safe to eat? Some plants will make you

sick, or kill you outright."

"My moman taught me. She knew a lot about herbs and other plants and their uses."

"She a conjurer?"

"Yes, Mamzèl."

"She pass that to you?"

"Yes."

"Who sent you here?"

"Squire Jean."

She laughed. "That old goat."

"He sent me to a Seer named Agatha Mae first, and that was good for a while, but traveling with *le cirque* she and her husband belonged to didn't end well."

She studied my face and shook her head with pursed lips. "What should I call you?"

"Jacqueline."

"Pleasure to meet you, Jacqueline. You can call me Aurora. Help yourself to some cornbread and greens. I'll heat some water on the stove; you need a bath. Better check for ticks since you been sleeping in the woods. I can lend you some clothes until we wash and mend yours."

Aurora was an unusual name. How many Negroes could there be that answered to it? Moman had taught me there were no such things as coincidences. If something seemed familiar, there was a reason.

Too hungry to ponder if this woman was indeed my grandmother, the only other person I knew to have that strange name, I gobbled up three pieces of cornbread and a plate of collards. They tasted just like Moman's.

The steaming water in the tin tub made me sleepy. The knots in my muscles began to loosen and the crust of filth embedded in the crevices of my neck, behind my ears, between my toes, and under my fingernails flaked away as I used Aurora's homemade lavender soap to scrub myself pink. Aurora scolded me when I drifted off.

"You gonna catch cold if you fall asleep in that dirty water."

I raised my head, but my eyelids fought me at the effort.

"Come on, get dry by the fire."

She wrapped me in a clean white linen sheet as she helped me out of the bath. I stood by the hearth until my hair and skin dried, and she gave me a worn, but freshly laundered nightshirt.

"There's a bed up in the loft. You can sleep there."

"It's nice to be warm and safe inside a house again."

"When was the last time you felt safe inside a house?"

I had to stop and think. Safety had been an illusion my whole life, and was dependent on the whims and moods of others. People who felt cruelty was a God-given right. I had never been safe. I lived moment-to-moment waiting for the next punishment or humiliation.

"Don't go fooling yourself into thinking that just because you've outrun the men who are after you now there won't be more like them willing to take up the chase."

"We'll move on in a day or two. We don't want to cause any trouble."

"The only trouble I'd worry about if I was you, is that dead man you got yourself mixed up with. What you think is going to happen if you stay with him?"

Again, I had no answer.

"Misery. That's all a creature like that can bring you."

I didn't argue. Instead, I climbed the wooden ladder to the loft and collapsed on the bed. It was cold up there, but the wool blanket soon warmed me. Before I drifted off I heard Carlos's voice inside my head.

Sweet dreams, my love.

I almost wished Carlos were next to me in the loft. His company could be nice at times. Well, at least on the nights he wasn't slaking his thirst in the arms of one of his victims. Violence was part of his true nature. His behavior wouldn't change just because I wanted it to. He needed blood, and I wasn't about to stand in the way of that need. He'd threatened me a few times, but had never taken advantage of me. I couldn't help thinking he knew something about our relationship that I didn't.

He put up with my refusals as if he knew I would eventually give in and let him have his way with me. A voice inside me screamed "no" every time his touch lingered a little too long on my skin. It got harder and harder to say no each time he tried to bed me. Especially after drinking his blood.

I pushed my thoughts aside and allowed myself the pleasure of a good night's rest. I didn't even dream. It was a welcome rest from the nightmares. No Ogden brothers, no chattering masks, and no Old Nick. I slept like the dead.

Chapter 29

The comforting smells of hot coffee, frying bacon, and fresh-baked biscuits greeted me at dawn. Sleep still hung heavily over my eyes as my bare feet hit the cold, rough floorboards.

"Come down and get some food in you."

Aurora raised her voice above the sound of eggs frying in a large iron skillet. She poured coffee into two clay mugs on the table.

I climbed down the ladder slowly, still unable to shake off the cobwebs of sleep.

"Wash up out back and get warm by the hearth." Her voice was commanding, but gentle, a natural mothering tone not unlike Moman's.

The pump gave me a little grief before water began to flow and I thought back to the plantation. Spilled water on the dry earth had earned me two days locked in the corn crib with rats. My arms and legs still bore the scars of their bites and scratches. I splashed cold water on my face to chase sleep and memories away.

My breath misted in the early morning air. I'd lived in the heat of Louisiana all my life, and I missed the sweltering days. I could get used to the weather up north if it meant freedom from slavery. I'd survived Lottie's hatefulness and Lynch and Jimmy's violent invasions of my body. If I could live through the horrors I'd experienced as a slave, a little cold weather wouldn't kill me.

Across the yard sat the newly raised barn where Carlos slept. Its timbers were fresh and unpainted. He would be safe there until dark. Soon, he would need blood, and with that thirst came the promise of murder. Maybe he'd find a neighboring town full of unsuspecting strangers and leave the townspeople of Freedom alone. It never hurt to ask. A smile and a gentle touch on his knee seemed to encourage him to heed my words. Growing up at Lottie's side had taught me much about manipulation, and she was practically a scholar when it came to her abilities for swaying the minds of men. Coquetry was a science as far as my half-sister was concerned, and she had excelled in her chosen field of study.

Back inside, a tin plate of eggs, bacon, and warm biscuits waited for me. I came up for air when every scrap of food was gone. Aurora poured me more coffee and offered me a hand-rolled cigarette.

"Sleep good?"

"Yes, Mamzèl."

"Glad to hear it. You can help me chop wood and gather eggs this morning. You know how to cook?"

"I learned to cook at Moman's side in the plantation kitchen."

"You can help me prepare the noon meal for the men when they get home from the mines. Just biscuits, beans and collards, but there's a lot of mouths to feed and I'm getting too old to do all the cooking by myself."

"Do you work for white folks?"

"No white folks here to work for. This here's a colored settlement. Free Negroes live here. I'm cooking for free black men because I want to, not because I have to."

"Only black folks live here? Who tells them what to do all day?"

Aurora threw her head back and laughed so hard I could see how many teeth she had missing.

"How far you run from?"

"All the way from New Orleans."

"No wonder you so tired. You been with that vampire all this time?"

"Most of the way, yes."

"You tried to get rid of him, didn't you?"

"He refused to leave me alone. Said he didn't want to be without me," I said, exhaling smoke out of my nose.

"What happened to your owners?"

"Got killed."

"Did he kill them?"

"He wanted to, but a *loup-garou* beat him to it."

"Why'd he take you?"

"I don't know. Maybe it's because he knows my secret."

"What secrets you got at such a young age?"

I didn't answer.

Aurora tended the fire and cleared away the dirty breakfast dishes. She was quiet for a long while.

"After supper tonight, I want you to tell me your whole story. Everything you can remember."

I wasn't sure why this dark-skinned, white-haired stranger wanted to know my life story, but I wanted to tell her.

I dressed in the clean work clothes she loaned me. The men's trousers, shirt, and boots all fit comfortably with a little extra breathing room. She gave me a knitted hat to pull down over my ears before I went back outside to split logs. It felt good to work again. My muscles craved the activity. I soaked up as much fresh air and winter sunlight as I could. The labor warmed me quickly and I soon developed a rhythm to the swing of the ax.

Before nine o'clock, I had enough wood split and stacked next to Aurora's house to last a week. I hefted the last logs onto the pile and stretched. Another kink gone from my spine. Sleeping in the woods for three days had been brutal on my bones. Aurora's hospitality erased some of the pain and stiffness.

I found her collecting eggs in the hen house. She cupped fuzzy yellow chicks in her hands and sang sweet words to them.

"They were born last week. A little too early, but spring's coming soon."

"Won't they freeze out here?"

"They got plenty of fresh straw and they snuggle up together with the chickens at night. They're tougher than they look. They'll survive."

I wondered if I would. Lottie and her husband were dead. They couldn't hurt me anymore. If I could figure out a way to free myself from Carlos, I wouldn't have to worry about Gale either. Would Jimmy and the Ogden brothers still come after me?

Close to eleven o'clock, Aurora put me back to work. She'd already built a fire in the stove and rolled out dough for biscuits. She gave me a biscuit cutter, a brush, and a pot of melted lard.

"You get them biscuits cut, and I'll start the beans. Collards'll be ready soon."

"How many biscuits you need?"

"As many as you can cut. Try to get as many as you have fingers four times."

"That's 40."

"You know your arithmetic?"

"I can read, too." The words slipped out of my mouth before I could stop them.

"Is that one of your secrets, too?"

"Yes. I don't talk about being a Mambo either."

"Don't ever be ashamed of your power, girl."

I felt I could trust Aurora, but even among black folks it wasn't wise to brag about knowing certain things. Even if there weren't any whites in town, knowing how to read could still cause problems for a runaway slave.

"Where you learn how to read?"

I didn't respond.

"Listen, I'm not going to tell anyone what you can or can't do. If you want it to be a secret, I'll keep it a secret."

"Moman taught me. She wasn't born a slave. Her daddy taught her. But, when her daddy died, she got sold at auction and soon after that she was carrying me. She always hoped I'd have a better life, but never forgot the world is a dangerous place. She taught me lots of ways to protect myself if I ever got into trouble. I wish I could read all the time, but it isn't safe."

Aurora's eyes rested on my back as I cut the dough. I sensed she wasn't judging me, just trying to understand me. Moman used to look at me like that sometimes when she couldn't figure out what was going on inside my head. She worried about me a lot. I missed her like a runaway slave misses an amputated limb. I could still function and get along without her day-to-day, but a dull ache lingered in my side where she used to stand next to me.

"Folks around here could benefit from that kind of knowledge. Not many of us have that skill."

Again, I focused on my work.

"Who knows, maybe you could make a life here for yourself teaching folks to read. Preacher's been talking about building a school, but we don't have any teachers in town. Until you came."

"I'm no teacher. I never went to school."

"You know how to read, and you know how to count. That's a

start."

Maybe she was right. Where else did I have to go? I couldn't run with Carlos forever. Besides, I was never going to be like him. I didn't want that life. Killing folks, drinking blood, and never seeing another sunrise. I wanted more. I wanted to get an education, buy my freedom, and see the world. I was tired of running. Carlos would be angry, but he didn't need me to go on with his life. He could go anywhere in the world. He was a white man who could charm almost anyone into doing what he wanted, and a vampire to boot. Fear inspires people to do just about anything. It was probably one of the oldest emotions, and it was the driving force behind slavery.

"Hurry up and get those biscuits in the oven, girl."

"Yes, Mamzèl." I handed her a finished pan and got another one ready.

"We got lots of hungry mouths to feed soon."

Once the biscuits were in the oven, I helped stir the big pot of beans on the stove and fill tin pitchers with water from the pump. Aurora set up two long wooden tables behind her house and covered them in a blue and white gingham cloth. A stack of wooden plates sat at the end of the table with the pitchers of cold water.

"Beans and collards are ready," Aurora called from inside.

Together we hefted the big cast iron pots off the stove and carried the food outside. I could get drunk off the inviting smell of her pot liquor. Big chunks of bacon rind and ham hock floated to the surface and made my mouth water. The idea of giving up such wonderful treats to survive on nothing but blood filled me with sadness. How could Carlos live forever without enjoying the pleasures of home-cooked meals? That wasn't living.

Aurora straightened her apron and tucked a stray braid behind her ear. She took a good, long look at me and seemed to be making calculations in her head.

"After lunch, I'm going to take your measurements, and we're gonna make you a dress."

"I was just going to mend my old one."

"A young girl like you needs to look nice if she's gonna attract a husband. Besides, that old rag you showed up in looks like something a runaway would wear. If you don't dress like a runaway, maybe no one will come looking for you."

Her logic seemed silly, but I could never say no to a new dress.

"There are lots of good men in this town, Jacqueline. What we don't have is enough strong, good-looking girls like you."

I listened, but had nothing to say.

"When these young men get a look at you they'll be tripping over their own feet to stand at your side."

Aside from Jimmy, Lynch, and Carlos, my experience with men was very limited, but usually ended in violence. Carlos had only kissed me, but I could hear his thoughts —and none of them were pure. Would he be jealous if I showed affection for another man? He was a predator by nature, but I did not wish to be his prey. At least, that's what I kept telling myself. Jimmy had savagely taken the one and only possession that mattered to me, my innocence. I hated him. Picturing him dead widened the smile on my face. Aurora probably mistook it for eagerness to meet the young men in town.

Soon after the food was assembled on the tables, the dinnertime church bell rang and men of all shapes, sizes, ages, and hues entered the yard at the back of Aurora's house. Clothes covered in coal dust, they jockeyed for a position at the pump to wash their hands before helping themselves to the delicious spread of food. I hurried inside to bring out the still warm biscuits and fresh honey butter.

Men old and young pulled their own forks and spoons from worn pockets and dove into their steaming plates of beans, greens, and biscuits. *Soul food*, the old woman called it.

Aurora had favorites among the men. As I helped her serve, she gave a little extra meat to this one or that one, an extra biscuit to the handsomest, and she smiled and flirted like a young girl receiving courters on a Sunday afternoon. I couldn't keep the smile from my face.

"Who's your new helper, Aurora?" A tall, light-skinned man asked. He wore a red hankie around his neck and had the brightest eyes I'd ever seen.

"This here's Jacqueline, Percy. She came to town last night looking for work and a place to stay."

"Nice to meet you, Miss."

I smiled without showing any teeth and nodded at him. My eye contact was brief, and I focused on serving greens to the next man in line.

"Maybe I'll see you at church on Sunday, Miss." Percy directed his words at me.

"Maybe."

I smiled again, and he walked towards an old oak where his friends were sitting, shaded by the branches.

"Percy sure would make a fine husband."

I ignored Aurora and kept filling plates until all the men had been through the line at least once. Percy kept stealing looks at me while he ate and talked with his friends. He seemed agreeable. I wasn't sure what qualified him as a good husband. He wasn't hard to look at. Tall, strong arms, a solid frame, skin as light as mine, and those beautiful eyes. Handsome as the day was long.

Lottie would say that handsomeness was one of the most

important qualities to look for in a husband. I wasn't sure I agreed. Of course, a handsome man was easier to get close to when the need arose. It didn't matter how handsome Jimmy or Lynch were, because I rarely had to look at their faces when they had their way with me. Any man is as handsome as you imagine him to be if he takes you from behind.

Chapter 30

Once I knew I could trust Aurora, it was easy to open up to her. There were too many coincidences between us. She agreed we must be kin. Did Squire Jean know he'd sent me to my grandmother? Her house was my home as far as she was concerned, and she was happy to have me there. But, no matter what I said in Carlos's defense, he was still unwelcome.

He tried to win her trust with gifts and acts of kindness, but no amount of whiskey, tobacco, or firewood she didn't have to chop herself swayed my grandmother's belief that he was pure evil. Maybe she was right, but it didn't change the way I felt about him. Nights I spent by the hearth with Aurora were nights he would spend alone. Parts of me missed him. We had grown closer and had learned to rely on each other after we ran from New Orleans. On the road, we talked of a time in the future when we could rest and enjoy each other's company without the threat of Aleister Gale at our heels. Here in Freedom, it seemed like that time had come, but instead of spending my nights with Carlos, I was learning about my ancestry from Aurora.

"Your granddaddy was the kindest and gentlest man I ever knew. Smart, but stubborn." She smiled, a far-off glint in her eye. "You need to find a man like that. Kind, strong, dependable, and skilled at love-making." She giggled and covered her mouth like a schoolgirl. I wondered if she meant someone like Percy. She definitely wasn't talking about Carlos.

"He gave me the name Aurora. Said my eyes shone like the lights he saw flashing in the night sky up in the wilds of Canada. Most beautiful thing he ever saw," she continued. "Well, that is until your mama was born. That child could do no wrong and your granddaddy spoiled her something awful."

"Moman's still pretty, but she ain't spoiled no more. No matter what the other slaves say."

"I bet it was hard on her being sold after living free all those years."

"How old was she when it happened? When granddaddy died?"

"No more than eleven. Still a girl. Is your daddy a slave?"

"No, Mamzèl. Bunch of us light-skinned slaves just fell from the sky the way folks on the plantation acted. Master's got more slave children than white."

"Well, that ain't nothing new. Your granddaddy wasn't the first white man to have his way with me. But he was the only one to ask permission first."

Again I thought of Carlos. I watched how he treated the women he fed upon. He never asked their permission. When he knew he was in control of their choices, he took what he wanted from them. Money, sex, blood, trinkets and gifts for me, it didn't matter, it was all his for the taking. No one said no to him, even if they wanted to. All I knew was he never put his hands on me without asking or making a proposal. He provided me with choices, no matter how unacceptable they were at times. He never took anything from me without giving me something in return. I didn't know why, but I was certainly thankful for that. His bloodlust and anger was terrifying. I'd seen him unleash it on the Williams family. I never wanted him to bring that wrath down upon me. It was not only pleasurable to be in his favor, it was the key to my survival.

"Are you still with me, Jacqueline?"

I stared at Aurora for a moment, lost in my thoughts about Carlos. Where could he be? Out hunting, but not in Freedom. I had forbidden him from feeding off the residents of the town soon after we arrived. He agreed, but teased me with the knowledge that he would need to travel to other towns. I wouldn't be around to make sure he didn't fall in love with someone else.

"Sorry, I was just...."

"You were thinking about that vampire."

I nodded my head and took a sip of coffee.

She stared into the fire, gathering the words she needed to persuade me once again to stay away from him. I liked that she wanted to protect me. Moman always looked after me when my head got full of wild ideas. I knew it was dangerous to feel the way I did about Carlos, but you can't choose who you love or what you desire. You can only deny yourself the pleasure of seeking out your passions. Like so many others in my life, Aurora wanted me to be happy, but only if it was on her terms.

"Girl, I'm only going to say this one time. I care about you, because you're my blood. And you will always have a safe place to go, as long as I draw breath and have a roof over my head. But, if you give in to that man and let him turn you into what he is, you'll never be welcome in my home again."

And there it was. The one promise I wanted to keep but wasn't sure I'd be able to. I didn't want to be a vampire. Not because my grandmother threatened to disown me, but because I believed it would be a betrayal to myself. Slavery was the one thing that kept me from living up to my full potential. And as far as I was concerned, becoming a vampire was just another kind of slavery. Sure, Carlos was ageless, strong, powerful and almost indestructible, but forever is a long time. Drinking the blood of your fellow humans is quite a price to pay for immortality. Life could be really lonely sometimes. Imagine living as long as Carlos without the comfort of friends, family, or even lovers that lived for more than one night. A slave to his desires, bound to his cravings, damned to walk the Earth forever. My fear of that kind of sadness lodged a lump in my throat that made it impossible to swallow. I knew I couldn't be the only girl he ever cared for, but how many times in his long existence did he lose someone to old age, sickness, madness, or a simple careless mistake when blood and passion became confused in his head? I didn't want that kind of life. I also didn't want to belong to some white man just because a piece of paper said so.

Aurora meant well. She cared about me. How could she know what was best for me, though? Percy was a nice man, but he would never make my heart beat like Carlos did. For her sake, I'd make an effort and get to know the handsome miner better and keep the peace in my new home. She deserved my respect and I owed her my word.

"I promise not to become like him." As I spoke the words, I hoped I wouldn't have to break that promise any time soon.

Chapter 31

After supper, I went to find Carlos. I narrowed my eyes against the darkness before entering the barn. I couldn't see him, but I could feel him, smell him. Stale blood and that strange scent of decaying flowers, and a lingering musk of sex greeted me as I stepped into the large open space. My footfalls were silent to my own ears, but I knew he could hear me coming. I took a deep breath and a moment to gather myself before approaching the ladder that led to the loft where he slept. The sun had been down for an hour, but he waited for me instead of going to hunt in the next town over, Butcher's Falls.

He made no sound, no movements, and my legs trembled a little as I waited to hear his voice above the pounding of my heart. Darkness loomed in every corner, pressing toward me. I worried it might swallow me up. I should have brought a lantern from Aurora's kitchen. It was silly to be afraid of the dark when I knew the only thing hiding in it that could hurt me was Carlos.

"Come," he called from above.

I took another deep breath and climbed the ladder slowly. It was sturdy enough to hold me, but my balance was off. Asking Carlos to leave me alone at *le cirque* hadn't been easy, but now it would be even more difficult. My pulse throbbed in my throat, as I got closer to the top of the ladder. What was I going to say? Would Carlos be angry enough to hurt me? I deserved a chance at a normal life.

At the top of the ladder, a soft glow of lantern light danced about and cast a halo around Carlos's head of curly, raven hair that framed his pale serene face. He sat facing me on the edge of the brass bed he'd carried up the ladder on his back a few days after we came to Freedom. He explained that just because he was sleeping in a barn didn't mean he had to live like an animal. His white shirt was open at the collar and tiny black hairs traced a pattern of swirls across his solid chest.

I felt his eyes upon me, taking in each part of my body like an artist preparing to paint his model. I shifted from foot-to-foot, unable to stand still.

"Are you afraid of me?" He asked.

I nodded my head and refused to meet his stare.

"I am not your Master. I do not wish to punish you."

I remained silent and unable to look at his handsome face.

"Come here," he said.

I obeyed and took small steps across the wooden floor to stand before him.

"Take off your dress," he said.

I met his gaze. "No."

"I know why you have come. You like it here in Freedom and want me to go."

"Yes."

"I know you do not desire me the way I desire you, but I thought our friendship meant more to you."

"It does, but your world and my world are too different. I can't live in both and be true to myself."

"May I kiss you?"

I thought about Aurora's story about my grandfather. How he was the first man to ask permission to touch her.

"Why?"

"Because this may be the last time we see each other. I would like to have a fond memory of you before I go."

I sensed his touch before his icy fingers grazed the skin at the base of my neck and he drew me in to gently urge my mouth open with his tongue. His lips were cold like his fingers and shivers ran along the backs of my arms. Tremors quaked behind my knees. The kiss was deep and passionate, but more than his usual hunger lingered behind this kiss. A moan rumbled in my throat and I drew him closer to me. His hands slid down my body to cup my breasts and I grasped his hips to pull him closer to my body. I hated myself for wanting him.

He stopped kissing me to offer me a taste of damnation yet again.

"Let me turn you and be mine forever."

"How can you ask me to give up my mortality?"

"How can I allow you to leave me?"

"I don't belong to you."

"We'll see what the law has to say." He produced a copy of the wanted poster with my description and reward and waved it in my face.

"You're a murderer. You feed on people like slaughtered hogs!"

"Hogs don't usually get treated to indescribable pleasure before they die."

I thought of Mrs. Williams and her daughter. Did he honestly believe he was doing these women a favor? Rape and murder weren't gifts, no matter how you wrapped them up. He gained pleasure from what he did, but his victims didn't. It became clear to me at that moment he made no distinction between his victims and me. He wanted to kill me, too. By turning me into a monster like him, he believed I would accept what he was.

"Do you love me?" He asked.

"I'm not even sure I know what love is."

"Don't lie to me. Tell me the truth."

The truth was, my heart beat faster when Carlos was near. I denied this fact every chance I got. How terrible would it be to accept his offer? I would lose Aurora's trust, but I would be true to my desires. Still a slave, but on my own terms. Enslaved by a need for blood and the desire to lie next to a man I feared. I craved Carlos's touch like a dying man hungers for his last gasp of air. Each time I denied myself the pleasure of falling into his arms, the hotter the fires deep inside me burned. What was the drawback to saying yes? Temptation couldn't possibly lead to ruin every time. Could it?

"From the waist down, my body is telling me to pack my things and run away with you. But, from the neck up I know that choice will only lead to more tears, more heartache, and misery."

Carlos stared, studying me with his lips pursed tight. I'd been a mystery to him since the day we met. He still couldn't figure me out. Maybe that's what kept his interest. I was a puzzle for him to solve.

"I've only ever wanted for you to be happy," he said. "If building a life here makes you happy, then I will go."

I wanted to believe his words. I knew him well enough to know he wouldn't stay away forever.

"Thank you," I said.

"Stay with me tonight. Let me enjoy your company for just a little while longer. I will go to Butcher's Falls before daylight and take a room there."

"Why? How long are you planning to stay?"

"Until I know you're settled and safe. Then I'll move on."

He still wouldn't be out of my life, but I hoped he was sincere about moving on.

Chapter 32

The next day I woke up alone in the barn. Relief washed over me. If Carlos really cared about me, he would stay away.

"He gone?" Aurora asked, when I entered the house.

"Yes."

She didn't push me for details.

It was Sunday. After breakfast, Aurora took me to church. The day before, I'd baked three apple pies. She suggested I bring one to share with the congregation. She combed and braided my hair, but wouldn't let me wrap it in a *tignon*.

"This ain't the plantation. No need to hide your beauty here in Freedom."

I wore a gray wool skirt and a white blouse, with a dark blue knitted shawl. It was pretty, but it also kept me warm in the cool morning air.

"You look nice. Percy will be at church." She reminded me for what seemed like the hundredth time. I'd only spoken to the man once and all we'd talked about was cornbread and greens. Now I guessed we'd talk about pie.

On our walk to church we passed the graveyard, which was close to the edge of town. There was a new grave dug with fresh, upturned soil piled at its side.

"Poor Nellie Johnson." Aurora shook her head and made the sign of the cross over her heart.

"What happened to her?"

"She worked as a maid for a white family in Butcher's Falls. It's about five miles from here, on the other side of that hill to the south. A lot of our womenfolk go there to find work. She'd been working for the family for about a year when she got mixed up with the eldest son. They fooled around, and before you knew it, she was carrying his baby. Well, he couldn't tell his folks about the baby and tried to get her to quit her job. But Nellie thought she was in love with that white boy and begged him to run away with her. I guess he got worried his parents would ask who the father was when she started to show, so he waited for her after work one night. Said they needed to talk. He offered to walk her home to Freedom. They were walking along the road, just after dusk, when they ran into a group of his friends. Those boys did terrible things to her. Can't even have an open casket for the poor girl's family."

"Why did they kill her?"

"Don't always need to be a reason, Jacqueline. You know that. Whites get an idea in their heads, and even if it don't make no sense, they go ahead and do it anyway. That's their way."

"Why didn't she just get rid of the baby?"

"She was in love and wanted the child. Love makes people do stupid things."

"You can't blame her for loving him."

"No, but he didn't love her back. At least, not enough. Chasing after colored girls is a game to some white boys. Some kind of perverse rite of passage. They're sick, Jacqueline, and you need to stay away from men like that."

I thought back to all the times Lynch had made me lie with him. It made me angry. He and Jimmy had managed to humiliate me and make me feel like garbage. I pictured that boy and his friends taking turns and cheering each other on while they brutalized

Nellie. They must have beat her so bad all she could do was die.

A hot, angry tear slid down my cheek. "How can you stand it?"

"Stand what?"

"Being free and still not being able to do a damn thing about those disgusting pigs who control our lives?"

"I take one day at a time, child. That's all I got to work with, and until a time comes when I can do more, that's all I'm gonna do."

"It makes me so angry. I still feel dirty inside, like I'll never be clean again."

"You need to learn to love yourself enough to make that feeling go away. Give it time. It gets better. You'll see."

I wanted to believe her. All the love in the world wouldn't wipe away the memories of what Jimmy and Lynch had done to me.

Carlos believed he could take my pain away. I doubted that was true, but he'd made every effort to convince me he could wash away the filth and poison I carried inside me. Wash it away with his blood.

We were both quiet the rest of the way to church. Nellie's broken body on our minds. I didn't know her when she was alive, but I would damn well attend her funeral. What else could I do? It didn't make sense to take revenge on the men who killed her. Lynch was dead, and I still didn't feel much relief. Nellie took her pain to the grave.

Sunlight filled the one-room, clapboard church. The parishioners talked and laughed, and wished each other good morning. The buzz of gossip, news from other towns, and stories about masked mobs of white men snatching black folks from their homes and burning down towns filled the air and made the church feel like a hive. Aurora sat on a pew near the middle of the congregation. People smiled and nodded at her respectfully, but few spoke to her. I thought for sure we'd have the pew all to ourselves until Percy Thomas came in, hat in hand, and asked Aurora's permission to join us.

"Please, Percy, sit next to Jacqueline."

"Yes, Ma'am."

Percy left a respectable amount of space between us on the wooden bench. He nodded to me and smiled. "Miss Jacqueline. You look very pretty this morning."

"Thank you, Mr. Thomas."

He gestured towards the apple pie in my lap. "Did you bake that?"

"Yes, I brought it to share after church."

"It looks delicious, I hope I get the first bite."

"You're welcome to eat the whole thing if you like."

He shifted a little closer to me on the bench and lowered his voice slightly. "I'd be delighted to eat your pie. It's probably the sweetest one in church today."

I'll admit that I'm not worldly and have been naïve on more than one subject, but I knew he wasn't talking about the dessert I baked. I blushed and looked away to hide the idiot grin on my face. Percy was a handsome man and he smelled like wood smoke, sunshine, and the muskiness of a freshly shaved face. His clothes were clean and pressed, and he sat up straight and tall in the pew next to me. He would make some nice girl a perfect husband someday. I envied her.

When the preacher was done telling the congregation we were all going to Hell, Aurora wandered off to talk to some of her neighbors. She smiled over her shoulder and was gone. I was left alone with Percy.

"Would you like to join me for a walk in the orchard behind the church?" His voice was sweet and steady. He was confident I would say yes.

"I'd like that."

He stood and offered me his hand. His kind action allowed me to enjoy the rare opportunity of being treated like a woman. Outside the church he placed his hat on his head and gestured for me to link arms. I slipped my arm through his and he guided me away from the church.

"How long you fixin' to stay here in Freedom?"

"Not sure. Aurora says I can stay as long as I like."

"And that man who came to town with you? Is he staying, too?"

When would he have seen Carlos?

"This town is too small for him. He'll move on soon."

"Will you go with him?"

"No. I like it here."

"I'd like if you stayed. Aurora says you're smart as a whip and can maybe help out if we ever finish building a school."

Had she told Percy my secret? "She sure has been talking to you a lot about me. I didn't know the two of you were so tight."

"She's sweet on me. Says if she was ten years younger, she'd marry me."

"Ten? More like twenty." We both laughed until our sides hurt.

"Your grandmother cares about you and wants you to be happy. And safe. She thinks I can provide both, happiness and safety. But, if I'm not what you're looking for, then it doesn't matter what I have to offer."

I was quiet for a minute or two. He made a good point. He might be the best man that ever lived, but my happiness depended on me, not him. If I wasn't ready to settle down and start a life with him, but did it anyway, neither of us would be happy.

I must have looked perplexed by my thoughts, because Percy smiled and gently raised my chin so my gaze could meet his.

"We don't have to figure everything out today, Jacqueline. I have all the time in the world. Besides, we don't live on the plantation no more. You can be your own person out here. We can get to know one another and decide if we really would be good for each other. Maybe I'm just blinded by your beauty."

I blushed again and tried to cover a giggle, but he stopped me.

"Your smile is too pretty to cover up like that. If you're happy, don't be afraid to show other people. So what if people get jealous. Let them. Laugh, smile, live a good life. Give folks something to be jealous about." He took the pie from me and helped himself to the biggest bite he could, right out of the middle. And then we laughed some more.

Percy ate the whole apple pie and ended up walking me all the way home. He made me laugh so many times on our walk I thought my stomach would burst. I couldn't remember ever laughing so much in my whole life. Laughter felt good. I learned something new about myself that day. Not only did laughter take away a lot of the pain I stored up inside me, but the fact that Percy could make me laugh made him ten times more attractive than the first day I met him. His coal black hair, dark, almond shaped eyes, brown sugar skin, and tall muscular build made him elegant and handsome. But his flirtatious words and teasing humor made him desirable.

Percy and I said our goodbyes at Aurora's front door. I invited him to join us for supper the following Saturday evening. My heart fluttered slightly when he removed his hat and kissed my hand. So gentle, so polite. I stood and waved as he made his way back across the street and down the road to his own house. He was barely out of sight when Aurora opened the door and I stumbled backwards inside.

"So, how did things go with Percy?"

"Fine." I regained my balance and steadied myself against the doorframe.

"Are you going to see him again?"

"He's coming for supper on Saturday."

"Oh good. I really hope the two of you get along. He'd be good for a girl like you."

That was the first time she'd phrased it so specifically and I wasn't quite sure what she meant. Was she referring to the fact that I was somehow tainted? I suspected she meant something a bit more judgmental than that, but I didn't know what.

"Well, he is a nice man."

"And handsome, too!"

"No denying that. He's smart and makes me laugh."

She smiled and patted my arm. She looked like she might have something else to say to me, but hurried into the kitchen instead to put on coffee and fix our lunch. She made extra biscuits that morning, so we had ham sandwiches and a slice of one of the remaining pies.

Chapter 33

After lunch, we drank more coffee by the hearth, and she smoked her pipe. The wind had picked up outside and clouds had moved in to chase away the sunshine. We'd have rain by nightfall. I wanted to ask her why no one sat with us in church, except for Percy, but I didn't want to offend her.

"What's on your mind, child?" She blew smoke out of her nostrils and set her gaze steadily upon my face.

"In church today, I saw you talking to a few folks, but no one wanted to come sit with us. Why?"

She took another long drag off her pipe and held the smoke in her mouth for a few seconds before exhaling. "Most people are superstitious. They think that when they're in the Lord's house they can't mix with people who are different like you and me."

"How are we different?"

"What color are your mother's eyes?"

"Why should that matter?"

"What color?"

"Golden, almost yellow, why?"

"Your eyes will turn soon, too."

"What do you mean?"

Aurora drained her coffee cup and fetched a bottle of whiskey from the cupboard. She poured a healthy dram and offered me the bottle. It was barely past two o'clock, and Sunday to boot. I downed the rest of my coffee and held out my tin cup. She poured the amber liquor. She took a long, deep swallow from her cup and refilled it before setting the bottle on the table.

She looked at me for a long time before she spoke.

"Some stories you can start in the middle, or near the end, and you might be able to follow along just fine, but other stories need to start at the beginning. I'm going to tell you my story, because now it's your story, too."

I followed her example and took a hefty pull from my own cup. I threw another log on the fire and wrapped my shawl a little tighter around my shoulders. The wind tried to pry its way between the logs of the cabin, but the house held its ground. I got comfortable.

"I was born in Africa. I never even saw a white man until I was twelve or thirteen when I was taken from my home and brought across the sea, into slavery. Before that happened, before my first blood came, my father took me to see a very powerful shaman. You see, the people in my village knew I was a witch. That is the last thing you want people to know when you are a young girl in a tribal society. In fact, that's true for any girl living in any society."

"How did they know you were a witch?"

"I had these dreams. Nightmares. And sometimes they came true. No one had ever told me to keep that kind of thing a secret, so I told people about my dreams, and when they came true, people became afraid of me. They wanted my father to kill me."

"But you didn't do anything wrong. You couldn't control the things you dreamed about."

"No, but I *could* keep the dreams to myself."

"Sometimes my dreams come true."

"I'm not surprised. Your mother's dreams came true when she was a child. I'm sure that's another secret you kept between you."

"That's right." I was excited to talk about things I'd only talked about with Moman.

"That's why your mother is so good at her craft. I bet she has lots of people who come to her for help."

I rested my chin in my hands, waiting to hear more of her story.

"We have a natural ability to see things, know things, and understand things before others do. And, we have a knack for learning and practicing magic with little effort. That's why you can read so well, and bake such delicious pies, and use herbs for things beyond cooking. You and your mother get that from me."

"Why did your father take you to the shaman?"

"People in our village became angry with him when he didn't kill me. They threatened to do it themselves if I stayed. So, he took me to the shaman and asked for help."

"Did he help you?"

"Yes, and no."

"What happened?"

"I stayed with the shaman for a long time. He lived in a cave at the base of a mountain. It took two days for my father and me to walk there. I thought my father was taking me there for help, but my father gave me to the man. There were tears in his eyes when he left, but I never forgave him."

She took another drink from her cup and smoked her pipe. I watched her face and waited for signs that she would continue.

"Each night I dreamed, and each morning, I told the shaman what I'd seen in my dreams. He needed proof that I was able to see the future. When he got his proof, there were other tests. For weeks, he listened to my dreams, fed me, and gave me a place to sleep at night in his cave. He never once tried to touch me even though I understood my father had given me to him as a bride. Unlike some of the men in my village, he wasn't comfortable with the idea of having sex with a child."

I refilled my cup and poured Aurora more whiskey. She smoked and stared at the fire as she chose her next words.

"Because he treated me so well, I was shocked when I discovered what he had planned for me. One night, on a full moon, he woke me from sleep and told me to follow him outside. He'd made a circle of stones in front of the cave and there were symbols drawn around and inside the circle in red soil. I'd never seen symbols like that before. He told me to undress and lie down at the center of the circle."

"What did you do?"

"Exactly what he told me to do. I removed my dress and got inside the circle. That's when I noticed the stakes in the ground and the tethers tied to each one. He bound my arms and legs and spoke words I didn't understand. He made cuts along my arms, legs, and stomach with a large knife and my blood ran into the dirt."

Chills raced along my back and arms as she described what I recognized as black magic. Moman rarely called upon the dark spirits, and she always warned me against it unless it was absolutely necessary. She told me never to practice black magic for money or personal gain. It was only to be used for revenge against an enemy or to protect someone you cared about deeply.

Aurora continued her story. "The shaman called up an evil spirit. He said we needed it to protect us."

"Protect who?"

"All of my people. You see, I'd dreamed that white men came in boats and stole people from my village. The dream frightened the shaman, and he believed that calling the spirit would prevent it from happening."

"Why did he need you?"

"He needed my body to contain the spirit. I was the only one strong enough to hold it inside. Me, a young girl, with no voice, and no choice in how I would live out my future, I was the savior of my people. And they wanted me dead."

She closed her eyes and took a deep breath. Even after all those years, I could see that the memory still haunted her.

"That night, the shaman bound the spirit to my soul. In exchange for his promise to protect our people, the spirit made a pact with the man. They cursed me and my children to live with this spirit forever inside our bloodline."

"Do you still have it inside you?"

"Yes, and when I die, your mother will have it inside her."

"How?"

"It will leave my body and find your mother because her blood is my blood. She is a witch like me. And when she dies, it will seek you out."

"I thought the spirit was supposed to protect your people, but the white men still came and took you away."

"The spirit lied."

"What does it want?"

"It wants to take control of our bodies and do evil things."

"Do you do what it tells you to do?"

"No. Only once did I heed the spirit's voice and allow it to take control of my body." She finished the whiskey in her cup.

"What happened?"

"It killed every man, woman, child, and animal on the plantation where I lived. That's how I became free."

"Why hasn't it taken control again?"

"Because I don't let it," she said plainly. "Root work keeps it weak. Squire Jean helped me figure out the right spell, and I've been keeping it asleep ever since."

Spell work or not, keeping a demon from taking over took a lot of power. I hoped to be as powerful as Aurora when it became mine someday.

"Does Moman know about the demon?"

"No."

"Why not?"

"Because I was foolish enough to believe that I could find a way to stop it from passing from me to her. To you."

"But you've found a way to weaken it?"

"Yes."

"Will you teach me?"

"Yes, and you must promise to teach your mother if you can. Once I die, the demon will pass to her and if she doesn't know how to control it, it will control her."

As much as I enjoyed the fantasy of seeing Moman kill Master, his family, and the overseer, she would never forgive herself if she took the lives of innocent slaves and animals in the process. From what Aurora described, the demon had killed without distinction.

Chapter 34

Percy came for supper the following Saturday. Aurora dipped into her sugar reserves again and we baked apples stuffed with raisins, walnuts, and brown sugar. The whole house smelled like Christmas or some other holiday when Moman and I made special foods for Master and his family. Aurora even sprinkled cinnamon over the apples before placing them in the warming oven to slowly cook while the rest of the meal came together. She laid a clean linen tablecloth on the table by the hearth, and then she fussed over my clothes and hair for what seemed like the tenth time. She wanted me to look perfect for our guest.

"That man won't have a choice but to fall in love with you," she teased.

"Do you really think he could love someone like me?"

"I saw the way he looked at you after church, you got that man on the hook."

"Maybe."

"He's looking for a wife so he can start a family. Don't you want a normal life?"

What entitled me to a normal life? Why did I believe I wanted one? If I settled down in Freedom, my best chance for happiness would be as Percy's wife. He worked hard, built his own house, and went to church every Sunday. Percy was smart and didn't mind that I could read. Encouraged it, even. He smelled nice too, and when he spoke, his eyes always met mine instead of measuring me up like other men did. Lottie was right about one thing: A woman with a good husband had little to worry about. If I had Percy to look after me and I had him to care for, I wouldn't need Carlos anymore. I could put the idea of giving myself to him right out of my head.

Percy arrived early. He brought tobacco for Aurora and flowers from his garden for me. She was so excited she almost forgot the chicken frying on the stove. I didn't know what she was conjuring, but I saw her cut the throat of that chicken. She sprayed the blood on a flat stone with *véve* drawn in brick dust behind the house. She didn't mention the spell work and I didn't ask her about it. Sometimes it's better not to know.

The three of us sat at the table, and before we ate, Percy said Grace.

"Oh, Heavenly Father, we thank you for this wonderful bounty before us to fill our bellies and give us the strength we need to live the lives you have chosen for us. We thank you for bringing us together and providing what we need to prosper in this life. Amen."

"Amen," I said.

"Pass the biscuits," Aurora said.

"This is a fine meal you've made for us, ladies."

I passed the biscuits to Percy, and Aurora passed me the platter of chicken.

"Aurora did most of the cooking."

"I can't take all the credit. Jacqueline made the dessert."

I took a sip of water and waited until everyone was served before I began to eat.

"I'm still dreaming about your pie!" Percy took a bite of his chicken and winked at me.

"Jacqueline's gonna stay on in Freedom. She might outgrow my house soon, though. She'll need a place to live."

"I'm glad to hear you're staying," Percy said. "There's plenty of room at my house. The attic is finished, and I just put in a new wood stove. Kept the whole house nice and warm all winter. I could use some help around the place."

"Are you offering her the attic? How much would she need to pay for room and board?"

People were always talking about me. Around me. Over me. I may as well have been invisible. I should have been used to it after a lifetime of being ignored and having other people make plans for how I would live my life. Instead, each time it happened the rage inside me grew a little darker, a little deeper. I understood Aurora was trying to look out for me and help me find a safe place to live, but the way she talked about me to Percy made me feel like I was standing on the auction block. Her praise of me was kind, but auctioneers rattled off the strengths and weaknesses of slaves up for sale: strong back, hard worker, a full set of teeth, still of child-bearing age, no complaints of disobedience, but she may have killed her last owner. Would Percy be my new master?

"What do you want to do, Jacqueline?" Percy turned his full attention to me and waited for my reply.

Surprised by this unexpected desire to hear my thoughts on the subject of my own life, I was at a loss for words for a beat or two. "I can be useful around your house, if you have room for me. I could come live in your attic. I mean, if that's what Aurora thinks is best."

My grandmother had a lot of wisdom I only dreamed to possess someday. My conjuring skills were no match for hers. I still had a lot to learn from her. Not just about magic, but about life, love, and men, too.

"I'll need you to prepare meals, keep the place tidy, tend the garden, and see to the animals," Percy said. "During the week, I work in Butcher's Falls. I leave early Monday and come home late Friday. You'd have the place to yourself most days, so I hope you don't get lonely too easily."

"If I have books, I don't need too much company."

He smiled and turned back to Aurora out of respect for her authority as my grandmother. She was grinning like a fool.

"I guess it's settled," he said. "With your permission, Jacqueline's welcome to come live in my house."

"Free of charge?" Aurora said.

"There's a lot to be done around the house. Helping me care for the place is payment enough. Besides, every other man in Freedom will be so jealous, my ego will get a boost every day she's living under my roof."

"Oh, Percy, you rascal," Aurora laughed.

I didn't laugh. Again, I felt like a prize, and I guess Percy was the winner. I liked Percy. He would treat me nice and I would have a safe place to live. No one mentioned marriage, but a girl like me would be a fool to turn down a proposal from a man like him when the time came. And it would come. Aurora was right. I'd hooked him.

After deciding my fate, we sat at the table and enjoyed the meal. Percy and Aurora moved onto other topics. I chimed in from time to time, but I preferred to listen to their stories. Aurora had so many to tell. And Percy told us all about the town where he worked. It was the same town where that poor dead girl had worked before she was murdered for loving the wrong man. I hoped I never had any reason to go there.

I didn't trust most white folks. I worried about Percy's safety. Black men had even more to worry about than black girls. I knew what it was like to be raped, beaten, used, and hated simply because I was female and the wrong color. I could never understand the fear Percy must have carried in his heart.

The burden of his birthright, being born black and a slave, was all the excuse *les Blancs* needed to blame the ills of their own lives on him. Now he was free, they hated him even more. It would now be my job to worry about him. I would do whatever I could to keep him safe. At the very least, I would take care of his house so he had somewhere special to come home to.

Chapter 35

A week later, I was living in Percy's house. It wasn't big or fancy, but it was the most beautiful home I'd ever been in, because now it was mine. At least, Percy was kind enough to make me feel at home and tell me I was free to do as I pleased. We moved what little I had into the attic after church on Sunday. By Monday morning I was settled in and making breakfast in the kitchen.

"Sure is nice to wake up to the smell of bacon and biscuits cooking," Percy said.

He sat down at the small table in the middle of the cozy little room, and I poured him coffee. It was early. Sun was barely up, but he had a long trip into Butcher's Falls. If he left early enough, he could catch a ride with Cyrus Sampson. Cyrus had a wagon and a team of horses. He charged a nickel to ride people in Freedom to the next few towns over so they could work, buy goods, see family, or catch a train further north. If Percy missed Cyrus, it was a long walk. But he didn't need to worry. The old wagon driver liked him and would always stop by the house to see if he needed a ride.

"Morning, Percy. Miss Jacqueline." Cyrus took his hat off and wiped his feet at the door before he sat at the table with Percy. I poured him a cup of coffee and packed two lunches, one for each man. I even threw in a couple extra biscuits with bacon for their early morning ride. It was chilly, and the fog hadn't lifted yet. A warm biscuit in his hand would make Percy's ride less uncomfortable.

"We better get going. Sun's almost up," Cyrus said.

"Thanks again for breakfast, Jacqueline," Percy said. He put on his coat and hat and grabbed his haversack. We stood in the doorway and stared at each other, not sure what we should do. We weren't married, so a kiss in front of Cyrus wouldn't be appropriate. A hug maybe, but we settled for a handshake. Percy put two dollars in my palm and told me to use the money for emergencies. I tucked the money into my apron and waved to the men as they climbed into the wagon. Most weeks, Percy stayed in town to avoid traveling back and forth. I wouldn't see him again until late Friday night.

One thing for sure, being a slave had prepared me for domestic life. I'd spent my youth serving others and barely had time to do things that really mattered to me, like reading, conjuring, and taking care of the people I loved. There were times when Moman and I could rest, make special treats for each other with the scraps we saved from Master's house, and best of all, sometimes she would tell me stories. With Percy gone, I didn't have anyone to tell stories to, but I did have time to read. I had plenty of work to do around the house, but no one stood over me, watched my every move, or hoped I would mess up. Chores felt different now that I could decide when to do them and how hard I wanted to work to get them done. I took more pride in my work, because it was mine.

Once Percy was gone, I went outside to tend his garden. It was nice, but I could make it better. I got down on my hands and knees to weed, replant, and prepare the soil for new seeds I needed to sow. Percy wasn't a conjurer, so there were lots of things I normally used in root work and healing that he wouldn't have planted.

Days were getting longer and warmer, and soon it would be

time to bake berry pies, can tomatoes, and shuck beans. I knew it wouldn't get as hot as Louisiana, but that was fine by me. Thoughts of summer breezes and salads with fresh green lettuce filled my head as I worked in the garden and sang the hymns I'd learned in church. Aurora told me I didn't have to believe everything I heard in the pew, but in a small community like Freedom, it was important to show others that we at least respected their beliefs. I didn't mind going to church. I liked the stories and seeing all the people, and there was usually music of some kind. But Aurora was right. I didn't believe everything I heard there. There were passages in the bible that said slavery was God's will and that to run away from your master was a sin. Bullshit. Slavery itself was a sin, and anyone who thought it was a good idea or owned slaves could go straight to Hell. If that meant I wasn't a Christian, I didn't want to be one anyway.

Aurora came for a visit the second day Percy was gone. That woman always knew what I needed. She brought clippings from her herb garden, seeds from her pantry, fresh eggs, one of her best hens, and a blessing spell for the house. Seeing her brightened my day. We planted the herbs and seeds side-by-side, built a small coop for the hen, and worked the spell together all before noon. I'd made a pie the day before. Aurora ate two slices for lunch.

"Girl, Percy is one lucky man. Your mother taught you right when you learned how to make a pie crust. Mine are good, but never as good as this."

"Thank you for the herbs, Aurora. You must have read my mind."

We laughed out loud. She could have read my mind, but didn't need to. In the short amount of time we'd known each other she'd learned more about me than most people would in a lifetime.

"So, how are you settling in?" She asked.

"I like having this place to myself, but I think I miss Percy a little."

"He'll be back in no time. Besides, you stay here with him long enough; a time will come when you look forward to him leaving each week. He's a good man, but at some point, all men get on your nerves."

"Do you ever miss your husband?"

"Which one?"

"My granddaddy."

"I do. I don't think of him often, but when he comes to mind, my heart hurts a little. He didn't run off on me or treat me bad. He loved me. He loved our children. When he died, there were days I thought I might join him. But with four children to worry about and protect, I didn't have time for such foolish thoughts. One of these days you'll have children of your own and you'll know what I mean."

I refilled her coffee cup and cleared away our plates from the table. She smoked, and I rocked in the chair by the hearth. We enjoyed each other's company well into the afternoon. Before suppertime, Aurora headed home. I made a quick meal for myself from the leftover pie and fell asleep next to the fire with a book in my lap.

Chapter 36

I woke to the rain beating on the roof like angry fists. The chill in the air made me wrap my shawl a little tighter around my shoulders. I'd need more firewood soon, but going out in the downpour to fetch it from the shed behind the house meant getting soaked to the bone. The sky had been dark all day with storm clouds threatening to let loose their fury, and now that it was after dusk, the sky had turned an inky black. I was glad to be inside by the fire and dressed in warm clothes. I'd get more wood when the rain let up.

Every few minutes, long, jagged lightning bolts split the darkness with a sharp crack and an eerie glow, and the smell of damp earth and sulfur cut through the crisp sweetness of spring rain. Thunder rolled up through the valley and bounced off the hills. Storms always made me a little uneasy. I wouldn't be able to sleep until this one passed. The raging weather kept me on the edge of my seat, like I was expecting something. It would be a good night for conjuring, but my concentration was off. I kept reading the same two sentences over and over each time I picked up my book.

I gave up on the book and decided to make tea. Something to calm my jangled nerves.

I put the kettle on the stove and took a tin cup down from the shelf. There were several small glass jars of dried herbs in the pantry, and the one I needed was near the back. I took a candle to cut through the shadows and found the little jar of catnip, chamomile, and lemon balm. On my way back to the stove, I peered out the front window to see if the rain was starting to slow, and another flash of lightning lit up the entire sky.

A man in a wide-brimmed black hat stood in the front yard under the apple tree. I almost dropped the glass jar, but managed to set it on the table before the knock came upon the front door. How had he moved so quickly? A good three hundred yards stretched between the apple tree near the front gate and the threshold of the house. No man could cross that distance in such a short span of time.

I liked being alone in Percy's house up until that moment when the man outside knocked again. Visitors who weren't neighbors were rare in Freedom, especially on a night like this. Everyone I knew was safe and warm inside their own houses. No one would be out in the storm unless it was a matter of life and death.

The house was protected. Aurora and I had seen to that. Whoever was on the other side of that door thought it was important enough to come out in this downpour to see me, which meant he probably wasn't bringing good news. My curiosity got the better of me, and I opened the door.

Carlos stood in the doorway of Percy's home. My home. He needed me to invite him in, but I wasn't sure I wanted to do that. I stood facing him and although he was happy to see me, his smile faltered and there were questions brimming behind his eyes. He could see the indecision on my face.

"Aren't you going to invite me in?" He asked.

His coat was sopping wet and rainwater ran down the side of his hat in great streams. If he were a living, breathing man, I would have worried about his health.

"Why did you come?"

Shocked by my greeting, he stared at me with his mouth open. He tested the strength of the invisible barrier between us. Blue flames shot out from his fingertips as he passed them over the threshold. He jerked his hand back.

"Your magic is much stronger," he said.

"Aurora helped," I said.

"I came seeking your company. Would you turn me away on a night like this?"

"You were gone for weeks. I didn't think you were coming back."

He gestured wildly at the doorframe like it was a gaping chasm and tilted his head dramatically in anticipation of my invite.

"It's not getting any drier out here, and I really want to talk to you." He paused before speaking his next words. "I missed you."

My gut screamed at me to turn him away. Once he crossed the threshold, I wouldn't be able to keep him out. He could come back any time he liked. Percy wouldn't like that. I didn't want Carlos interfering with Percy and me. My gut was right, but my desire to see Carlos, to be near him, to hear my name upon his lips stamped out the sanity of my instincts.

"The fire's dying down. Fetch more wood from the shed out back and you can come in," I said with my hands on my hips.

He threw his head back and laughed loudly. As always, his smile softened his features and made him appear devilishly playful, yet somehow angelic at the same time. His laughter was contagious.

"I will fetch more wood if you promise to offer me a drink by the fire."

"Bring as much as you can carry," I called over my shoulder as I turned and moved away from the door to grab the whistling kettle off the stove. In less than two thudding heartbeats, he was back at the door with an armload of wood. Again, his smile undermined my resolve to keep him out. I invited him in.

He removed his hat and ducked his head to enter. A river of rainwater spilled from the brim onto the dry floorboards. He shrugged off his coat and it fell to the floor in a sodden mass of black wool. I glared at him for making a mess and went to find something dry for him to wear. Percy wasn't as tall as Carlos, but they had similar builds. When I returned from Percy's bedroom, Carlos was standing before the fire stark naked sipping something from a tin cup.

He turned to me without a care for his nudity and pointed to the open bottle of whiskey on the table. "I hope you don't mind, I helped myself."

"I'll take some of that, too," I said, and sat the dry clothes on the rocking chair by the hearth. "Those are for you."

"You didn't say you missed me," he said, and took a step closer to me.

I couldn't ignore how beautiful his body was. It was a temple to sin, and every part of him beckoned for me to touch it. I accepted the cup of whiskey he poured for me and took a hefty pull from it. The liquid burned the back of my throat and warmed my chest on its way to my belly.

"I did miss you, but I'm with Percy now."

He took another step closer and sniffed at the air around me.

"I don't smell him on you, so you must not be too close to him yet."

"Don't." I turned my back to him and closed my eyes trying to get the image of his strong slender form out of my head. I shuddered at his icy touch on my shoulder.

"Jacqueline, you know as well as I do that we are not like other people. We want more from this world than small towns can provide. You don't honestly think you'll be happy here as this man's wife, do you?" His irritation grew with each word.

I crossed my arms and took a deep, calming breath. Carlos was agitated. I needed to choose my words with care.

"Percy is a good man. He cares for me and I feel safe when I'm with him. I feel normal."

He sighed and took his hand off my shoulder. His feet padded slowly across the floorboards back toward the fire. A rustle of fabric meant he decided to get dressed.

"No one can keep you as safe as I can. Besides, if you allow me to give you my blood again, you won't need any man to protect you. You'll be strong enough to protect yourself. We'll be equals. If you stay here, all you'll ever be is a wife."

"This world is frightening enough without creating more monsters. I don't want to be like you. I've fought too hard and put up with too many humiliations in order to be free. You aren't free. You're a slave to your hunger."

"That may be, but with you at my side I know life could be so much more. Have more meaning and depth."

I turned back around to face him. He was slipping a clean white shirt over his head. Still tempting, but at least he was dressed.

"What makes me so special?"

He frowned and shook his head. The gap between us closed quickly and again he stood before me. With his free hand, he lifted my chin so that I couldn't look away from him.

"I have been alone for as long as I can remember. I have known many women and men intimately. I have befriended them, taken them, and even killed them, but I have never loved a single one."

"What does that have to do with me?"

A shadow passed across his face, he was getting impatient,

almost angry.

"Are you mentally deficient? I love you. I want you to be mine forever."

I backed away from him and laughed cruelly.

"You don't love me. How could you? I'm a runaway slave, barely a woman. All I know about the world comes from books I've stolen or borrowed. You've lived for more than four hundred years and traveled the world. You may be a vampire, but you can still walk down the street in any town and blend in. I can't. I don't look like the men who have all the power. You do. What is it you think we have in common?"

Rage replaced the confusion on his face. He took another step closer and leaned down until his nose touched mine and he glared as the words he gathered to throw at me formed upon his twisted mouth.

"I thought you were an intelligent and loving girl with a passion for discovery. The energy force growing inside you gets a little darker each time we meet, and I like that. Your beauty radiates from inside out and I know your fears and desires."

I tried to back away. His voice was getting louder with each word. He grabbed my arm and held me still.

"You didn't run from me when you found out what I was."

He looked like he was about to cry. Was he able to feel sadness?

"Where would I run to? I was a prisoner in my sister's home."

"You kept my secret." His voice softened slightly, but his grip on my arm was beginning to hurt.

"I didn't tell anyone for fear that you would kill me," I whispered.

His eyes widened in surprise and his grip got tighter on my arm.

"Liar," he spat the word at me. "You knew all along that I would never hurt you. If I wanted to hurt you, I would have had you and eaten you the first night we met."

"But you didn't. Why? I wasn't sick, or feeble, or with child. Lynch practically handed me to you."

"You think carrying a child would have kept me from seducing you? If only it were that simple. Do you have any idea how many expectant mothers I've had in my four centuries on this Earth? They were always a little sweeter to me, more wanton in their fecund states. Snuffing out two lives at once made my cock twice as hard."

I slapped his face and regretted it immediately. He slapped me back hard enough that I fell backwards and landed on the floor. My head bounced against the solid wood and I saw stars after I bit my tongue. Then he was upon me, pressing me down into the floorboards and prying my thighs apart with his knee. He shoved his hand under my dress and tore at my underclothes. I tried to push him off me, but his strength was inhuman.

"If you won't give me what I want, I'll take it from you," he leered down at me.

I was terrified, but more than that, I was devastated. He knew that the one thing he could do to me that would break me was to take me against my will. I told him how much I feared and hated the men who raped me. I was wrong to trust Carlos. Time and again, my instincts had told me not to, but I refused to listen to my gut where he was concerned.

"Don't," I whimpered.

He unfastened his trousers and pinned me to the floor. I kicked and screamed. A trickle of blood ran down my face from my nose. An animal stared down at me with an expression somewhere between lust and rage. He licked the blood from my face and uttered a moan that vibrated through his entire body.

"I knew you would taste sweet. I've never drank blood so full of life."

He closed his eyes and sniffed at the air around me again. His mouth was open like he was savoring my scent. I could see his sharp teeth as he leaned closer to me. He would drink from me while he raped me. Sweat broke out all over my body and the fabric of my calico dress clung to me.

"Please stop," I begged. Tears poured from my eyes. "You're scaring me."

"That's the point," he growled, and tore into my neck with his teeth.

My body stiffened and my heartbeat raced like a team of horses at a gallop. I felt the quick thud of my pulse at my throat where he drank, in my temples, and to my shame and disgust, I felt it between my thighs. My breaths came in and out of my mouth so fast I thought I might faint.

He's going to kill you.

Aurora's voice rang out inside my head and dragged me out of the fog I slipped into from loss of blood. Carlos remained latched onto my neck grunting and moaning as he took pleasure from my slow death.

You hear me, girl? Do something before it's too late.

I heard her, but I didn't know what to do. Carlos was stronger than me on a good day. Now I was trapped under him and he was draining away my life. There wasn't much chance for me to escape.

Use the storm.

What did she mean? Use the storm? I closed my eyes and concentrated on the wind and rain beating against the house. Lightning split the sky open again and thunder vibrated the foundation beneath me. I suddenly understood what she meant. The floor shook again with a distant roar of thunder and I knew I had to absorb the power of the storm like the floor absorbed the vibrations of the thunder rolling across the valley. I had to focus on the lightning outside and try to ignore the agony of Carlos's teeth tearing into my flesh.

As the blood flowed out of my body and into his mouth, I pictured it coursing through my body. I needed the power of the storm to flow through me.

Silence everything else around you and draw the energy into yourself.

Aurora's words gave me courage. I took a deep breath and listened carefully to the storm raging outside. After the next rumble of thunder, I counted in my head like Moman had taught me, to figure out how many seconds there were between lightning strikes. She said the higher you could count, the further away the lightning was. I counted: one, two, three, four, five, six. Lightning struck outside. I counted again: one, two, three, four, five. Again, lightning flashed through the sky. The storm was getting closer. Moman had taught me about drawing in energy from the natural world to strengthen my own power. She said I had to use my imagination. If I wanted to draw down the rain, I could picture myself as parched earth—cracked, dry, and thirsty. If I wanted to harness the power of birds in flight, I could picture myself as a field of fresh sunflowers swaying in the breeze on a hot summer day; bright, inviting, and heavy with seeds. What I needed was the power of lightning to charge my magic, a burst of energy to cast off the monster stealing my life.

I counted once more: one, two, three, four. This time I was ready for the lightning. I pictured myself as a lightning rod on top of the house. A ramrod straight shaft of iron stabbing the night sky with shining metal appendages shooting out from my sides to grasp the lightning and draw it down into my body to let it concentrate at my core.

He would not have me. Not like this. Not ever.

As the lightning cut across the sky, I summoned the *loa* Sogbo and Bade, inviting them into my body with a prayer. When the *loa* mounted me my back arched off the floor and my skin became hot and feverish. I heard a voice, not my own, speaking the words: *It is I who am the gunner of god; when I roar, the earth trembles.*

Carlos stopped feeding long enough to stare at me like I'd gone insane. Blood, my blood, smeared his mouth and nose, and his eyes were completely black. I saw what was happening around me, but I moved like a sleepwalker, trapped in a dream.

"What did you say?" He asked, barely above a whisper.

Again, the voice issued from my mouth: *It is I who am the gunner of god; when I roar, the earth trembles.*

This time, when the words were spoken, my body became rigid and the power of the storm coursed through me. A voice inside my head, maybe it was Aurora's, but I'm not sure, told me to press my palms against Carlos's chest and release the energy building inside me.

A tingle at the base of my spine and at the top of my skull like icy fingers glided over my flesh, and as my mouth uttered the words again, a charge built up in my spine that raced along my arms and coursed through my fingers. When I released the power, Carlos flew back away from me and slammed against the wall. The impact shook the timbers and sawdust fell in tiny clouds from the ceiling. He sank to the floor and didn't move. Somehow, I was standing in the middle of the room, but I didn't remember getting up from the floor. My hair blew about my face from the wind rushing all around me. The frame of the house shook again with the vibrations of the storm outside and raging inside me.

Carlos righted himself and sat with his back against the wall.

His mouth hung open in disbelief, the blood on his face slowly drying into a reddish brown stain. His eyes were wide and he shifted into a crouch, like a cornered animal, ready to attack when threatened.

My mouth opened and the *loa* chuckled. Their mocking laughter made my body tremor. *Leave this place, demon. Your invitation has expired.* Again, they spoke through me.

"Jacqueline...?" Carlos stood from his crouch, his back still against the wall, his face a mixture of fear and confusion. His body was poised to fight. Like a predator surprised by its prey's ability to fight back, he edged closer to the door, never taking his eyes off me.

The spell was weakening. My grasp on the *loa* was slipping. I had to hold on a little longer. It took all my remaining strength to keep them tethered to my body. If he witnessed a moment of weakness, Carlos would attack again and Percy would find me dead.

"How did you...when did you learn how to do that?" Carlos took another step toward the door.

Be gone, demon. You are welcome no more.

Their power was fading, but they still spoke through me.

Carlos was in the doorframe. He grabbed his hat and coat from the floor without taking his eyes off me. The wide-brimmed hat still dripped water when he put it on his head. He was taking his time to get back out into the rain.

I wouldn't be able to hold on much longer. If he didn't go soon, I was going to collapse on the floor and be at his mercy. Again, I imagined myself as a lightning rod and drew in more power from the storm to recharge and managed to float myself a few inches above the floor. I had enough power to propel myself toward the door, which made him back up again so that he almost disappeared into the darkness. The night and the black wool of his traveling clothes framed his pale, bloodstained face. Raw rage and fear stared back at me.

"One day, you'll need me. Maybe not tomorrow or next week or even next year, but the day will come. When it does, I won't be there to help you." He spat his words at me.

Go!

The voice rumbled from deep inside my body. I think Aurora added her voice to the choir as well. With that final word and my last ounce of strength, he turned his back on Percy's house, my house, and vanished into the night. As soon as he was gone, the *loa* left my body, and I collapsed to the floor where I lay all night. Outside, the storm raged on.

Chapter 37

Aurora found me lying curled up on the floor in front of the hearth in my torn dress. The fire had died down to tiny orange and red embers and the charred skeletal remains of the logs. I had stared at the fire for hours trying to gather enough strength to lift myself off the cold hard floor and climb the stairs to my room. I couldn't. Not after expending so much energy fighting off Carlos. Not after he treated me like every other man I'd ever met in my whole miserable life. He said he loved me. He didn't know what love was. Love required trust. Love meant longing, and the willingness to ignore your basest desires in order to keep your pride intact. Love was more than passion and carnal knowledge. Love was shared secrets, and acts of kindness without expectations.

I'd fooled myself into thinking Carlos felt the same way I did about him and almost died because of it.

I remained motionless on the floor like a piece of chewed up meat, spat out and left to rot. Unlike most of his victims, I lived. The dead ones were lucky. Memories of his violent acts died with them.

"Girl, you still alive? You need to get up off that floor," Aurora said in a stern voice.

I didn't respond. Kept staring at the dying fire. Lost in my thoughts.

Some folks would be scared after encountering a monster like

Carlos. I was nauseous with disappointment. My head hurt from crying long after the tears had dried up. Black-and-blue marks in the shape of his fingers ringed my wrists, and even though I couldn't see them, I felt bruises forming between my thighs where he'd forced my legs apart. Lynch had always been careful when he helped himself to my flesh. He didn't want to leave behind any marks for Lottie to see. Jimmy didn't care about leaving signs of his filthy hands on my skin. That was his way of showing others that I belonged to him—off limits to everyone else. Did Carlos mark me for Percy to see? Would Percy think I'd given myself to Carlos willingly? I had no way to prove that I had fought him off. I wasn't untouched. My innocence had been stolen from me long ago. How can a girl prove she isn't a whore when every man who touches her tries to turn her into one?

"Go on and lie there if you want, I'm gonna stoke the fire and make tea." Aurora walked outside to fetch water and left me in front of the hearth.

Would he regret it? Mourn his actions while he slept his unnatural death-like sleep? My stomach tightened as I thought of him prying my legs apart and sinking his teeth into my neck. He knew about Lynch and Jimmy. I'd told him everything about me on the long nights we'd spent together running from New Orleans to Freedom. My secrets had given him power over me and he'd chosen to use that power to destroy me.

"How can I face Percy when he gets home?"

"I'll tell you how you're gonna face Percy," Aurora said. She placed a pail of water by the stove and added logs to the fire. "The first thing we're gonna do is wash that devil's stink off you. Once we get you clean, you need to eat and rest."

I still didn't move.

"As powerful as you were last night, there's no reason for you to ever fear or worry about what a man thinks of you. You summoned the storm and controlled the *loa* that rode you last night. I've never seen so much power coming out of a small girl like you before," she said.

She was proud of me. I shifted my eyes from the embers to meet Aurora's gaze. I didn't move another muscle.

"It's fine to feel the way you do, Jacqueline. You loved that man and he finally showed you his true face. I warned you. I was so happy when you sent him away and decided to live here with Percy. We aren't like other women, but that don't mean we don't deserve the love of a good man. That thing that hurt you last night isn't a man. He's a demon walking around in a dead man's body."

She added more wood to the fire and put the kettle on. When she turned back around I was sitting up.

"He...he almost killed me," I whispered. "I've never been so afraid."

"All you been through, that's hard to believe isn't it? The evilest thing about him is how he gained your trust. The devil won't appear to us as our greatest fear, he'll arrive in the guise of what we want the most."

"I stopped him." I said the words a little louder this time.

Aurora wrapped a shawl around my shoulders and kissed my forehead. Tears welled up in my eyes again. Comfort given without the expectation of something in return was a rare experience for me. Since leaving Moman, I hadn't felt that safe with anyone.

"Yes, you did," she said, and rubbed my arms and shoulders gently. Pins and needles tingled under her touch. My body was numb from lying on the floor all night.

"How many women has he done that to?"

"Too many for you to count or be worried about," she said.

"He wanted to kill me!" My voice caught in my throat. Tears

welled up, but I fought to keep them from falling. I'd wasted too many on him already.

"But he didn't. There's still fight left in you," she said.

I wanted to believe her, but I was so tired. Sadness folded over me like a heavy, wet blanket. The weight was unbearable. All I wanted to do was sleep, but I knew I wouldn't be able to shut my eyes without seeing Carlos's face leering down at me covered in my own blood. Nightmares were waiting for me behind my eyelids.

"I'm going to help you through this." Aurora slowly took the braids from my hair. "We aren't going to tell Percy. He doesn't need to know."

I agreed but had no idea how I would hide the fact that I was attacked. My body was covered in bruises, cuts, and bite marks. I would have trouble walking for at least a few days. Percy would be back before I could heal.

"How can I lie to him about what happened when I have these?" I showed her my throat where two large puncture wounds throbbed with pain under my jaw.

"You let me worry about that. I just need you to rest. Best thing for healing a body is sleep. And a little root work."

I stared at the growing fire Aurora had built and wondered ... if I could summon a storm, what else could I conjure to aid me in my spell work? Could I harness the power of fire and use it to protect myself and grow stronger? If it could be done, I was ready to learn how.

I slept all day. Aurora's tea kept the nightmares away and lulled me into a deep and restful sleep. She stayed by my side and worked on healing my body. We didn't have Carlos's blood to heal me quick, but I had grabbed a fistful of his hair in the struggle. Aurora used it to drain energy from Carlos to make me stronger. That kind of magic was dark, but necessary. She needed to work another protection spell to keep him from returning to Freedom. He'd try killing me again if he had the chance. No matter what lies he told himself about loving me, if I said no too many times, he'd slit my throat and ravage my corpse. He was worse than his enemy, Aleister Gale. Even though he wouldn't tell me the nature of their quarrel, I knew Carlos must have done something awful. Gale was driven by such an unbridled desire for revenge. I knew how much pleasure Carlos took from his victims' pain. I'd caught a glimpse of it in the Williams's house, but to experience that level of cruelty up close made me certain I'd never feel anything but disgust for him as long as I lived.

Chapter 38

Percy came back after five days. While he was gone I planted herbs and flowers in the garden, baked bread, fed chickens, milked the cow, sewed a new dress, and read three books. Anything to stay busy and keep my mind off Carlos. Each time I closed my eyes, he was lurking there, his face stained with my blood and a mixture of lust, rage, and fear. It was that fear I'd seen in his eyes before he ran from Percy's house that kept me from cowering in a corner waiting for him to return and finish killing me. He had been afraid of me when he left. That gave me hope that he might be afraid enough to stay away. Maybe Aurora was right. Maybe I was strong enough to keep myself safe from the monsters.

Dinner was waiting on the table when Percy came home late Friday evening. I greeted him at the door with a cup of hot coffee. Water heated on the stove for his bath after the meal. I knew he'd be tired and would want to clean up a bit before heading to bed. All day, I hurried to get ready for his arrival. I looked forward to seeing him and wanted everything to be perfect. I wore my new dress, and Aurora had plaited my hair that afternoon.

Making Percy happy was my number one priority. If I was ever going to be his wife, I knew my job was to keep the house clean, warm, and welcoming. He didn't need to know that Carlos had tried to rape and kill me. It would only anger him and make him go off and do something stupid. It was my burden to carry alone.

Carlos showed me exactly what I needed to see to help me make the right choice. I would stay with Percy.

Even though I was glad to see Percy, when I greeted him at the door the smile on my face was forced. The pain I felt was too intense, and I struggled to keep my mask from slipping off. His shoulders slumped with the burden of his bag and his hard work as he crossed the threshold into our home. I sat him down in a chair and took off his boots. His feet were swollen, and I had to tug hard to get the worn brown leather to come loose. He sighed and wriggled his toes before the fire as he sipped his coffee.

"Dinner smells wonderful, Jacqueline. And the house is so clean. You were busy while I was gone."

My chest swelled with pride at his compliments. There was so much I wanted to say, but I sat quietly at the table and waited for him to take a bite before I ate. I was happy to have him back home, safe and well. All week, I'd had nightmares about faceless white men hurting him. They dragged him out into a busy street and took turns beating him with their fists and kicking him while he lay face down on the ground. A crowd gathered to cheer the men on, and soon they called out for blood. They wouldn't be happy until another Negro died. I woke up sweating each night before they strung him up and left him to dance at the end of a rope. I couldn't get the images of leering white faces out of my mind.

"Can I get you any more to eat?" I asked.

"Couldn't eat another bite. It was delicious, but I'm too full."

"I'll get the washtub ready," I said, and stood to clear the table.

He placed a gentle hand on my arm. "Is everything all right, Jacqueline?"

I couldn't look him in the eye.

"Yes, I just want you to rest after your long week."

He glanced around the room and rubbed the fabric of my new

dress between his thumb and forefinger. "It looks like you had a long week, too."

"Don't worry about me, I rested when I wasn't busy."

"Tell me about your week," he said, and slipped a rough hand into mine.

I stared down at the chapped skin of his warm hand and took a deep breath. He wanted me to relax with him and enjoy this moment. I smiled and he squeezed my hand a little tighter.

"Not much to tell," I lied. "I planted herbs and flowers in the garden. I read three of your books. And I made this dress." I stroked the soft, cotton fabric at my shoulder, and thought of the torn, blood-stained dress I'd burned in the hearth.

"Sounds better than my week, but I earned a little extra money," he said as he reached into his breast pocket, then placed a pile of bills in the middle of the table. "That's ten dollars, which should cover any household expenses for the next few weeks. We'll save what I earn next week."

"Save for what?"

"Our wedding," he said, and stood up from the table.

He moved over to the stove where the water had begun to boil. He poured the water into the tin tub sitting a few feet from the fire. Steam rose from the tub as he added cooler water from a bucket I had brought in from the pump. He hung his jacket on the hook by the door and slid his suspenders off his shoulders to hang at his slim waist. His white shirt was stained with dirt and sweat. When he raised it over his head, he uncovered the muscular back and shoulders he'd earned from hard labor. He caught me staring at his beautiful body and smiled, pleased by my adoration.

"Will you join me in the tub?"

I wanted to go to him, but I was afraid. Carlos had rekindled my fear of men. I knew Percy wouldn't hurt me, but trusting anyone would be difficult after Carlos betrayed me.

"If you're uneasy, that's fine. We can wait until after we're married."

His words put me at rest and gave me an excuse to decline his offer. Cautiously, I wrapped my arms around him. What I felt for Percy was friendship, respect, and love. I knew there were stronger feelings in the world – rage, fear, hatred, despair – and I didn't want to feel those anymore.

I mended a hole in his pants while he soaked in the bath, and he told me about his week. He said a white girl had gone missing in Butcher's Falls, and people were getting angrier by the day. Soon, they'd need to punish someone.

"I saw that man you came to Freedom with last night. He was on his way into a tavern. He recognized me, but I couldn't remember meeting him. We talked for a bit, then he went about his business."

"What did he say?" I prayed Carlos hadn't mentioned coming to see me.

"Mostly, we talked about you. He asked how you were doing and if you needed anything."

"Did he say anything else?"

"He made small talk to be polite, but he seemed to be in a hurry. That may be because he was on his way to see a prostitute. He even offered to treat me, but I declined," he said.

Carlos could have killed Percy, but didn't. Maybe he was toying with him like a true predator. If Percy had accepted his invitation, he probably would've killed him in the brothel.

"Did he say if he'd be staying in Butcher's Falls long?"

"He said he'd be moving on at the end of the month. He seemed to think you were in good hands."

I suddenly felt like I couldn't breathe, as though a hand had tightened around my throat. I tried to swallow and felt tears rise up at the corners of my eyes. He'd told Percy he was leaving, but I didn't believe it. I knew his true feelings. He'd never stand by and watch me love another man. He'd kill us before he let that happen. The day after he attacked me, Aurora had put the protection spell back in place and doubled its strength. I prayed to the *loa* he would stay away.

"I invited him to visit us, but he said he doubted he would have time," Percy said.

"It's probably for the best," I said. My heart pounded in my throat.

"Do you miss him?"

"Not as much as I thought I would," I whispered, choking back tears.

"Do you love him?"

I didn't know how to answer him.

"Jacqueline, nothing would make me happier than your staying here with me. But, if you love him, I won't stand in your way. Maybe you should talk to him before he leaves, tell him how you feel."

What I had felt for Carlos Velasquez wasn't love, it was hunger. Now all I felt was shame and rage. Carlos was dangerous. Everything about him spoke to the darkness inside me. Percy made my light shine brighter. I knew where I belonged.

"If you go to him, I won't be angry," he said. "He cares about you. I heard it in his voice when he spoke your name."

"I belong here with you. This is my home."

Percy finally gave in to his exhaustion and headed to bed. I wasn't far behind. Pretending to be happy and whole for Percy had worn me out. I listened to his gentle snoring through the floorboards beneath my own bed in the attic and stared into the darkness waiting for the nightmares.

Chapter 39

I awoke in darkness. Someone was knocking on the front door. My heart pounded as I sat up quickly. I knew it wasn't Aurora, because she was sleeping downstairs. I couldn't bear to be alone in that house after Percy left for work Monday morning. I was terrified Carlos would come to finish me off.

"Stay here." Aurora's voice was gentle, yet commanding outside the attic door. A candle's flame created a crown of light around her stark white hair. She went downstairs to answer the door.

The second knock was more insistent.

"Hold on," she shouted.

I knew Carlos couldn't enter the house without an invitation. He'd worn out his welcome during his last visit. But I couldn't stop shaking. I listened for Aurora to open the front door.

"Who is it?" She didn't lift the latch.

The door muffled a man's voice. I couldn't make out the words.

"What do you want with her?" Aurora demanded.

I still couldn't hear what he was saying, but his voice was familiar. He sounded impatient, but not angry.

Aurora called to me. "It's Aleister Gale. Says he needs to speak to you right away."

I climbed out of bed and hurried downstairs. Aurora waited for me to make a move. I placed my index finger over my closed mouth and with the other hand, I pointed to the rifle above the hearth. I took a moment to gather myself while she fetched the gun. I couldn't show the *loup-garou* how afraid I was.

"What do you want?" My voice trembled.

"Is Velasquez with you?"

"No."

He was silent for a moment.

"Do you know where he is?" His voice was calm.

"Far away, I hope."

Aurora stood behind me pointing the rifle at the door.

"Look, Jacqueline, I'm sorry for all the trouble I've caused you. I didn't mean to mix you up in all of this. I need to find Velasquez. Can you help me?"

I wanted to believe he was sorry, but each time I'd put my trust in a man, I'd been betrayed. So far, the only man who hadn't done that was Percy. And he should have been home by now. I was worried sick.

"Please open the door and talk to me."

Gale wouldn't leave until he got what he came for. I opened the door a crack and peered out at him. He took off his hat and fidgeted with it until he saw my face. Aurora's healing spell had worked wonders, but all the crying and sleepless nights had left dark circles under my eyes. When Percy was home, I wore high-collared dresses, but my nightdress couldn't hide the black-and-blue finger marks that still circled my throat. The puncture wounds under my left ear were still tender even though they had turned greenish yellow. Soon, the bruises would fade, but the scars from Carlos's teeth would remain.

"What happened?" He was shaken by my injuries.

I opened the door wider to show him Aurora and the rifle. He acknowledged her and showed her both of his hands. He came inside to get a better look at me, but kept a polite distance while examining me. His eyes widened when he caught a glimpse of my neck. "Velasquez did this to you."

I didn't confirm or deny what Carlos had done. I didn't want to talk about it. I relived that night each time I closed my eyes. I was afraid to talk about Carlos. If he knew I was thinking about him, he might come back.

"I hope you aren't still protecting that monster," Gale said. "Not after...not after he tried to...." His voice trailed off and he placed his warm hand on my injured neck. It was a gesture of concern, and tenderness. I broke down crying and crumpled to the floor.

"Happy now?" Aurora set the rifle down and wrapped her arms around me tightly while she scolded Gale.

"I didn't...I wasn't.... Please tell me what I can do." His voice softened, and he knelt beside me.

"Find Percy and bring him home," I choked out between sobs.

"Percy?"

"He's the man who owns this house. He works in Butcher's Falls. Should have been home yesterday. Girls have gone missing in that town and they'll be looking for someone to blame," Aurora said.

"Velasquez," Gale spoke through clenched teeth.

"Maybe he's the one responsible, but the residents of Butcher's Falls haven't figured that out yet. When white girls get raped or end up dead, black men get blamed."

"Not if I can help it," Gale said.

"It takes a little over an hour to get there on horseback," Aurora said.

"How long on foot?"

"You can ride with Cyrus when he makes his morning run."

"I could transform and run the distance. I'll leave now."

"Transform into what?" Aurora reached for the rifle.

"He's a *loup-garou*, but he won't hurt us. He killed Lynch and Lottie."

"Monsters sure do love your company, don't they?" Aurora was still holding the rifle.

"I'm not here to hurt you. I want Velasquez."

"Lots of well-meaning people aren't always in control of their actions. The last monster my granddaughter trusted loved her so much he almost killed her. You seem like a nice man, and I appreciate you wanting to help her, but I'll kill you myself if you hurt her."

A heavy silence fell between us. Aurora was right. Monsters, even pure-hearted ones, make dangerous company. But I needed Gale's help if I was going to stop Carlos from killing me or anyone else. And, I needed to know that Percy was safe.

"I fought Carlos off. Think I scared him a bit. He won't stay scared forever. He'll keep coming after me until I either become like him or end up dead."

"You fought him off? How?" Gale asked.

"*Vodun*," Aurora said.

"You used magic?" He sounded skeptical.

"I drew down a storm and asked the gods to mount me."

"Mount you? Do you mean *possess*?"

"Yes, but once the spell ends, the *loa* leave your body."

"Isn't that dangerous?"

"It was worth the risk," I said.

"You've come quite a long way from salt circles and protection spells." Smiling, he offered me a hand up.

"Bring Percy home to me."

"This man, what is he to you?"

"He wants to marry me."

A wistful look replaced his smile. I didn't know what had happened between the *loup-garou* and the vampire, but I knew Carlos had hurt someone very precious to Gale.

"Do you have a picture of him? I need to know who I'm looking for."

I handed him a daguerreotype of Percy in his Sunday best.

"Cyrus can take you to Butcher's Falls in the morning, Mr. Gale. Sun won't be up for a few hours. You hungry?" Aurora stoked the fire and put hot water on to boil.

"I don't want to be any trouble," he said.

"Nonsense," Aurora said. "Sit down at the table. Jacqueline baked a pie yesterday. We'll all have something to eat before we get some sleep."

He obeyed and set his hat on the table. I stood by the fire trying to burn the chill out of me. Staring into the flames, I pictured Carlos's face covered in my blood. I shivered despite the heat of the coals.

Gale placed a hand on my shoulder. I recoiled from his touch. He removed his hand and shoved it into his pocket.

"I'm sorry. I should have known better. It's just...I wish I could offer comfort. Take away some of your pain." He stood next to me, but gave me space.

"Who's going to take away your pain?"

He sighed. "I wish I knew."

"I'm sorry. I didn't mean...."

"Don't apologize. You have every right not to trust me. I haven't told you anything about myself or why I'm after Velasquez."

"True, but you didn't do this to me." I touched the wounds on my neck.

"Velasquez wasn't the first monster to hurt you," he said.

He knew me better than I thought. We didn't need to say anything more on that subject.

"I'll find Percy and bring him home. And I promise, Velasquez will pay for what he's done to you."

We stared at the fire in silence until Aurora poured the coffee and sliced the pie. Gale and Aurora got acquainted while I sipped my drink. She had a lot of questions about his *condition*. I was too worried about Percy to listen closely. Worried that Carlos may have hurt him. Worried that Carlos would come back and try to ask for my forgiveness like some insane jilted lover.

"Try to get a little sleep, Mr. Gale," Aurora said.

He stretched and yawned.

"A few hours of shut-eye might do me some good. Thanks for the pie, it was delicious."

I went upstairs and found an extra blanket in the cedar chest at the foot of Percy's bed. The smell of the wood had seeped into the wool, and the earthy scents calmed my nerves a little. I pressed the fabric to my face and breathed deeply. I was reminded of how important it was to take pleasure in the little details of living. A little more than a week ago, I'd almost lost my life. Tonight, I'd gained an ally. An ally who recognized my pain, respected it, and wanted to help carry the burden if he could. Could I trust Aleister Gale? Only time would tell.

"Sorry I can't offer you a bed, Michié Gale," I said.

"Please, call me Aleister. I'll be fine by the fire." He took off his coat and folded it. He settled down next to the hearth like a man who is used to making do and tucked the coat under his head after wrapping himself in the cedar-scented blanket.

Aurora made sure the door was locked and headed back upstairs to sleep. I followed in her footsteps.

"Pleasant dreams, Jacqueline."
"Good night, Aleister."

Chapter 40

When they brought me Percy's body, his head was all wrong. The delicate skin of his beautiful brown face was ruined by purple bruises and had turned an ashen gray. His eyes were swollen shut and most of his teeth were missing. I stared at him for an hour, maybe two. His hands were black as coal where they'd been tied. The skin of his palms and knuckles was covered in scrapes and cuts.

He'd fought back when they came for him. A dark ring scarred his neck where the rope had silenced his screams and choked out his life. At least they hadn't burned him or cut off his privates. He was badly beaten, but still whole.

Aleister and Cyrus paced silently outside in the yard. Aurora sat smoking her pipe beside the fire. They waited for me to tell them what to do next.

I cleaned the dried blood from Percy's face with warm water and tears. My sobs were so heavy at times I thought I might stop breathing. *Wanted* to stop breathing. I never got the chance to love him the way I wanted to. He was so kind, respectful, and caring. I guess I wasn't meant to be happy. How could I be? Born a slave, cursed with intelligence, and yet foolish enough to believe in love. I'd suffered the brutality and humiliation of rape with a smile on my face just to stay alive. How many times could one heart break?

Happiness was for other people. People who lived in books. No one I'd ever met was truly happy. Not in this miserable world. I was out of lies to tell myself. I didn't care about surviving anymore, because I had nothing to live for. The cruelty of love is that even after the person you care for treats you like garbage or up and dies on you, the feelings you have for them don't just stop or go away. The feelings stay the same —or get stronger until they choke you.

Carlos almost killed me because he couldn't stand the thought of losing me to another man. He'd rather see me dead and rotting in the ground than belonging to someone else. Seeing Percy's broken body lying on the kitchen table made me wish Carlos had finished me off. Only death would take the pain away. I looked upon death sweetly. But before I welcomed death to my door, I would see Percy's murderers punished.

Aurora got up from her rocking chair to stand beside me. She put her arms around me and held me until the tears finally stopped falling.

"I'm going to kill them." My voice rasped out of my throat, dry as a bone.

"You're gonna need a lot of strength."

"I'll find it."

Aleister poked his head round the door but stayed on the other side of the threshold.

"What can I do?" His voice was steady and strong.

"We're gonna need the rope they used to hang him, and the names of the bastards who did it," Aurora said.

"And I'll need you to take me to Butcher's Falls," I said.

Aleister stared at me in silence for a moment and then nodded his head once.

"Velasquez is as much to blame for this man's death as the men who killed him."

"What did that demon have to do with Percy's lynching?" Aurora asked.

"He killed the women in Butcher's Falls. Percy died for the vampire's sins."

"Where's your proof, *loup-garou*?"

Aleister stepped inside and loomed over Aurora. "I'll take Jacqueline to see for herself."

I knew what Carlos was capable of. I'd seen him kill and take pleasure in it. Saw the lust in his eyes when he tried to kill me. The thought of his being aroused while draining my blood made me sick. "He's a monster, but he isn't stupid," my voice came out harsher than I expected.

"What's that supposed to mean?"

I took a step closer to Aleister and could feel his breath on my face.

"I mean he likes to kill, but he doesn't leave bodies lying around like bread crumbs leading to his door."

He pitied me.

"Velasquez almost snuffed out your life, and still you protect him. Do you love him?"

"What's in my heart doesn't matter. My gut tells me he probably did kill those girls, but he's too smart to get caught."

"You're too smart to be fooled by that villain," he said.

"I know Carlos killed those girls. I'm saying there's a reason he was careless. He wanted Percy to take the blame. He wanted to punish me for choosing Percy instead of him."

Aleister clenched his fists and suppressed a growl that rumbled deep in his chest.

"How could you ever love a creature like that?"

I was tired of being judged by men who had enough of their own sins to pave their way to Hell.

"Should I find comfort in your arms instead?"

His unspoken answer hung heavily in the air between us.

"Cyrus," I called to the open door.

"Yes, Miss Jacqueline?"

"We're going back to Butcher's Falls. Have the horses ready in twenty minutes."

"Yes, Miss."

I turned to Aurora and handed Aleister some paper and writing charcoal. "Tell him everything we'll need for conjuring. When the time comes, I'll need you here, guiding me like you did before."

"What you gonna do?"

"Change my clothes and gather what I need for the ride."

Aurora listed the items for Aleister to write down.

The town was unusually quiet for a Saturday night. When Cyrus pulled the wagon into the square, there wasn't a soul in sight. A leftover chill from winter lingered in the air, but the days were getting longer, and the sun hadn't quite faded behind the horizon. There should have been people out on the street going to supper or church or visiting the shops that stayed open into the evening.

In the center of town, not far from the post office, general store, police station, and courthouse, grew an enormous apple tree with big, burly limbs and ancient bark. I stared up into its branches and could see the tortured souls of the men and women who'd died hanging from its strong boughs. Percy's face floated among the death masks. Part of the rope the townsfolk had used to murder him was still clinging to a branch.

"Cut that down," I said to Aleister. "We'll need that."

Taking advantage of the empty streets, he used his unnatural strength and quickly shimmied up the trunk of the old tree to grab the frayed rope, returning to my side in a matter of seconds.

"Nice tree, but strange fruit they got hanging from it in these parts," he said, handing me the rope.

"Can you see them?"

"No, but I can smell their fear," he said.

We both grasped onto the frayed rope, and an electrical shock passed between us. Magic flowed freely, and the bolt of energy raced up my arm and jerked my elbow so hard it felt like I'd slammed it against something solid. I winced and rubbed my arm.

Aleister shook his hand as if trying to release the energy from it.

"You felt that, too?" I asked.

"What was that?"

"No time to worry about that now. We need to gather the other ingredients for the spell and find Carlos. Percy told me he'd seen him in town, staying at a hotel."

"A brothel seems more likely."

Aleister asked for directions from the only person out on the streets, a young man of eighteen or nineteen. I tried to remain unseen, and allowed him to take charge. Irishmen weren't too much higher on the social ladder than me, but his features allowed him to masquerade as white more than mine did. I kept quiet and stayed a few feet behind him as we walked through the streets of Butcher's Falls. Subservience, while I despised it, came naturally to me and served our purposes well. No one gave me a second look as I kept my eyes to the ground and my mouth shut.

"The brothel should be on the next street over," Aleister whispered to me over his shoulder.

"I hope he hasn't sensed us coming."

"I won't let him hurt you."

I wanted to believe Aleister could keep me safe, but now that Carlos had tasted me, nothing would stop him from doing it again.

A bribe got us access to Carlos's room. The bartender seemed happy to help Aleister, especially when he explained he had a score to settle. The Madame made him promise not to wreck the room or he'd be responsible for the damages.

"Two of my best girls have gone missing since that bastard took up residence here. I don't have any proof, but I'd bet he's responsible," the Madame explained.

"Do you think the missing harlots have anything to do with the other deaths in town?" Aleister asked.

"Everybody's up in arms about the murders, because they were good Christian girls. Nobody cares about a few missing whores. They strung up that nigger the other night, but I don't think we'll see the last of these killings."

Nellie Johnson, the dead black girl they'd buried on the outskirts of Freedom with her unborn child, came to mind. Nobody cared about her either, but her death had nothing to do with the girls who turned up dead in Butcher's Falls. Carlos had raped and murdered those white girls. He would pay for Percy's pain and suffering.

So would the monsters who strung him up in that tree.

Chapter 41

I smelled Carlos on the dead woman's body. He'd left the corpse strewn across the bed, face down, naked, and drained of blood. Mixed among the musky odors of decay and sex in his rented room, were the salty tang of blood and the scent of funeral flowers I always associated with Carlos's skin. I cupped my hand over my nose and mouth to filter out the smell of death. I swayed, but Aleister's strong hands steadied me.

"Maybe you should wait outside."

"I'll be fine."

His hands lingered on my shoulders. He reassured me I wasn't alone. I crossed the room, trying not to look at the dead woman, and opened the dingy window. I gulped down the fresh air and opened the top two buttons at my collar. Thankfully, my station in life didn't require me to wear a corset.

"I apologize for the untidy state of my room, but I was not expecting company." Carlos pushed past Aleister and entered the room.

"You're getting careless," I said with a slight tremor in my voice, and gestured towards the corpse.

"Or more brazen," Aleister added.

"I was out of bourbon." Carlos held up the unopened bottle of amber liquid. "May I offer you and your cur a drink?"

"I'm not here for your hospitality."

He crossed the room and set the bottle on the windowsill. He loomed over me, but left a sliver of light between us in the dimly lit room.

"Have you come to apologize?"

I felt Aleister's hackles rise as a ripple of his rage vibrated the air around me. I shot a warning glance at him and he gritted his teeth in response. I swallowed my revulsion and forced myself to make eye contact with Carlos.

"Apologize? For what?"

He touched my cheek with his long, pale, icy fingers. I held in a scream as an image of his face covered in my blood flashed through my mind.

"For so rudely interrupting our love-making, you fickle little temptress."

Aleister crossed the room in two strides and slapped Carlos's hand away from me. I grabbed his arm and stopped him from striking Carlos again. He turned on me.

"Are you going to allow him to speak to you like that?"

"We don't have time for an argument, Aleister."

He glared at me and then at Carlos, and raised his hands above his head in defeat.

"Why have you come if not to apologize? Are you seeking my blessing to bed Gale?"

Aleister reconsidered his truce and flew at Carlos, punching him in the face before I could intervene. The blow drew blood. Carlos licked the blood from his lips and laughed as Aleister cupped his fist in the palm of his other hand. He wasn't used to feeling pain when he struck someone.

"Not as tough as you think you are, eh, Gale?"

"We'll see how tough I am after I transform. I'll tear your head off."

"Enough!" I stopped their bickering with one word and a little well-placed energy. They slid across the floor until they were on opposite sides of the room. Both looked surprised by the strength of my will to physically separate them without the use of brute force. Carlos stared at me with just a hint of the fear that lingered from the last time we'd met. And yet, he provoked me.

"I can't give you my blessing if you're already bedding Gale. What's that old saying about putting the cart before the horse?"

"Percy is dead."

Carlos's face was blank.

"How?"

"A lynch mob that was meant for you," Aleister shouted.

I turned my back on them to hide my tears.

"What do you expect me to do?" Carlos tried to get close to me, but Aleister stopped him.

"I expect you to help us find and kill the bastards who killed Percy."

"If I help you, will Gale call off his bounty hunters?"

"That's the best part, Velasquez. You'll be the bait to lure them to Freedom. We're going to kill them all in one night," Aleister said.

"How can I trust you not to double-cross and kill me too?"

"You owe me," I said, and walked into the hallway.

"Your whore isn't getting any fresher," Aleister said, and slammed the door behind him.

Chapter 42

"Whatever happens tonight, you have to kill the vampire."

Aurora got straight to the point, but her words weren't designed to hurt me. I needed to be strong and accept the truth. Carlos had to die. He killed for pleasure, not just for sustenance. It didn't matter that he deluded himself into believing that his victims achieved new heights of passion while he violated them. Facts are facts. Carlos Velasquez was a rapist and a murderer. Just because he said he loved me, didn't mean I wouldn't end up dead in his arms. And he was the reason Percy was dead.

"How will I kill him?" I hated the tremble in my voice.

"I have a few ideas about that," Aleister chimed in, a little too quickly.

On the table, he placed a wooden case about the size of a shoeshine box. An iron clasp held it shut. I stepped closer to get a better look. My hand hovered over the latch.

He gestured toward the box. "Open it."

Old scars were ingrained into the wood. The clasp showed similar signs of wear. Eager to see inside, I flipped the metal latch and opened the box. The interior was lined with red velvet. Tiered compartments of various shapes and sizes contained a collection of unusual objects. A small book bound in black leather with faded letters tooled into the hide occupied the first compartment. It reminded me of the bibles at Aurora's church. There were small glass bottles with faded labels: dead man's blood, silver nitrate, and holy water. Other compartments contained dried garlic bulbs, rosaries with silver crosses, sharpened wooden stakes with flecks of dried blood on the points, and a heavy wooden mallet.

I touched each item with wonder. "What is all this?"

"My vampire hunting tools," Aleister said.

"You hunt other vampires besides Carlos? How long have you been hunting them?"

He took a step closer, placed a hand on my shoulder, turned me to face him and held my gaze. His eyes glittered with unshed tears. He didn't speak about his past, but I knew it was as dark as mine. Unlike Carlos, Aleister wanted to fight his monstrous nature. I wanted to believe that each death on Aleister Gale's conscience served a purpose. Wanted to believe he was trying to do some good in the world. Carlos killed for pleasure and every one of his victims had suffered.

"I've been killing vampires ever since Velasquez killed my beloved Delores. I didn't even know they existed before that. I'd heard stories, but I never believed any of them."

Aurora spoke up. "Disbelief costs lives."

"Aye, right you are," he said, with sadness in his voice.

"Tell me what happened."

He hesitated for a second and nodded with his eyes closed.

"Should I bring out the whiskey?" Aurora asked.

He laughed. "If you're offering, I'm drinking."

She grabbed the bottle and I found three clean tin cups. Aurora poured generously and we all had a drink before he began his tale.

"My Delores and I were to be wed the second week of June. Our families were happily planning the big day. But, the fields still needed mown, animals needed fed, and stone walls don't repair themselves. I had plenty to do besides getting ready for my wedding."

He took another drink and Aurora refilled his cup.

"A few local lasses had gone missing, but no one was worried until their bodies were found floating in the Grand Canal. They didn't turn up all at once. Velasquez must have kept them hidden for a few weeks. He may have grabbed a few at a time to stock his larder."

Carlos probably gained as much pleasure from taunting the townspeople by letting them find the bodies of his victims, as he did killing them. It was a game to him.

"Mind you, we have a fair number of suicides in Dublin, but all the bodies pulled from the canal were drained of blood and missing large sections of their throats. At first, rumors spread about werewolves and people pointed fingers at their neighbors. Rather than looking for strangers among us, we wanted to blame each other."

"Mustn't be any black men in Dublin if they blamed werewolves first," Aurora said.

Despite the gravity of his tale, Gale laughed.

"Were you...had you become a *loup-garou* at this point?"

"No." He remained silent for several heartbeats. "That happened much later."

He didn't offer any further details.

"What happened to Delores?"

He wanted to tell me, but had trouble finding the words. Even if I managed to kill Carlos, Aleister's pain would never go away. I touched his forearm to let him know I was listening.

"Velasquez didn't grab her and hide her away like the rest of the girls. He toyed with her in plain sight for several weeks. By the time I found out what he was, it was too late."

He paused again and drank from his cup.

"While everyone busied themselves hunting werewolves, Velasquez used the chaos to his advantage. Delores was a beautiful girl, kind and generous, and maybe a bit too trusting of strangers. She believed his lies."

"It's easy to fall under his spell," I said, barely above a whisper.

Aurora cleared her throat. "Almost dark."

Carlos would awaken soon, and an angry mob of faceless cowards would come to burn down Freedom.

"We're running out of time," Aleister said. "You need to decide how you're going to kill him. I have proven methods and I'm willing to be at your side, but I don't think he'd allow that to happen. He's too smart for that."

"I know a way," Aurora spoke up. "Stronger than the spell you used to chase him away. This time, you're gonna steal his power."

"His power?" I asked.

"Whatever keeps him alive. It can't be that much different from the energy floating all around us. If you can pull energy from a storm, you can do the same to a vampire and steal his essence."

"You mean his soul?" Aleister was intrigued.

"No offense, Mr. Gale, but I'm not sure creatures like you and he have souls. What he does have is eternal life. Dark forces allow that dead man to walk, so we need to conjure up some dark magic of our own and use it against him."

Even though I was terrified, I would face Carlos. I wished Aleister could be by my side, but he was right. Carlos would never allow the two of us to trap him. But his arrogance would enable me to get close enough to kill him.

"Do you have everything we need?" Gale asked.

"The only thing we need is for you to get those bastards who killed Percy to come to Freedom," I said.

"Aye, it won't be hard to do. Jimmy and the Ogden brothers

will have them riled up already, all I have to do is show them the way here."

"Did you convince the vampire to come?" Aurora asked.

"He'll come," I said.

He'd come because he wasn't finished with me. I'd told him he owed me, and he believed it. But he thought I owed him my heart, or maybe my life. Unlike Jimmy and Lynch who only wanted my body, Carlos wanted every part of me. He wanted me to belong to him, body and soul.

"Good. I'll guide you like I did before, but you'll need to call down the *loa*."

"*Loa*?" Aleister looked to us for answers.

"The African gods we call upon to help with our conjuring," Aurora explained.

"Will Jacqueline be safe? I got too close to the darkness and it changed me forever."

"You're a good man, Mr. Gale," Aurora said. "You just have a curse upon you."

"I wish it were that simple," he said.

The sun sank deeper toward the horizon.

Aurora took charge. "Mr. Gale, take one of Cyrus's horses and warn the neighbors about the mob. Tell them to get their guns, but stay inside. I don't want the citizens of Freedom getting hurt while we settle a score."

Aleister paused before heading out the door. He fumbled with his hat, then turned around and strode quickly across the floor until he was facing me.

"If you don't kill him now, you'll regret it the rest of your life."

"You sound like you speak from experience," Aurora said.

"It's always hard to kill someone you love, no matter how monstrous they become."

Did he mean Delores? Killing her outright wouldn't have been cruel enough by Carlos's standards. She was special to him, like me. Carlos would have turned her.

"You didn't find Delores dead, did you?" The words tasted like ash in my mouth.

"No."

My heart broke for Aleister, because I understood what he had suffered through.

"She was the first vampire you killed," I said.

"Aye, a day doesn't go by without Delores haunting my dreams." His voice caught in his throat and he choked down a sob.

"I can't bring Delores or Percy back, but Carlos will pay for what he's done to both of us."

Aleister gently kissed my forehead. I tensed, startled by this unexpected show of affection.

"Call my name when you're ready," he said, and placed his finger on his temple.

Time was not on our side. Carlos and the mob would be there soon. Aleister reassured me that even if he wasn't by my side, he would be with me that night. His kindness gave me a reason to want to see the dawn.

When he was gone, Aurora and I got to work.

Aurora kept chickens for eggs, meat, and magic. Like Moman always said, if a spell is gonna come out right, some chickens have to die. Blood always made magic stronger. It was a fact. Each morning, I gathered eggs for Aurora, just like I'd done on the plantation. We ate eggs almost every day for breakfast, or sometimes she'd hard-boil them for our lunch. We counted on the chickens to lay eggs, and we treated them well. Aurora taught me the song she sang to them, an old song she'd learned as a girl in Africa. The sounds were similar to the clucks the chickens made, so it was like speaking to them in their own language. They were fat, happy birds, and they yielded a lot of eggs. Those hens laid so many eggs we could sell some to our neighbors too. A nickel for 6, and a dime a dozen. Sometimes when a chicken got too old to lay eggs, we'd eat it. But not before we used its blood for conjuring. The blood would spoil overnight if you didn't use it right away. If you wanted a spell to work, you needed fresh blood.

Chapter 43

Blood covered every inch of Carlos, but I wasn't sure how much of it was his. His injuries were minor compared to those of the men who'd been hunting us. Their shattered limbs and battered bodies littered the grass outside.

"Gale set us up," he shouted, and wiped gore from his face. Blood lust blackened his eyes. A gluttonous demon stared back at me.

Aleister and Jimmy led what was left of the mob—slave catchers, bounty hunters, and the cowards who'd lynched Percy— toward the barn where we hid. I trusted Aleister, but the sight of thirty men in white hoods, with black holes where their eyes should be, terrified me. Could he keep them under control long enough for me to finish my conjuring? Nervous excitement brewed inside me like a storm.

Carlos Velasquez would pay for his crimes. I would steal his power to destroy the men coming to kill us. Until then, if Carlos wanted to kill more men, I wouldn't stop him.

"Aleister is on our side," I insisted.

Carlos grasped my shoulders and forced me to look at him. "Have you fallen for his do-gooder charm? Such a fickle girl you are, Jacqueline. There is no telling where your loyalties lie."

I didn't fully understand my feelings for Aleister Gale, but I knew we wanted the same thing—to see Carlos Velasquez dead.

"You spurned me for Percy, Percy is barely cold and, in the ground, and now you are snuggling up with that Irish dog."

"Shut your mouth!"

His look of surprise strengthened my confidence.

"How long are you going to keep telling yourself this lie that lives between us?" I took a step closer to him. He stood his ground.

"Which lie are you referring to?"

I laughed.

"The poisonous lie you've been trying to feed me since we first met—that we're meant to be together. The lie you use to justify the torment you've put me through," I said.

"The same lie you told my Delores before you murdered her on our wedding day." Aleister stepped inside the barn with a torch in his hand, ready to set fire to Carlos.

"Aleister, don't," I commanded.

"I told you he betrayed us," Carlos spat.

"Not us," I said.

Carlos ran at us, prepared to attack. I grabbed Aleister's hand and channeled the spark of magic that surged between us. Carlos flew into the air and slammed against a beam in the middle of the barn. My magic held him in place.

"Enough," I screamed. "Is Aurora ready?"

"Yes," Aleister said.

I opened the small bundle he handed me. Inside was salt to cast a circle, a single candle, and matches to light it when I called down the *loa*.

"You'll need this, too," he said, handing me a wooden stake.

"I expected Gale to betray me," Carlos yelled, "but not you, Jacqueline."

"You tried to rape and kill me!" Angry tears fell down my cheeks.

"I love you, but you refused to show me affection in return."

"Liar!"

"I do love you," he whispered. He fought to free himself from the beam, but my magic was too strong.

"Stop saying that!" His words sent me into a rage.

"But it is true. I do love you. All the others have been nothing more than entertainment or food. *You* are different," Carlos pleaded.

His lies taunted me, but helped me focus on the task at hand. I tightened my grip on the wooden stake and took a step toward the vampire. My legs were shaking, but my resolve was strong.

A gunshot split the silence outside the barn. The mob was done waiting.

"What's taking so long, Gale?" Jimmy's voice frightened me more than the gunshot.

We needed more time.

Aleister called to the men outside. "They aren't in here, they must have escaped out the back."

"We came for a lynching, Gale. If we don't kill someone soon, these men will get bored. Plenty of niggers around here to keep us entertained, though," Jimmy said.

Sickening male laughter rose up outside like a chorus of demons.

No way in Hell I was going to let Jimmy, the Ogden Brothers, or anyone else outside that barn hurt the people of Freedom. The men and women of that town worked hard and fought for the right to live their lives by their own rules. I would not allow a bunch of cowards to destroy what they'd built.

"We got an eye-for-eye situation out here, Gale. Too many dead white men and not enough dead niggers. I don't like that arithmetic," Jimmy said.

I cast a wide circle with salt, placed the candle at its center, and lit it. I knelt inside the circle and rested my backside on the heels of my feet.

"How much time do you need?" Aleister asked.

"A few minutes. Once I connect with Aurora it won't take long for the *loa* to mount me."

"How long do you think it will take *me* to mount you once Gale walks out of the barn?" Carlos asked. "Do you expect me to just wait for you to kill me?" He fought against his invisible restraints.

"You won't get inside that circle to harm her," Aleister said. He doused his torch in a watering trough and undressed.

I focused my attention on the candle flame and called to Aurora with my mind.

It's about time. I thought you'd changed your mind.

I ignored her jab and prepared to call upon Baron Samedi, the spirit of death and resurrection.

Did your mother teach you the banda dance?

"Yes," I answered out loud.

I stood inside the salt ring and swayed my hips in inviting circles—a dance to entice the god of the afterlife and erotic energy.

"Feel free to follow Gale's example and take your clothes off," Carlos said, licking dried blood from his lips. "If you will not let me touch you, at least I can watch."

Aleister was captivated by my movements, but snapped back to reality when Jimmy's voice got louder and closer to the barn.

Jimmy spoke above the chorus of angry voices. "These men came seeking justice, now they're looking for revenge."

Aleister dropped to all fours and a ripple of energy bounced off the circle protecting me. A deep growl rumbled up from his gut, and his body changed. Thick, dark hair sprouted from his skin. The transformation mesmerized me. I wasn't sure if all *loup-garou* had the power to will themselves into wolves, but Aleister had mastered control over his shape-shifting. Familiar golden eyes stared back at me before he turned and disappeared into the darkness outside. Shots were fired, but I was sure none of the men had thought to bring silver bullets.

Focus! Aurora shouted inside my head and her voice jarred me back to the task at hand, calling down Baron Samedi. Once the spirit rode me I would control the souls of the undead. Carlos had died at the hands of a vampire four centuries ago. Dark magic kept him alive.

Magic that would soon be mine to wield.

I danced and Aurora chanted inside my head. My eyes were closed, and I saw the ritual she performed in her kitchen. We'd created an altar that afternoon with some of Baron Samedi's favorite foods—salt fish, hot peppers, and roasted corn. Bananas were hard to come by in Freedom, but she had a black chicken from her own coop to offer up, and a little tobacco.

Caught up in the spirit, my dance became more suggestive. I heard drums like the slaves played down in the bayou at Moman's secret meetings.

Baron Samedi mounted me. The base of my neck tingled as if a lover had planted a kiss between my shoulder blades, and the spirit slid inside me like a hand into a soft leather glove. Aurora helped me guide Baron Samedi, and together we worked our wills to subdue Carlos.

"Come to me, vampire," a deep, seductive, male voice poured from my lips.

Rage and lust mingled on Carlos's face. His cravings were minimal compared to the hunger raging inside Baron Samedi, inside me.

"When I get my hands on you," Carlos taunted, "the carnage you witnessed in the Williams's bedroom will seem like a romantic interlude."

A deep, booming laugh shook my shoulders. "If you're looking for romance, vampire, speak to Erzulie, not me."

Using the *loa's* power, I lifted Carlos into the air and levitated him before me.

"I sense great anger in this child, you must have done her a great injustice," Baron Samedi spoke through me.

"All I ever wanted was to give her pleasure, but she kept resisting me." Carlos acted like a jilted lover.

"She made a sacrifice, performed the rituals, I do her bidding. Two conjurers, powerful daughters of Africa, mean to end your life tonight."

Carlos could not move. Panic and rage coursed through him.

The spirit looked around the barn. Through my eyes he took in his surroundings. He made note of the ring of salt and the objects inside the circle. The wooden stake I clutched in my hand. He showed it to Carlos.

"Funny how something so simple can strike fear into a creature like you," the spirit said.

"Jacqueline," Carlos begged. "Please stop. Gale is using you to exact his revenge."

Baron Samedi filled the space with his deep, booming laughter. "How long have you been a monster?"

"Four-hundred years."

"And how many people have you killed in that time? Can you remember them all?"

"I did not ask to be like this," Carlos cried out.

"Maybe not, but to cheat Death that long, you must have been cut out for this kind of...existence. It suits you."

"I love this woman, but she refuses to love me back," Carlos screamed.

"I think you confuse love with lust, vampire. It's a common mistake. None of that matters now. She conjured me to end your unnatural life."

I ignored Carlos's pleas for mercy and continued to work on him with my mind. Unable to step outside the salt circle, I slammed him back against the post in the center of the barn and ripped open his bloodstained shirt. With Baron Samedi's help, I plunged the wooden stake like a dart into Carlos's chest. The stake didn't penetrate his breastbone. Baron Samedi was hungry, but he wanted to take his time and savor the death.

"Please, Jacqueline. I know you have feelings for me." Carlos's face was stained with tears of blood.

He was right; I did have feelings for him—anger, disappointment, and shame. I willed my energy forward and pushed the stake deeper into his breastbone. It cracked under the pressure. He screamed as the sharpened end of the wood pierced his heart.

Aleister entered the barn naked and covered in viscera. He stumbled, exhausted and injured, toward the salt ring. The men fought back before losing their lives, one-by-one.

"Welcome, shape shifter," Baron Samedi greeted him. "Your enemy is about to meet his end. Any last words for him?"

The wooden mallet lay on the floor next to Aleister's discarded clothes. He grabbed it in a blind rage and ran at Carlos. When it connected with the dull end of the stake, it split Carlos's heart in two. Blood gurgled out of the monster's mouth and spilled down the front of his chest.

"I'll see you in Hell," Aleister spat.

Baron Samedi didn't waste a moment. Carlos clung to this

world by a thread. The *loa* of death summoned the vampire's soul from the ether. A ball of green energy appeared and danced before my face. Baron Samedi forced open my mouth and made me swallow it whole. It fluttered like moths in my stomach.

Once Carlos's soul was safely inside me, Baron Samedi drained the dark energy from the vampire's body into mine.

Blood leaked from every pore on Carlos's body and I choked it down. Baron Samedi feasted on the blood and black magic like the vampire had feasted on so many others. Aleister stood slack-jawed and watched Carlos shrivel up and collapse upon himself, until nothing remained but a dried out husk, no bigger than a newborn baby.

"Are you still with me, shape shifter?"

Still dazed, Aleister turned to face Baron Samedi and me.

"When I release this child I ride, you must keep her safe. The vampire's soul and dark magic are trapped inside her. She will be tempted by the darkness. Promise me you will watch her."

"Why did you trap his soul inside her?"

"In a time of great need, his knowledge will prove useful to her. With the right root work, she can put him back inside that husk."

"She wanted him dead, to send his blackened soul to Hell!"

"It is not for you to decide what happens to the vampire. She will know what to do when the time comes."

Aleister listened, but did not respond right away.

"Will she...will his darkness change her?"

"You care for her a great deal, shape shifter. Good. She needs all the love, strength, and understanding you can provide."

"Can he still hurt her?"

"She is strong, she will be able to fight his influence."

"Influence?"

"I must depart and allow this child to rest."

Aleister stepped closer to the salt circle. "What am I supposed to do?"

"You accused the vampire of not knowing how to love her. If you consider yourself worthy of her love, you must do everything in your power to keep her safe."

"I...I will," Aleister said.

"This child has power beyond anything I've seen. I will be watching to make sure no harm comes to her. Am I clear, shape shifter?"

"I'll protect her life as if it were my own."

Chapter 44

The large, brown alligator valise was lighter than it appeared. I could have carried it myself, but Aleister insisted on being a gentleman. Or, maybe he didn't trust me with the contents. Carlos's desiccated remains were protected by complicated spells. He wouldn't be harming anyone any time soon. The husk inside the case would take several days to revive once all of the preparations were made. Careful planning and patience would be needed to resurrect him. After that, I had no idea how long it would take for a vampire to regain its strength. I didn't want to find out unless it was absolutely necessary.

"Are you sure you want to keep...it?"

Aleister wanted to throw the case, contents and all, onto a bonfire. He couldn't understand why I needed it. The night before, he'd begged me to destroy it and leave our past behind us. He wanted a clean slate. Needed one. As far as he was concerned, his enemy was dead and should stay that way.

"I'm sure."

I thought about burning Carlos's remains but remembered something Moman had taught me. There were things far worse than death, like eternal hunger, enslavement, or longing for something unknown. If Carlos remained bound to me, he could never truly rest. He would suffer the same torments and cravings, but he wouldn't be able to satisfy his thirst—a fitting punishment for someone who'd indulged in the pleasure of hurting others. Besides, I didn't want the dark magic inside me forever. Knowing I needed somewhere to put it guaranteed the vampire's corpse would stay in my possession until I decided to make use of it. I knew the risks of keeping his dark soul imprisoned inside my body, and I didn't care. My instincts told me that I would need Carlos Velasquez someday.

I knew where Carlos was, but the same couldn't be said for Jimmy. After Baron Samedi released me and I had a chance to rest, Aleister, Aurora and I began burning the bodies scattered all over Freedom, with the help of the townspeople. There could be no evidence of what happened there. We searched for half a day and could find no sign of Jimmy among the dead. Aleister didn't want to talk about the possibility that he had survived, but only because I knew he feared the worst.

Aleister offered me his hand and helped me onto the train. We were headed northeast to New York City. We could stay with his cousin in Five Points until we earned enough money to buy passage on a ship across the ocean. Aleister made his ancestral home sound like a mystical place. I caught glimpses of it in his thoughts. Now that Carlos was dead, or at least no longer a threat, Aleister could move forward with his life.

"You'll love Dublin, Jacqueline."

He settled next to me on the padded bench in the Negroes-only section of the train. The conductor had given him a hard time about not sitting with the other white passengers. Aleister had threatened the man's life using some very descriptive and colorful terms. Their argument created some unwanted attention for us, but it was worth it to be able to sit together. The more time I spent with Aleister Gale, the more I enjoyed his company. Was it possible to find my happily ever after with *Le Grand Méchant Loup*? Only time would tell.